MW00416363

THE FALCONI EFFECT

A MODERN NOVEL ABOUT THE DAYS OF THE MESSIAH

by

CATRIEL SUGARMAN

acatriel@netvision.net.il

First published in Israel in 2016

Ketoret Publishers

Copyright © 2016 by Catriel Sugarman

Cover design and layout: Judy Shafarman

A Ketoret Publication

ISBN 13: 978-0692531884

To Heidi

...זכרתי לך חסד נעוריך
אהבת כלולותיך
לכתך אחרי במדבר
בארץ לא זרועה.
ירמיהו 2:2

Preface

A Personal Note from the Author

One *Tisha B'av*, I was walking from the Jewish Quarter of the Old City of Jerusalem down to the Western Wall Plaza. I paused and looked up. I saw an outlandish eight sided blue building with a golden dome perched on *Har Habayit*, the Temple Mount, and site of the destroyed first and second Temples. But instead of being overwhelmed by sadness, I thought of the future *Tisha B'av* whose destiny it is to be a time of exultation for *Am Yisrael*. Then, on the anniversary of the destruction of the first and second Temples, we will celebrate *Bayit Shelishi*, the Third Temple, which by Divine promise will never be destroyed. I remembered the prayer of Rabbi Akiva, that incurable optimist, the great sage who lived and taught in the shadow of defeat, death, and destruction.

> Let us live unto other festive seasons and holidays, which shall come to meet us in peace, we shall be happy in the building of Thy city and joyous in Thy worship. May we eat there of the Passover feasts and sacrifices whose blood shall reach the wall of Thine altar for acceptance. And may we thank Thee with a new song for our Redemption ...

Then at that moment, in my mind's eye, I "saw" the reconstructed *Beit Hamikdash,* the Temple complex, in its entire splendor, and, at the same time, almost like an epiphany, the plot of *The Falconi Effect: A Modern Novel about the Days of the Messiah* filled my brain.

For many years, I had a studio-workshop in downtown Jerusalem where my staff and I crafted fine Judaica from rare woods. We frequently incorporated elements of silver, gold, and mother of pearl. We made elegant mezuzot; ornate spice towers and Torah pointers, spectacular *Seder* plates and *sefirot ha'omer* counters, inlaid *megillah* covers and *graggers* which graced the homes of collectors and museums all over the Jewish world. From time to time, we restored priceless antique wooden Judaica. The most important of these commissions came when we were approached by the Breslov Hassidim who asked us to repair and refinish the original carved chair of the legendary Rav Nachman. Even so, I always felt that my work – as creative and magnificent as it might be – was somehow incomplete. I had a fantasy. I wanted to build an exact model of the *Beit Hamikdash*, a very time consuming and expensive proposition. Then one day, the long-hoped-for opportunity arrived; one of our major customers came through the door and said, "Catriel, build me the *Beit Hamikdash!*"

Once we started cutting wood and crafting the literally hundreds of (gilded) silver and bronze parts (and there was quite a bit of preparation *before* we reached that comparatively advanced stage), the project took us a year and a half to complete. As month followed month, we saw the *Beit Hamikdash* gradually take shape in all its detail and majestic beauty. Finally with great joy (and relief), we finished the project. Seeing the *Beit Hamikdash* laid out before me, I thought, "The *ge'ulah sheleimah* – the Final Redemption – is so close that I can taste it."

In fact, I have long been fascinated by the subject of the *ge'ulah sheleimah,* which will culminate in the coming of *Mashi'ach,* the Messiah, the complete ingathering of *Am Yisrael,* the people of Israel, in *Eretz Yisrael,* the land of Israel, and the return of the Divine Presence in a purified *Beit Hamikdash.*

The Rambam (Maimonides) – codifier, commentator, and philosopher – wrote, "Regarding these matters, no one knows how it will be until it will be. For these matters are unclear in the writings of the prophets. Even the Sages themselves did not have a tradition regarding these matters and could only attempt to understand the verses quoted from the prophets. Therefore there were disagreements in these matters (*Hilchot Melachim 12:2*).

Nevertheless, since the time of the destruction of the *Beit Hamikdash,* people have speculated on how the Messianic era will come about and sometimes with horrific consequences. Besides wondering *how* this will come about, there are many other tantalizing questions as well. For example, how will the *Beit Hamikdash* function in the age of the Internet, SMS text messages, Facebook, and modern technology? And will the nations of the world have a role to play in the unfolding drama of the *ge'ulah sheleimah*?

I have been a "Temple buff" practically all of my life. Irresistibly drawn to the messianic prophecies of our *nevi'im,* I struggled to conceptualize these prophecies graphically. Speculating about the glorious future they promise *Am Yisrael,* I contemplated their practical meaning and tried to picture how they might be fulfilled in our modern world. In *The Falconi Effect: A Modern Novel about the Days of the Messiah,* I

3

attempted to hypothesize as to how the Final Redemption and the rebuilt *Beit Hamikdash* will impact our daily lives.

The book I am placing before you may well be the beginning of a new genre in Jewish literature. We have a plethora of historical novels and many children's books about the Second Temple. But there are no futuristic novels about life in the era of the Third Temple. As far as I know, no contemporary author has presented a possible scenario of how it "might be." Yet...

But know that this is a serious book and many important concepts germane to the age of *Mashi'ach* are examined within its pages. It is my hope that you will find this book not only enjoyable, but also stimulating and thought provoking. And as you continue to read, I pray that you too will come to yearn for the *ge'ulah sheleimah*.

> And it shall come to pass in the end of days that the mountain of the House of the Lord shall be established as the chief of the mountains, and shall be exalted above the hills; and all nations shall flow unto it ...
> (*Isaiah* 2:3)

May we be worthy of greeting *Mashi'ach* and ascending to the new *Beit Hamikdash* three times a year!

Catriel Sugarman,

Jerusalem the Blessed, Israel

Prologue

It was a cold winter's day and a driving rain beat against the windows. Chanina, scion of an ancient priestly family, stood before the dean of Yeshivat Sha'ar Shamayim, his *Rosh Yeshiva* Harav Eliyahu Kagan. Chanina's parents sat across the desk from the *Rosh Yeshiva*. Chanina was tense; he could not imagine what he could possibly have done to warrant bringing his parents all the way from Tzefat, far in the North of Israel, to the *Rosh Yeshiva's* study in Jerusalem – and on such a day! Had he done something wrong? As he stood there waiting for the *Rosh Yeshiva* to speak, Chanina looked over the *Rosh Yeshiva's* head for a moment and gazed at *Har Habayit*, the Temple Mount, in the distance.

Through the pouring rain, he saw the familiar eight sided blue building with the golden dome brazenly ensconced atop the site of the destroyed *Beit Hamikdash*, the Holy Temple. The sight of that reproach to *Am Yisrael,* to the entire Jewish people, perched on the site of the *Mikdash* always made Chanina grit his teeth in indignation. *How dare they! Am Yisrael* has been praying for the return of the *Mikdash* for almost two thousand years. Wasn't it enough? *Ad matai*? When will we merit having the *Beit Hamikdash* back?

Chanina's reverie was interrupted when the *Rosh Yeshiva* started to speak, "Chanina, I have called you here together with your parents because I have something very important to discuss with you." Chanina could no longer contain himself. Despite his consternation, he remembered to speak in the formal third person, customary when addressing a rabbi of great stature.

"*Kavod Harav*, have I done something to displease the *Rosh Yeshiva*?"

"No, Chanina." Rav Kagan smiled, putting him at ease, "Not at all. You have met and surpassed all the great expectations we had when you first came here."

"Then why has the *Rosh Yeshiva* called us?" Chanina asked.

"Chanina, please pay close attention to what I am going to say to you. In a few years, *Hakadosh Baruch Hu*, the Holy One blessed be He, is going to cause monumental changes in our world and in the life of *Am Yisrael*. You, Chanina, will be at the center of all this and you will play a most vital role. You have been chosen, and *because* you have been chosen, you must acquire the knowledge and expertise that you will need to fulfill the essential tasks that in time will be placed before you."

"What is the *Rosh Yeshiva* saying? I thought learning Torah was the way!"

Rav Kagan smiled, "Chanina, listen to me. You have been learning in our yeshiva for many years. But now that you have a firm foundation in learning, it is time for you to prepare for the next stage in your destiny. You must leave the yeshiva!"

"Leave the yeshiva? *Kavod Harav*, I don't understand. I love learning Torah. I want to stay here in Sha'ar Shamayim!"

"I know you do, Chanina. Your intense love for Torah and for our yeshiva shows in everything you do. But the time has

6

come when you must take that love and prepare to serve *Hakadosh Baruch Hu* and *Am Yisrael* with the Torah that you have learned and the inborn talents that you possess in a new way. You must begin by learning business administration."

"Business administration? Is the *Rosh Yeshiva* expelling me from the yeshiva?" Chanina asked plaintively, his eyes dampening.

"No! Never think that even for a moment! I am giving you this mission because you are the best student here, and one day you will understand why I am doing this. Listen to me. You must learn business administration, accounting and computer science. You must learn how to administer very large institutions and be fluent in English and other languages. You must master the latest technologies and gain experience in modern management techniques. We will discuss how you will do this in the very near future. We will help you with tutors and getting you admitted to the institutions where you will study. And we will be in constant contact."

Chanina was stunned. He gripped his chair to steady himself. His head reeled; he felt dizzy as he struggled to understand what Rav Kagan had just told him. *Whatever he had expected, it wasn't this!* He looked at his father for encouragement, but his father only gestured in the *Rosh Yeshiva*'s direction. His mother looked at him with shining proud eyes.

The rain continued lashing the windows. There was a flash of lightening and the rumble of thunder in the distance. Branches of the trees swayed back and forth in the howling wind. Saddened and confused by the *Rosh Yeshiva*'s words, Chanina lowered his eyes. For a few minutes, he was lost in thought. The room was quiet. Finally, Chanina raised his head,

"*Kavod Harav*, I will do what you ask of me. *Im kach nigzar alai, ani mekabeil et zeh be'ahavah!* – if such has been decreed for me, I accept it with love!"

Rav Kagan pulled his *talmid* over and embraced him warmly, even exuberantly, "It will not be easy, you know. I am asking a lot of you."

"*Rebbe*, thank you for having faith in me," Chanina whispered with a tear in his eye.

"Thank *you* for being who you are and what you are," Rav Kagan answered, embracing him again. "*Be'ezrat Hashem*, with God's help, I know that you will succeed."

Fifteen years had passed since that day in his *Rosh Yeshiva*'s office, and more had changed in the world than Chanina could ever have imagined.

Tall, and broad shouldered, with a wide strong mouth, deep black eyes, and raven black hair and beard, Harav Chanina Abulafia was now the *Segan* - the highly regarded administrator and trusted assistant to his teacher Harav Eliyahu Kagan, *Kohen Gadol*, the High Priest of the *Beit Hamikdash,* the rebuilt Third Temple.

Sitting in his work room overlooking the *Beit Hamikdash*, Chanina recalled every word of his conversation with Rav Kagan years before. He smiled; his *Rosh Yeshiva* had known *exactly* what was going to happen.

But Chanina also remembered something else.

Something extraordinary happened that day.

When the *Rosh Yeshiva* had finished speaking, Chanina looked up and gazed though the window overlooking *Har Habayit*. The rain had stopped and a brilliant sun glowed with a supernal brightness. *But the eight sided blue building with the gold dome was enveloped in thick dark clouds, and in fact, was invisible to the eye.* In another moment, the clouds disappeared and the building was visible once more.

Though it did not occur to him at the time, over the years, Chanina came to believe that the brief invisibility of the blue eight sided building with the gold dome was a clear sign from Heaven.

Its days were numbered.

Chapter One

Overhead the first streaks of dawn lit up a purple and crimson sky; a new day had begun in the *Azarah,* the Temple Court. Meir Hakohen, dynamic assistant to *Segan* Chanina Abulafia, watched the hustle and bustle around him. It was the third day of the Hebrew month *Sivan,* and summer was just beginning. "How did it get to be the third of *Sivan* already? It seems like *Pesach* was just last week!"

During those hectic first few years after the restoration of the *Beit Hamikdash,* Meir Hakohen thought of himself as one of the dreamers referred to in the oft recited *Shir Hama'alot,* the hundred and twenty-sixth Psalm.

Am Yisrael had waited and prayed for the renewal of the *Beit Hamikdash* for almost two thousand years, and in his lifetime, *in his lifetime,* it happened! Looking around the incomparably splendid white and gold *Mikdash* complex, he sometimes had to pinch himself to make sure that he was awake, and that the rebuilt *Beit Hamikdash* was not just a beautiful dream that would vanish with the morning mist. But the *Mikdash* **was** real! With his own eyes, he saw the *Kohanim,* enthusiastically yet meticulously, performing the *avodah,* the Temple service. With his own ears, he heard the matchless music of the new Levitical choir as they sang *Tehillim* – the

Psalms of David – and played their instruments while the sacrifices, the *korbanot*, were offered. Daily, he saw tens of thousands of Jews joyously flooding into the courtyards of the new *Mikdash* with their sacrificial animals.

Even better, as a *Kohen*, Meir lit the Menorah, blessed the people, served at the altar, and offered *korbanot* on behalf of *Am Yisrael*. And just as the Zohar described the fiery pyre on the sacrificial altar in the days of the First Temple, so too now, the flames shooting up from the blazing woodpile took the form of a lion! Best of all, Meir had even offered *ketoret*, the fragrant incense used in the Temple service, on the golden altar in the *Heichal*, the Temple sanctuary - an honor allowed a *Kohen* but once in his lifetime.

At that moment, when he offered *ketoret*, his eyes became riveted to the rising column of smoke. Miraculously, the column of fragrant smoke that emanated from the sizzling coals ascended in a straight vertical line, and then curved and entered the most sacred area of the Temple, the *Kodesh Hakodashim*, the Holy of Holies. The Sages said that would happen, and it really did!

Meir felt that all the years of his life he had waited only for this!

Ever since that wonderful day, Meir replayed the scene in his mind again and again. How he wished that camcorders and digital cameras were permitted to record that momentous event for posterity, or at least for his family. But the Sanhedrin ruled that, due to the extreme holiness of the *avodah*, no cameras or recording equipment would be permitted on *Mikdash* grounds or even on *Har Habayit*, however unobtrusive such apparatus might be.

When Meir was still learning in the Sha'ar Shamayim yeshiva, he was troubled by the Sages' statement that the Second Temple lacked five things that existed in the First Temple: the *aron habrit*, the Ark of the Covenant; the *shemen hamishchah*, the sacred anointing oil compounded by Moses in the wilderness; the fire that descended from Heaven to consume the *korbanot* on the altar; the visible manifestation of the Shechinah, the Divine Presence; and the *urim ve'tumim*, the sacred Temple oracle, worn by the *Kohen Gadol*. Even so, *Pirkei Avot*, the Ethics of the Fathers, *did* list ten miracles that regularly occurred in *Bayit Sheini*. Over the years, the young Meir must have asked his teachers a hundred times if these miracles would return when the Temple was rebuilt.

He need not have worried.

The new *Mikdash* had all the miraculous hallmarks of the earlier Temples – *Bayit Rishon* and *Bayit Sheini* – and more! The sacrificial meat never spoiled even in the burning summer sun and there were no flies in the area of slaughter. Even though the *lechem ha'panim*, the showbread, was exposed to the open air in the *Heichal* for an entire week, it remained as fresh as the moment the expert bakers of Beit Garmu removed it from the oven.

Although the sacrificial altar was outside in the open air, the sacrificial fires were never extinguished, even when the winter rain came down in buckets and even during raging blizzards. The strongest of winds did not scatter the smoke rising from the sacrificial pyres on the altar; the smoke rose to the heavens in a mighty column as straight as the trunk of a date palm.

Meir remembered how astonished he was the first time he witnessed it. Mouth open, he had blurted out, "*Ha'avodah!* The smoke really does go straight up!" He raised his eyes up, up, up, towards heaven, as he followed its progress.

The first Yom Kippur in the new *Beit Hamikdash* was unbelievable!

It seemed like the whole world was trying to get into the *Ezrat Yisrael* - the portion of the Temple Court where *Yisraelim*, layman not of the Priestly class, entered. People were not just standing on the stone floor; they floated in a sea of humanity jammed against each other. Yet when the people prostrated themselves in prayer, there was plenty of room for everybody, just as the Mishnaic tractate *Pirkei Avot,* said that there would be. Logically, and in accordance to the laws of physics, that was physically impossible. But as Meir had come to realize very quickly, the new *Beit Hamikdash* operated under its *own* laws of physics. It was a new and different world, and Meir Hakohen was excited to be part of it.

Meir recalled that exhilarating first *Tisha B'av*, the fast day memorializing the destruction of the First and Second Temples, after the *Beit Hamikdash* had been rebuilt. It truly *had* been transformed into a day of great joy! We read *Eichah,* the Book of Lamentations, as did our forefathers in the days of the Second Temple, simply as a commemoration of a tragic historical event. Though we prayed that there would never be another *churban,* we no longer wept and abstained from food and drink. On that first *Tisha B'av*, we read *Eichah* sitting on chairs, not huddled on the floor. We celebrated Jerusalem's new found glory and exulted in the new *Beit Hamikdash*. We gave thanks to *Hashem* for His kindness and expressed our growing confidence in the imminent coming of *Mashi'ach* and the Final Redemption. Rejoicing instead of mourning, we invited all our family and friends for a *se'udah,* a festive meal, and we ate *kodashim,* sacrificial meat!

But still, it felt so strange **celebrating** *Tisha B'av* instead of mourning and fasting. But why should I have been surprised? Did not our prophets tell us that would happen when the *Mikdash* was restored? And to think that the prophecies of our *nevi'im* have been fulfilled in my lifetime!

The four solemn fasts that commemorated the destruction of Jerusalem and the *Mikdash* were now days of rejoicing!

While going over a list of minor repairs completed by Yehoshua and his maintenance crew that day, Meir asked himself, "Why didn't we take our *nevi'im* more seriously? Yechezkel – the prophet Ezekiel – had already told us that 'the nations shall know that I am the Lord that sanctifies Israel, when my Sanctuary shall be in the midst of them forever.'"

In pre-*Mikdash* days, before the appearance of the Third Temple, the nations of the world would not even admit that Jerusalem was the capital of the Jewish people. Now every country in the world was building palatial embassies here.

Meir laughed to himself, "I guess they want to be where the action is!" How the world and its attitude towards *Am Yisrael* has changed! Today Jerusalem, the undisputed capital of Israel, is now universally acknowledged as the world's political, technological, and scientific center. And who would have thought only a few years ago that we would become an "energy superpower," exporting vast quantities of natural gas and oil to dozens of countries in Europe and the Far East? And *baruch Hashem*, Depression II, the financial meltdown that is wrecking the economies of virtually every country in the world, seems to have passed us by.

And the *Mikdash* has become the pre-eminent religious and moral center of the world! Yeshayahu – the prophet Isaiah said that would happen. Why didn't we believe him? He declared that the new *Mikdash* would be the world center of Torah and not only for *Am Yisrael*. Teaching ethics, philosophy, and *Sheva Mitzvot B'nei Noach* (the Seven Noahide Laws), every day, *Shidurei Hamikdash* - Mikdash Broadcasts and the countless educational websites set up by the Mikdash Committee for Universal Education, reaches hundreds of millions of Jews and non-Jews. Through the Internet, the message of the *Beit Hamikdash* has spread to every corner of the planet.

Not too long ago, there were even Jews who wanted to give away Yehudah and Shomron, the heart of *Eretz Yisrael*, to our enemies. Treacherously, they even tried to activate foreign powers, NGOs, hostile journalists, and contentious academics to help them. Not surprisingly, these same people wanted to sever every connection the Jewish nation had to Torah as well. This guy Pringsheim or whatever his name is, their standard bearer, is still beating the drums and spouting his poison, but *baruch Hashem*, hardly anyone listens to him anymore. He's more of a joke than anything else. *Ha'avodah!* He and his coterie used to be so popular and so influential. What a contrast to only a few years ago!

But even though the *Beit Hamikdash* is rebuilt, and *Am Yisrael* is putting down ever deeper roots in the holy soil of historic *Eretz Yisrael*, North, South, East, West, the world still had its share of festering sores.

Yesterday, the *Segan*, his manner unusually brisk and businesslike, invited Meir to his office to sit in at a meeting with Raphael Nachum, one of the *Mikdash* representatives who had just returned from Europe. The *Segan's* immaculate office was a spacious well-lit white room with a breathtaking view of the *Mikdash*. The office contained a massive desk, an ergonomic office chair, three white arm chairs for visitors, and the requisite water cooler. Neatly arranged on the *Segan's* desk, the nerve center of the *Beit Hamikdash* administration, were family pictures, a large computer screen, a keyboard, a telephone, a few books, and incongruously, a graceful thin-necked, white vase holding a dark red rose. In a corner sat an overstuffed couch, a coffee table, and three comfortable club chairs. An enormous plasma screen covered one of the walls. After Raphael Nachum, a tall wiry man with prematurely white hair, brown eyes, and a tanned face, had answered all the *Segan's* questions about the *Mikdash* educational programs in Europe, the *Segan* asked him:

"Reb Nachum, what's happening in Europe, politically I mean?"

"Reb Chanina, things there are not what they seem. At the moment Europe seems relatively placid despite all the unemployment, societal breakdown, constant altercations between the burgeoning Muslim migrant communities and the declining indigenous population, recurring financial crises, soaring debt, demonstrations, and civil unrest. Make no mistake, Depression II has hit hard. Under the surface things are stirring."

"Can you be more specific?" Meir asked.

"Everywhere in Europe, there is a feeling of real unrest and danger. It's eerie. There is a tension in the air that just doesn't go away."

"What form does this tension take?"

"Quiet cities erupt without warning. Violent mobs fill the streets, disrupting business and traffic, and whole towns are shut down. Then suddenly everything returns to normal. The mobs simply vanish. Stores reopen, planes take off, trains, and busses begin to run again, and everyone goes about their normal business."

"It sounds like someone, somewhere, is flicking a switch on and off. Maybe this is a dress rehearsal for something much bigger," the *Segan* commented dryly with a ghost of a smile.

"Many people think so," Nachum agreed nodding his head, "And I think they're right."

"Who's behind all this?" Meir asked.

"People in the know say that the anarchists are behind it. Some political analysts claim that a Sicilian professor is the real mastermind and manipulator behind these disruptions. The professor's name is Antonio Falconi. He's very popular and influential. They say that he has literally millions of followers on Facebook. So far there is no direct proof linking him to the unrest. He's too smart for that. But he hasn't made any public appearances lately."

"Europe seems quiet now," the *Segan* said thoughtfully.

"Yes. For the moment it *is* quiet, but everyone's afraid of what'll happen next. It's an inherently unstable situation," Nachum concluded.

Sighing, Meir shook his head sadly; none of this was new to him, he'd heard it all before. *Beit Hamikdash* or not, tranquility in the world was still a long way off.

He pictured the very altar shedding tears.

Chapter Two

Meir Hakohen, a man of medium height with graying red hair and beard, apple cheeks, and penetrating sky-blue eyes, was a true *Yerushalmi*; he was descended from a family that had lived in Jerusalem for countless generations. However, a few years before Meir was born, his family relocated from their home in Yerushalayim Bein Hachomot, the old walled city of Jerusalem, to one of the new grape-growing settlements between Beit Rima and Shiloh in the Shomron, the hilly area north of Jerusalem. It was reputed to be the best grape growing region in the country.

Meir's father, Simchah Rabbah's, dearest wish was that one day he would be privileged to supply wine needed for *nisuch ha'yayin,* the wine libation that the *Kohanim* poured daily on the altar in the *Beit Hamikdash.* In anticipation of that day, he carefully followed the laws laid down in the Mishna for the production of wine destined to be used in the *Mikdash.* He did not train his vines on trellises. He never irrigated or fertilized his vines with night soil. He neither sweetened, nor smoked, nor cooked his wine. Nor did he add concentrates or any other chemicals. Inexplicably, his vines grew with a wondrously exuberant lushness that made him the envy of every other viniculturalist in the Shomron. And the quality of his wine was unsurpassed.

In pre-*Mikdash* days, Simchah Rabbah frequently took his family and friends to visit recently excavated wine vats dating back to the days of Yehoshua bin Nun, the Biblical conqueror of Canaan. Tall, lean framed, and bronzed by the sun, he possessed a persona which commanded respect, yet at the same time he emanated kindness with a warm smile. Simchah Rabbah wanted to demonstrate the longevity and authenticity of the tradition of Jewish viniculture in the Shomron, a tradition that went back thousands of years. In fact, the whole area teemed with ancient ruins of terraces painstakingly built by Jewish farmers in the days of *Bayit Sheini* and earlier, many of which had already been reconstructed and replanted by a new generation of energetic Jewish viniculturists over the last few decades. Simchah Rabbah never stopped explaining to anyone who would listen that renewed Jewish winemaking in the Shomron was one of the surest signs of the coming Redemption.

When he was a teenager, Meir's father took him to Shlomtzion Hamalka Street in Jerusalem, to visit the studio-workshop of a master craftsman who had fashioned an extremely accurate model of the Second Temple. The model, about the size of a large dining room table, was astonishing in its precision and beauty. For an hour, Simchah Rabbah and Meir kept walking around the model and studying it from all angles. Finally, with a smile, Simchah Rabbah pointed to a large domed building.

"Meir, what's this?" he asked.

"That's the *Beit Hamokeid*. Located on the north side of the *Azarah*, the *Beit Hamokeid* was a hostel for *Kohanim* who served the early shift in the *Beit Hamikdash*. They slept there the night before," young Meir pontificated.

19

"Very good!"

Nodding to Simchah Rabbah, the craftsman carefully removed the roof of the *Beit Hamokeid*.

"Look inside the *Beit Hamokeid*, Meir."

Meir saw a stone floor with a hearth in the middle of the room. Abutting the walls were high stone steps of a sort.

"The younger *Kohanim* slept on the floor around the fire. The older *Kohanim* slept on the step-like structures lining and built into the walls," the craftsman explained.

"I know that!" the young Meir exclaimed. "The stone step-like structures are called *rovdin shel even*. They're mentioned in *Middot*, the Mishnaic tractate which deals with the measurements of Temple buildings, courtyards, and the sacrificial altar."

Grinning, Meir pulled out a worn pocket Mishna out of the outer compartment of his bulging shoulder bag. Flipping through the pages, he quickly found what he was looking for. "Here it is: *Middot*; first chapter, eighth mishna, *rovdin shel even.* When we have the *Beit Hamikdash* back, I'll still be young. I'll sleep on the floor in the *Beit Hamokeid. Abba* will sleep on the *rovdin.* We're *Kohanim* and serving in *Bayit Shelishi*, the Third Temple, is our dream!"

Hearing his son's impassioned words, Simchah Rabbah almost burst with pride. His black eyes twinkled happily; his smile was as wide as the ocean.

"With young *Kohanim* like your son, our future is assured," the old craftsman said. "*Im yirtzeh Hashem*, God willing, we won't have long to wait."

In pre-*Mikdash* days, Simchah Rabbah coined the popular slogan, "Think *Mikdash*!" And true to his maxim, every year he put away a small quantity of his best wine "*zeicher le'mikdash*," in remembrance of the Temple. He did this in anticipation of the day when the *Mikdash* would once again stand on *Har Habayit* and it *would* become possible for him to donate wine made *be'kedusha ve'tahora*, in holiness and purity.

Meir also accustomed himself to "thinking *Mikdash*," and in that spirit he enrolled in Sha'ar Shamayim, the Jerusalem yeshiva of Harav Eliyahu Kagan. While Meir was not the most scholarly of Harav Eliyahu's students, he was definitely one of the most devoted. At Harav Kagan's yeshiva, Meir was assigned a *chavruta,* a study partner, named Chanina Abulafia, also a *Kohen* and several years older than Meir. The two young *Kohanim* learned well together and became fast friends.

◆

Chanina Abulafia's family history was interwoven with that of old Tzefat, the mystical city of the Kabbalah and the Holy Ari, high in the forested mountains of the upper Galilee. Tzefat was the city of poverty and earthquakes; expulsions, pogroms, and plagues; spiritual exaltation and intense Torah learning; narrow cobbled alleyways; picturesque arches; old stone houses with brass door knobs; ancient synagogues with ornate, breathtakingly beautiful carved wooden *aronot kodesh*; and kilometers of winding stone staircases with exquisite wrought-iron railings linking the various levels of the city.

Of slight build with glistening black eyes, silver beard and long side curls, Chanina's father, Ovadiah Abulafia, was an extraordinary personality in a city filled with extraordinary personalities. Every morning before sunrise, he immersed in the ice-cold waters of the *mikvah* of the Holy Ari, before

21

davening shacharit, the morning service, in the ancient Abuhav synagogue. While climbing the more than one hundred windswept stairs from the *mikvah* in the valley to the synagogue on the hill, he sang aloud the ancient *nigunim* of Tzefat that had been in his family for centuries. Usually Chanina accompanied him and they sang together. Later, Ovadiah and Chanina immersed a second time in a different *mikvah* before they parted company, Ovadiah to his studio-workshop and Chanina to the local yeshiva.

Ovadiah saw his studio as a kind of a miniature sanctuary. He believed that making *tashmeshei kedusha,* beautiful ritual objects out of silver and gold, for Jews to use in the performance of mitzvot was itself a mitzvah, and therefore had to be done in a spirit of purity.

When Chanina was still a young boy, Ovadiah realized that his son's talents were not in craftsmanship, but rather in organization and administration. By the time he was fifteen, despite his heavy schedule, Chanina confidently handled much of the studio's paperwork and even helped design the studio's website. Even at that age, during his infrequent breaks from yeshiva, he proved that he was able to deal easily with customers, suppliers, accountants, and various government agencies. By the time he was sixteen, despite his strict regimen of learning, Chanina managed the studio's entire financial, legal, and logistical documentation. Ovadiah signed wherever Chanina pointed his finger.

At midnight, Ovadiah would go to the centuries-old Sephardic Synagogue of the Holy Ari to recite *Tikkun Chatzot,* the midnight service of lamentation commemorating the destruction of the *Mikdash* and the exile of the Shechinah, the Divine Presence. In the light of flickering candles that cast fantastic shadows on the walls, Ovadiah and the *mekubalim* of Tzefat mourned for the lost Temple and the Shechinah, and prayed with fervor for their return. Young Chanina almost always accompanied his father on these midnight vigils. In his mind's eye, he saw the Holy Ari and his *talmidim* sitting there deep in the shadows mourning along with them. In the Ari synagogue, in the company of Tzefat's *anshei chein* – adepts of the Kabbala's hidden wisdom – Chanina's yearning for the *Beit Hamikdash* became almost an obsession.

Chapter Three

The advent of the autumn month of Elul meant that Meir Hakohen had to rearrange his full schedule to meet with the elders of Beit Avtinas, the priestly family responsible for preparing the *ketoret*, the incense required for the Temple service. Their annual conference was soon approaching, and since *ketoret* played such an important role in the *avodah*, attending their conference was a priority. Although they could be difficult to deal with at times, and Harav Azariah Abenatar, the imperious and totally dedicated patriarch of Beit Avtinas, simply impossible, their work was flawless.

Meir always looked forward to visiting Harav Azariah's realm high above the *Sha'ar Hamayim,* the Water Gate on the southern side of the *Azarah.* Meir's wife claimed that she always knew exactly when he had visited the Beit Avtinas' perfumery. When he came home, he had an unmistakable fragrance about him.

Although Rav Azariah grudgingly permitted computers in a side office, and tolerated such modern conveniences such as unobtrusive LED lighting and a top-of-the-line heating and air-conditioning system, he conceded almost nothing to modern technology in the actual preparation of the incense. The processing and the compounding of the *ketoret* were always done by hand.

Long tables carpeted with tins of rare incense, mortars and pestles, mixing bowls, measuring devices, scales, and various strange and fascinating tools filled the sweet-smelling workshop. Surrounded by the accoutrements of their trade, the *Kohanim* of Beit Avtinas worked soundlessly with incredible concentration. Their light-gray work clothes bore the embroidered logo of Beit Avtinas: a mortar and pestle and the Biblical quote, "Take yourself spices…" superimposed on the smoking golden incense altar.

As they worked, Rav Azariah repeatedly intoned the words of the Gemara, "Pound well, well pound. Pound well, well pound." The *Kohanim* carefully weighed the requisite ingredients, poured each of them into separate mortars, and thoroughly pounded them with pestles. Only then did they mix them in the exact proportions required.

To emphasize the importance of the *ketoret* to the *Mikdash* to his devoted team, Rav Azariah hung on the wall a quotation from the *Midrash Tanchuma*, an early homiletic commentary on the Torah, rendered in exquisite Hebrew calligraphy:

> R. Yitzchak ben Eliezer said, "Know that they built the *Mishkan* – the portable desert sanctuary constructed by Moses – and all its vessels, slaughtered and sacrificed the *korbanot* on the altar, placed the *lechem ha'panim* on the golden table and lit the Menorah. They did everything. However, the Shechinah did not descend on the *Mishkan* until they offered the *ketoret*.
>
> How do we know this? It is written, 'Awake thou North, come thou South, blow upon my garden that the perfumes flow out. Let my Beloved come to His garden

25

and eat His precious fruits.' 'Awake thou North' - these were the burnt offerings slaughtered north of the altar. 'Come thou South' – these were the peace offerings slaughtered south of the altar. 'Blow upon my garden that the perfumes flow out' – this is the perfumed *ketoret*. 'Let my Beloved come' – this is the Shechinah. 'And eat His precious fruit' – these are the now-accepted *korbanot*.

Said the Holy One Blessed be He, 'By means of the *ketoret*, you attained atonement in this world; so it shall be in the Future World.'

Meir shivered every time he read it.

Aside from a research library, which also served as a conference room and a *beit knesset* for the *Kohanim* of Beit Avtinas, Rav Azariah's workshop also included a refrigerated storeroom. Lining the chilly walls were shelves stacked with boxes containing the most exotic spices in the world, some of them literally worth their weight in gold. Equipped with insulated panels, the temperature controlled space was electronically monitored to prevent spoilage.

In a modest office off a side corridor was a state-of-the-art computerized information center directed by a Levite technician. When Meir entered, the IT was intently studying his computer screen showing the real time updates of Beit Avtinas's *ketoret* accounts.

"What's up?" Meir asked jocularly as he sat down.

"I'm just checking how much of each component of *ketoret* we have on hand," the technician answered. "The program just noted that our supply of frankincense and myrrh used to make the *ketoret* has reached a critical minimal quantity. Of course, we still have plenty on hand, but when we *do* reach the 'critical minimum quantity' of any of the required components, the *Mikdash* computers automatically place orders with our suppliers in Oman, Yemen, India or anywhere else in the world. This way we automatically maintain a sufficient quantity of the *ketoret*'s components to meet the *Mikdash*'s needs. And if there's a serious delay for any reason, we have alternate suppliers."

"So everything is under control."

"We're okay. In fact, this morning we brought in a new supply of *ma'aleh ashan*. That's that extra ingredient that Rav Azariah adds to the *ketoret* that causes the smoke to rise straight up instead of scattering. You know Meir, *ma'aleh ashan* is one of the miracles of the *Mikdash*. Nobody has the slightest idea why it causes the *ketoret* to act the way it does."

Meir smiled knowingly. He remembered his own amazement when *he* had offered *ketoret* on the golden altar in the *Heichal* and the smoke did not scatter.

Putt! The IT looked up with a grin. "Meir, I just received confirmation from our people in Oman and Yemen that these particular orders were received and processed. *Im yirtzeh Hashem*, we'll have our frankincense and myrrh by tomorrow evening," the loquacious Levite concluded.

"Great!"

Chapter Four

Pudgy with slightly freckled skin, dark eyes, brown curly hair and beard, Meshullam Hamalbish was responsible for the manufacture of *bigdei kehunah*, the white priestly vestments that the *Kohanim* were required to wear when performing the *avodah.* Optimistic by nature, Meshullam usually did not permit difficulties to upset him, but he was tense now. It was in the beginning of the summer, several weeks before *Rosh Chodesh Tammuz* when he told the *Segan* about a serious problem.

"Reb Chanina, the more *Kohanim* serving in the *Mikdash*, the more linen *bigdei kehunah* we need to outfit them," Meshullam began. "More *bigdei kehunah* means we need more flax fiber, the raw material from which we weave the linen. Reb Chanina, we're in trouble! We don't have nearly enough flax fiber to get by, and Rosh Hashanah, Yom Kippur, and Sukkot are already flickering on the horizon!"

Akiva Moshe, the Levite in charge of the *Mikdash* flax fiber warehouse, had called Meshullam on his emergency number early that morning. The Levite was very upset.

"*Kavod hakohen*," he began respectfully, "we have a high-priority problem here. Apparently, during the night, there was a serious malfunction of the cooling system and the dehumidifiers, which caused all of our flax fiber to get ruined. Please come over as quickly as possible, and I suggest you bring Chief Engineer Yannai with you. Something very strange has happened!"

In the shortest possible time, the anxious Meshullam arrived ˆwith an even more agitated Yannai, the brawny, slightly balding engineer. The moment they entered the building, they realized that it was far hotter and much damper than the procedures called for. It took them only a few minutes to verify that all the fiber had indeed spoiled and was unsuitable to be woven into *bigdei kehunah*.

"Akiva, what's the temperature in here?" Yannai asked, wiping his forehead.

"33 degrees centigrade."

"Humidity?"

"85 percent."

It was hotter and damper in the warehouse than it was outside. There was a pervasive smell of mildew in the air. Yannai and Meshullam wrinkled their noses.

"All right, Akiva, what happened?"

"*Kavod hakohen,* as far as we can determine, our initial analysis shows that both the cooling system and the dehumidifiers unaccountably malfunctioned at the same time. As a result, the excessively warm, damp air created the conditions enabling mildew to grow with incredible speed. Even so, the mildew developed far faster than we would have believed possible. We've gone over the data several times and we have no other explanation as to what happened."

"Akiva, what do you mean you have no explanation?" demanded the Chief Engineer. "The warehouse is insulated. The temperature and the humidity are continuously monitored electronically to prevent spoilage."

"Yes, I'm perfectly aware of that."

"Akiva, two backup systems were installed in anticipation of such an eventuality! Two! Each system is completely independent of the other! You have uninterruptable power sources, auxiliary power systems, and standby generators. You're telling me that they *all* failed at the same time? How do you explain that? The odds of all this happening at the same time are infinitesimal!"

"I know."

"So when the systems failed and you heard the alarm, why didn't you manually restart the system?" Meshullam demanded.

"There was no alarm," the fidgeting Levite replied.

Meshullam blanched, lips trembling.

"Two independent backup systems for the coolers and dehumidifiers and two independent alarm systems and none of them worked? The primary and the secondary systems all failed?" the Chief Engineer cried out in disbelief, hands on his hips.

"That's exactly what I'm saying," the troubled Levite answered nervously looking at the ground, "Check the logs and see for yourself."

"I'll do that," Yannai responded curtly.

With both Meshullam and Akiva looking on apprehensively, the Chief Engineer inspected the failed equipment's logs and ran a battery of tests. Aghast at his findings, the Chief Engineer checked the data once more and ran some more tests. He swallowed hard and shook his head: unbelievable! It was exactly as Akiva had said; there was absolutely no technical reason to explain why all the systems shut down simultaneously. It simply was not feasible!

Reluctantly, the Chief Engineer was forced to admit that Akiva's initial analysis was correct. The breakdown *was* inexplicable. The relieved Akiva was vindicated of any suspicion of negligence or wrongdoing.

Holding his nose, the chief engineer softly told the distraught Levite, "Look, you'd better get your people down here and start clearing everything out. And you'll have to fumigate the place."

Turning to Meshullam, he added, "Akiva is right. Something incomprehensible did happen here. And look at the mildew, it's a regular jungle! How is it possible for mold to grow and spread so quickly in a single night?"

Meshullam shook his head "I don't know. I've never seen anything like it. But it's peculiar that this happened now."

"What do you mean by 'now'?" Yannai asked slowly. "It would be peculiar if this happened any time."

"Didn't you hear what happened to the Canadian flax crop? In the last couple of weeks, a sudden outbreak of plant rust, actually a fungus, destroyed most of it. And another lethal fungus that attacks above-ground parts of the flax plant pretty much wiped out the rest. Then the fungi spread south across the border, effectively ruining most of the American crop as well. Now I've heard that these fungi plus a few other flax-destroying organisms have appeared in Europe and Asia as well. This year at least three-quarters of the world flax crop, probably more, is going to have to be written off."

"So it's a worldwide plague then," the Chief Engineer said thoughtfully as he watched Akiva in the distance assemble his staff of Levites and give them instructions. "Meshullam, how is this going to affect us? The *chagim* are coming, we need *bigdei kehunah* for our *Kohanim*. Do we have backup?"

31

"Look Yannai, the spoilage of all our fiber here is a serious financial loss to the *Mikdash*, no question about it. But we do have backup, although not in Israel. We have a year's supply of high-quality flax fiber sitting in a bonded warehouse in Dublin that we've already purchased from the Bodhrán Linen Company. It will be flown here in a couple of days. So even if there is a worldwide failure of the flax crop, we're covered."

But unexpectedly, Meshullam's reserve flax fiber supply disappeared. The Irish company claimed that there was a lacuna in the *Mikdash* contract which permitted them to divert the flax fiber to a Canadian firm. The *Mikdash* representatives in Ireland contacted Meshullam and told him the bad news: despite their best efforts, the Irish linen would not be forthcoming.

It was then that the stricken Meshullam informed the *Segan* of the seriousness of the situation. Upon hearing the news, the *Segan* immediately directed Meir Hakohen to appoint a special task force to locate suitable flax fiber, anywhere, regardless of cost. The *Segan* knew that unless he got fiber from somewhere fast, Meshullam's looms would soon be idle. The *chagim* were fast approaching: there was no time to lose!

After a frantic Internet search of the inventory systems of suppliers all over the world, Meir's office finally located several dozen huge crates of high grade flax fiber in a bonded warehouse in Milan, easily enough to tide the *Mikdash* over the current crisis.

"Meshullam, come on up here right away! We found your fiber!" Meir exulted over the intercom.

A few minutes later, Meshullam, out of breath, arrived at Meir's office. Meir and Avi Katz, the Chief Financial Officer of the *Mikdash*, sat behind a table intently studying a computer printout.

"Where did you find the fiber?" Meshullam asked eagerly.

"In a bonded warehouse in Milan," Meir replied, a twinkle in his eye.

"Before we go any further, I'd better check some details," the relieved Meshullam said as he sat quickly down at Meir's desk and pulled over the keyboard. While he carefully studied the specifications of the Milan flax fiber on the screen, Meir and Avi waited patiently for his verdict. Meshullam did not take long.

"I can't believe it!" he rejoiced as he clapped his hands gleefully and looked up from the screen. "*Baruch Hashem*, this fiber is Triple A grade, the highest quality on the market. It's exactly what we need! With the worldwide shortage of flax fiber, I can't believe someone didn't snap it up the minute it became available!"

Though the *Mikdash* ended up paying an enormous price for the fiber, both the *Segan* and Meshullam felt it was worth every gold shekel. Even Avi Katz, the frugal Chief Financial Officer of the *Mikdash*, reluctantly agreed.

However, one day before the containers were to be flown to Israel, a violent general strike broke out paralyzing the whole city of Milan. Within minutes, the well organized workers shut down Milan Malpensa Airport and all flights, domestic and international, were grounded. At first, Meshullam was not unduly alarmed; strikes frequently closed down cities in Europe. It happened all the time. Within a day, two days at the most, Milan would be back to normal and he would get his flax fiber.

But this time things were different.

33

Chapter Five

Over the last few years Europe, and indeed most of the world, had slid into a full blown depression. The average unemployment rate throughout the world rose to twenty-eight percent, the highest since the 30's of the previous century. Stock markets crashed and businesses were virtually paralyzed. The middle class became impoverished. Overwhelmed by mountains of debt, dozens of countries teetered on the verge of insolvency. Massive protest encampments clogged the streets of the financial districts in New York, Berlin, London, Paris, Geneva, Tokyo, and Beijing and many other cities. Banks and insurance companies thought "too big to fail" closed their doors as rampant inflation effectively wiped out the savings of hundreds of millions around the globe. The housing market fell to an unprecedented low, but nevertheless, untold millions lost their homes. They called it Depression II.

Under-funded pension funds, both government and private, collapsed, and student and housing loans ballooned completely out of control causing widespread hardship. Major cities in dozens of countries went bankrupt. After nine member countries of the EU jointly sought bailouts that were not forthcoming, for all practical purposes, the EU ceased to exist as a unified entity. The economy of virtually every country on earth was in free fall.

Angry and frightened, people demanded solutions. But people's faith in their governments had been destroyed due to rampant corruption and sheer incompetence. And it was well known that elected officials, judges, and law-enforcement agencies everywhere were closely linked to, and funded by, organized crime syndicates. Finding themselves without recourse, people took to the streets.

"The Wheels Have Stopped Turning," trumpeted Milan's *Corriere Della Sera*. In its last issue before being shut down by mutinous workers, Turin's *La Stampa* warned its readers that the unrest "could last weeks if not months." The normally staid *La Repubblica* published in Rome claimed that Italy "was on the brink of civil war." On blogs everywhere, countless amateur online journalists called for social revolution; the public responded.

The anarchists, who had long been inflaming tensions and fomenting unrest, quickly emerged from the shadows and expertly began to manipulate the emotional crowds. Articulate agitators incited civil disorder on a massive scale everywhere.

Tall and willowy, olive-skinned with a wide expressive mouth, silky moustache, long salt and pepper hair, a high forehead, and piercing big black eyes that radiated intelligence,

35

Professor Antonio Falconi was the mastermind behind the meticulously planned anarchist revolution. Though many condemned his arrogance, no one could deny his intelligence and erudition. Considered the leading intellectual of Europe, he was at the same time a formidable organizer, an accomplished academic, a philosopher, and a man of iron will. Ever glib, the charismatic Falconi used sophisticated argument, devastating flippancy, and trenchant mockery to excellent effect.

Whenever Falconi spoke in public - his voice was a powerful and skillful modulated baritone - his disciples jammed halls, theaters, and even football stadiums, and chanted slogans of support. Within minutes of his speaking, the social media flashed his message around the world, and millions of disks featuring his speeches were distributed everywhere. Not surprisingly, the always volatile university students joined the anarchists *en masse*.

Egged on by broadcasts over the Internet of Falconi's fiery tirades in five languages, maddened strikers in dozens of countries around the world overturned busses and trucks and set them on fire. Millions of students, office workers, small businessmen and farmers soon joined them. Resourceful, and mordant, Falconi used sophisticated argument, searing sarcasm, and crude invective to deliver his message. But he also could be charming, witty, sparkling, seductive, deliciously ironical, and always disturbingly moving. Under his magic spell, the rioters chopped down trees and ripped out paving stones and tram tracks to build hundreds of barricades in strategic locations in cities throughout Europe and around the world.

Meshullam Hamalbish was in his office despondently watching PrinceGlobal Media's anchorman Harris White on the popular program *Behind Today's News*. White was interviewing PrinceGlobal's representatives in various European cities.

Harris White: Sam Lombardi in Milan, are you there?

Sam Lombardi: Yes, Harris, I am. Right now, I'm overlooking the Piazza del Duomo, the main square of Milan. At this moment according to police estimates, there are about 450,000 demonstrators in the square, and they're still coming. The façade of the *Duomo di Milano*, Milan's Cathedral, is draped with anarchist flags, the now-familiar black flags with the "A" in a white circle in the middle and posters with revolutionary slogans. Here in Milan, Italy's second largest city, not a factory, office, or business is open. Huge barricades block the entrances of the nearby historic, glass-covered arcade, *Galleria Vittorio Emanuele II*. Dozens of the elegant shops in the arcade are boarded up.

Harris White: Professor Falconi's headquarters is in Milan, isn't it?

Sam Lombardi: Yes it is, but I have a real time update that says that he has once again dropped from sight. But even without him here, there must be tens of thousands of Falconi placards being waved around in the crowd.

Harris White: What about transportation facilities?

Sam Lombardi: The airport is hermetically sealed. Just yesterday, I visited the huge Milan Central Station, one of the largest train stations in Europe. Except for flocks of pigeons and nervous security men, it was completely deserted.

Harris White: Thank you, Sam. Adrienne Roux in Paris, are you with us?

Adrienne Roux: Yes, I am. Paris is shut down. And right now, several hundred thousand people with their fists raised in the anarchist salute are marching up the Champs-Élysées in sympathy with the strikers. In a couple of hours, they will be holding a huge rally in the Place de le Concorde, the center of Paris. The city is plastered with huge pictures of Falconi and anarchist flags are flying everywhere. All businesses, schools, universities, and government offices are closed.

Harris White: Adrienne, question: how has all of this unrest affected the famous Parisian night life?

Adrienne Roux: The cafés, the theaters, and even the hotels in Montparnasse are almost empty. Harris, here's something cute. A report just came in that says that the few guests remaining in the Ritz Hotel had to make their own beds this morning! If this is true, Paris, and indeed all France, is headed for serious trouble!

Harris White: Thank you, Adrienne. Now to Adela Castillo in Madrid.

Adela Castillo: Harris, this is Adela Castillo broadcasting from Madrid. I can see from here over a half a million *madrilènos* with raised fists in the anarchist salute, chanting slogans and singing *A Las Barricadas*, marching up the *Gran Via*, the main street of the city.

There are reports of serious violence in Barcelona, Valencia, Seville, and many other Spanish cities.

Harris White went on to report that there were demonstrations in virtually every major city in the world. And many of the protests were far from peaceful. In addition, taking advantage of the chaos, rampaging Muslim mobs were surging through the streets in dozens of cities throughout Europe and the United States, setting fires, looting, and wreaking havoc. Scandinavia, Belgium, Holland, Germany, the UK, and France were the hardest hit. Following recent practice, for the most part the security forces watched and took pictures, but made no serious move to halt the violence.

The PrinceGlobal Media anchorman also noted that there were sympathy strikes throughout North and South America, India, and the Far East. Dozens of countries throughout the world declared martial law.

Harris White always liked to end his programs on a positive note, "A release just in: 'Interpol reports that the anarchists, in a breathtakingly well coordinated worldwide offensive, said to be directed personally by Professor Falconi, have destroyed organized crime syndicates and their hangers-on everywhere.'"

But even the report of worldwide destruction of organized crime did not succeed in cheering Meshullam Hamalbish up. Sighing, he turned off the news.

Soon, there were real fears of food shortages. Lines at gas stations become longer and longer. Private cars ceased to circulate. The high-speed railways stopped running; ships stayed in port; airplanes ceased to fly; and trucks stopped hauling goods. In many cities, electricity was available only a few hours a day. The water supply became sporadic. Even the Internet collapsed. Torn by social strife, haunted by the prospect of greater civil unrest, Europe was rapidly falling into the abyss. Marching mobs swarmed everywhere, shouting slogans, smashing windows, battling police, and brandishing anarchist flags.

Every president, prime minister, and world leader tried to get in touch with the elusive Falconi to "make him see reason." Intelligence agencies and police all over the world tried unsuccessfully to flush him out of his hiding place.

Since Falconi was an Italian citizen, the bulk of the inquiries were directed to AISA, the Italian intelligence agency. Stung by widespread European criticism, AISA initiated a large-scale manhunt throughout Italy, but to no avail.

Finally, in desperation, the heads of all the European security services met in a seventeenth-century baroque palace in Warsaw's Old Town to pool their resources and exchange ideas. Centuries-old paintings depicting important events in Polish history, portraits of bewhiskered warrior kings, and faded coats of arms of extinct noble families lined the walls of their meeting room. Faded Polish battle flags from long forgotten wars and magnificent unlit chandeliers hung from the high oak beamed ceiling. The spooks looked around and shivered: the magnificent, vastly oversized, unheated room was *cold*.

In attendance were Hubert Diederich, the corpulent dour Director of the BND, the German Intelligence Agency; Achilles Papadakos, the swarthy Director of the Greek National Intelligence Service; Alonzo Caropoli, head of AISA; Gunter Overgaard, Director of the Danish Security Service; Axel Graumann, the cadaverous Director of Austrian Intelligence;

40

Marcel Bayrou, the dapper head of French Internal Security; Pierre Boulanger, the chief of Belgian Staff Intelligence and Security; and Mark Hollingsberry and Sir Eric Marshall, the two feuding Directors of British MI5 and MI6, respectively. The United States, China, India, Japan and many other countries sent representatives. The host was Jan Mickiewicz, director of the SKW, the Polish Counterespionage Agency.

Their mood was somber and their fatigued faces were edged with despair. Papadakos noted that two months before, Falconi had been seen twice in Salonika and then on the vacation island of Santorini. "He met there with union leaders but then he disappeared without a trace."

"What about the union leaders he met with?" Caropoli eagerly asked.

"They went underground," the Greek clarified. "But we know for a fact that they are involved in the current unpleasantness."

"We've had several sightings of him in Copenhagen in the last month or so," admitted Overgaard.

"He was reputedly seen here in Warsaw a month ago," Jan Mickiewicz remarked.

"There are sightings of him everywhere," Graumann added. "But few of them are confirmed."

"He has collaborators all over Europe," Bayrou said acidly. "And more important, he has sympathizers in the highest levels of government. There are no secrets from him. But I must tell you about a far more dangerous development."

All side conversations stopped.

"Three days ago, hackers we assume were working for Falconi successfully breached our computer systems. They were somehow able to penetrate our security. There is no question that these attacks were planned and executed by experts who had inside information. We know that Falconi succeeded in suborning some of our top people. The attackers used malicious software known as "Terminator 666." They struck our computer systems, including our central data bases, breaching all of our firewalls. They destroyed millions of files tying up our system resources. We haven't even *begun* to assess the damage. But we already know that a great deal of classified information is no longer secure. The identities of virtually all our agents in the field have been fatally compromised.

"I ask you, have there been similar cyber attacks in your countries? This is not the time to be reticent. We are facing a common enemy. That's why we're here. We are all professionals and we know how to be discreet. Our colleague and host Mr. Mickiewicz has assured us that the entire building has been thoroughly sterilized. There are no bugs, no listening devices here. We can speak freely."

Hollingsberry spoke up hesitantly, "Hackers shut down the computer networks of our Defense Ministry, the Foreign Ministry, Internal Security, and the National Intelligence Service for four hours yesterday. Since then, the systems are functioning only intermittently. But that's not all.

"Hackers infiltrated the most sophisticated systems inside MI5 and accessed and copied thousands of exabytes of top secret information. I must emphasize that some of this information was stored on non-networked secure computers. The very location of these systems is classified. As you know, high-security computers are physically isolated from network-connected computers. In order to pull this off, they had to have help from some of our senior people on the inside. We definitely ascertained that there was no undetectable 'time-bomb virus' programmed into the systems at the manufacturer's location before the computers were delivered to us. Monsieur Bayrou, I fear you are correct. There are no secrets from Falconi. We shut down all our systems and are checking for the source of the breach and we have instituted anti-hacking protocols."

"Falconi's no pussycat!" snapped Graumann. "Yesterday, hackers – we can only assume that they are Falconi's people – succeeded in penetrating our internal and external email systems, forcing us to take 180,000 accounts off-line."

One after the other, the intelligence chiefs admitted that their organizations, and their governmental computer systems, had been targeted by highly coordinated cyber-invasions over the last few days.

"This is just too much! Falconi's making fools out of all of us! We must get our hands on him and fast before even more damage is done!" shouted Hollingsberry, banging his fist on the table. Boulanger sharply reminded the participants that Falconi was known to use at least a dozen bogus passports. "They're technically perfect and can pass the biometric security check anywhere."

"And don't forget something else. He's a master illusionist," grumbled Hollingsberry.

Marshall sighed, "We know he's been in England several times but we never succeeded in catching him."

"One way or the other, despite our best efforts and his distinctive appearance, he just waltzes through security in every airport in the world!" the frustrated Carlopoli said angrily.

43

"Do you know there is a song about Falconi going around Europe now?" Marshall asked indignantly. "It's on radio, television and all over the Internet. It goes like this:

> Professor Falconi is the master of disguise.
> He can vanish right before your eyes.
> He can be in many places
> With a hundred different faces.

The directors of the Intelligence Agencies were not amused.

Popping a piece of chocolate glazed *baumkuchen* into his mouth, Hubert Diederich, the hitherto silent director of the German Intelligence Agency, looked up. His hair, a sandy blond, his face chubby with a double chin, brilliant blue eyes - subtly enhanced by tinted contact lenses - Herr Diederich slowly put down his ornate carved Tyrolean pipe.

"Gentlemen, with all due respect, I think you are overreacting. Our American friends might say that your behavior is 'over the top.' Even if it *is* true that Falconi has all these bogus passports, how can you be sure that he uses them to fly on commercial aircraft? Whatever else Falconi may be, he's no fool; he knows that we – and Interpol – are looking for him. How can you be so sure that the dozens of reports of 'sightings' all over the world are not simply lies, disinformation if you will, spread by his agents to mislead us? And I do not believe for a minute that he 'waltzes through security in every airport in the world.' It is impossible, even for him! Gentlemen, Falconi is indeed a master illusionist but not in the way you think. Have these so called 'sightings' of Falconi been properly authenticated? Have proper procedures been followed? Do you not put it past him to wage psychological warfare against us?"

The German's questions went unanswered.

They adjourned, having accomplished nothing. They agreed to meet again in the near future, but did not set a date.

An hour after they adjourned, the heads of the various intelligence agencies were appalled to hear that their deliberations at this supposedly top-secret meeting were being savagely ridiculed on the Internet everywhere, accompanied by the most acerbic comments imaginable.

The YouTubes went viral.

Chapter Six

Meshullam Hamalbish sat in his sparsely furnished office on *Har Habayit* listening to anchorman Harris White of PrinceGlobal Media on *Behind Today's News*. White was interviewing an anonymous high-level U.S. State Department official who just returned from Europe. Understandably, the official's identity had to be kept secret but he was unusually candid.

Harris White: Could you explain to our listeners what's going on in Europe now?

State Department Official: The situation in Europe is very fluid. One thing is certain: Falconi and his people are firmly in control of the insurgents. You really can't call them strikers anymore.

Harris White: Insurgents? Is it as bad as all that?

State Department Official: Yes it is, Harris. I witnessed what can only be called a pitched battle in one of Paris's northern industrial areas. Riot police with shields and clubs charged an angry, stone-throwing mob, and there were heavy casualties on both sides.

Harris White: Then what happened?

State Department Official: The police advance was stopped by solid barricades of oil drums and scrap iron, as well as a hail of ball bearings and engine parts. When the insurgents started shooting, the police backed off. The police began to run – I repeat, run – after three, *three*, of their helicopters were brought down by the insurgents. You probably saw the YouTube on the Internet.

Harris White: Yes I have, but up until now, we've been hearing about civil unrest and strikes. What you've described sounds more like civil war to me.

State Department Official: That's exactly what it is, civil war. I saw another street battle in Beauvais, an industrial city of 60,000, north of Paris. Despite their best efforts, the police units could not overcome the superbly trained and well-led anarchist militias. Incidentally, some of the policemen actually joined the insurgents.

Harris White: The insurgents sound very well-organized.

State Department Official: They are. Workers' Committees controlled by Falconi's people have taken control of factories and other work places throughout Europe and in many places in Latin America. They've seized most of the major transportation facilities, including nearly all the airports.

Harris White: The police can't dislodge them?

47

State Department Official: The police forces don't seem to be able to.

Harris White: What about the armies of the countries affected?

State Department Official: If army units were ordered into action now, they would likely side with the insurgents. The loyalty of even the most elite units is uncertain.

Harris White: I see. So, bottom line, where does that leave Europe?

State Department Official: If there are no major surprises, Europe is at the mercy of Antonio Falconi. I hope I'm wrong, but I think that the EU, what's left of it that is, and the various European governments will have to cut a deal with him sooner or later. They can't threaten him and they can't arrest him even if they find him. They can't risk making a martyr out of him. His base of support in Europe and around the world is too strong, and it's growing by the day. His people are everywhere, and they follow him blindly.

Harris White: But Falconi seems to have dropped from sight!

State Department Official: Falconi will come out of hiding when he chooses to, and not before. And when he does, governments throughout the world will have to negotiate with him one way or another. I don't think they will have a choice.

Sighing, Meshullam morosely turned Harris White off. He shook his head; he realized that he was not going to get his flax fiber as quickly as he had hoped. Haunted by a vision of idle looms and the *avodah* halted because the *Kohanim* lacked their requisite vestments, the Master Weaver sat slumped glumly over his desk with his eyes closed. The sun was setting and the shadows on *Har Habayit* were getting longer and longer. Overhead, the automatic lighting gradually increased to compensate. Looking around and tapping the side of his worktable, Meshullam slowly sat up and reached for his well worn *Sefer Tehillim,* his book of Psalms. Reciting King David's immortal words both comforted him and gave him strength.

Though there was much debate, the weak European governments could do nothing. In Brussels, after endless dithering, the splintering EU set up committees of inquiry. Well-meaning non-governmental organizations passed power-less resolutions. No one took them seriously, least of all Falconi.

The Russians, Chinese, Indians, Japanese, and Koreans were silent.

Mindless platitudes flowing out of Washington were treated with contempt. For years, hardly anyone had taken the United States seriously. The former superpower was seen as a stricken giant since its once-great economy had all but collapsed through incompetence, rampant debt, high unemployment, and inflation.

Savage riots in major cities around the world fed fears of revolution from both the left and right. Lisbon, London, War-saw, Athens, Mexico City, Detroit, Buenos Aires, São Paulo, Cairo, Tokyo, and Mumbai were all affected. Politicians

49

everywhere suddenly found excuses to leave their capitals for their summer homes in the countryside.

The atmosphere of fear throughout the world was palpable. Within only a couple of weeks Falconi had reduced the entire world to chaos.

Milan's Malpensa Airport was closed, grounding any transport planes capable of flying Meshullam's flax fiber to Israel. Phalanxes of scruffy, armed, iron-faced anarchists with black circle-A armbands blocked every entrance. They positioned fleets of trucks on every runway to prevent aircraft from landing or taking off.

Meshullam's old friends the *Segan* and Meir Hakohen entered his office as he was closing his *Sefer Tehillim.* Meshullam told them about the Harris White interview, and they shook their heads in commiseration.

"Reb Meshullam, Reb Chanina, we can't just sit here. We have to do something!" Meir Hakohen said, with resolve in his voice. "Let's tell the *Kohen Gadol* what's happening!"

Chapter Seven

There was no question in the minds' of Harav Menachem - the *Chacham Muflag*, chief sage of the Sanhedrin - and his learned colleagues as to who was most qualified to be *Kohen Gadol*. He was Harav Eliyahu Kagan.

Harav Kagan was the first *Kohen Gadol* to be anointed with the *shemen hamishchah* since First Temple days. Even the legendary Shimon Hatzadik, Simon the Just, who served as *Kohen Gadol* in the early days of the Second Temple, had not been privileged to be so anointed. During the closing days of the First Temple, King Josiah, the last righteous King of Judah, foreseeing all too clearly the coming destruction, concealed the *aron habrit*, the Ark of the Covenant, and the *shemen hamishchah* in winding subterranean chambers deep below the surface which had already been prepared by King Solomon, the Temple's builder. With the restoration of the *Mikdash*, the *shemen hamishchah* as well as the *aron habrit* miraculously reappeared.

Unassuming and modest, Harav Kagan had been the head of the Sha'ar Shamayim yeshiva in Yerushalayim Bein Hacho-mot for many years. Sha'ar Shamayim specialized in the study of *Kodashim*, the order of the Talmud dealing with the *avodah* in the *Mikdash*. Harav Kagan was the world's acknowledged expert in *dinei tum'ah ve'tahorah*, the laws of spiritual purity. Even in his youth, the illustrious "Eli" was regarded as an *ilui*, a brilliant child prodigy. It was also said that he was one of the great Kabbalists of the generation, though he rarely discussed this.

For centuries, the males in Harav Kagan's family married only women from families that were known to be of pure priestly descent.

In the new *Beit Hamikdash*'s first year, Harav Eliyahu Kagan exercised his authority as *Kohen Gadol* firmly but with great sensitivity and tact. He played the dominant role in reestablishing the *avodah* and setting up an efficient administration. Even more importantly, he was somehow able to reconcile the divergent opinions of the various halachic authorities. After hearing all sides, Harav Eliyahu made a ruling, and the Sanhedrin accepted it without argument.

Harav Menachem and his colleagues had ample reason to congratulate themselves on their choice of *Kohen Gadol*. Not surprisingly, in the first couple of years, there were some glitches in the functioning of the new *Mikdash*, even in how the *avodah* was performed. But under the *Kohen Gadol*'s energetic and firm guidance, the errors were soon corrected.

Many of the senior *Kohanim* such as Harav Azariah Abenatar of Beit Avtinas and Master Baker Harav Naphtali of Beit Garmu, venerable sages in their own right, had been Harav Eliyahu's study partners in their younger yeshiva student days. *Segan* Chanina Abulafia, Meir Hakohen, Meshullam Hamalbish, and many of the other leading younger *Kohanim* had been Harav Eliyahu's students.

♦

The *Segan*, Meir Hakohen, and Meshullam Hamalbish found the *Kohen Gadol* in his book-lined study on *Har Habayit*. Sitting on high-backed carved chairs around a long polished oak table, the *Kohen Gadol* and some of the members of the Sanhedrin were softly saying *Tehillim*. Lifting his eyes, the *Kohen Gadol* spotted the three *Kohanim* hesitantly standing at the door and invited them in.

"*Shalom aleichem*, Reb Chanina, Reb Meir, and Reb Meshullam. I've been expecting you." The *Kohen Gadol* made a sign with his hand and the Sanhedrin members closed their *Tehillim* and quietly left the room. With a broad smile, the *Kohen Gadol* warmly welcomed his three old *talmidim* and invited them to sit down. Despite their objections, he went into an adjoining room and brought out tea and raisin cake.

"Please have some cake. My wife baked it herself. It's delicious," he said with a proud smile.

"We don't want to trouble the *Kohen Gadol*," the three *Kohanim* insisted.

Ignoring their protests, he demanded of them: "Am I better than Avraham Aveinu or Moshe Rabbeinu? They served *their* guests!"

The three *Kohanim* said no more, and helped themselves; the raisin cake *was* delicious. In fact, Meir had a second piece and wrapped a third in a napkin and stuffed it into his pocket.

Anxiously the *Segan* began to describe the deteriorating situation in Europe and how their flax fiber was stuck in Milan. The serene *Kohen Gadol* merely motioned him to silence; he already knew about it. Not for the first time, the three *Kohanim* wondered if their *Kohen Gadol* was clairvoyant. Or did he really have *Ruach Hakodesh* like so many people said? No one ever heard him discuss secular matters or politics or saw him check the Internet news sources. Even so, Harav Eliyahu Kagan was always perfectly aware of what was happening in the world.

Stroking his silvery beard, the *Kohen Gadol* smiled again. "My friends, calm down."

The *Kohen Gadol*'s mood was anything but somber. In fact, he was effervescent with joy. He looked at them with glowing eyes.

"I understand your fears, but listen very carefully to what I am going to tell you. The seemingly impossible will become possible, as is said, 'and you shall see miracles.' We are living in a period of transition. Now that the *Beit Hamikdash* has been returned to us, we are entering a new age, a new world, a miraculous world – the world of *Malchut Yisrael*, the kingdom of Israel. The prophet Michah said, 'As in the days of your coming forth out of the Land of Egypt, will I show them, *Am Yisrael*, marvelous things.' We are entering *Yemei Hamashi'ach*, the Messianic Age: a world where *Am Yisrael* will wax greater and greater as all her lost children, both near and far, flock to her."

Thoughtfully gazing at the three solemn *Kohanim*, Rav Kagan continued softly, "All of our scattered people: the rebellious ones who turned their backs on *Am Yisrael*, those who knew Torah and cast it aside, those who never knew Torah, and even those who belong to *Am Yisrael* and do not know it. All of these lost souls wherever they may be will return to us!"

The *Kohen Gadol* suddenly rose to his feet and his voice became tremendous with enthusiasm, "The prophet Yechezkel said:

54

As I live saith the Lord your God,
Surely with a mighty hand
And an outstretched arm,
With fury poured out, will I be King over you;
And I will bring you out of the countries wherein
You are scattered,
With a mighty hand and an outstretched arm...

"I am telling you: not one single member of the House of Israel – not even one – will remain in the Exile!"

Catching his breath and reclaiming his seat, the *Kohen Gadol* turned to the *Segan*, "But remember, even though the *Beit Hamikdash* has been reestablished, we are still only at the beginning of the process. And remember what our Sages said, *'Kol hatchalot kashot*, all beginnings are difficult.'"

"*Ishi Kohen Gadol*, my lord High Priest, I know that the *Beit Hamikdash* is rebuilt. But look what's going on in Europe and all over the world!"

"Reb Chanina, the Final Redemption does not come about by flipping a switch! Did you not learn the *Yerushalmi?* Did I not teach it to you myself? Do you remember what Rav Chiyah Rabba said to Rav Shimon ben Chalafta when they walked through the Valley of Arbel? They watched the dawn before the light began to shine. Said Rav Chiyah to Rav Chalafta, 'So too unfolds the Redemption of Israel, little by little, and the more it progresses, the more it increases and grows.'

"Under the guidance of *Hakadosh Baruch Hu*, we are beginning the process. And as the process accelerates, we will see more and more physical manifestations of Divine favor."

"Like the miracles that happen in the *Beit Hamikdash*?" Meir asked slowly.

"Yes, Reb Meir, just like the miracles that happen in the *Beit Hamikdash* – except these miracles will be far greater in magnitude and power," Rav Kagan replied with a smile.

Slowly turning to the weary Master Weaver, he asked, "Do you really believe that the simultaneous failure of *two* independent backup systems for the coolers and dehumidifiers and the two independent alarm systems in our warehouse was just a coincidence? That both the primary *and* the secondary systems failing at the same time was just an accident? That the unprecedented destruction of flax harvests around the world by the fungi *melampsora lini* and *septoria linicola* was just by chance? Do you really think that the inexplicably rapid spoilage of the flax fiber in our warehouse just happened? *Mei Hashem yatzah hadavar!* This has come from *Hashem!*

"Do the actions of the Irish – wrongly depriving us of our already paid-for flax fiber – upset you? Know that by these actions *Hakadosh Baruch Hu* has set in motion forces which will cause the fulfillment of what was written by the prophet Zephaniah over twenty-five hundred years ago, 'I will make the peoples pure of speech so that they will all call upon the Name of God and serve Him with one purpose.'

"You will see it with your own eyes. Events are beginning to move very quickly now and soon they will climax in a great crescendo, the great *Hakhel,* just like in a symphony. We and all of *Am Yisrael* will be part of it."

> And it shall come to pass afterward,
> That I will pour out My spirit upon all flesh;
> And your sons and your daughters
> Shall prophesize,

Your old men shall dream dreams,
Your young men shall see visions...

With a broad smile and a tossing of his head, Rav Kagan continued in an almost jocular tone, "There is something else you should consider. Do you remember the Gemara? 'A man should not distinguish between his children. On account of the two *selas'* weight of silk from which the coat that Jacob gave to Joseph was made, Joseph's brothers became jealous of him and the matter 'rolled on and on,' eventually causing our fore-fathers to go down to Egypt.' Now, if the weight of two *selas* of silk – very little actually – could have such a powerful negative effect, why cannot a few containers of flax fiber have an equally powerful positive effect and help bring about the Final Redemption?"

The three *Kohanim* could not think of a reason; their eyes lit up and they smiled.

Looking warmly at his three former *talmidim*, Harav Kagan asked them, "Do you remember the words of the great Biblical commentator Rav David Altschuler, the *Metzudat David*? He said, 'You, Jerusalem, lift up your eyes and look around and see all your people gathering to come to you ... Your children will be coming from all sides; your face will light up with joy. Great wealth of the idol-worshippers ... will come to you ... The House of My Glory; this is the *Beit Hamikdash*, which will be glorified by the gifts the nations joyfully will bring to it.'"

He turned his eyes to the *Segan* and continued, "The nations of the world will vie with each other in offering gifts to the *Beit Hamikdash*." He turned to Meshullam again, "You'll see," he said with a sparkle in his eyes, "we will yet hear from the Irish!"

"But what about Falconi?" Meshullam demanded, raising his eyes. "He's shut everything down!"

The *Kohen Gadol* responded, "The great sage the Chofetz Chaim, once said, 'I envy Pharaoh of Egypt because through him, the greatest *kiddush Hashem*, the greatest glorification of God's name in history happened.'"

Pausing, he sipped his tea.

"Very soon, we shall all have reason to envy Professor Antonio Falconi of Sicily, because through him, there will be perhaps even a greater *kiddush Hashem* in the world than what happened in the days of Pharaoh!"

"But how?" the apprehensive *Segan* asked in a barely audible voice.

"Reb Chanina, I am going to speak to Professor Falconi myself and then I will tell you what you must do."

"Speak to him? But the whole world has been trying to contact him! How will you get through? And with all due respect, *ishi Kohen Gadol*, even if you get through to him, would he listen to you?" the *Segan* asked.

"Reb Chanina, I can reach him. And though I can't tell you everything yet, I have no doubt that he will listen to me."

Then something strange happened. Suddenly, the atmosphere in the room changed. The *Kohen Gadol* looked more majestic if that were possible. Looking around, Meir thought that even the air and light in the room somehow suddenly felt different. Both felt more intense. There was a new tang in the air that did not exist even a minute ago, a sweet fragrance. *Ketoret*? Here? Now? Impossible! He looked at the *Segan* and at Meshullam. Though they said nothing, instinctively Meir knew that they had sensed it as well.

He never felt so alive!

The three astounded *Kohanim*'s mouths dropped open in disbelief. They stared at each other as Rav Kagan said to himself, "Falconi" as he tapped a number into his smartphone. Despite their astonishment, they knew better than to ask exactly *how* the *Kohen Gadol* had gotten Falconi's private phone number.

The *Kohen Gadol* paused for a minute. Then, fondly gazing at the three still jittery *Kohanim* in his office, he said, "You seem surprised. You shouldn't be. Don't you remember the passage in the Book of Proverbs, 'The king's heart is in the hand of *Hashem* as the watercourses?' What King Solomon is telling us is that the heart of any man, even a king, can be compared to streams of water. Just like *Hakadosh Baruch Hu* controls the flow of rivers, He can guide the thoughts of men. Though Professor Falconi is in his own way a king and has great power, his heart still is subject to the *Rebono Shel Olam*, the Master of the Universe.

Chapter Eight

When Rav Kagan called, Falconi was sitting behind a battered walnut desk in the basement of an abandoned 17th century country house in an isolated valley in the Italian Alps. Decades before, the farsighted anarchist leader directed a little known front group to buy the property to serve as the secret redoubt of the growing anarchist movement. Without attracting attention, the anarchists added a whole complex of deep subterranean bunkers, storerooms for food and water, air circulation systems, diesel generators, and fuel tanks. The anarchists left untouched the shattered walls above ground and the original rubble, and carefully camouflaged the entrance tunnels leading to the underground facility. Mature trees were planted among the ruins, and with meticulous care, all traces of construction work were removed.

Falconi's technical wizards took extreme precautions to prevent electronic and thermal eavesdropping as well as potential cyber attack or spy satellite incursions. They sterilized the telephones and secured the computers. In fact, the scrambling technology Falconi used was the most advanced in the world; no intelligence gathering agency on earth had its equivalent. Nothing incriminating was written down anywhere in the compound, and everything of importance was stored on dedicated impenetrable encrypted hard-drives. Alert but unobtrusive security men discretely patrolled the area. Hidden surveillance cameras, infrared sensors, and motion detectors surveyed the single access road and the surrounding pine forests twenty-four hours a day.

Several weeks before the outbreak of the anarchist revolution, activists clandestinely re-supplied the facility.

The interior walls, floor, and ceiling of Falconi's subterranean workroom were made of poured concrete which in places poked through a flaking light green patterned wallpaper. Falconi's desk, cluttered with papers, a miniature supercomputer, and a cluster of state of the art electronic equipment, was in the center of the room. A folding cot, buried by a mass of disheveled dark blue covers, stood in a far corner. The only other pieces of furniture were four white plastic chairs, a shaky wooden table, and a grey metal bookcase. Striking revolutionary posters blanketed the walls. Three swinging florescent bulbs hanging by chains from the ceiling furnished the only light.

Sipping a glass of Marsala, a Sicilian wine, Falconi looked intently at his computer screen. A tough veteran of countless street brawls, his chief lieutenant and bodyguard Eliodoro Russo, sat in a corner painstakingly oiling a semi-automatic weapon. He was a tall man with a scarred face, a close-cropped military haircut, massive hands, a rigid demeanor, and the body of a prize fighter. Intensely loyal and an organizational genius in his own right, he never let Falconi out of his sight.

Seemingly oblivious to the presence of his aide, Falconi leaned back in his chair and with a growing sense of satisfaction read reports of anarchist successes in Europe and elsewhere. The news from Latin America was particularly encouraging. Observers called the continent a "volcano ready to blow at any minute." Just within the last two days, his partisans launched major attacks in Mexico City, Buenos Aires, Sao Paulo, Rio de Janeiro, and many other Latin American cities. Some observers claimed that Cuba, Southern Mexico, Venezuela, Peru, Bolivia, and Paraguay were "overrun by the anarchists" though this last was not yet confirmed by independent sources. Falconi pushed the keyboard aside, slowly put down his glass, and began to think.

He thought of Sicily, the lost world of his childhood.

Beautiful Sicily. Sicily of ancient Greek and Roman temples; Sicily of magnificent Byzantine amphitheaters and variegated, multi-patterned vibrant mosaics studded with gold; Sicily of melancholy dark Norman castles, crenellated moss-covered stone walls, and mysterious resplendent medieval churches; Sicily of the endless orange groves, vineyards heavy with luscious purple grapes, and long white unspoiled sandbank beaches. Sicily, the splendid, the glorious.

Sicily, island of corruption, murder, and death, the land of the *Cosa Nostra*.

Falconi fell into a reverie...

The image of his adored, long dead father and mother filled his mind; he visualized them bending over his cradle and singing him a lullaby in Siculu, a little-known Sicilian dialect:

> Hush, little one, and fold your hands.
> The sun has set, the moon is high;
> The sea is singing to the sands,
> And wakeful oranges are beguiled
> By many a fairy lullaby...

Falconi mused to himself:

Some forty years ago, my father, may he rest in peace, had an orange orchard in the southeastern corner of the island in the Siracusa district. One day when he was alone in his orchard, a *Cosa Nostra* sniper picked him off with a high powered rifle with a telescopic lens from three hundred meters away. One bullet in the back sufficed to kill him.

That morning my mother, may she rest in peace, had asked me to drive to Siracusa to buy some food in the market, and on the way back, pick up some fresh bread from Bruno the baker. When I came back, I found her weeping over my father's dead body. Holding each other and swaying back and forth, my three younger sisters were standing behind her wailing uncontrollably. Paralyzed, I stood there helpless. In front of my eyes, I saw my adored father lying there dead under the orange trees he so loved. His overturned basket and picked fruit were scattered around him, but the wooden ladder he used to reach the higher branches was still standing upright.

We buried him quickly, without ceremony, that same day.

The local police took no interest in my father's murder; nor did the politicians in Siracusa or Palermo, the seat of government in Sicily, for that matter. That night, I heard shooting outside our house. Terrified by the shots, my mother and my sisters huddled together in my parents' bedroom. I stood guard with my father's old rifle in hand.

Someone cut our phone line. There were no cell phones in those days, certainly not in rural Sicily.

At midnight Vito, an old friend of mine who had contacts with the *Cosa Nostra*, came to our house. Breathing heavily, he knocked softly on the door.

"Open up! Open up, quickly! It's Vito!"

I looked through the peephole. Seeing Vito's familiar gaunt unshaven face in the dim overhead light, I hurriedly unbarred the stout wooden door.

"What are you doing here? Why have you come?" I demanded.

"Antonio," Vito burst out, "I know about your father! You must leave Sicily at once!"

"I have to see my father's murderers brought to justice!"

"Antonio, grow up! That's not going to happen, at least not in this world!"

"But the police?"

"Antonio, the police are on the *Cosa Nostra*'s payroll. All the politicians are on the *Cosa Nostra*'s payroll. You won't get any help from them!"

"Then I'll have to do it myself!"

"Don't be a fool! Not only is your life at stake, but the lives of your mother and sisters as well. Think of them. Don't destroy yourself by trying to fight wicked men more powerful than you. You can only lose, and they will kill your family as well. Then what will you have accomplished?"

"Vito, my old friend, what would you have me do?"

"Take your mother and sisters and leave Sicily now. Before dawn, if you can. You can't stay here any longer. Antonio, you must understand, they are coming to kill you!"

A cold chill ran up my spine.

Bowing my head, I sighed. Vito was right. I had no choice.

Like refugees from a war zone, we fled Sicily that morning, before it became light. We left behind virtually all of our belongings. Later I heard that the next night, the *Cosa Nostra* burned our house and orchard. Nothing was left. We could never go back.

We relocated to Roma where a kindly uncle helped us find a place to live, jobs for my mother and me, and suitable schools for my sisters. After an eight-year hiatus in my education, I enrolled in the Sapienza University in Roma, where eventually I earned Ph.D.s in political science, sociology, history and an advanced degree in law. I was considered the most brilliant student in the university's history.

But for the rest of my life, I castigated myself because I had left my father alone in the orchard, which led to his death. I built up a titanic hatred for all criminal organizations and their police and government protectors that permitted their crimes to go unpunished. I promised myself that one day I would get even. One day I would exact a fearful revenge on all of them. And I would build a new world, a just world, on the ashes of the old.

Then Falconi smiled as he recalled an even earlier memory.

I was seventeen and my father was still alive. In a few weeks I would leave home to attend university in Palermo. It was a hot, humid day. The air was heavy with the scent of deep summer; the sun was golden overhead and the clouds rose like white tree tops from

65

behind the distant mountains. Four birds flew overhead in formation. I was working in my father's orchard pulling weeds. Suddenly I sensed that someone was there, and I looked up to see a stranger.

He was an old blind man, shabbily dressed, sitting on a tree stump. He was wearing a tattered gray shirt with a frayed collar, blue trousers held up with a thick leather belt, brown sandals, and a wide-brimmed straw hat. I was sure that I had never seen him before. His strange luminescent face frightened me.

"*Mio padre*," I asked politely, "who are you and where are you from? I'm sure you're not from around here. May I help you?"

"No, Antonio," he smiled, "I am not from here."

"*Signore,*" I asked him with surprise, "How do you know my name?"

"Who I am or what I know does not matter. What does matter is who *you* are." Nodding his head, he slowly rose to his feet and gently took my hand. His grip was surprisingly warm and firm. "Magnanimous Antonio, I do have a request. Could you take me to the bus stop to Siracusa?"

"*Mio padre*, unfortunately, our truck is in the garage being repaired so I can't drive you. However, I'll gladly walk with you there if you wish and I'll wait with you until the bus comes. But if we do go on foot, it will take almost an hour and it's mostly uphill. Are you sure you're up to it? Perhaps I can offer you something cold to drink before we start?"

A sweaty hour later we arrived at the bus stop to Siracusa. I was soaking wet and exausted from the heat of the blazing sun, but to my amazement, I saw that the blind man showed absolutely no discomfort at all. I looked at him closely and marveled. Then he gazed at me with his sightless eyes and opened his mouth to speak. I mentally prepared myself to listen very carefully. Without thinking I bowed my head.

Somehow, instinctively, I knew that what he was going to say would be of great importance and I didn't want to miss a single word. At that moment, I felt that my senses were heightened a thousandfold. The sunlight was dazzling and the verdant Sicilian countryside was an unnaturally bright green. Even the stones seemed to sparkle like diamonds. The very air, suddenly redolent with the sweet fragrance of orange blossoms, had an electrical quality about it.

At that moment, my entire universe came to a complete halt. My eyes riveted on the blind man. I watched as he slowly raised his right hand heavenward in benediction and then he began to speak, emphasizing every word.

"Magnanimous Antonio, as you have been gracious to he who is seen but does not see, so may He who sees but is not seen be gracious to you. Know that you have been chosen to help rebuild and purify His world!"

The blind man's blessing made me very uneasy. My face fell and I shuffled my feet. As rivers of perspiration rolled down my forehead, I bit my lip. I looked up and said softly, "*Mio padre*, I am sorry but I am not a believer. And what do I know about rebuilding and purity?"

"My son," he smiled gravely, "you may not believe in Him but He believes in you. You have been chosen to further His will among men and magnify His glory on earth!"

"Chosen for what? *Signore*, what are you saying? I do not understand."

"Antonio," he replied in a whisper, "One day, perhaps far in the future, it will all be clear to you."

Then, right before my eyes, the blind man vanished! I looked up and down; he was nowhere to be found! I looked behind the trees, the bushes, and around the ramshackle ivy-covered bus stop. There was no place for him to hide. Frustrated, I shook my head. Had I imagined the whole thing? Was it all a hallucination?

But later, when I had been a student at Sapienza University for a number of years, the long-forgotten blind man began to fill my thoughts. Stripped of the supernatural veneer, the strange blind man, if he really existed, simply told me that I was destined for great things. And when I, the despised son of a Sicilian orange grower, easily surpassed the graduates of the best schools in Europe and excelled in my university studies far beyond anyone's highest expectations, I began to take his unusual words as a kind of prophecy.

I began to see myself in a new light. I would be the man anointed by History to build a new world. The power of human will and intellect would play the decisive role – *my* will and *my* intellect. I came to believe fervently in the words of the blind man. My father, may he rest in peace, always said that every man has his destiny. I had found mine.

It was then I made contact with the anarchists and became active in their movement. It did not take me long to become their chief ideologue, and later, their unquestioned leader. After the university appointed me a full professor while I still was in my mid-thirties, I began to churn out books and articles. Invitations to speak - and honorary degrees - arrived from all over the world. Soon I was the darling of the media and my name was on everyone's lips. Within a few years, I became an oracle to hundreds of millions all over the world.

♦

When the phone buzzed, Russo jumped. It was a new phone number and experts, *real* experts, had once again sterilized *everything* only a few hours before. The number had not yet been given out to anyone. Furtively, almost instinctively, he looked around the room searching for enemy prying eyes, electronic or human, staring at him. The anarchist facility, set up with great expense and protected by the most advanced technology on earth, was supposed to be completely impervious to the outside world. He shivered. If there really *was* a security blowout, *his* head would be on the chopping block. Falconi looked up, a quizzical expression on his face. Frowning angrily, his eyes darting fire, he signaled to Russo to answer.

"*Si? Chi è là?*

"*Sono il rabbino Eliyahu Kagan. Sono sommo sacerdote del tempio di Gerusalemme.*" ("This is Harav Eliyahu Kagan. I am the High Priest of the Temple of Jerusalem.")

"How did you get this number?" Russo demanded.

"*Signore* Eliodoro Russo, trusted aide to Professor Falconi, the mere fact that I have it at all should tell you something."

"How do you know who I am?"

"If I know this number, why shouldn't I know who you are?"

"All right, High Priest, what do you want?"

"I wish to speak to Professor Falconi immediately."

"High Priest, the whole world wants to speak to Professor Falconi immediately. Why should *he* want to speak to you?"

"There are reasons. But enough idle chit chat! Tell Professor Falconi – who is sitting right there – that *il rabbino* Kagan, the High Priest of the Temple of *Gerusalemme*, wishes to speak with him this very moment! Tell him that I will brook no delay!" Rav Kagan said with a voice booming with authority.

There was a pause on the other end of the line. "Very well, I will ask the *Professore* if he will talk to you."

Back in Jerusalem, in the *Kohen Gadol's* office, the three entranced *Kohanim* sat stunned. An aide of Antonio Falconi, the anarchist leader, speaking to the Jewish High Priest? And since when did the *Kohen Gadol* speak Italian?

"*Professore*, it is the High Priest of the Temple of *Gerusalemme!*"

"The High Priest from *Gerusalemme*? How did he get this number?" Falconi demanded.

"I don't know!" Russo answered nervously.

Taking a deep breath, Falconi got up, testily pushed Russo out of the room, and shut the door after him. He stopped to think for a minute and then, as he sat down, very slowly picked up the phone.

"*Si*"

"*Buona sera*, good evening *Professore* Falconi."

"Lord High Priest of the Jews, how may I be of service?" Falconi asked, his voice dripping with sarcasm.

The *Kohen Gadol* made a sign and the three *Kohanim* quickly left the room.

"Professor Falconi, listen to me very carefully, 'He saw a skull floating upon the water. He – the Sage Hillel – said to it: 'Because you have drowned others, they have drowned you; and those who drowned you in turn will be drowned.'"

"High Priest, make it quick! What are you trying to tell me?"

"I am telling you that the Mafia boss who ordered your father's death and the man who actually shot him were killed two weeks after you fled Sicily. And your friend Vito, whom you thought they murdered because he warned you to flee, is alive and well. He is living in Chicago. He has four children and eleven grandchildren. The *Capo di tutti capi*, the boss of all bosses, of the Sicilian *Cosa Nostra* discovered that a considerable amount of drugs was missing from a shipment that they were going to smuggle into the United States. When a conference of the *Cosa Nostra* families could not find out who stole them, the *Capo di tutti capi* decided to take matters into his own hands and murdered the heads of the three families whom he suspected of stealing the drugs."

Rav Kagan had Falconi's complete attention. The *Kohen Gadol* continued.

"The first to die was the Mafia boss who ordered your father's death. This triggered a war between the families in which many *Mafiosi* were killed, including your father's assassin and the *Capo di tutti capi* himself. The otherwise apathetic Italian government was forced to intervene when many innocent bystanders were killed in a Mafia street battle in Siracusa. As a result, they arrested all the surviving *Mafiosi*. And after a long and thorough investigation, the Italian authorities sentenced virtually all the policemen and most of the politicians of Siracusa and Palermo to life imprisonment for 'breach of trust' and 'aiding and abetting corruption.'

"By order of the Italian Government, all news of the *Cosa Nostra* war in Sicily, and the subsequent investigations of its criminal activities, was strictly censored. The Minister of the Interior ordered a total blackout, so as not to 'undermine the public's confidence in the integrity of the Sicilian law enforcement agencies.' That is why it was not publicly reported. And for once, and probably the only time in history, the Italian government succeeded in preventing leaks."

Falconi was silent.

Rav Kagan began to sing softly in Siculu, the Sicilian dialect:

> Hush, little one, and fold your hands.
> The sun has set, the moon is high;
> The sea is singing to the sands,
> And wakeful oranges are beguiled
> By many a fairy lullaby...

"High Priest, how can you possibly know that song?" Falconi asked incredulously, "How do you even know Siculu?"

"Antonio, I am the High Priest of the Temple of *Gerusalemme*. I bear on my chest the *choshen mishpat*, the be-jeweled Temple breastplate which envelopes the *urim ve'tumim*, the sacred Temple oracle. It is given to me from On High to know things."

"*Signore*, I have not heard that song since I was a child in Sicily! My parents wrote lullabies for all of us. That was my lullaby! My sisters each had their own. The melodies were my mother's and my father put them to words. That was the lullaby they would sing to me at night!"

72

"I know." Rav Kagan replied softly, "Antonio, your father was a good and honest man though perhaps naïve. He ignored all threats from the local *Cosa Nostra* extortionists and refused to pay protection money to the local boss. He even tried to organize resistance to the *Cosa Nostra* since the Siracusa police and the politicians in Palermo were clearly not interested in helping the beleaguered orange growers. Your father was a brave man."

"Yes, he was. *Signore*, I loved and honored my parents and I always remembered what they did for me. By great personal sacrifices, they sent me first to the newly-opened experimental school in Siracusa – I was one of only six children in the first class – and then afterwards, at great expense, they sent me to the university in Palermo. Aside from my parents, no one in our village cared very much about their children's education, certainly not the orange growers."

"Very true. Antonio, your parents were different. They saw your academic triumphs as their triumphs. They were happy to provide you with the educational opportunities most did not care about. They were good parents, loving parents, and you were a good son," Rav Kagan said.

Falconi smiled. He thought of his parents and sisters. "*Signore* High Priest, the lullaby, could you sing it to me again please?" he asked.

The *Kohen Gadol* began to sing softly in Siculu:

Hush, little one ...

This time, ever so tenderly, Falconi sang with him.

"Antonio, I know that it has been an open wound in your heart all these years, but you cannot continue blaming yourself for your father's death. *Era un bon figlio.* You were a good son. Did you not show him the greatest honor and respect? Did you not return home from the university and help him in the orchard whenever you could?"

"Yes, I did."

"Your mother asked you to go into town and buy food. You were a dutiful son and you obeyed her. Did you not need food in the house? Did you not need bread? Could either you or your mother have foreseen what was going to happen, that the *Cosa Nostra* would strike so suddenly and so brutally?"

Falconi was silent.

"Antonio, *mio figlio*, I repeat my question. Was there any way that either you or your mother could have known what was going to happen?"

Falconi hesitated, his eyes dampening. "No, my lord, *il rabbino* High Priest, there wasn't."

Then with tears in his eyes, Falconi began to talk to Rav Kagan as he had not spoken to anyone since he was a little boy sitting on his father's knee so many years ago. To his surprise, he found that opening his long-closed heart to the High Priest of the Temple of Jerusalem was the most natural thing in the world.

At that moment, Falconi felt that in his heart all things were created anew. He felt a sweet inner peace filling his soul, like the juice freshly squeezed from the best Tarocco blood oranges picked by his father in Sicily nearly forty years before.

All these years he had misunderstood what the blind man had said to him! Still holding the phone in his hand, he raised his eyes and looked around. The atmosphere in the room had changed somehow. And the light! It was more intense! He looked again. Physically, everything in the room seemed to be the same: the ratty furniture, the peeling green wallpaper, the screaming revolutionary posters on the walls, but at the same time they were ... different. They were from another world, a world no longer his own.

He took a deep breath. How was it possible?

There was an aroma in the air that had not existed even a minute before, a familiar scent: the honeyed perfume of orange blossoms filled the bunker with a heady fragrance.

He blinked. The hate and bitterness that had envenomed his soul for almost four decades were gone!

He never felt so alive!

"*Il rabbino*, Lord High Priest of the Temple of *Gerusalemme, mio padre*, what would you have me do?"

Several hours later Rav Kagan hung up. Falconi sat for a few minutes gazing into the distance thinking of the import of the *Kohen Gadol*'s words. He rubbed the back of his neck, a nervous reaction he always had when facing a difficult decision. He pushed his chair back, lifted his glass, and sipped the last of the Marsala. He shook his head; he tapped his foot against the floor. This was not going to be easy. Then taking himself in hand, he took a deep breath and resolutely pushed a button. "Russo, make the necessary preparations! We return to Milan at once!"

Chapter Nine

After Rav Kagan finished speaking to Falconi, he called the *Segan*, Meir Hakohen, and Meshullam Hamalbish back to his office. He told the *Segan* and Meir to return to the *Segan*'s office and wait. Falconi or one of his aides would contact them there. It was going to be a long night for everybody.

Despite Meshullam's protests, the *Kohen Gadol* ordered him to go home and get some sleep; his real work would begin soon enough and he would need all his strength. There was nothing he could do at this point anyway. One way or another, Meshullam would get his fiber.

To the *Segan*'s amazement, the *Kohen Gadol* instructed him to email an authorization with the proper codes to Falconi empowering him to act on the *Mikdash*'s behalf in Milan.

"Listen to me carefully," the *Kohen Gadol* concluded, "Our contact with Professor Falconi is to be kept secret as long as possible. Tell absolutely no one, not even your wives. When the story breaks, the world media will besiege us. You must keep them away. Tell our people that they are not to give interviews to anyone, anywhere, under any circumstances, about anything. There are to be no casual 'conversations' about the *Mikdash* with strangers either. There must be no exceptions or accidents. Remember, journalists are persistent, ruthless, and above all, deceptive.

"All journalists are to be kept out of the *Mikdash*. Make sure the Levites at the gate understand this. Be sure to explain the reasons for my prohibition to all our people. Emphasize that this ban is a direct order from me. And remember, we still have to prepare the *Mikdash* for Yom Kippur and Sukkot. Reb Meir, this is your responsibility."

The three *Kohanim* hurried out the door into the cool Jerusalem night.

After they left, a crowned regal figure arrayed in purple and gold, venerable, splendid, and awesome, emerged from the shadows.

"Eliyahu, you have done well."

"*Hod Malchutecha*, Your Majesty," the *Kohen Gadol* replied with a gesture of great respect. The regal figure withdrew into the shadows.

The *Kohen Gadol* picked up his *sefer* and resumed reciting *Tehillim*. Sitting in his office by the dim light of an ornate brass chandelier, he smiled, stroked his silvery beard, and slipped into his own thoughts.

Europe, Latin America, and much of the world were still in flames.

♦

The *Segan* and Meir Hakohen waited in the *Segan*'s office and started going down their lists of *Mikdash* department heads. By pushing three buttons simultaneously, Meir was able to SMS them all at once. Public Relations warranted a phone call.

Time passed slowly. On the wall, an old fashioned square black clock with white numbers, a souvenir from the *Segan*'s boyhood home in Tzefat, ticked off the minutes. Restless, they stared at the ever so slowly moving hands of the clock. Meir paced back and forth. The *Segan* got up and sat down repeatedly. They downed endless cups of tea.

Finally, the *Segan* said, "We're being ridiculous. Let's do something useful." He handed Meir a *Sefer Tehillim.* Nodding, Meir smiled as he opened it.

The phone buzzed; the *Segan* jumped.

"Yes."

"Will you be home late tonight?" asked Chavatzelet Hasharon, the *Segan*'s wife.

"Chavi, I'm expecting an important call, a very important call. Please go to sleep. I won't be home tonight."

"Have you eaten anything?"

"No, but we'll send out for something."

The two *Kohanim* had been so involved with the crisis in Milan that they had totally forgotten about eating. The *Segan* did not even remember when he had his last meal, probably at breakfast. Meir could not even remember if he *had* eaten breakfast.

"Don't forget. You do have to eat. Can you tell me what's going on?"

"No, but you'll find out soon enough. I don't even know myself."

"I know you've been very busy, but have you heard the latest about what's happening in Europe?"

"I sure have," he sighed wearily.

"I understand. All right then. Good night."

Ten minutes later the phone buzzed again and this time the *Segan* picked it up very slowly.

"Good evening. Is this *Gerusalemme*? Is this *il rabbino* Chanina Abulafia?"

"Yes. Yes it is."

"*Signore*, I am Eliodoro Russo, assistant to Professor Falconi."

The *Segan* and Meir Hakohen looked at each other in amazement. Despite their trust in the *Kohen Gadol*, they honestly did not expect that they would hear from Falconi's people; they felt ashamed of their initial skepticism.

The *Segan* touched an icon on his phone; Russo was on speaker.

"Thank you for calling. Please tell us what's happening," the *Segan* anxiously asked the Italian.

"Our people are now in the warehouse. They found your containers and they're loading them on to trucks as we speak. We have drivers who will take them to Malpensa Airport as soon as possible. We will meet them at Malpensa to help move things along. Also, at the request of *il rabbino* Kagan, *Professore* Falconi is returning to Milan. I will call you when I have more news. *Che Dio la benedica!*"

Russo hung up.

An hour and a half went by. The phone rang again.

"We are at Malpensa. The mechanics are checking out the airplane now. When they are finished, we will load your containers on to the aircraft."

An hour later, the phone rang again.

The now familiar voice of Eliodoro Russo echoed from the speaker.

"The plane has taken off. It should land in Israel in approximately four hours. Now I must go with *Professore* Falconi. He will be holding a press conference. Please listen to it. We will broadcast it all over the world at noon Milan time, 11:00 a.m. GMT."

"I will."

"*Grazie mille.*"

Emotionally drained, the two *Kohanim* fell back on the couch and closed their eyes. A minute later, they opened them and looked at each other. Then with real feeling, they recited the *berachah* that the Sages ordained upon hearing good tidings, "*hatov ve'hameitiv*" – He who is good and does good.

"Truly a night of miracles," the *Segan* said. "In a few hours, Meshullam should have his flax fiber!"

In their excitement, the *Segan* and Meir Hakohen completely forgot about the press conference. Besides, their flax fiber was in the air already, why should a press conference in Milan concern them?

Had the *Segan* and Meir Hakohen been in Milan that evening, they would have been even more convinced that it was a night of miracles. As soon as Professor Falconi got off the phone with the *Kohen Gadol*, he made a few calls and sent a few SMS's. Then he contacted the warehouse where the *Mikdash*'s flax fiber was stored, located the chief of the Anarchist Warehouse Workers' Committee, directed him to find the Temple's containers, and prepare them for transport. Enrico Aquarone, one of his adjuncts, would be arriving at the warehouse shortly. The members of the Worker's Committee were to obey his orders implicitly without question. "Trucks with fast drivers and a motorcycle escort are already on their way to the warehouse," Falconi reiterated. "By the time they arrive, I want the Temple's containers in the loading area and ready to be put on the trucks! There must not be any delay!"

Miraculously no one argued.

Once Enrico Aquarone arrived, he supervised the loading of the flax-bearing trucks and jumped into the cab of the lead truck. The speeding trucks, accompanied by the motorcycle escort sped to Malpensa. Falconi's lieutenants were already waiting for them at the entrance. At their terse command, the striking workers rolled aside the iron gates and removed the barricades enabling the trucks to reach the aircraft. While the ground crew fueled the airplane and the mechanics prepared it for flight, workers swiftly moved the crates to the aircraft's cargo deck. Everyone worked with eager efficiency.

Miraculously, no one argued.

"What's so important about these boxes?" the workers asked Enrico Aquarone.

"These boxes contain flax fibers to make fine linen for the *abbigliamento elegante* – the elegant vestments needed for the priests of the Temple of *Gerusalemme*."

Chapter Ten

The Segan and Meir HaKohen sighed with relief when they heard that the aircraft was in the air. Exhausted, they dozed off on the couch in the *Segan's* office. A couple of hours later, they awoke bleary-eyed. But there was no time to waste; there was work to be done.

Meshullam was overjoyed to hear that the flax was on its way. After concluding *Shacharit*, the morning service, together with the *Segan*, Meir Hakohen, and hundreds of other *Kohanim* in the Chamber of Hewn Stone, he gulped down breakfast, and hurried to his workshop to prepare for the long day ahead. With Meir Hakohen at his side, he anxiously awaited the arrival of the flax fiber and instructed his staff to be on call.

When the aircraft landed in Israel, the ground crews quickly unloaded the containers and waiting Levite drivers trucked them at top speed to Meshullam's workshop. Upon seeing the containers, Meshullam bowed his head and offered a silent prayer of thanks. Then calling over a crew of Levites, he told them to open the containers and remove their contents. As the Master Weaver ran his hands over the bales of fiber, he was filled with growing excitement.

"Meir, I can't believe it! I've never seen such high quality fiber in my life! *Baruch Hashem!*"

"So what happens now?"

"This is raw flax fiber. We process it before we can make thread from it. Meir, look over there."

Meir watched as Levites swiftly moved bales of flax fiber over to conveyor belts.

"Before making *bigdei kehunah*, we transform the flax fiber into linen thread. First, we rid it of impurities, clean it, and straighten it. Once we've spun the yarn, we bleach it. *Bigdei kehunah* must be pure white. All the preparatory work is mechanized and computerized now. Thanks to recent technological advances, we'll have our first batch of linen thread in a few hours. Even a couple of years ago, it took much longer. Then in compliance with the Torah's command, we wind the thread into six ply strands. And our weavers must create the required checkerboard pattern as well."

"Sounds complicated."

"It is, especially since we don't make *bigdei kehunah* from several pieces of fabric like ordinary clothing. Every one of the four priestly garments that our *Kohanim* require is hand woven out of one piece of cloth. In other words, they are seamless. The only exception is the sleeves of the robes. We weave them separately and then sew them on."

"It really *is* complicated!"

"Meir, we must prepare each set individually. And every *Kohen* needs several sets, and each set must fit him perfectly. They can't be too long or too short. At every step of the way, the weaver must make a special declaration of intent: '*Le'shem mitzvat assei assiyat bigdei ha'kehunah*, this is for the sake of the positive commandment to make the priestly garments,'" Meshullam concluded.

With an expanded staff and three shifts - as well as a special budget authorized by the *Segan* - the production of *bigdei kehunah* ballooned. Seeing all the frantic activity around him, Meshullam Hamalbish felt immense relief and a sense of deep pride in his superb staff. He took a deep breath and ran some projections. It would be close, very close, but *be'ezrat Hashem*, he would meet his deadline, and every *Kohen* serving in the *Mikdash* would have all the *bigdei kehunah* he needed for the *chagim*.

◆

That morning, while the *Kohen Gadol* was saying *Tehillim* in his room and the *Segan*, Meir Hakohen, and Meshullam Hamalbish were hard at work in their offices, news outlets all over the world unceasingly trumpeted the news. At noon Milan time, 11:00 a.m. GMT, Falconi was going to break his long public silence and hold a press conference at Proudhon Hall, the anarchist center in Milan. Though no one knew what he would say, everyone feared the worst.

Chapter Eleven

An hour before the press conference was to begin, select reporters from virtually every network and news service in the world were permitted, upon presentation of passports, to pass through the barricades that encircled Proudhon Hall. As they neared the building, the sharp-eyed journalists noted that while there were many tens of thousands, maybe even hundreds of thousands, of Falconi's supporters in the streets, there were no army or police to be seen. They also noticed loudspeakers and large electronic billboards affixed to the façades of many of the surrounding buildings. Squads of tough looking, stubble bearded anarchist security men with battle-scarred AK-47 assault rifles slung across their chests were visible everywhere. Anarchist helicopters and drones flew overhead. As the journalists entered Proudhon Hall, security men once again carefully checked their passports against a prepared list. Other security men roughly rifled through the contents of the journalists' bags; they paid particular attention to laptops and cell phones. They were not particularly polite.

The anarchists made little effort to accommodate the media. The poorly lit press room was overcrowded as reporters kneed and elbowed their way forward to the few available grungy chairs up front. The wheezing air conditioning was dysfunctional, the sealed windows were draped with heavy blackout curtains, and the air was stale. The light from the few antiquated wire cage imprisoned florescent lights was inadequate. Black, green, and gray electric cables snaked across the dirty tiled floor. Hot and frustrated, clutching their lap tops, the reporters who had not found seats lined the walls or stood impatiently transferring their weight from one foot to the other.

The room had a low stage accommodating a red and black swathed table and a dozen dented aluminum chairs. The table was strewn with anarchist pamphlets, disks featuring Falconi's speeches, bottles of tepid *Levissima* mineral water, and some plastic bags filled with paper cups. A brown wooden lectern with a microphone stand – its angled surface scratched and worn – stood to the right of the table. Huge colorful posters of Pierre-Joseph Proudhon, Mikhail Bakunin, Georges Sorel, Sacco and Vanzetti, Buenaventura Durruti and other anarchist icons covered the walls. Falconi's choice of pictures did not bode well for the peace of Europe.

As the bells of a nearby church tower rang in the hour, the journalists heard ear-shattering applause outside. Electrified by the sight of their leader, tens of thousands of his excited followers were enthusiastically cheering and giving the anarchist clenched-fist salute. The crowd parted as Falconi and his entourage approached the building with long, confident strides. Acknowledging their adulation with a brisk wave of his hand, the anarchist leader and his entourage disappeared through the back entrance of Proudhon Hall. The cheering became an earth-shaking roar.

Rhythmic cries of "Fal-co-ni, Fal-co-ni," filled the air.

At 12:05, a side door to the stage opened, and flanked by dozens of aides and brawny bodyguards brandishing assault rifles, Falconi pushed into the room. Quickly, Falconi and his aides seated themselves at the table on the stage and the bodyguards took up their positions, their practiced eyes coolly surveying the crowd. Other security men sealed off all the entrances to the building. Falconi looked up and raised his hand for silence as he slowly got up walked to the lectern and adjusted the microphone.

Within seconds, the dropping of a pin would have sounded like thunder in the hall.

Seemingly oblivious of the hundreds of people who jammed the sweltering room, Falconi poured himself a glass of *Levissima*. He thought of the mysterious blind man who had blessed him so many years before and bowed his head. How could *he*, the great intellectual, the idol of tens of millions, have so misunderstood his message? How? He fell into a reverie.

> *Mio padre*, forgive me, I failed to understand the true meaning of your words. In my arrogance I thought we could build a new world of peace and justice with hatred, violence, guns, bombs, and cyber-warfare. But I know now that such a world would be inherently evil and could not survive. It would not deserve to survive.

Then for the first time since his childhood, his lips moved in prayer, "God of *Rabbino* Eliyahu Kagan, High Priest of the Temple of *Gerusalemme*, help me to do what I have promised."

Falconi raised his head and stood to his full height. Gripping the lectern, he opened his eyes and contemplated the crowd. He tapped his foot. He fitfully touched the back of his neck. Uncurling his fingers, he let his arms drop very slowly. He took a deep breath. He could wait no longer; the time had come. His wire-rimmed spectacles reflecting light from an overhead spot light, Falconi began to speak.

"Brothers and sisters, please listen to me with an open heart and mind because I speak to you from my heart. What is spoken from the heart should enter the heart. What I am about to say may seem out of character for me as the anarchist leader, but even so, please listen carefully.

"From the earliest times of human history, mankind fought for survival. We struggled against the adversarial forces of nature, the weather, and disease. We struggled to find food and shelter and we battled wild and ferocious animals. Our struggles were difficult, and often unsuccessful. Failure was more frequent than success.

"But our hardest struggles and battles were not against the infinite powers of the universe, but against other men. Resources have always been limited and they have never been easy to come by. There have always been famines, and men frequently slaughtered other men for a few stalks of wheat. How many wars have we fought over water? How many wars have we fought over trade routes and for gold and for silver? Can one eat gold? Can one drink silver? What did we *not* fight each other for?

"As time went on, we began to argue about the nature of God. We persecuted and killed each other because of differences of belief. Later countless tens of millions of innocent men, women and children died because fanatical devotees of social ideologies espoused by secular 'prophets' - *you know who they are!* - murdered them. This time, the victims were not religious heretics; they were 'biological heretics,' or economic heretics, or political heretics!

"Brothers and sisters, over the last few years, hundreds of millions of people around the world looked to me as their leader. As I grew older, I came to realize that I did not deserve this honor, and – despite what some people have said – I never pursued personal glory, certainly not wealth. But you found that my aspirations were your aspirations. I believe that I have said nothing that your hearts and souls did not instinctively know to be true. My words struck a chord with you. Though my lips cried out in bitter tones, your ears heard harmonious music.

"Think of what we have done together! We energized hundreds of millions of men and women throughout the world who have sought relief and salvation from their hopelessness. We made them conscious of their power and gave them back their dignity. We led the fight for a better and meaningful life for us all. We took up the cause of the oppressed against their oppressors, and the weak against the strong. There are so many good, kind, and sincere human beings, men and women – workers, members of the middle class, small businessmen and farmers – all over this great world of ours, who have so little, yet deserve so much more. They ask for the basics: a roof over their heads, jobs with security and honor, decent schools for their children, a clean environment, honest government, and impartial judges.

"The lack of response from the ruling classes left us with no choice but to take to the streets. We wanted our fair share and we wanted respect.

"Unfortunately, our just struggle was violent and many innocent people were killed. Who more than I understand the impact our struggle had on peoples' lives? Who more than I comprehend the extensive damage we did to the infra-structures of almost every country in the world? I feel the pain of the guiltless!

"However, our recent struggles have succeeded, and we achieved far more than what we dreamed possible when we began. We started with a small band of ragged anarchist revolutionaries and we gradually became the representatives of many hundreds of millions of men and women all over the world. We succeeded in mobilizing hundreds of millions of men and women, previously passive, inarticulate, and frightened, to rise up and defend their human rights. Today, governments, multinational corporations, and banks will listen to us and, although they still hate us because of their irrational fears, they have already begun to implement those very policies that we have advocated. We have seen our impact in the business world, in the promotion of human rights, and in improvement of a vast number of social issues.

"For personal reasons, I am especially proud to say that we eradicated the cancer of organized criminal cartels – including the *Cosa Nostra* – everywhere. The murderous drug lords and their minions, many of whom succeeded in evading justice for decades, are no more!

"There will be no turning back now.

"We are almost there! We have nearly attained our fundamental goals. We are in a far better place than we were 20 years ago, no, even 20 days ago. For the first time, the powers that be everywhere take us seriously. We are no longer the dust under their feet!

"But now, it is time for new strategies and new tactics. There is just a short way to go to finish the job that we began. We have reached the point when we must do things differently, and I need all of you to support me through this very difficult transitional period. Help us ascend to the next level, the level of negotiation and peace.

"Brothers and sisters, I will now tell you an extraordinary story and you must believe me that what I say is true. You must decide for yourselves whether you believe me or not. But, I say the following with all my soul and being, and you know that whatever else I may be, I am honest. I have always spoken the truth. I stand here before you and tell you with all my heart and soul that I have experienced nothing less than a revelation.

"If you wish to believe that I have 'sold out' or been bought off or that I have been threatened, I assure you that it is not so. You know me better than that. I speak to you with a message which is so true and so correct that you must accept it. It is as pure as freshly fallen snow, and as profound as anything I have ever spoken – perhaps as profound as any man has ever spoken in all of human history.

"Last night I received a telephone call. It was the most unusual call I ever received in my life. To my astonishment, the man on the other end of the line knew things about me that no one on this earth could ever possibly know. We spoke for hours.

"There were no tricks or illusions. There was no manipulation. This was real.

"The man who called me spoke to me about my father and my mother, may they rest in peace. He spoke to me about my boyhood, things which were never spoken of by anyone, any time. He even sang to me a lullaby in Siculu – a Sicilian dialect – that my late mother sang to me when I was a small child in Sicily so long ago. We discussed at length what I have done in the past and he explained to me what the future held for me, and indeed for all of us. He explained to me with a luminous clarity the true meaning of a vision I had in Sicily many years ago.

"Was this all a hallucination? You may believe so. I do not. I have seen magic acts, but this was no act.

91

"I, the anarchist, the arch-rationalist, believe with all my heart that I spoke to a holy man – a prophet and a man of God. What can I say? I felt like the cells in my body were rearranging themselves. I felt truth ricochet through my soul.

"Like many in the West, as I matured, I abandoned the faith of my fathers. You know that from the days of Auguste Blanqui, Pierre Joseph Proudhon, and Mikhail Bakunin, there was no place for God in the anarchist universe. But when this prophet of God spoke to me of Moses, Isaiah, Jeremiah, Ezekiel, and God's plan for all of us, I remembered my childhood and I responded.

"I say to you today that the man who spoke to me was not just one of the many charlatans who throughout the ages claimed to speak to God. They lied; the man who spoke to me spoke the truth. He told me what we must do.

"Brothers and sisters! We now ascend to the next level, the level of reconciliation, negotiation and consolidation of our gains.

"Brothers and sisters, for this reason, I am calling for a halt to the strikes and demonstrations. The barricades in the streets are to be dismantled; factories and businesses must reopen; schools, universities, and businesses must open their doors; trains and busses are to begin running immediately, airports are to be reopened. The anarchist flags everywhere are to be lowered. Workers must return to their jobs at once in a spirit of trust, honor, and reconciliation. I, Antonio Falconi, assure you, your forbearance will be rewarded. We begin negotiations with the powers that be for a final settlement, a just settlement for all, immediately. Take my word for it. For the first time in history, they will negotiate with us seriously.

"As we speak, my aides are contacting our people all over Europe, Latin America, and throughout the world. Let every man and every woman who hears my voice share enthusiastically in the building of a new and better world, not by violence but by good will, kindness, and yes, love. Brothers and sisters, we must change direction, and we must – and we will – do it together!

"Brothers and sisters, I implore you! As you followed me to revolution, follow me to resolution. Follow me to the new world which we will build together, a world of good will, kindness, and love. Together, with God's help, we can defeat Depression II and build a new and better life for all of us!

"Che Dio la benedica!

"God bless you all!"

On cue, Falconi's aides, led by Eliodoro Russo, started tearing down the anarchist posters on the walls.

When Falconi finished, there was silence while the journalists tried to absorb what had just happened. At first, flabbergasted, they could not believe what they just witnessed. Then all at once, they leapt to their feet and began screaming out questions.

Oblivious to the uproar around him, Professor Falconi stood at his podium, smiling quietly with a euphoric look in his eyes. He took a deep breath. *Grazie a Dio!* Thank God, he did it! *Rabbino* Eliyahu Kagan will be pleased! Exhilarated, he laughed out loud: the blind man would be proud! After a few seconds of private mirth - he almost danced a jig in his excitement - he raised his hand for silence. It took several minutes until the astonished journalists quieted down.

All over the world, people listened and watched the news conference. They could not believe what they had heard.

Falconi's supporters in the streets surrounding Proudhon Hall, who had watched the press conference projected on the huge screens, stood at attention, inhaled the fresh air, and cheered. But they did not raise their fists in the anarchist salute.

Political commentators all over the world were speechless. Incredulous government leaders everywhere contacted each other to ask what was going on, but none of them had an explanation. Within minutes, in response to Falconi's appeal, all over Europe, Latin America, and around the globe, people poured into the streets and started dismantling the barricades.

Miraculously, no one argued or tried to stop them!

As Workers' Committees throughout Europe took the first tentative steps to reopen the factories, and bus drivers starting reporting for work, the extraordinary press conference continued.

"*Signore e signori*, if you can remain calm for a few more minutes, I will take questions," Professor Falconi said politely, as he sipped more *Levissima.*

Tall and slender with chiseled facial features, high cheek bones, coal black hair pulled back in an elegant chignon, internationally-known correspondent Samantha the Cat, sprang to her feet, her intense almond-shaped green eyes fixed on Falconi. There was a sudden hush in the hall as she stood there, svelte and poised, with the supreme self confidence of someone who knew that she was at the top of her profession.

"Professor Falconi, I think that I can speak for all of us here when I say that we are stunned by your total about face. Just yesterday you demanded revolution and blood in the streets, yet now you are calling for reconciliation, negotiations, and good will. You had Europe and indeed, the world by the throat and suddenly you, the anarchist leader, offer the hand of peace.

94

What made you change course? Was it really this ... this prophet?"

There was total silence.

"Yes it was. I indeed spoke to a prophet, a holy man," Falconi said simply.

"A holy man?" she gasped.

"Yes," he said, nodding. "A true man of God. He showed me the error of my ways. He touched my heart."

An uproar broke out again. It took a few minutes until there was quiet. Tens of millions around the world heard Professor Falconi's words with disbelief.

Samantha continued, "Did you go to this ... holy man? Or did he come to you?"

"I told you, he called me last night."

"He called you last night ... Professor Falconi," Samantha asked in a wondering voice, "May I ask you who this holy man might be?"

"Yes, you may. He is *Rabbino* Eliyahu Kagan. He is the High Priest of the Temple of Jerusalem."

"The High Priest of the Temple of Jerusalem? How did he manage to brainwash you with one phone call?" she blurted out without thinking, her voice rising a few decibels.

"No one 'brainwashes' me with a phone call!" snapped Falconi. Then his voice softened, "Young woman, have you heard of the prophet Ezekiel?"

"I can't say that I have."

"*Signorina*, with all due respect, that says little for your education. Ezekiel is a prophet in the Holy Bible. He said, 'And I will give them one heart, and I will put a new spirit within you; and I will remove the stony heart out of their flesh, and will give them a heart of flesh; that they might walk in My statutes and keep My ordinances and do them; and they shall be My people, and I will be their God.'"

He looked at Samantha and asked kindly, "Do you think Ezekiel's beautiful prophecy only applies to the Jews?"

Taken aback, Samantha the Cat fell back into her chair.

Someone called out, "Professor, what about the flax fiber?"

Though he had not mentioned the flax fiber, Falconi was not at all surprised that news of it leaked out. He raised his hand for silence.

"I am descended from a very old family. We trace our lineage back to Roman times. It's likely that my forefathers helped destroy the second Temple of Jerusalem almost two thousand years ago. Did you know that in the Temple they offered seventy sacrifices to effect atonement for all the nations of the world? The Jewish rabbis say that if the nations of the world had known what benefit *they* derived from the Temple, instead of destroying it, they would have built a belt of fortresses around it to protect it. In my old age, I have come to believe them. If I could not help in building the Temple as atonement for the sins of my fathers, at least I am privileged to help out in other ways.

"I arranged the transport of containers of flax fiber to Israel because the Temple priests need flax fiber to make linen for their holy vestments. Without the necessary priestly garments, they cannot conduct the Divine service in the Temple properly." Shrugging his shoulders, he asked the amazed journalists, "What else could I do?"

An Italian-accented voice called out, "Professor Falconi, now that you've called a halt to the violence, what's your next step?"

"*Ascolta con la tua anima*, listen with your soul. I will call my teacher, *Rabbino* Eliyahu, in Jerusalem and ask him to offer a sacrifice in the Temple on my behalf and on behalf of all of you. Then I will do my best through negotiation to bring about peace, justice, and good will in Europe, Latin America and everywhere in the world. And with the grace of God, I will succeed."

Absent-mindedly pushing a strand of hair out of his face, Falconi gazed at the assembled journalists and said in a soft voice, "In my old age, I have come to understand that *Salvezza*, salvation, is indeed of the Jews. Ladies and gentlemen, thank you very much for your time."

For a moment, there was shocked silence in the hall, and then pandemonium broke out again. Professor Falconi and his aides, taking advantage of the chaos, slipped out the side door and were gone, leaving behind only the torn anarchist posters on the floor and a couple of opened bottles of *Levissima* on the front table.

Falconi never did take questions in Italian.

As the dazed correspondents stumbled out of the dank hall into the golden sunlight, they saw men, women, and children cheerily dismantling the huge barricades blocking the entrance to Proudon Hall. Owners of nearby stores were jauntily raising their rolling metal shutters, and public parks were re-opening. Pedestrians and motorists alike smiled, laughed, and happily called out to each other. And in the distance they heard the ringing bells of a moving tram.

Miraculously, no one argued.

Chapter Twelve

Newscasters everywhere literally raved about "the phone call that saved Europe." The next day, more than two hundred newspapers around the world ran the identical headline: "Jewish High Priest Saves World from Chaos." Professor Falconi's words were quoted everywhere on the Internet and were the main topic of blogs and chat rooms. His Facebook page was inundated by massive waves of "likes" and favorable comments. The YouTubes went viral.

But now that order was returning to Europe, and the economies of dozens of countries around the world were starting to function more or less normally again, the world's attention turned to the mysterious High Priest of the Temple of Jerusalem and the vital role that he had played in "saving Europe" from revolution or worse. The commentators emphasized how extraordinary it was that a Jewish High Priest from Jerusalem and not a religious leader in Italy exerted such influence on Falconi. They recalled Falconi's quote, "Salvation is of the Jews" and wondered.

Busy in their offices on *Har Habayit*, the *Segan* and Meir Hakohen were blissfully unaware of the world's sudden interest in the *Kohen Gadol* and the Temple of Jerusalem. They had their own work to do, and plenty of it. Intensely involved in preparations for the approaching *chagim*, they put Falconi out of their minds until Meir's wife called excitedly.

"Meir, quick, Google the news!"

The screen on the wall lit up. And there, before Meir's unbelieving eyes, was Professor Antonio Falconi telling the world about his late-night telephone call with the High Priest of the Temple of Jerusalem and how, because of their conversation, he had ordered a halt to the violence. Meir watched in growing astonishment.

He pushed the intercom button. "Reb Chanina, turn on the news! Fast! You must see this. I'm coming right over."

But a stunned Reb Chanina was already watching Falconi's press conference when Meir called. By the time a rather winded Meir burst into the *Segan*'s office, one pundit after another was commenting on "the phone call that saved Europe." They spoke deferentially of the "Jerusalem High Priest's great moral authority." Reporters noted how people, rich and poor from every nationality and religion, everywhere, were now working together in harmony to repair the damage. They commented about the "new spirit" that animated them.

The commentators also mentioned how government leaders around the world were trying to contact the High Priest without success.

Stupefied at what they had witnessed, coming on the heels of an eventful, exhausting night, the two *Kohanim* collapsed on the couch. Meir turned to his old friend and said slowly, "Rav Eliyahu knew that this was going to happen. He said that we would see miracles, and we have! This is the great *kiddush Hashem* he talked about when we saw him last night."

"And this is only the beginning!"

The two *Kohanim* sat in silence for a few minutes, each lost in his own thoughts.

"Didn't he also say that the world media would be banging on our door?"

At that minute, as if in answer to his question, all the telephone lines listed in the *Mikdash* public directory lit up. The media siege had begun.

Not surprisingly, many of the reporters who attended Falconi's press conference in Milan tried to get to Jerusalem by any means possible. Without bothering to take a change of clothes and madly waving their passports, they raced to the chaotic offices of El Al and Alitalia at Milan's newly reopened but barely functioning Malpensa Airport, with the indefatigable Samantha the Cat leading the pack.

The journalists soon discovered to their dismay that there were no tickets to Israel to be had. Apparently anyone who wanted to fly to Israel booked their seats well in advance. Every available seat was taken and now there were long waiting lists.

A few of the more intrepid - and lucky – journalists managed to charter a small private plane.

Chapter Thirteen

A luxurious suite of offices occupies the two top floors of a thirty-four-story oval-shaped skyscraper with a unique red granite and stainless-steel exterior on Third Avenue in midtown Manhattan. The offices belonged to George Prince, CEO and sole owner of PrinceGlobal Media. A beefy man of powerful build with a heavily seamed face, a strong chin, hard piercing eyes, and a glistening shaven head, George Prince was known all over the world as Big George, the Media Mogul. A shrewd judge of character, psychotically ambitious, and absolutely ruthless, he was also a brilliant strategist, and a superb tactician.

Despite the commanding view of Manhattan from his office, the antique furniture, the Persian carpets, and the costly old masters hanging on the walls, George Prince was not happy. Along with everyone else, Falconi's unprecedented press conference had taken him by surprise. Worse, Samantha the Cat, whom even he could not deny was one of the best in the business, was not one of his people. He still smarted at how she had made a fool of him in London five years before. He sat up with a start. He really must be slipping; five years later and she's still an international figure!

And who was this holy High Priest Falconi kept babbling about? Prince sat there watching the conference on the huge screen that covered almost an entire wall in his office. The chatter about "the phone call that saved Europe" exasperated him. In his aggravation, he chomped down on his omnipresent cigar and bit off the tip. He made a grimace of disgust as he spat out the soggy butt. He threw the rest of the cigar across the room. Undeterred, he pulled out a new cigar, lit up, and continued thinking.

Falconi's flip-flop in front of the entire world was the biggest story in years, and his people had botched it! He gritted his teeth in anger. Freelancer Samantha the Cat got all the publicity: his overstaffed and overpaid European Bureau got nothing! However, as Prince realized, all was not lost; he knew that the world's attention would very rapidly shift to Jerusalem. What he needed for PrinceGlobal to get back on top was an exclusive interview with this High Priest: pictures, life story, and some shots of the Temple.

Prince called in his much-abused right-hand man Peter Bernard, "What do we have on this priest?" Prince bellowed, his eyes flashing menacingly.

Bernard, a tense man of medium height, thinning dirty blond hair, sallow skin and deep-set brown eyes, pulled out his keyboard and started tapping. He researched Eliyahu Kagan, high priest, Temple of Jerusalem, and other related topics. Angrily puffing his cigar, chest puffed out with legs apart, arms akimbo and stony faced like an Easter Island monolith, the shaven headed Media Mogul waited impatiently.

"Mr. Prince," Bernard said anxiously, afraid that his boss was on the verge of one of his famous rages, "there's surprisingly little on him for a man in his position, a few bare facts, that's all. There *are* a few articles that people have written about him in recent years, but nothing special, and he's never given a single interview, anywhere."

"The man who saved Europe with one phone call? And there is virtually nothing on him?" Prince asked with a flick of his newly lit cigar.

"That's right, sir."

"Pictures?"

"There are a couple of generic pictures on the Temple website."

"I don't believe this! Is our man Bernstein back in Jerusalem yet?"

Bernard tapped his keyboard a few times and looked up, "Yes, he just got back."

"That twerp! Get him on the phone!" Prince shouted, his grey eyes narrowing.

Two fat pigeons who recently built a nest on the window ledge outside Prince's office began flapping their wings. Then they stopped and glared at him. Angered at their avian insolence, Prince threw a yellow legal pad in their direction, but it bounced harmlessly off the reinforced glass. The pigeons paid no attention. Flapping their wings again, they seemed to be laughing at him. The antics of the two uppity birds did not improve his temper.

Six thousand miles away in Jerusalem, Dave Bernstein's cell phone buzzed. Sighing, he answered it and heard a familiar and not particularly welcome voice. His hands dampened.

"Bernstein! Prince here."

"Yes sir," Bernstein answered, groaning inwardly but mentally snapping to attention. He had expected this call.

"I suppose you heard about the Falconi press conference in Milan by now," barked the furious voice on the other end of the line.

"That's all people are talking about here. High Priest Eliyahu Kagan is a very popular man over here. He is ..."

Prince cut him off. "Look, let's not waste time. I want you to get an exclusive interview with this High Priest. I want to know what he talked to Falconi about. I want pictures. I want his life story, all you can get. Get help if you need it but do it fast."

"Excuse me. There may be a problem there."

"What sort of problem?" Prince snarled.

"The High Priest has never given an interview to the public media. They have their own media company, *Shidurei Hamikdash* – Mikdash Broadcasts. And as far as I know, he's never been interviewed on television or on the Internet even by his own people."

Prince snorted. He knew all about Mikdash Broadcasts. Not nearly as large as PrinceGlobal Media, still, it was an important communications empire with extensive websites and distance learning programs followed by tens of millions of people all over the world and growing fast. And there were strange persistent rumors about them as well. Experts claimed that "Mikbro" – as people in the industry called it – was far more advanced technologically than PrinceGlobal, the supposed world leader. He grimaced. Mikdash Broadcasts had been a perpetual bone in his throat for years. It suddenly occurred to him that for some incomprehensible reason he had always avoided picking fights with them. Stroking his chin, he wondered why. Maybe the time had come.

"Bernstein, can you reach this High Priest some way?" Prince asked impatiently.

104

"I don't believe so, sir. He almost never leaves the Temple Mount. Falconi is right; he is some kind of holy man."

"Don't give me that garbage! There's no such animal," Prince scoffed.

"I bég to differ," Bernstein said nervously.

"Really now?" he said, rolling his eyes. "All right, so what about doing a spread on the Temple?"

"Aside from what they post on their websites, there's not all that much available. And I repeat, they don't deal with the general media," Bernstein replied.

"What difference does that make?" Prince asked in a hectoring tone of voice.

"It means there will be no interviews with any Temple official."

"Bernstein, what's the matter with you?"

"And if they think that I'm trying to go in just to scout the place out, they won't even let me in," Bernstein continued.

"Look holy. They won't know the difference."

"Mr. Prince, I'm telling you that the Levite guards at the Temple gates know who's supposed to be there and who's bogus. I don't know how they know, but they know. And I'll tell you something else. All these media guys who will be banging down the door to get in there? Every last one of them will be stopped. I tell you, these Levites know."

"Look, Bernstein. Do I have to get somebody else?" Prince growled in a low menacing voice.

"You can try but I don't think that's going to help. Strange things go on there. The High Priest has assistants. Maybe, just maybe, I can squeeze something out of one of them, but I don't think so. They have this policy of no cooperation with the public media. But I'll do my best."

"What about pictures?"

"That's something else you should know. They don't permit cameras or recording equipment on the Temple Mount. And even if you take pictures of the Temple from a safe distance with a camera fitted with a telephoto lens, for some reason, they are always too blurry to be of any use. Not even pictures taken from satellites come out! It's bizarre. There are a few generic pictures on their websites, but again, everybody has access to them. For all practical purposes, the Temple authorities ignore the public media entirely. None of their people give interviews. No press conferences, nothing! Anything they want to say to the world, they say it on Mikdash Broadcasts, and plenty of people listen. Mr. Prince," Bernstein said lowering his voice, "inexplicable things go on in that place."

"Yeah, like what?"

"I'll give you an example. Every day when the priests offer sacrifices on the altar in the Temple Court, the fire makes a lot of smoke. But instead of scattering in the wind like you'd expect smoke to do, it rises straight up like a column – a ramrod straight column of black smoke. Even on the windiest days, the smoke from the sacrifices does not scatter. It just goes straight up. I couldn't believe my own eyes the first time I saw it."

"Is that a fact?"

"Yes, sir, it is," Bernstein replied, manfully trying to control his temper and barely succeeding, "That altar is out in the open. There's no way that it can be faked. I first saw the smoke myself rising straight up when I was on the Temple Mount the first time. I couldn't believe it myself. And it was a real windy day. There are other strange things that go on there as well. There are. ..."

"Bernstein, cut it! Are you telling me that those priest guys are legit? Hey, are you getting religion in your old age?"

"It seems that Falconi did!" Bernstein retorted.

"Hmmmm. All right, Bernstein, get what you can, and do it fast! Get help if you need to."

Prince clicked off his BlackBerry. He put down his cigar, and began to think feverishly. He had to admit that Bernstein was a first-class journalist, earning two – or was it three? - Pulitzer Prizes for investigative reporting in seven years, some kind of record. You couldn't take that away from him. But somehow those priests had made a believer out of him. Even more incredible, the High Priest made a believer out of Antonio Falconi! Something peculiar was going on in Jerusalem. What could that High Priest have said to Falconi? That press conference in Milan could not have been a set-up.

Prince alerted his aides and secretaries that he was not to be disturbed.

Chapter Fourteen

Sitting alone in his office, George Prince flicked on the screen once more. Again and again he watched Falconi's press conference and especially his exchange with Samantha the Cat. He thought for a moment. Maybe he should give her another chance. He had to admit that the woman had spirit. He remembered the spat they had at that stupid benefit in London years ago. What a mess that turned out to be, but he had to admit – albeit reluctantly – that had he been in her shoes, he would have done exactly the same thing she did.

Falconi always fascinated him. A tough old bird, brilliant with strong convictions, they called him the leading intellectual of Europe, maybe even the world. Over the years, Prince's people had written numerous feature articles on Falconi, always sympathetic to the anarchist cause – as long as they did their dirty work in someone else's backyard. Bernstein was right though. Falconi appeared to have gotten religion in his old age. The anarchist leader had become a disciple of the High Priest!

Prince remembered an odd historical tidbit: when General Cornwallis surrendered to George Washington at Yorktown in 1781, effectively ending the American Revolutionary War, the pipers and drummers serving with the British army played an old English ballad, "The World Turned Upside Down."

"Maybe the pipers and drummers should have played it at Falconi's press conference," he snickered. "Falconi and the High Priest sure turned the world upside down!"

He listened again to the exchange with Samantha. And there, before hundreds of the top correspondents from all over the world, Falconi, the anarchist-in-chief, was quoting the Biblical prophet Ezekiel.

Grabbing his keyboard, Prince searched for "Ezekiel and prophet" and pulled up the reference.

He read, "And I will give them one heart, and I will put a new spirit within you; and I will remove the stony heart out of their flesh, and will give them a heart of flesh; that they might walk in My statutes and keep My ordinances and do them; and they shall be My people, and I will be their God."

"That might be all right for Falconi. He's only an intellectual! I have a business to run," Prince smirked. He looked at the screen and read the passage again.

"A new spirit ... remove the stony heart out of their flesh and give them a heart of flesh"... Prince mused as he put his cigar down. He thought of all the bodies he had climbed over through the years, all the reputations he had destroyed, all the people he had ruined to get to where he was today. He had come a long way. Prince laughed.

> No one took me seriously in those days. They still thought that I was some kind of lightweight. That was their mistake. At the age of forty, I succeeded in organizing the greatest coup in Wall Street history. After years of meticulous preparation, I simultaneously mounted successful takeovers of *The New*

109

York Times, Time-Warner, Fox and *The Washington Post*. Slowly, very carefully, I managed to co-opt many of their key people, making them for all practical purposes part of my organization. And it gave me particular pleasure to smash CNN. My strategy and tactics worked perfectly. Machiavelli would have been proud! Hah! Atila the Hun would have proud!

I succeeded by working through tiers of straw men, fictitious shell companies and corporations, plus some very fancy stock manipulation. I didn't forget to pay off judges, legislators, and journalists. Eventually, everything just fell into place.

In Washington, dozens of people whom I had taken care of ran interference for me – "friendly" legislators and judges; various officials of the SEC, FTC, and FCC; and dozens of "public servants" and top media people in the United States and all over the world. Paying off all of these leeches cost a fortune, but it was worth it, as I knew it would be.

After taking over the major media companies, I went after the independents. For all the tough talk around town about my "brutality" and my "predatory methods reminiscent of the notorious robber barons of the nineteenth century," no one wanted to tangle with me. I was now Big George, the "Media Mogul," and I made sure everyone knew that, like an elephant, I never forget.

One thing for certain, Prince was no saint. He thought of his two failed marriages and his children who despised him but happily took his money. He pushed those thoughts away, and refocused on his Upper East Side apartment, his estate in

110

Cannes on the French Riviera, his mega-yacht, his Dutch Solid aiR private jet, his fawning flunkies, and his thousands of employees.

Suddenly, out of nowhere, the chorus from an old song popped into his head, "Is that all there is?" He thought of Falconi again. Maybe there really was more to life than possessions, money, power, and fame. "I guess that's one thing I'll never find out," he cackled.

The telephone rang. Prince stiffened.

"Now who could that be?" he muttered. Calls were never supposed to be put through to his office unless they were vetted first. And today he had given strict instructions that he was not to be disturbed.

Someone slipped up, and someone would be fired.

Though he never answered a call without knowing who was on the line, this time, impulsively, he grabbed the phone. "Prince here," he snapped.

It was a vaguely familiar voice out of his past, his distant past.

"Griesha Shmu'el, it's been a long time."

Griesha Shmu'el? Who could be calling him Griesha Shmu'el? It had been years since he had heard that name. He took a deep breath, his jaw dropped. He couldn't believe it. It was his mother, whose voice he hadn't heard in forty-five years! Her voice sounded somewhat different, but there could be no doubt that it was her.

He gritted his teeth. *How did she get this number anyway? And how did she get through?* he wondered.

"I'm sorry, Ma, I've been busy," he answered lamely wishing she would hang up and go away. Yet for some reason

111

he could not fathom, something inside him prevented him from hanging up.

"It's almost impossible to get through to you."

"Well, you got me now. What do you want?" Though he replied in a brusque tone, he shifted nervously in his chair. He was thankful that she could not see him squirm.

"What do I want?" the voice on the other side of the receiver asked with barely controlled fury. "Your father died five days ago and you, his only son, missed the funeral. We're still sitting *shiva*."

"Okay, I should have been there," replied Prince boorishly. "But what can I do about it now?"

"What can you do about it now? You can come here and say Kaddish for your father. That's what you can do about it!"

The phone went dead in his hand.

He ground his teeth together and slammed the phone down. His heart racing, he closed his eyes. Maybe he could make the telephone disappear and pretend that the conversation never happened. Maybe it was a bad dream. He took a deep breath and, like a little child standing over a candle-covered birthday cake, made a wish. He waited a minute and opened his eyes. The wretched phone was still there. He had to face the truth. His mother really *had* called him up. He looked around his office and then out the window. The two fat pigeons were staring at him. He had the nasty feeling they were laughing at him.

His mind exploded with long suppressed memories. He tapped his foot against the leg of his chair and glanced at the window again. The pigeons starred at him intently. And he, Big George, the great Media Mogul, couldn't get rid of them!

112

He ran his tongue nervously around his lips and thought of his once-beloved father lying dead in the cold ground. Staring at the telephone, he fidgeted restlessly in his chair and played with his unlit cigar. Why had he picked up the receiver anyway? What made him break his policy of not answering unless he knew in advance who was at the other end? Why?

For the first time in decades, George Prince felt that he was the servant of events rather than their master. How was it possible that one telephone call could turn him – *him* – into a shaking bowl of jelly? He shook his head; he had lost control. Like a leaf that had fallen into a rapidly cascading river, he felt that he was being swept downstream in a raging current. Unavoidably, he was being pushed into something he did not want to do. He did not like the feeling one bit. Finally, after long minutes of fevered thought and passionate denial, he angrily threw down the papers that he had been tensely fingering and, giving in to the inevitable, pushed the intercom button.

"Tell Fred to bring the limo around to the Third Avenue entrance," he barked as he nervously relit his cigar.

Driving through the less than elegant Brooklyn neighborhood, his chauffeur was amazed that *this* was where his boss wanted to go. But he knew better than to say anything. When they sped down Eastern Parkway, a few raindrops hit the windshield as the sky got darker. A couple of blocks away from their destination, Prince had the driver pull over. As he slowly got out of the car and turned off his smartphone, he looked up and down the familiar street. The trees had grown a bit but the old red-brick apartment buildings and the brown phalanxes of row houses lining the street still looked the way he remembered them, though somewhat shabbier. There was an air of neglect, and the street was full of potholes. Like

113

everywhere else, city services in the old neighborhood had been cut back drastically since the advent of Depression II.

Dark gray clouds swiftly raced across the sky, and the branches of the Norway Maples shading the sidewalks moved back and forth in the wind. He could hear the rumble of thunder in the distance. Any minute the heavens would open up. He had better move it. The wind picked up and so did the rain. As he accidently stepped on the ribs of a discarded broken umbrella, it ricocheted off his leg, almost causing him to lose his balance on the slippery sidewalk.

Only after he was certain that his driver was out of sight did Prince hurriedly cross the street and look for the house. As he felt the rain on his face, he noticed a familiar telephone pole on the corner covered with damp, tattered Hebrew, Yiddish and English notices about past and coming events in the community.

One of the notices caught his eye. He looked at it with a start. It was a partially torn notice announcing his father's funeral. Yes, this was for real! His father really was dead. He took a deep breath; this was going to be harder than he thought. In vexation, he made a fist and smacked his palm. Looking up and down the street, he straightened up to his full height. Breathing hard, he took a final puff on his cigar.

"All right, let's get this over with," he said out loud as he threw the still lit cigar into the gutter.

After all these years, Prince's mother still lived in the same second-floor apartment in the same red-brick, two-family row house on Carroll Street where he had grown up. Seeing the old house, he reeled.

After forty-five years of repression, the nightmare returned in full force. He was fourteen years old again.

One stormy evening after dinner, I was returning to the yeshiva to learn with a friend. Visibility was almost nil and the driving rain made huge puddles on the streets and sidewalk. The gutters had turned into flowing rivers. I was so intent in trying to prevent my umbrella from turning inside-out because of the strong gusts of wind that I did not pay attention to running footsteps behind me. Suddenly, I heard a hiss, "Hey, Jewboy, give us your money! Now!"

I looked up. Three towering thugs surrounded me. Their heads were covered with dripping wet black stockings with narrow slits for their eyes. I was so scared that I couldn't move or say a thing.

At that moment, there was a deafening clap of thunder followed instantly by a flash of forked lightening. Almost if that was some kind of signal, without warning, they started beating me. They hit me on the head, punched me in the stomach, and pummelled me all over. The pain was indescribable. The last thing I remembered before I passed out was seeing my Gemara laying facedown in the mud and hearing a siren wailing in the distance. Then everything went black.

I was unconscious for many hours, maybe even days. When I came to at Kings County Hospital, my parents were sitting on either side of my bed; my father watched me closely and held my hand; my mother was softly saying *Tehillim*. A translucent plastic IV bag hung on a hook over my head and sunlight streamed in through a barred window. I tried to move my legs but the effort was too great. I was bandaged up everywhere. A tall blonde nurse stood at the foot of the bed holding a clipboard.

Full recovery was long and painful. I required three operations and months of intensive physical therapy. While there was no permanent physical damage, my mental health suffered greatly. Though my family, and teachers and friends from the yeshiva visited me daily and tried to cheer me up, I continued to brood about the attack. I seethed with anger.

One day while still in the hospital, I asked my father a question.

"*Tati*, why do they hate us so much?"

"Greisha, who hates us?"

"You know, the *goyim*, everybody. Why does everybody hate the Jews? Those guys who beat me up, what did I ever do to them?"

"Greisha, the answer to your question is found in *Tehillim*; 'They repay evil for the good that we have done for them.' ... They hate us because we pursue good and because we bond closely with God and His Commandments. Our forefathers asked that question already in the days of King David. Listen carefully to what I am going to tell you. The *navi* says, 'You are My witnesses saith *Hashem*, and My servant whom I have chosen.' Greisha, *Hashem* chose us to be His witnesses on earth when He gave us the Torah at Sinai. At Sinai, He selected us to be the teachers of humanity, to spread morality and the concept of justice in the world.

"Think what we have taught the nations of the world: the belief in the one God, ethics, a weekly day of rest, the rule of law, the concept of a fair trial, that all human beings are of equal worth, not to murder, not to steal, sexual purity, charity; to this day Jews are among the most charitable people in the world. We taught them them the concept of *tikkun olam* – the belief that people can work together to improve society and make it better. All that is from our Torah."

I pondered over my father's words for a few minutes, "For this they hate us?"

"Yes, Greisha, for this they hate us. Our sages tell us that the word 'Sinai' is related to the Hebrew word *sina*, hate. The nations of the world who refused to receive the Torah on Mt. Sinai hate us because *we* did. As the *navi* said, we are the servants of God and sometimes the servants suffer because the nations of the earth do not want to hear the message of the Master. We do not call upon them to be Jews but we *do* call upon them to rise above themselves, practice a higher morality, and strive for a more just society."

"For *this* they hate us?" I repeated.

"Yes Greisha, this is the orgin of their hate. We are an embarrassment to them because we remind them that there is a God in Heaven who judges His creations and very often they simply do not want to be reminded. For this reason they resent us. But it is our Divinely-ordained destiny to be God's witnesses on earth and we must be faithful servants until, in His good time, the Final Redemption will come. And when it does come, we will be vindicated in the nations of the worlds' eyes ... and our own."

Looking at my bruised body, I whispered. "I don't want to suffer that way."

"Greisha Shmu'el, you have no choice. It is the Jew's role in the world. We must accept our destiny because we have been chosen, especially you, because from birth, you have been set aside to *Hashem* for a special purpose."

117

The half-open curtains around my bed were suddenly whisked aside. Robin, the tall blonde nurse, poked her head in and chanted in a singsong voice, "Get ready Greisha, the doctors are coming!"

As I sat up with difficulty, I whispered again, "I don't want to be a suffering servant."

The conversation with my father ended. The doctors were making their rounds and when they finished with me, Robin wheeled me out for some more tests. Finally, they allowed me to rest. But even though my body rested, my mind gave me no peace. I could not stop brooding. It became an obsession with me. Whatever else happened, I was not going to suffer like that again. I wanted out.

My parents loved me so very much. I knew that they would never accept my leaving our community. I understood what my running away would do to them, and it broke my heart. I wept for my parents, but my attitude had changed permanently and irrevokably: the break would be total. In the meantime, I would continue as before, learning in the yeshiva. I was still too young to do anything else. I would bide my time.

Chapter Fifteen

George Prince was jolted back to the present when he saw the familiar front door of his childhood home. The heavily painted green door with the tiny peep hole and the blackened metal mail slot on the bottom were exactly as he remembered. Even the large plastic wrapped mezuzah on the doorpost looked the same. As he climbed the steep stairs, he smiled grimly: they still creaked just like they did when he was a boy. The wallpaper in the stairwell was the same familiar pattern of little red roses on a pale yellow background. It was eerie, like going back in time: *nothing had changed*. Finally he reached the top of the stairwell. When he touched the tarnished brass door handle, he paused, his heart thumping with trepidation.

"Why am I doing this?" he said out loud. On the other side of the door, he heard the steady hum of voices. Reluctantly, he curled his fingers around the door handle and slowly opened the unlocked door.

When he entered the room, everyone gaped and became quiet. No one knew who this burly bareheaded stranger with the shaven head was. He had this image of himself as the local gunfighter with a price on his head pushing his way into an old Wild West saloon and stopping all conversation by his mere presence. Noticing the attire of the bearded men sitting there, he felt as out of place as a polar bear in the Sahara Desert.

Looking up, he saw his mother in another room surrounded by dozens of solicitous women. His mother was obviously a respected woman, honored in her community. The women had brought mountains of food with them.

One of the women noticed him, touched his mother's shoulder, and pointed in his direction. Lifting her head, his mother saw him, and paused for a moment. Limping slightly, she slowly came out of the room, touching the walls for support. At first she was not even sure who he was. He had changed so much.

Finally, nodding somberly in recognition, she haltingly gave him a black velvet *kippa* she saw lying behind some books. Wincing as he balanced it on his shaved head, he mentally kicked himself for not remembering to bring one. Prince looked at her; she looked so old and so tired that he barely recognized her. Her eyes were red, her face, puffy. Obviously, she had been crying.

To his surprise, a wave of primitive emotion engulfed him. For the first time in decades, he felt pangs of guilt. He should have at least hired a housekeeper to help her out a couple of times a week, or maybe a nurse.

She embraced him. "Grieshke, I'm glad you came. Go sit with the men for now. I'll talk to you later," she said, turning away, crying.

"Okay, Ma."

The first man who came over to him was his older cousin Chaim, whom he remembered as a lanky newly married scholar always with his nose in a book. Chaim, now much older, had a slight paunch and his intelligent face was trimmed with white hair specked with gray and a white beard. Prince pursed his lips; in his youth, he had looked to Chaim as a role model.

Upon recognizing him, Chaim nodded stiffly, took a sharp knife, and with a pull and a cut made a long rip in George's left lapel, before he could stop him.

"Are you crazy?" Prince cried out.

"Good of you to come Griesha Shmu'el," Chaim calmly said as he put the knife down. "The halachah requires that mourners tear their garments as a sign of grief before the funeral, but since you couldn't make it to your father's funeral, you have to do it now. This cutting or rending of the garment is called *kriyah.*"

Uncharacteristically restraining himself, Prince looked at his ruined jacket with dismay. It had cost fourteen thousand dollars. Even the best New York tailor couldn't repair that rip.

Then he looked closely at Chaim's inscrutable face.

Chaim had personally assumed all the family responsibilities that George shirked all these years. While Chaim saw to George's mother's comfort and had taken care of her affairs in the years when his father was sick, George was busy acquiring various Internet companies, television and radio networks, and newspapers. While Chaim and his children consoled George's mother when her husband – *his father* – was dying in the hospital, George was in Singapore negotiating some contract or another.

How many hours had Chaim's wife sat with George's mother over the years? It was Chaim, not George, whom his mother would ask to order his father's tombstone. And it was Chaim, at his mother's request, who said Kaddish as his surrogate at the funeral. In the years of George's absence, Chaim became the son George refused to be.

No wonder Chaim looked at him with such contempt.

Prince had come too late for *shacharis*, the morning service. He would have to say Kaddish some another time. But at least he did not have to put on tefillin in public. He didn't think he remembered how, and it would have been too embarrassing to have Chaim or someone else show him. Besides, he didn't even own a pair.

People came over to George and said the traditional *Hamakom yenachem eschem be'soch sha'ar avelei Tziyon ve'Yerushalayim*; May the Omnipresent comfort you among the mourners of Zion and Jerusalem.

But they did not start conversations.

He just wanted to get out of there, but he felt like a fiery sword was blocking his path.

Chaim sat him down on a low bench near his father's two brothers, who had flown in for the funeral. He looked at them; they had rips in their lapels. Now he fit in; he had one too.

He looked around. All the mirrors in the apartment were covered so his father's disembodied soul could not come back from the next world and somehow be trapped in this one. All the pictures were taken down, revealing oval, square, and rectangular discolorations on the walls. Five sad *shiva* candles representing the five mystical levels of the soul flickered on the old dark sideboard in front of his father's worn leather Vilna *Shas.* One of his uncles passed out *mishnayos* books and began to learn various *mishnayos* which started with the same Hebrew letters that constituted his father's Hebrew name.

Someone leaned over and explained to him that the word "Mishna" contains the same letters as the Hebrew word *neshamah,* soul. "Studying Mishna on your father's behalf will deliver his *neshamah* from any harsh judgments that may have been decreed against it and raise it to a higher level in *Gan*

122

Eden, in paradise. It's a *tikkun*, a spiritual rectification for his *neshamah*."

Automaton-like, Prince nodded, but he did not have the slightest idea what the man was talking about.

Like his mother, his father was a highly respected figure in the community. He was a well known *Rosh Yeshiva* whose writings were read eagerly all over the Jewish world. Relatives, colleagues, and former students had flown in for the funeral, the funeral that *he* missed, from Chicago, the West Coast, and even Australia and Israel. The outpouring of love shown by so many people to his mother overwhelmed him.

"Who will come to my funeral? Who will say Kaddish for me?" Prince suddenly asked himself.

He knew perfectly well: no one.

People loved and honored his father, Harav Haga'on Yehudah Pressman. His son George Prince was feared and despised, but not honored, and certainly not loved. Not even his children cared what happened to him so long as their fat allowances came on time. On the contrary, like circling vultures, they were just waiting for him to drop dead so they could help themselves to all the goodies. While his passing would rate a substantial obituary in *The Wall Street Journal*, *The Financial Times*, and *Forbes*, no one would say Kaddish for him. Not even realizing, he started humming the song, "Is that all there is?"

Chapter Sixteen

After the Mishna lesson was over, Chaim and the other men in the room rose to say *Kaddish de'Rabbanan,* the special Kaddish recited by mourners after learning Torah. Prince also got up and started mumbling along with them, hoping he could fake it. He couldn't. Shaking his head, Chaim looked at him out of the corner of his eye with tightened lips; he was not fooled for a minute. He looked again.

> I couldn't take my eyes off of him. Greisha Shmu'el had come back! Uncle Yehudah always said that he would someday, even when years and decades passed and we never heard from him.
>
> Uncle Yehudah and Tanta Menucha were childless for over ten years before Greisha Shmu'el was born. All that time, they never lost hope of having children. When people came to see the new baby, the proud parents lifted him high above their heads and quoted Channah, the mother of the prophet Samuel, "For this child I prayed; and *Hashem* has granted me what I have asked of Him. So now I give him to *Hashem*; as long as he lives, he is lent to *Hashem.*" As he grew up, everyone said he was a child prodigy, an *ilui* and eventually he would be a *gadol ha'dor* – one of the leading Talmud scholars of our

generation. He was well on his way until he was mugged.

I guess being beaten up and left for dead in the street does something to you. After he came out of the hospital, he was never the same, always restless and never sitting still. But nevertheless, I was the only one not surprised when he ran away. After he disappeared, his parents did everything they could to find him, including putting out an appeal in the newspapers. The police scoured the area again and again, but it was as if the earth had swallowed him up.

When it was obvious that he really was gone, Uncle Yehudah and Tanta Menucha seemed to age ten years in one month. But despite everything, they believed that he was safe and that he would return one day. "After all," they would say, "Greisha Shmu'el is lent to *Hashem* as long as he lives. He *has* to come back!"

We found out that Greisha Shmu'el was in New York only many years after he had come back to the city. We have our own newspapers and magazines, and rarely read or watch non-Jewish news sources. But once by chance I saw a picture of George Prince on someone's computer screen at work. I recognized him at once. I was shocked! Our little Greisha Shmu'el had become the notorious scandal-mongering George Prince! Of course, he had changed completely since the last time I'd seen him, but without a doubt, it was him. I couldn't believe it.

I tried to think how I would break the news to Uncle Yehudah and Tanta Menucha. It wasn't easy.

"Shall I try to get in touch with him?" I finally asked them.

"No, the time has not come. But at least we know he's safe."

"Uncle, tell me, when will the time come?"

"When he is ready and not before." With that my uncle ended the conversation.

I simply could not understand their serene confidence that Greisha would return some day, and I began to follow his career closely. There were many scandals; the less said about them, the better. He was constantly in the public eye, his escapades filling the gossip columns. He married a supermodel and within three years he was divorced. Not long afterwards, the news broke of Greisha's second marriage to a non-Jewish movie star with a plummy British accent. "Now we certainly will not contact him. Do you expect us to recognize this woman as our daughter-in-law? But Chaim, you'll see, he *will* return. He has to. He belongs to *Hashem*!"

I nodded sympathetically, but I did not believe it. Greisha's second marriage, like his first, did not last long.

Greisha's conglomerate, PrinceGlobal Media, became more and more powerful but did nothing to counter the new anti-Semitism we felt bubbling up all around us.

When Uncle Yehudah became terminaly ill, I disobeyed him for the first time and tried to contact Greisha, but it was impossible to reach him.

Uncle Yehudah believed to his last day that Greisha Shmu'el would return.

George felt Chaim's blistering stare and reddened. The front door of the apartment slowly opened and fifty or sixty young men with jackets and black hats crowded into the room, students from his father's yeshiva.

Someone leaned over and explained to George that it is a great honor for the departed when students study Torah on behalf of their teacher. Aside from learning in the *shiva* house, they took it upon themselves to divide and study all the tractates of the Mishna and complete it by the end of *Shloshim*, marking thirty days after the funeral.

"It's good for your father's *neshamah*."

Who will learn Torah for my neshamah? Prince suddenly asked himself, as he wiped his forehead with a silk monogrammed handkerchief.

He knew perfectly well; no one.

Unbearably hot and crowded, there was standing room only. Taking advantage of the resultant chaos, Prince slipped out unnoticed, promising himself that he would return as soon as he could. Having dismissed his driver, he took a local car service to his apartment in Manhattan, wolfed down a sandwich, and threw some things into an overnight bag. Then, with the iron discipline that characterized his business career, he would force himself to go back to his mother's home.

While in his apartment, he called his office.

"Bernard, what's happening?"

"Mr. Prince! Where have you been? I've been trying to reach you on your cell. The chairman of the *Credit Suisse* bank and his people are due here in a half hour," came the nervous reply.

"Call them up and reschedule!"

"Reschedule the chairman of *Credit Suisse*?" Bernard asked in amazement.

"Bernard, you blockhead, are you deaf? I said reschedule him. Make it the beginning of next week."

"Mr. Prince, I don't think they'll still be here then," Bernard answered in a timorous voice.

"Then they'll have to make some other arrangements. Today, tomorrow and Saturday are out."

"Whatever you say, sir."

There was one more thing Prince had to do before returning to the *shiva*.

Chapter Seventeen

Prince briskly walked down Lexington Avenue, and quietly approached a huge white trailer parked near the corner. On the sides of the vehicle were enormous pictures of a white-bearded sage with a black hat. External loudspeakers attached to the roof of the trailer blared out *klezmer* music. Prince paused for a minute, folded his ripped jacket over his arm, and then slowly climbed the metal steps of the trailer. Opening the door, he saw three young men wearing black jackets, white shirts and black fedoras sitting around a small table having a snack. Dark blue velvet bags, brochures and cards with information about various aspects of Judaism lay in neat piles on metal shelves. More pictures of their spiritual leader covered the interior walls.

As the young men rose to greet him, Prince laid his jacket on a white plastic chair and said quietly, "You're going to have to help me with this. I haven't put on tefillin in over forty-five years." Nervously taking a black *kippa* from a cardboard box on the table, he clumsily balanced it on his shaved head. He rolled up his left sleeve.

"Please remove your watch so nothing will come between the tefillin and your body," the young man requested.

Prince slipped off his antique gold watch and dropped it into his pocket.

Okay, you put on a tallis first," one of the young men said gently, taking a tallis out of its blue bag. "Can you read the *berachah*?"

"Maybe you'll do it with me?"

George Prince and the young man read the blessing slowly together. The young man draped a white tallis with black stripes over Prince's shoulders. Then he took a pair of tefillin out of a smaller blue velvet bag.

"Look here." the young man said as he held one of them up. "You unwrap the straps – they're called *retzu'os* – of the *tefillin shel yad* first. That's the one you put on your left arm. You're right handed, yes?"

Prince nodded. The young man proceeded, "Okay, now we put the box, the *bayis*, over the biceps muscle of your arm so that the leather piece sticks out on the side closest to your shoulder. The knot goes on the top of the biceps muscle towards your body. That's it. A bit tighter; otherwise, it'll fall off. A bit more. Perfect. Now we'll say the *berachah*. We'll do it together: *Baruch atah...*"

As they recited the timeless Hebrew words together, something jogged in Prince's memory. He looked at the young man showing him how to put on tefillin and he remembered his father doing the same thing. His father also had a black beard and wore a black jacket.

But for the life of him, he could not recall his father's face.

The young man then wrapped the strap seven times around Prince's arm. "Make sure that the straps don't touch each other," the young man warned. After the seventh turn, he wrapped the rest of the strap around Prince's hand and Prince held it in place with his thumb.

"Now we're going to unwrap the *tefillin shel rosh*. That's the one that goes on the head. Now look in the mirror."

Prince looked.

"The *bayis*, the black box, should be on top of your forehead and centered between your eyes. The knot is positioned in the back of your head. Then we put the *retzu'os*, the straps, one over each shoulder. That's it. Okay, now we'll say the second *berachah* together: *Baruch atah...*"

"Now, we're going to finish the hand," the young man said. He unwound the strap on Prince's palm.

"Wrap the strap around your palm and then three times around your middle finger. The way you do it is to wrap the strap once around the lower part of that middle finger, once around the upper part near your finger tip, and one more wrap around in between." Then he helped Prince do it.

Prince looked at himself in the mirror again: a Jewish man wearing tallis and tefillin looked back at him. He did not look as funny as he thought he would. In fact, he did not think he looked funny at all.

With considerable help, Prince very slowly read through the *Shema* and some of the other prayers. After he took the tefillin off, he asked if the young man could help him put them on again, he needed practice; it had been a long time. The young man agreed happily. Then they did it a third time. Finally Prince felt he could confidently put them on himself.

"How much do tefillin cost?" Prince asked. "And I'll need a tallis too. I want the top of the line."

The young man hesitated. "Well, the top of the line tefillin are of very high quality. They're expensive."

"It's okay," Prince replied. "Just tell me the price for both the tallis and tefillin. I want the best. That's the way I do things."

The young man checked a price list and told Prince the cost of both items.

"No problem."

Prince wrote out a check and the young man ran it through the automatic scanner, verified it, and put it into the cash box without even looking at it.

"Could you read the Kaddish over with me a few times?"

They read the ancient Aramaic prayer together out loud several times. *"Yisgadal ve'yiskadash shmei rabba...."*

A real tongue-twister, Prince thought to himself. *Aramaic is even harder to pronounce than Hebrew is!* He would have to read it out loud somewhere in private a few more times before he dared recite it in public. When they finished, he thanked the young men for their help, retrieved his jacket, and took some brochures.

After Prince left, the young man looked at the check and gasped. Then he showed it to his friends, and they all gasped. The check was made out for twenty-five thousand dollars!

"This is *gevaldig*! I can't believe this!"

"Hey guys! Look whose check this is!"

They read: "George Prince: PrinceGlobal Media."

"Wow!"

"I thought he looked kind of familiar!"

"I didn't know he was even Jewish!"

Chapter Eighteen

The next day, Friday, Prince put on tefillin and said Kaddish unaided.

At his mother's insistence, George agreed to spend Shabbos with her. He even slept in his boyhood bed, back in his old room. Then, as now, the bed stood next to a big white bookcase, full of *sefarim* that he received as bar mitzvah presents. They were still there after all these years. The door of the closet still scraped on the worn wooden floor. The bathroom mirror with the chipped white frame still had a tiny crack in the upper right hand corner. Sitting up in bed and humming a tune just as he did as a child, he looked through the window and saw the familiar cat-ridden back yard. The old unpainted wooden fence was still there, separating their yard from their neighbors', the Goldsteins. *Good fences make good neighbors*, George mused.

Friday evening he accompanied his cousin Chaim, his sons and grandsons to the old yellow brick *shtibel* on Empire Boulevard where he had become a bar mitzvah. Unbelievably, the Hispanic dry cleaner next door with the flickering red and green neon sign was still there. The old shul had not changed since his bar mitzvah; the walls were still light green and the *aron kodesh* was dark stained mahogany, just as he'd remembered. *Sefarim* filled book cases still lined the walls. When he opened the siddur that one of Chaim's grandsons handed him before *davening*, he was saddened by how little he remembered.

Walking back to Chaim's house after shul, he saw that the old neighborhood was even more Jewish than he remembered. Looking around, a tsunami of memories flooded his brain. The whole area teemed with Jewish book stores, glatt kosher restaurants, and travel agencies offering impossibly low fares to Israel. Kosher pizza shops were interspersed with Judaica emporiums, matchmaking bureaus, and countless *shtibelach*. But that wasn't all. George also saw boarded-up stores, abandoned houses, broken street lights, and garbage in the streets. The old neighborhood was not unaffected by the economic crash that had traumatized America. The streets were still wet from the previous day's rain and the air smelled fresh and clean.

As he climbed the stone stairs leading to Chaim's red-brick house on Montgomery Street, it suddenly occurred to him that he had not entered such a modest dwelling in over twenty-five years, aside from his mother's apartment just the day before. But once inside Chaim's home, George saw the interior of a palace! Immediately he was entranced by the smells of Shabbos, so long forgotten – the mixed aromas of chicken soup and freshly baked challah. As George entered, he saw a long table which stretched from the dining room into the living room. The table was covered with a white tablecloth and was set with beautiful china and silver. Two enormous twisted challot, partially hidden by a gold-fringed embroidered cover, adorned the head of the table along with sparkling crystal wine decanters filled with red and white wines. A score of lit Shabbos candles in silver candlesticks graced the table. Even the little girls had lit candles in honor of Shabbos. Everyone was dressed in their Shabbos best.

A huge picture of the *Beit Hamikdash*, the Temple of Jerusalem, hung on the wall over the buffet.

Chaim's five children, all grown and with families of their own, lined up before their father to be blessed. Then they in turned blessed their own children. Watching Chaim blessing his children brought back poignant memories. His father also used to bless him when they returned from shul Friday night. Taking their places at the table, everyone sang *Shalom Aleichem*, welcoming the angels who had escorted them back from shul. Seated next to his mother, George saw her eyes shining with pride, but at the same time dimmed with sadness, since her husband, his father, was no longer at her side.

Chaim sang *Eishet Chayil*, King Solomon's immortal words of praise for the woman of valor. George noticed that while Chaim sang, he looked at Yehudis, his life's companion for almost fifty years, with the affection of a newlywed. Yehudis, elegant in turban and pearls and courtly as a *fin-de-siècle* noblewoman, looked at her husband the same way. As they fondly gazed into each other's eyes, unspoken messages of love passed between them. Prince's heart contracted as he remembered his two messy divorces and the lurid publicity that surrounded them.

Then Chaim, followed by his sons and his older grandsons, recited Kiddush. After everyone drank the Kiddush wine, they

135

rose from the table, lined up, washed their hands using brass two handled cups set aside for only this purpose, and returned to their seats. Everyone remained silent while Chaim chanted the *berachah* over the twisted loaves, sliced them, and placed the pieces on a silver tray. He took a slice of challah, dipped it in salt, took a bite, and then with a smile gave a slice to his wife. Then with a nod, he passed the tray around to everyone at the table. No one said a word until they took a piece of the challah, dipped it in salt, and taken a bite.

The ritual was exactly as George had remembered. Suddenly he was ten years old again and his *tati* was sitting at the head of the table.

During the meal, the main topic of discussion was the weekly *parshah* from the Torah. The grandchildren relayed what they had learned in yeshiva since the previous Shabbos. George enjoyed seeing all the kids participating actively. These kids literally jumped up and down with excitement. They could not wait to answer the questions that their *zeidi* asked them. Then with a jolt, George remembered that long, long ago, he too had jumped up and down with excitement at the Shabbos table when he knew the answers to his *tati's* questions.

The food prepared by Yehudis, her daughters and daughters-in-law tasted better than any that he had eaten in the most prestigious and expensive restaurants in Europe.

Between courses, they sang the old *nigunim*.

They chanted the mystical Aramaic hymn in praise of the Shechinah written by the Holy Ari, Rabbi Yitzchak Luria of Tzefat. They sang his father's unique *nigun* which had been in his family for seven generations. George remembered that he had never heard anyone else sing it with that same haunting melody. As the family sang, George looked at the English translation in his *bentcher.*

> *Azameir beshevochin, le'mei'al go pishchin...*
> I shall sing hymns to enter the gates
> Of the field of apples of holy ones.
> A new table we prepare for Her,
> A beautiful candelabrum sheds its light upon us.
> Between right and left, the Bride approaches
> Decked in holy jewels and festive garments....
> She is adorned with seventy crowns
> But the King is above Her
> That all may be crowned in the Holy of Holies
>
> Exorcised and cast out
> The unclean powers,
> The frightening demons
> Are now in chains.

Prince gasped for breath.

Who will exorcise the unclean powers within me? Who will cast out my demons? he suddenly cried out to himself, almost in a panic.

He noticed that his hands shook uncontrollably. Embarrassed, he quickly slipped them under the table. They were ice cold. Furtively, he looked around. Thank God, no one had noticed. Then he looked up. There on the wall facing him, he saw a picture of his father; a suffocating sensation tightened his throat.

He shuddered as he suddenly remembered a long forgotten incident.

> I was about eight or so and a much older boy – not Jewish – had knocked me off my new bicycle and

137

grabbed it away from me. The bully stood there waving the bicycle up and down and laughing at me. Then he slowly walked off, carrying the bicycle and leaving me crying. But *tati* had seen what had happened from the window. Totally out of character for such a sweet and gentle man, he raced down the stairs and chased the bully down the block. And he caught him! And when he did, he gave him a good thrashing! I never was so proud of my *tati* as when he came marching back with the bicycle under his arm.

Prince smiled wanly, but then he remembered something else and his smile abruptly vanished.

I was sitting across from my father in his book-lined study. This was two years after they beat me up.

My father had a sad look in his eyes.

"Griesha Shmu'el, your *rebbe* in yeshiva spoke to me today. He is very unhappy with your progress. He says you have by far the most brilliant mind he has ever seen, and he's been teaching Torah for forty years. Why are you wasting such a brilliant mind?"

"I want to do more with my life than learn Gemara."

"What *do* you want to do?"

I looked straight into my father's eyes. Clenching my fists, I said in a firm voice, "I want to conquer the world!"

I was not even thinking when I said it.

That was the first time I had articulated the thoughts that had been coalescing in my mind ever since they beat me up. A few days later, early on a Shabbos morning, I ran away from home. I had been planning this for some time so I had already withdrawn my bar mitzvah money from the bank, and I also took whatever other money I managed to scrape together.

The first thing I did was to shave off my hair and *peyos* and change my clothes so no one would recognize me. Later on, long before it became popular, the shaven head became my trademark. To make sure they couldn't find me, I avoided all Jewish communities and forced myself to eat forbidden foods and desecrate Shabbos. It was hard at first, and eating unkosher foods literally made me sick. There were times I even threw up, but I persevered.

I had a goal, and I was going to achieve it come what may. I was going to conquer the world. First I had to disappear, and for that I had to blend in with the *goyim* and divest myself of any traces of *Yiddishkeit*. It wasn't easy, and a few times I almost slipped up. There were many things I had to unlearn as well as learn. But only by doing that could I succeed. And I wasn't going to be squeamish about how I was going to do it either. Looking back, I can only say that a demon must have possessed me.

I fled to Los Angeles to avoid detection, and got a job at one of the film studios as a messenger boy, at less than minimum wage. Me! A messenger boy! I didn't remain a messenger boy for long, but that *was* the start of my career. I knew that I had to acquire a new identity. To get anywhere, I could not remain an "undocumented worker" forever. A few years after I began working at the studio, a smart young lawyer on the make – who even then realized I was worth befriending – arranged a falsified identify for me, seemingly out of thin air. I still can't imagine how he did it.

One day he called me into his office and handed me a sheaf of papers including a Wisconsin birth certificate, high school and college diplomas, a driver's license, a social security card, and a valid passport. There were even bank records! And not only was there a paper trail, there was even a computer trail, though computers were little used in those days. "Memorize all the info as soon as possible," he laughed. "You're a new man now! Don't forget your new birthdate. You've just aged five years." Magically it seemed I was fully documented and appeared on every data base in the country. I owed that lawyer big time, and over the years I made sure that he never had reason to regret what he did for me. Later on he became my right arm, and my most trusted collaborater. Now I was officially George Prince, and for the first time since I had run away, I felt secure. I was on my way!

That day Griesha Pressman the yeshiva *bochur* died, and George Prince, the future CEO of PrinceGlobal Media was born. I was a fast learner and I was amazed how over the years everything fell into place. I succeeded in everything I did. It did not take long for people to start whispering that I had the Midas touch, and I did! Everything I touched turned to gold. Everything I bought shot up in value and my holdings grew almost by the hour. *The Wall Street Journal* called me "the Rocket," *The Financial Times* called me "the Genius," *Forbes* dubbed me "the Bulldozer" and when I made the cover of *Time* – that was even before I took it over – they called me "the Titan of Wall Street, the Media Colossus that Bestrode the World."

By the time I was forty, I was "Big George, the Media Mogul." Things moved so fast even I couldn't believe it. The *Rosh Yeshiva* was right: I *was* vastly smarter than everybody else. In my new life, no one even suspected that I was Jewish. I even laughed at all the sick anti-Semitic jokes I heard all around me. Many years passed before I returned to New York, and by then I had totally changed beyond recognition.

I never saw my father again.

Sitting there contemplating his father's picture, Prince continued thinking. His hands still shook under the table.

Could anyone have made a greater effort to willfully cast aside Torah and mitzvos than I did? Isn't the level of rebellion against the Torah the factor that determines the seriousness of the transgression? The Torah said to Israel, "If you leave me one day, I will leave you for two." It's so true. The one time budding Torah scholar couldn't even put on tefillin without help. The one time budding Torah scholar can barely read from the siddur. At the shiva, *I didn't even remember what kriyah was. And God help me, to my eternal shame, in my perversity I even hardened my heart when the* Beis Hamikdash *was restored!*

It was hard to explain, but at that moment something inside George Prince broke. An inaudible sob burst forth from his depths of his soul.

Suddenly PrinceGlobal Media did not seem so important to him anymore. He had succeeded in his dream of conquering the world, big time, but to what end? Did he really need all those multimedia companies, cable networks, film studios, publishing houses, newspapers, magazines, and theme parks? His Dutch Solid aiR private jet? The estate in Cannes? What good did they really do him?

"Be a mensch," his father had told him.

Sitting there, George Prince covered his eyes to hide his tears.

Whatever else he had been in his ostensibly super-successful career, he had not been a mensch. He looked up and noticed his cousin Chaim's eyes. They were beaming with pride.

Holding on firmly to the old traditions that George had thrown into the garbage, Chaim had a good life. Though he and Yehudis were not particularly affluent, they were wealthy in every other aspect of their lives. They had raised five good solid kids who had followed in their footsteps, children that they could be proud of. Unlike George's own miserable brats who led dissolute lives without purpose, Chaim's children had grown up and started beautiful families of their own with a mission in life. Why should George have expected anything else? He had only given his parents grief, so why should his own brood be any better? *And now his father was dead.*

George looked around. Chaim had a couple of dozen Jewish grandchildren, and no doubt the first great-grandchildren would be arriving in the not too distant future.

His children, the only grandchildren of his father, Harav Haga'on Yehudah Pressman, and his mother, Rebbetzin Menucha Pressman, were not even Jewish as defined by halachah, since their mothers had not been Jewish! In his unbridled arrogance and limitless contempt, he had chopped off a branch of the House of Israel! How was "Big George," the scion of great rabbinical families on both sides for generations, going to explain *that* in *Beis Din shel Ma'alah,* the Heavenly Tribunal? His stable of wildly overpaid lawyers would not be able to help him up there!

142

He closed his eyes and he was studying *Perek* with his father on a rainy Shabbos afternoon. Graced by a decorative cut glass vase with a spray of red and yellow tulips, the table for *Seudas Shelishis*, the third Shabbos meal, had already been set. Breathing heavily as he looked at his father's picture, Prince whispered the passage they had learned together.

> Akavia the son of Mahalalel used to say: Reflect upon three things and you will not come to sin. Know from where you came, where you are going, and before whom you are destined to give a judgment and accounting. From where you came, from a putrid drop; where you are going, to a place of dust, maggots and worms; and before whom you are destined to give a judgment and accounting, before the supreme King of Kings, the Holy One, blessed be He.

What excuse will I be able to give the King of Kings, the Holy One, blessed be He?

George Prince, usually so good with words, had no answer.

Sitting there with bowed head and closed eyes, George trembled. Shaking, he tightly gripped the arms of his chair.

A soft sound interrupted his musing, *ting, ting, ting*. A moment later, it started again; *ting, ting, ting*. He opened his eyes.

Chaim was standing at the head of the table and gently tapping his fingernail against the side of a crystal glass. "*Kinderlech, eineklech*, can I have quiet please? I have something to say." As Chaim cleared his throat, everyone in the room respectfully quieted down and looked up.

"*Baruch hatov ve'hameitiv*," Chaim began, reciting the blessing ordained by the Sages upon hearing good news. Everyone's ears perked up.

143

"Yesterday we got word that our homes in *Eretz Yisrael* are finally finished! I couldn't mention it before because we were still sitting *shiva* for Uncle Yehudah. But now I can tell you that the contractor notified me that the painters have completed their work, and the kitchen cabinets and closets have been installed. The electricity and water are connected, and everything passed inspection. The contractor says that we can move right in.

"Now that we've passed the last hurdle, *im yirtzeh Hashem*, and *be'ezrat Hashem*, we can make our final arrangements. We will make aliyah as soon as possible. There is absolutely no reason to stay in *galus* even a minute longer than we have to!"

Chaim turned to his excited wide-eyed grandchildren sitting at the end of the table and said with a warm glow in his sparkling eyes, "*Eineklech*, after Shabbos, start packing!" He turned towards Prince's mother, and smiled, "Tanta Menucha, your new bedroom *will* have a southern exposure."

All the grandchildren cheered loudly. Yehudis and the children were radiant. They had been planning this move for a long time. Spontaneously, everyone burst into song, "*Veshavu vanim, veshavu vanim le'gelvulam* - and the children shall return to their borders."

Pointing to the picture of the *Beit Hamikdash* hanging on the wall, Chaim cried out, "*Kinderlech, eineklech, Eretz Yisrael* is calling her children home!"

The cheering became even louder and some of the *eineklech* got carried away and started banging on the table.

Prince was stunned. Chaim and his family were leaving Brooklyn and moving to Israel! Like many of their friends and neighbors, they were relocating to the growing garden city of Har-El in *Eretz Binyamin* – the land allotted to the tribe of

144

Benjamin by Joshua – ten kilometers north of Jerusalem. And after all these years, his mother, Tanta Menucha, as they respectfully called her, would be leaving Carroll Street and going with them. Of course he had known nothing about any of this. George noticed that mixed with the feelings of joy, there was also a sadness in the air. His father, the beloved Rav Pressman, had not lived to fulfill his dream of living in *Eretz Yisrael*.

As Chaim began eulogizing Rav Pressman, Prince wondered who would eulogize *him*. His assistant Peter Bernard? The chairman of *Credit Suisse*? The editors of *The Wall Street Journal*? *Forbes*? He controlled all sorts of media outlets, yet he felt a void. Chaim had children and grandchildren he could be proud of. Who was the real winner in the casino of life? Chaim's quiver was full: his was empty. Chaim had a family he loved and who loved him. Chaim was an honored member of a community and part of an eternal people. George Prince, for all his power, for all his money, was a barren tree, a solitary atom floating in space. He had thousands of employees and fawning flunkies all over the world, but he did not have one real friend, not one, whom he could really talk to. Not a single one.

Sitting at Chaim's table, George made a decision. He would take himself in hand and try to salvage what he could. He would try to become the mensch his father had wanted him to be. There was more to life than multimedia companies, television stations and theme parks. He considered himself an intelligent man. Why had it taken him so long to understand this?

He suddenly realized that he actually enjoyed observing Shabbos. It was so restful, so peaceful. He even learned *Pirkei*

Avos with Chaim before *Seudas Shelishis*. When the three stars came out on Saturday night signaling the end of Shabbos, he felt real regret. That night, before he returned to his empty apartment in Manhattan, he had a long talk with his cousin Chaim, his wife Yehudis, and his mother. He was astounded by how easily he could talk to them. He was amazed to find out how perceptive and intelligent they really were.

Chapter Nineteen

Early Sunday morning, Prince's chauffeur drove him to a synagogue on Lexington Avenue between 94th and 95th. He chose this particular synagogue to *daven shacharit* in because it was less ostentatious than the larger, more affluent one closer to his Upper East Side apartment, and he knew that here he would attract less attention.

Exiting the car and holding his new tallis bag, Prince instructed his bodyguards to wait for him outside. After the service was over, he reflected as he removed his tallis and tefillin. He had fulfilled his filial obligation, and said Kaddish for his father. He smiled; *im yirtzeh Hashem*, he had helped his father's soul to ascend to even a higher level in *Gan Eden*.

In a sunny mood, he asked his chauffeur to drive him to his office. There he found Peter Bernard silently preparing the week's appointment schedule for approval. Apparently, the people from *Credit Suisse* had flown back to Zurich; Prince had missed them. Never mind, he would get back to them another time.

He paused and thought for a moment. Up until a couple of days ago, had he missed the chairman of *Credit Suisse*, he would have gone on a rampage like a wounded bull elephant.

Those days are over, he vowed to himself. *No more bullying people and no more temper tantrums. It's time to grow up.*

"*Be a mensch*," his father said.

Closing the door to his office, he sat behind his desk. He thought about his parents, the *shiva*, his cousin Chaim, his wife Yehudis, and their beautiful family.

Images of Falconi and his Milan press conference flickered through his brain. It took real courage to do what Falconi had done, repenting and changing course. And doing it in front of the entire world!

"That Falconi has all the luck. I wish the High Priest would have called me instead!" he said out loud. He thought for a few more minutes and made a decision. If Falconi could do it, so could he.

Prince brought up the Temple website. He followed the instructions, filling in all the required information. He paused when he had to make one particular choice. Finally he selected "lamb."

Like Antonio Falconi, he had (albeit electronically) requested and authorized the priests of the Temple of Jerusalem to offer a burnt offering on his behalf. He noted that the Temple would email him back the exact time when his sacrifice would be offered. The site also informed him that at the specified time, he had to be awake. After all, Jerusalem was quite a few hours ahead of New York. Once awake, he had to put himself into the right frame of mind and have the proper intentions. The Temple site provided step by step instructions on how to accomplish this. If he did not do so, the site warned, the sacrifice in the Temple would be a meaningless gesture, and in fact, counterproductive.

"Be a mensch," his father said.

Looking around his palatial office, he made another decision. He always prided himself that he paid the lowest salaries in the industry. *That was going to change as of now.*

148

First thing tomorrow morning, he would call in his people from human resources and the legal department, as well as his financial experts to discuss how the change could be effected as quickly and as efficiently as possible. He also knew that his best people deserved real bonuses aside from mere increases in salary, beginning with the long-suffering Peter Bernard.

"Plenty of pasture for all the sheep!" he chortled.

He laughed when he imagined their reactions. *That will blow them away.*

Pushing a button, George said, in language and a tone of voice he had not used in years, "Excuse me, Peter, could you come in here for a moment, please? There is something I would like to discuss with you."

Peter Bernard practically fell off his chair; his boss had not spoken to him in such a polite tone in twenty years. He was even more shocked when he heard what his boss wanted. Hours later after a jubilant Peter Bernard had long gone home, Prince remained at his desk, letting his mind run free. He couldn't remember when he felt so good, maybe twenty years younger. He felt, well, rejuvenated.

Today, perhaps for the first time in his life, he had been a mensch. His father would have been proud.

Behind the computer on his desk, he noticed the brochures that the young man who had helped him put on tefillin gave him. He picked them up and slowly read them cover to cover. Then, nodding and smiling, he reached for the telephone.

The urgent phone calls and emails from the chairman of *Credit Suisse* went unanswered.

Chapter Twenty

Somewhat behind schedule, Meir Hakohen was finally able to report to the *Segan* that the last of the thousands of temporary holding pens south of Jerusalem and the huge aluminum prefab hangers were in place. The hangers were well-stocked with fodder for the tens of thousands of sacrificial animals needed for the *olei regel*, pilgrims who would ascend to Jerusalem for the holidays. IsRail train service had assured him that they could handle all the extra trains required, both passenger and freight. In fact, the special trains transporting the sacrificial animals to the holding pens were already running.

Upon hearing the news, the *Segan* sighed with relief. *Baruch Hashem*!

There would even be extra trains filled with palm branches for *s'chach* for roofing sukkot and *mehudar* etrogim, coming from the vast date and etrog plantations belonging to the scores of flourishing new settlements that dotted the northern Sinai and New Greater Gush Katif. The newly-expanded Atarot International Airport was now ready for the expected influx of people. The high-speed rail system that now spanned the country was running perfectly. The ports of Haifa and Ashdod would also be working overtime, as more *olei regel* came to *Eretz Yisrael* by ship every year.

The Mikdash Home Hospitality Committee worked around the clock for weeks, yet the lists of *olei regel* requesting home hospitality only grew longer. The Jerusalem Municipality estimated that hospitable Jerusalemites and their guests would be building tens of thousands of sukkot for the holiday on just about every available sukkah porch, roof, driveway, and sidewalk in Jerusalem.

Elimelech Eizenman, media advisor to the *Segan*, launched a massive publicity campaign to induce Jerusalemites to host *olei regel* in their homes. He based his campaign on the well-known passage from *Pirkei Avot*, "No man ever said to his fellow: 'The place is insufficient for me to stay overnight in Jerusalem.'"

Eizenman challenged present day Jerusalemites, "Will **our** *olei regel* be able to say the same?" Eizenman's campaign was promoted everywhere: on the Internet, in print and in the mass media. In neighborhoods in close proximity to the *Mikdash*, whole walls papered over with colorful posters hammered Eizenman's message home.

And the Jerusalemites responded! The number of families offering home hospitality spiked. Swamped with Jerusalemites' requests for guests, the Mikdash Home Hospitality Committee matched up the ever-increasing numbers of *olei regel* with an unprecedented number of families eager to host them. The ancient tradition of Jerusalemites extending home hospitality to *olei regel* was back in full swing! "It will be tight but, *im yirtzeh Hashem*, every *oleh regel* and his family will have a roof over their heads during the *chagim*," the committee chairwoman informed Eizenman. Eizenman passed the news on to Meir Hakohen. Meir's shoulders, previously tight with tension, relaxed, and he relayed Eizenman's good news to the *Segan*.

Surveying the top-level project management results, the *Segan* exalted, "Things are starting to jell! *Im yirtzeh Hashem*, we'll just squeak by."

In his office down the hall, Meir Hakohen was carefully checking his management reports. Did an *oleh regel* from Ra'anana or Rio de Janeiro have the slightest idea of the planning that went into preparing Jerusalem and the *Mikdash* for the thrice-yearly flood of *olei regel*? A thousand things could go wrong! Could an *oleh regel* from London or Los Angeles even conceive of the enormous amount of additional food that had to be brought into Jerusalem during the *chagim*? And the food had to be efficiently distributed according to a strict time schedule so the supermarkets would not be caught short. *Olei regel panic when they see empty shelves*, Meir laughed to himself.

They also needed sufficient animals for *korbanot* as well. Ah yes, *korbanot*. Meir needed to make sure everything was under control on the *korbanot* front as well. He bestirred himself.

Sitting up in his chair, Meir noted a few significant differences between the forecast quantities of each animal and bird needed for the sacrifices and the projected supply. He then sent a quick email to one of his aides, requesting that he clarify the matter and report back to him immediately.

Ever the perfectionist, Meir ruefully thought to himself that however computerized the system is, there still could be the occasional slip-up. Meir shivered when he recalled how one day during *chol hamo'ed Pesach* a couple of years ago, they had almost run out of *solet*, the fine flour required for the meal offerings. Fortunately, Supply was able to provide what was needed from emergency storage.

But it should not have happened.

After Meir reviewed his management reports for the third time, he smiled. The Levites had just finished moving the extra supply of the purest fine olive oil needed for Yom Kippur and Sukkot from the vast *Mikdash* subterranean storehouses into the *Lishkat Hashemanim,* the special chamber where oil and wine were stored in the *Ezrat Nashim* in the outer Temple court.

This morning, the Master Spice Apothecary, Harav Azariah Abenatar of Beit Avtinas, had confirmed that the requisite *ketoret* needed for the *chagim* was already compounded and in place. The extra wine, some from Meir's father's winery, needed for the *chagim*, would be moved into the *Lishkat Hashemanim* tomorrow morning. And as of yesterday, the *Mikdash* storerooms were bulging with fine flour.

Meir noted with pleasure that *av bayit,* Reb Yehoshua and his team of artisans, finished refurbishing the sacrificial altar. This semi-annual renovation and re-plastering of the *mizbei'ach* required extra fine-tuning, as this had to be done in such a way as not to interfere with the daily *avodah* of the *Kohanim.* And after a thorough inspection, the *Mikdash* stonemason inspectors verified that no flagstone in the *Azarah* floor was loose or had developed cracks. This was of particular importance because a loose or cracked flagstone in the *Azarah* floor invalidated the *avodah* of the *Kohen* standing on it.

Putt! An email just arrived; it was from Radash and Leilush, the two *Mikdash* Master Goldsmiths. All ninety-three new gold vessels ordered by the *Kohen Gadol* for the coming year were ready. "If you send us Levites and transport to take them to the *mikva'ot,* they can be purified. Please get back to us so we can make arrangements." Meir made a note in his calendar to attend to it.

Meir sat back in his chair and his smile grew wider. In the next few days, six hundred and forty-eight young *Kohanim* would be finishing their final exams. In an impressive ceremony in the *Lishkat Hagazit,* the Chamber of Hewn Stone, they would receive their certificates of validation from the Sanhedrin authorizing them to serve in the *Beit Hamikdash.* This certificate also signified that the Sanhedrin accepted the documentation that the young *Kohanim* had submitted, attesting that they were indeed descended in the male line directly from Aaron, the first *Kohen Gadol.* Then, after a number of *divrei Torah,* the *Chacham Muflag* and his colleagues, together with the *Kohen Gadol,* the newly-certified white-clad *Kohanim,* their families and guests – all in a state of purity – would rise and cry out in unison:

> Blessed is the Omnipresent, blessed be He, for no blemish has been found in the seed of Aaron. And blessed be He who chose the seed of Aaron to stand and serve before *Hashem* in the House of the Holy of Holies!

The ceremony would be followed by a lavish *se'udah.* Grinning, Meir marked in his calendar to reserve two places. A few days after the *se'udah,* he would begin integrating the new *Kohanim* into their respective *mishmarot,* just in time for the *chagim.*

Putt! Another email appeared on Meir's screen: Master Weaver Meshullam Hamalbish was finally able to assure him that every *Kohen* serving in the *Mikdash* over the *chagim* would have all the *bigdei kehunah* he required. There would even be a few extra sets.

Meir's face lit up. *Baruch Hashem*, everything was under control.

Meanwhile, like a mighty stream, masses of *olei regel* were flooding into Jerusalem. Singing songs of welcome, children met the special trains bringing the visitors. Proud to have a role to play, the children shouted with delight as they distributed refreshments. Levites in light green robes were on hand to answer questions and efficiently speed the *olei regel* to their destinations. Everyone, especially Meir, was in a holiday mood.

Chapter Twenty-One

Meir Hakohen glanced at the clock. In another two hours he would have his daily conference with the *Segan*. Today, they were going to review the main points of Meir's report on the revamping of the Mikdash Purification Centers which he just completed.

That morning, Meir had been interviewed on Daniel Natan's popular *Shidurei Hamikdash* – Mikdash Broadcasts radio program *Mah Chadash Be'Mikdash?* (What's New in the *Mikdash?*). The new procedures at the Purification Centers were one of the topics they discussed. Meir reviewed the interview in his mind. He leaned back in his chair, sipped some orange juice, and played back the recorded program.

Daniel Natan: Ladies and gentlemen, this afternoon we are happy to have with us Harav Meir Hakohen, the administrative assistant to *Segan* Chanina Abulafia. Harav Hakohen will tell us about the newly refurbished Purification Centers. The centers have been re-designed to make the ritual purification of *olei regel* before they enter the *Beit Hamikdash* smoother and more efficient. Since the *chagim* are nearly here, efficient and halachically correct ritual purification is a subject of

156

concern to all of us. *Kavod Hakohen*, welcome to *"Mah Chadash Be'Mikdash?"*

Meir Hakohen: Thank you, Daniel. It's my pleasure to be here.

Daniel Natan: Before we begin, would you mind giving our listeners a little background regarding *dinei tum'ah ve'tahorah*, the purity laws? Can we really aspire to understand their rationale? To many of us, these halachot are, well, mystifying to say the least.

Meir Hakohen: Of course. *Dinei tum'ah ve'tahorah* belong to the category of halachot called *chukim*, "statutes" or divine decrees. *Chukim* are Torah laws for which we are not given a reason *why* we should observe them. The true reasons behind these laws are beyond our comprehension. We accept *chukim* with the realization that they transcend human intelligence.

Daniel Natan: Now aren't the laws of kashrut – the dietary laws – also *chukim*?

Meir Hakohen: Yes, they are. The Torah doesn't give us any reason *why* we should observe the kashrut laws either. Nevertheless, that does not diminish their importance.

Daniel Natan: If I remember correctly, the Rambam – Maimonidies – postulates that the Torah often gives priority to *chukim* over other categories of halachot because they demonstrate in no uncertain terms the Divine authority that is the basis of Torah law.

Meir Hakohen: Yes, that's true.

Daniel Natan: You said that the purity laws are *chuckim*, halachot beyond our comprehension, but what *are* they really?

Meir Hakohen: First, let me explain what the laws of ritual purity are not. Ritual purity – *tahorah* – is not the same as physical cleanliness. I'm sure your listeners are familiar with the adage, "Cleanliness is next to Godliness." It's true! But when we discuss *tahorah* we are speaking of a *spiritual* state of cleanliness, which we can't achieve by simply taking a shower.

Daniel Natan: Well, if ritual purity was simply a matter of soap and water, we wouldn't need *mikva'ot* or Purification Centers at all!

Meir Hakohen: No we wouldn't. Before immersing in the *mikvah* – the "purity pool" if you will – or entering a Purification Center – a man or woman must already be physically clean. That's a basic prerequisite for ritual purity. And it's vital to understand that the performance of these 'esoteric' halachot must be done with our minds fully in gear. The psychological aspect of these halachot must not be overlooked.

Daniel Natan: Psychological? *Kavod Hakohen*, could you elaborate on this?

Meir Hakohen: Yes, of course. In our busy lives, we may tend to do some mitzvot without careful focus. That's wrong! We should always strive to perform mitzvot with a high level of concentration, not robotically. We must fully engage our hearts and our minds in serving God. I'd like to quote the Rambam in *Hilchot Mikva'ot* if I may.

Daniel Natan: Please.

Meir Hakohen: I ask our listeners to pay careful attention, since the Rambam is teaching us a very deep concept here. I quote, "Immersion as a means of removing impurity is an inexplicable divine decree, because ritual impurity is *not* mud or filth which

158

dissolves in water. Proper performance of these Biblical decrees (*chukim*) depends on *kavanah*, the special intention of the heart. Therefore the Sages have said that if a person immersed himself and did not have the proper intention, it is as if he never immersed himself at all. But if he immersed himself and had special intention, he becomes ritually pure even though there is no physical bodily change; he immersed with the intention of cleansing his soul from spiritual impurities such as wicked thoughts and evil philosophies. When he immerses, he takes it upon himself to abandon these doctrines and by doing so, elevates his soul to a state of purity."

Daniel Natan: In short, what the Rambam is telling us is that immersion is – or should be – a process of spiritual regeneration.

Meir Hakohen: Exactly right.

Daniel Natan: Does this psychological element, the necessity for special intent on the part of the person undergoing purification, apply to all forms of purification?

Meir Hakohen: Yes, it does. True spiritual purification is not a physical act; true purification is an act of spiritual transformation. And getting back to what we were saying before, even though the purity laws are inexplicable divine ordinances, many great sages including the Rambam himself, encourage us to try to find rationales for them.

Daniel Natan: Does the Rambam offer us a rationale for the purity laws?

Meir Hakohen: Yes, he does. In his *Moreh Nevuchim* (*Guide for the Perplexed*), the Rambam hypothesizes that the purity laws were ordained in order to emphasize the concept of distance between us and the *Beit Hamikdash*. These laws prevent us from entering the *Mikdash* casually, without spiritual preparation. The act of ritual purification assures us that we will enter the *Mikdash* "with a sense of awe," and the effort involved will "most assuredly result in the intended sense of submission before God."

Daniel Natan: That's very powerful.

Meir Hakohen: But there's another rationale I once heard which I like very much. To my mind, it even enhances the significance of the Rambam's words. I would like to share this with your listeners if I may.

Daniel Natan: Of course!

Meir Hakohen: There are twelve *avot ha'tum'ah*, twelve primary sources of ritual impurity. Three of them are connected with the *avodah* in the *Beit Hamikdash*, but virtually all the others are somehow associated with the birth and death cycle, the hallmarks of human mortality.

Daniel Natan: Yes, I've heard that.

Meir Hakohen: It says in *Pirkei Avot*, "Against your will you were fashioned, against your will you were born, and against your will you will die..." Birth and death are divinely ordained. Therefore it is never sinful for an ordinary Israelite to be in a state of ritual impurity caused by "exposure" to the birth and death cycle unless he enters the *Beit Hamikdash* or eats sacred food such as *kodashim*, sacrificial meat.

Daniel Natan: But sometimes we can become ritually impure by doing something which is very praiseworthy, even a mitzvah.

Meir Hakohen: Absolutely! The classic example is a *Yisrael* – a Jew – who is a member of a *chevra kadisha*, a burial society, who helps prepare a corpse – a *meit* – for burial. By doing this, he performs a tremendous mitzvah. But at the same time he acquires the severest form of ritual impurity: *tum'at meit* or "corpse impurity."

Daniel Natan: That makes sense. Obviously, a *meit,* a corpse, is the most compelling reminder of the transience of human life there is.

Meir Hakohen: Right. And that explains why the purification process necessary for divesting oneself from *tum'at meit* is the most exacting of all *Mikdash* purification proceedures. In fact, it is the only form of impurity which requires a special Purification Center.

Daniel Natan: When a *Yisrael* purifies himself from *tum'at meit,* must he *mentally* divest himself of all thoughts of mortality as well?

Meir Hakohen: Yes, he does. Only when the *oleh regel* divests himself of all thoughts of mortality can he enter the *Beit Hamikdash.* Daniel, the *Beit Hamikdash* is the House of the Immortal One, the Creator of All Life. When the *Yisrael* enters the holy courts of the *Beit Hamikdash,* he or she is entering the house of eternity.

Daniel Natan: Are these concepts explained in greater detail on the *Mikdash* website?

Meir Hakohen: Yes they are. You can download the newly released e-book from the *Mikdash* website entitled, *Mikdash Purification Manual for Olei Regel: Practical Instructions and Frequently Asked Questions.* I urge all *olei regel* to visit our website and familiarize themselves with the material posted there *before* they initiate the purification process. It will make the purification process – and indeed the entire *Mikdash* experience – that more meaningful.

Daniel Natan: *Kavod Hakohen*, last year, there were bottlenecks at some of the Purification Centers. There were complaints about the long lines.

Meir Hakohen: Unfortunately that's true. But because of last year's overcrowding, we appointed a special committee to find ways to upgrade the efficiency of the Purification Centers while at the same time not compromising the halachic validity of the purification process.

Daniel Natan: Please continue.

Meir Hakohen: First we verified that each Purification Center has sufficent amount of *mei niddah*.

Daniel Natan: *Mei niddah* is the purifying spring water mixed with the ashes of the red heifer necessary for purification. Do I have it right?

Meir Hakohen: Yes, you do. Also each center must have a sufficent quantity of the hyssop sprigs required for the purification process. At the same time, we devised a series of simulated exercises at each center to clock how long it actually took for each *oleh regel* to be purified, and we took that into consideration. We also critiqued our traffic control procedures. As a result, we were able to initiate a more efficient system.

Daniel Natan: So *Kavod Hakohen*, what can we look forward to now that the *chagim* are approaching?

Meir Hakohen: When *olei regel* arrive in Jerusalem they will be briefed on the laws of purity, and given copies of the *Mikdash Purification Manual for Olei Regel* which I mentioned earlier. Then they will be assigned to a Purification Center near where they will be staying. Teams of Levites will be on hand to answer questions.

Daniel Natan: Do *olei regel* have the option of registering on line?

Meir Hakohen: Without question! In fact, the vast majority of *olei regel* already register on line from the comfort of their homes, well in advance of their arrival in Jerusalem. This is a trend we strongly encourage. It saves them and the Levites a lot of time. Information on how to register on line is available at the *Mikdash* website under "Purification Information." Read it carefully! Everything an *oleh regel* needs to know to prepare himself to enter the *Beit Hamikdash* is explained there clearly, in simple language.

Daniel Natan: Then what?

Meir Hakohen: Once the *oleh regel* arrives in Jerusalem, he or she must make sure to avoid anything potentially contaminating. The halachot are all explained on our website under "Purification Information" in the *Purification Manual*. By avoiding ritual contamination for three days, the *oleh regel* has already begun the purification process. At that point, the *oleh regel* visits his assigned Purification Center for the first of his two sprinklings. The Purification Centers are now housed in spacious halls strategically located throughout Jerusalem.

Daniel Natan: *Kavod Hakohen*, how are these sprinklings actually done?

Meir Hakohen: Every Purification Center contains a series of stations. Supervised by *Kohanim*, volunteers man each station. Posted arrows indicate the route that *olei regel* must follow once they enter the building. Each volunteer stands next to a large stone vat of *mei niddah* and holds three stems of hyssop. As each *oleh regel* steps forward, the purifier dips the hyssop into the *mei*

163

niddah and sprinkles him or her with special intent to purify.

Daniel Natan So an *oleh regel* does not have to immerse when he is in the Purication Center?

Meir Hakohen: No, he doesn't. Unlike a conventional *mikvah,* where the individual who is to be purified must immerse completely, even a single drop of *mei niddah* suffices for the *oleh regel*'s purification process from *tumat meit* if it touches any part of his body. Except for the tongue, that is.

Daniel Natan: And the *oleh regel* has to return on the seventh day?

Meir Hakohen: That's right. On the seventh day, he returns for his second sprinkling. Only *after* the second sprinkling, the *oleh regel* immerses in a conventional *mikvah*. At sunset the purification process is complete. The next morning, the now ritually pure *oleh regel* may enter *Mikdash* grounds.

Daniel Natan: *Kavod Hakohen*, our time is running short. Do you have any final words for our listeners?

Meir Hakohen: Yes, I want to emphasize that *olei regel* are only permitted to enter the *Beit Hamikdash* in a state of *tahorah* – ritual purity. This is a Torah command! The Levite guards at the *Soreg* entrances of the *Mikdash* will turn back anyone who tries to enter *Mikdash* grounds in a state of ritual impurity.

Daniel Natan: Question: may I ask *how* the Levites know who's ritually pure and who isn't?

Meir Hakohen: Let's just say that they know. Take my word for it.

Daniel Natan: Good enough. *Kavod Hakohen*, thank you for joining us on *Mah Chadash Be'Mikdash?* this afternoon. We look forward to having you again soon.

Meir Hakohen: Thank you. It's always a pleasure to be here.

Meir looked up at the clock. He still had some work time before his meeting with the *Segan*. He turned to his monitor and looked at it with dismay. He frowned when he saw the long list of emails. *Ha'avodah!* Where did they all come from?

Chapter Twenty-Two

A handful of irrepressible journalists fresh from Falconi's press conference succeeded in finding transportation to Israel. Upon arriving in Jerusalem, they piled into the crowded media hangout, the American Union Hotel. The few lucky ones shared rooms; the less fortunate slept on mattresses in the hotel's dingy, long unused air-raid shelter. They did not complain. Well, not too much. After all, they *had* reached Jerusalem, and were thankful to have any accommodations at all.

Early the next morning the journalists, hoping somehow to blend into the vast crowds of *olei regel* from abroad, joined the long lines already forming outside of *Har Habayit*. As they approached the Temple Mount, while they were discomforted when they saw the signs banning cameras and recording equipment, they were simply scandalized when told that they would have to remove their shoes and socks before entering Temple grounds.

Dave Bernstein, the top PrinceGlobal representative in Jerusalem, had positioned himself outside the main entrance to the *Mikdash* compound and blithely watched his colleagues as they tried to smuggle themselves into the Temple complex in the guise of *olei regel*. Watching from a distance, Bernstein took it all in and chuckled.

Bernstein had the look of an American journalist himself, dressed in a sports jacket and button-down shirt. He was tall and handsome, with light wavy hair, hazel eyes, faint laugh lines around his wide mouth and an air of self-assurance. His thin frame emanating his characteristic restless energy, Dave Bernstein carefully watched the lines of *olei regel* entering the Temple complex. Laughing softly, he adjusted his beige Tilly-Mesh hat, his signature trademark.

The weather was warm, although the sky was slightly overcast. A stiff west wind was blowing.

The thousands of *olei regel* and the sprinkling of reporters moved forward on *Har Habayit* until they came to the large openings in the *Soreg*, the low wall surrounding the *Mikdash* compound. There, just as Dave Bernstein had predicted, all of the journalists were stopped and removed from the line. To their amazement, the teal-blue robed Levite guards knew exactly who they were. Even more amazing, the flustered journalists did not even protest. Even they themselves could not understand their sudden docility in the face of the Levites. To their chagrin, they stood in a small, forlorn group on the side, and watched the Levites wave the genuine *olei regel* through the openings in the *Soreg* without a second glance.

Bernstein stayed put, wondering how things would play out. Unnoticed, an old acquaintance standing in the shadows was eyeing him.

The acquaintance came over.

"Hey, Bernstein, it's been a long time!"

It was Nimrod Pringsheim, who seemed to have aged since Bernstein last saw him. A man of medium height, with probing brown eyes, pale skin, long graying hair, and a slight stubble on his face, he wore the small round glasses popular in certain intellectual circles. Despite endless sessions on the treadmill, persistent use of a rowing machine, and periodic draconian diets, he had a round belly, and flabby arms and legs. A former professor of political science at Tel Aviv University, Pringsheim was a well known veteran leftist activist, a journalist, and a prolific author. Regarded in Israeli leftist circles as a genius, he had been their prominent ideologue for many years. Like many other members of the "enlightened community" – that's what they called themselves – Pringsheim frequently published vitriolic anti-Israel articles in Europe and America; his recorded YouTubes proliferated exponentially. His contempt for the Jewish religion was proverbial.

That morning something he could not explain drove Pringsheim to visit the Temple Mount, a place he always assiduously avoided. In fact, he detested Jerusalem altogether, and was amazed that people could actually *live* there, especially now. Jerusalem was the Middle Ages; Tel Aviv, or better yet, Paris, was the real world.

Pringsheim had left his swanky Sderot Rothschild apartment in Tel Aviv early that morning, took a cab to the train station, and immediately boarded the gleaming new high-speed rail. Twenty-eight minutes later, the train pulled into the lower level of Jerusalem's Binyanei Ha'uma station. He crossed the platform and waited for the Temple Mount express shuttle which would take him directly to the Har Habayit terminal. Upon arriving, together with hundreds of other Tel Avivians, he quickly exited the building and joined the jostling crowds that were streaming towards the Temple Plaza. With the unceasing media hullabaloo about the High Priest and the Temple, he was not surprised to see Dave Bernstein there.

"Hey, Prings! Great to see you again."

"What's up?"

"Some unhappy people over there," Bernstein said as he gestured in the direction of the stymied journalists. Pringsheim glanced at the group, recognizing most of them.

"Why couldn't they go in?"

"The Levite guards stopped them at the gate."

"How come?"

"They're not Jewish. Non-Jews are not permitted to enter Temple grounds."

"Oh, I didn't know that. What about you? Are you going in?"

"Not now."

"Well," Pringsheim sneered contemptuously. "I'm here already. I might as well go in."

"Somehow, I doubt that," Bernstein replied with an ironic smile.

"Why not?" Pringsheim snapped just a shade too quickly, his lips tightening.

"Have you purified yourself? You have to be ritually pure before you enter Temple grounds."

"Ritually pure? Give me a break! What's that supposed to mean?"

"Get into line and you'll find out!"

"Hang on Bernstein!" Pringsheim said with a sharp tone. "You're serious, aren't you? Okay, I'll get in line and they'll let me in. You'll see."

"I'll be right here," Bernstein called after Pringsheim's back.

"Don't bother. I'm going inside and I'll take a look around. Maybe I'll even write it up. How does 'My Experience in the New Jewish Disneyland' sound?" Pringsheim laughed.

Bernstein grinned knowingly as Pringsheim turned to get into one of the lines of *olei regel* waiting to pass through the *Soreg* and enter *Mikdash* grounds. Pringsheim noticed that the Levite guards waved virtually all of them through without looking twice

A good sign.

Chapter Twenty-Three

Waiting in line, Pringsheim began to wonder what he had gotten himself into. He had known Bernstein for years. They even collaborated on some projects in the past, and probably would do so again in the future. Pringsheim knew Bernstein to be a straightforward guy, but somehow he was getting the impression that this time Bernstein was setting him up. Bernstein seemed to know something that Pringsheim did not. This was more than just ritual purity, whatever that was. Well, he would nail him on it when he came out.

A better question: what was the enlightened freethinker, Professor Nimrod Pringsheim, doing here, waiting in line with a bunch of primitives to get into a temple where they sacrifice animals? They even made him take off his shoes and socks!

"For the life of me, I don't know!" he exclaimed out loud as he contemplated his naked toes. Several heads turned in his direction but he paid them no attention. All he knew was that he had this sudden overwhelming impulse to connect somehow with the *Beit Hamikdash*, and it had nothing to do with Bernstein. For reasons he could not explain, he felt he *had* to do it. Something inexplicable was driving him.

Looking around, he prayed that he would not bump into any of his political associates, colleagues from the university, or former students. He would never live it down. He could not explain what was going through his mind at that moment. Falconi's crazy press conference shook him more than he cared to admit, a lot more. Falconi! How *could* he? Covering his eyes, he recalled Falconi's press conference with horror.

The line was long but it moved quickly. The Levite guards didn't seem to be paying attention at all; they kept waving everyone through the *Soreg* entrance. Once he passed through the *Soreg*, another few steps would bring him to the Eastern Gate of the *Ezrat Nashim*. Once he passed through that gate, he would be on Temple ground! He'd show Bernstein a thing or two! Another three, four minutes should do it. In front of him, two *olei regel* families with their sacrificial animals just about ran through the *Soreg* entrance in their eagerness to get in. The smiling Levites barely looked at them. Now it was his turn.

As Nimrod Pringsheim started to enter, he came face to face with six stern broad-shouldered Levites blocking the entrance.

"*Adoni*," one of them said in polite Biblical Hebrew, "Excuse me, sir, please step to the side."

Stunned, sheepishly he obeyed. He moved a couple of meters to the right. Out of the corner of his eye he noticed that the Levites kept whisking the people behind him through the *Soreg* entrance. How did the Levites know to hold *him* back? Did Bernstein tip them off somehow?

Speaking in the extremely formal third person, the Levite continued, "May the master forgive me, but he is in a state of ritual impurity. His Excellency may not enter the holy courts of the *Beit Hamikdash*."

"What? Why, why not?" Pringsheim stammered.

"Anyone who wishes to enter the holy courts of the *Beit Hamikdash* must be in a state of ritual purity. If he is not, he must purify himself first. His Excellency failed to do so."

"What exactly do you mean?" Pringsheim asked, taken aback. "What about all those people you just let through? How do you know that they're all so pure?"

"Even Jews who observe the mitzvot fastidiously and live in *Eretz Yisrael* are assumed to be *temei'im*, ritually impure," the Levite explained patiently. "That's why before entering the holy courts of the *Beit Hamikdash*, they must purify themselves. The people whom we are admitting to *Mikdash* grounds did so, and therefore are in a state of ritual purity."

The Levite looked Pringsheim straight in the eye. "In your case, yet another factor comes into play. May I remind his Excellency that he traveled abroad recently? The Gemara notes that the sages Rav Yosi ben Yo'ezer and Rav Yosi ben Yochanan decreed that *eretz ha'amim*, all lands outside of *Eretz Yisrael*, are *te'mei'im*, are impure."

"How do you know I've been abroad?" Pringsheim asked suspiciously.

Pointedly ignoring Pringsheim's question, the Levite continued, "Furthermore, his Excellency attended the funeral of a Jewish colleague who was killed in a car accident five weeks ago in Paris. The funeral was held in the Montmartre cemetery on Rue Caulaincourt. When a Jew enters a cemetery, attends a funeral, or comes in contact with the dead, he acquires the severe form of ritual impurity, *tum'at meit*, corpse impurity. While it is not a transgression for a Jew to be ritually impure in his normal day-to-day life, he may not enter the *Beit Hamikdash* in that condition." Before sending him on his way, the Levite invited Pringsheim to visit one of the new Mikdash Purification Centers. He even recommended one.

Stupefied by the Levite's exact knowledge of his attending a funeral in Paris, Pringsheim staggered away. It was incredible. Bernstein had no way of knowing about the Paris funeral. *Ergo*, he could not have tipped them off. On the other hand, there was no way that Pringsheim could believe that the Levites had attended the same funeral in Paris, and recognized him a few weeks later on the Temple Mount. That was asking too much of coincidence. Pringsheim started to shiver. There was no way the Levites could have known. But somehow they clearly did!

Bernstein approached the completely bewildered Pringsheim, put his arm around him, and gently led him away.

A sudden gust of wind whirled dust into the air, and the sky clouded over. There was a golden luminosity that hovered over the Jerusalem stone. Pringsheim shivered again.

How could they have known?

Pulling himself together, Pringsheim pointed at a strange phenomenon in the distance. Nodding his head and his mouth open, he stood there studying it in fascinated astonishment. "Dave, look at that column of smoke going straight up even though it's so windy. How do they do that?"

"Prings, you really haven't been here before? Come with me and I'll tell you all about it."

Bernstein took Pringsheim to a well known café off the Ben Yehudah Midrachov in downtown Jerusalem. Over bagels and lox they had a long discussion about the Temple and Jewish topics in general. The café was large and airy, with light streaming through the high windows that faced the street. The walls were of red brick and the ceiling had an intricate beam

174

overlay. Embossed brass and copper trays hung on the walls. The light beechwood tables and chairs were comfortable and solid. As Bernstein continued talking, Pringsheim sat quietly and listened intently. And to Pringsheim's amazement, his story of how the Levites stopped him from passing through the *Soreg* did not faze Bernstein at all. In the distance, they heard a series of clangs announcing the light-rail approaching its stop on Jaffa Road.

Pringsheim asked many questions. Bernstein, though hardly an expert, answered them as accurately as he could. Despite himself, Pringsheim listened respectfully and attentively. Bernstein hailed a waitress, and asked for a pitcher of ice water. She returned with a tall pitcher and a few glasses. Nearly two hours later, Bernstein finally stopped talking and took a deep breath.

"Fascinating!" said a familiar female voice.

They were so engrossed in their conversation that they had not even noticed that a third person had pulled up a chair and silently joined them. Startled, they looked up. It was their old buddy Samantha the Cat.

"Hey, Sam. When did you get in?"

As she answered, she poured herself a glass of water. "I got in last night," she said, taking a few sips. "What a flight! But I'll tell you about it some other time. Let's get down to business. What do you guys have on the H.P?"

"H.P. is it? Come on Sam, show a little respect! You think you'll get an exclusive with him?" Bernstein needled her.

"Bernstein, nobody's getting an exclusive with him," she retorted. "Don't you do your homework? He never talks to the media. He's never given an interview. No one can get to him. He doesn't go anywhere where the press, or anyone for that matter, can ambush him. I think he just goes from the Temple to home and back."

"Sam, believe me, I know he's impossible to get a hold of," Bernstein sighed. "Last night Big George called me up all hot and bothered, and demanded that I get an exclusive with him and find out what he talked to Falconi about. He wants pictures, his life story, everything. And of course he wants it yesterday."

"Does he now?" Samantha tittered. "And what did you tell him?"

"What do you think I told him? I said it couldn't be done. I told him that neither the High Priest nor any of his people deal with the general media, period."

"Big George must have loved that."

"No, Sam, Big George did not love it. He was his usual pleasant self, if you get my drift."

Samantha nodded. She understood perfectly.

"Bottom line, he said to get what I could and get help if I needed it."

There was a sudden gleam in Samantha's eye, "Really?"

"Yes, really. I just have to figure out a way to get to that High Priest," Bernstein muttered.

Samantha shook her head vigorously. "No chance! The High Priest is locked up tight. The next in line is his assistant, *Segan* Chanina Abulafia. He's a priest but he doesn't minister in the Temple much. He's in charge of the day-to-day functioning of the place, the chief administrator. He's more like a successful CEO of a major corporation than anything else, and he doesn't talk to the general media either. He only gives interviews on Mikdash Broadcasts, the Temple broadcasting company. There's no way to get to him."

Bernstein looked at Samantha with respect. "It sounds like you really *have* done your homework, Sam. So where do you think the High Priest is now?" Bernstein asked.

"I told you. He's either at his home or somewhere in the Temple."

"Okay, the High Priest is at home or in the Temple. His assistant, the *Segan* doesn't talk to the general media. So where does that leave us?"

"Us? Did you say 'us?' Dave, are you suggesting that I join you in this little project?" Samantha asked with an impish grin. "You *did* say that Big George said you should get help!"

Bernstein reflected for a minute and then slowly nodded. Bernstein knew that Samantha the Cat was not exactly one of his boss's favorites, not by a long shot. But on the other hand, she *was* a media superstar, especially after her well-publicized exchange with Falconi in Milan. And she obviously *had* done her homework.

He looked at his watch. There was no way he could reach Prince now anyway. Besides, Samantha had the reputation of being able to charm an exclusive out of a stone. He would go out on a limb; he decided to collaborate with her.

On her part, Samantha knew that despite her resourcefulness and brief assignments in Israel in the past, she had little knowledge of Israeli society. Bernstein, on the other hand, over the years had come to know Israel intimately. While she could not speak a word of Hebrew, Bernstein spoke it fluently. Besides, for all her bravado, instinctively, she sensed that the High Priest was somehow on a different level than the people she was used to dealing with. Bernstein and Samantha simultaneously raised their glasses and clinked them together.

"Good, that's settled then," Samantha said airily as she put her glass down. "After the High Priest and the *Segan*, the next in line is a guy called Meir Hakohen. He's the *Segan*'s assistant. We'll have to concentrate on him. Maybe we can camp outside his door. He lives on Rechov Hatamid in the Jewish Quarter."

"Bad idea," Bernstein said, shaking his head emphatically. "The whole place is crawling with Levite guards." At the mention of the Levite guards, Pringsheim gave a start, spilling his water glass, a puddle quickly formed on the floor.

"Hey, Prings! What did I say?" asked Bernstein.

There was a pause. But in a flash, Bernstein understood *why* Pringsheim had reacted the way he did. He touched Pringsheim's arm.

"Prings, tell Sam what happened."

In the background, they could hear the other patrons of the café chatting noisily over the clatter of dishes and cutlery. There were fewer of them now. The lunch crowd had thinned out and the evening crowd had not yet arrived. A baby howled in the distance.

Pringsheim drained his glass. He signaled to the waitress, and ordered a beer. He had developed a raging thirst. He looked at Samantha and opened his mouth to talk, but then closed it again. He shook his head slowly.

"C'mon. Tell her!" urged Bernstein.

Pringsheim grimaced. "I had a run-in with the Levites this morning."

Samantha turned towards him, "Really? What happened?"

178

Chapter Twenty-Four

Nervously scratching his chin, Pringsheim began by describing his dismay when the Temple was restored thereby negating everything he and his followers believed in.

"Guys, I can't tell you how we felt when the Temple appeared. One morning, there it was, standing on the Temple Mount just like the *dosim* said it would. The crazy euphoria that swept the country! The excitement! The hysterical reaction of people all over the world! But for us the *Beit Hamikdash* was a nightmare! The sudden breakdown of everything we swore by caused many of our best people to enroll in yeshivot specializing in teaching *ba'alei teshuvah*, you know, the born-again types. That really hurt."

"It *must* have been a shock," Samantha cooed sympathetically.

"It was. Even *I* was shaken. Sam, you know my background. I'm a red diaper baby from Ramat Aviv. My parents were classic leftist ideologues, Stalinists even. We were secular to the core. I went to the best schools in Israel. I did my doctorate in political science at Tel Aviv University, post-doc at Harvard, and later I did work at the Sorbonne in Paris. Then I returned to Israel and started teaching at TAU, but I found Israel too confining, provincial even."

"Then what?"

"I went back to Paris and worked under Professor Falconi for five years. Then I returned to Israel and organized the United Peace Movement, the Freethinkers' Society, and other front groups for Falconi's mission. I got grants from the EU and various progressive foundations. Money was never a problem for us. It just flowed. Most of the people who joined our organizations had no idea who ran the show behind the scenes, or who funded us. And they never asked. The people who joined us were what we call in Israel *'yefei nefesh,'* which literally means they had 'beautiful souls.' At least they thought they did. Anyway, they meant well, but they were totally naïve. We used to call them 'useful idiots,'" Pringsheim smirked.

"'Useful idiots,' Lenin coined that phrase, didn't he?" Samantha asked.

"Yes, he did. And who knew more about establishing front groups than Communists? We were determined to recreate Israeli society in our own image. After brainstorming with Falconi and his people in Paris, I realized that the best way to do that in Israel was to leave academia entirely and become an 'intellectual' journalist and commentator. I quickly became a media personality and then I started a political party. Being Falconi's man in Israel opened a lot of doors for me in academia, the judiciary, among political leaders and not least, in the media."

"Tell me," Samantha asked, "When you went to school, did you ever study the Bible?"

"Maybe we should have, at least a little bit, but we didn't. After all, the Tanach, the Bible, was for *dosim*, you know, those religious nut jobs. Actually, my father played a major role in *reducing* the number of hours allotted for Bible study in the secular Israeli schools. You know, we didn't even have a Tanach in our house! In the schools I attended, we never studied Tanach. We studied excerpts from the *Bhagavad-Gita*, the *Avesta*, and the *Buddhavacana*, the Hindu and Buddhist scriptures. We thought they were so cool, so full of spiritual insight. We used to quote them all the time."

"What about Jewish history?" Samantha asked.

"To use a hackneyed phrase, we considered ourselves citizens of the world. We were what was then called transnationalist. We didn't think of ourselves as Jews at all. We didn't even think of ourselves as Israelis, we were beyond that. We were transnationalists, citizens of the world, cosmopolitans. Sam, before the *Beit Hamikdash* reappeared, the political elite in this country pretty much danced to our tune. And I'm talking about cabinet ministers, members of the Israeli parliament, judges, you name it, from the top on down. The cultural elite were in our pockets - academics, writers, columnists, historians, artists, pundits. Most of them were card-carrying members of our front groups and NGOs.

"Remember the social critic Harold Rosenberg? He popularized the phrase 'the herd of independent minds.' It's truly an apt description. To put it bluntly, despite their pretensions of being boldly independent thinkers, they became our echo chamber," Pringsheim said with pride in his voice. "They were like puppets on a string. We told them that we transcended politics and they believed us."

"Then what happened?" Samantha asked cautiously, giving him a searching look.

Pringsheim shook his head and took a gulp of beer.

"Everything we built up fell apart," Pringsheim said, shaking his head. "With the Temple back and the resultant uproar, the intellectual atmosphere here became just unbearable. No one paid attention to us anymore; they wouldn't even listen. To sum it up, we were totally marginalized. Like beached whales! And then, there were the enormous political changes that took place here, none to our liking," he said vehemently. Bernstein and Samantha waited for him to continue.

Pringsheim's mouth began to tremble. He tried to cover it with a weak smile but did not succeed.

"We felt that history was getting away from us and somehow we were being left behind," Pringsheim said raising his voice.

"Calm down, Prings."

"No. Let me continue." Pringsheim said, taking another gulp of beer. "If the appearance of the Temple on the Temple Mount wreaked havoc on our philosophic pretensions, Falconi's public about-face was an absolute catastrophe."

"Why?" Samantha asked.

"With the Temple back, Falconi was our last hope. In the past couple of days since Falconi betrayed our cause, and let me tell you," Pringsheim said wagging his index finger, "that u-turn he took, *really* was a betrayal – more of our people have become interested in this High Priest thing, the Temple, and the whole shebang.

"Guys, you've got to understand what this all means," Pringsheim said, leaning forward. Sweat trickled down his forehead, and not from the heat. "We'd been following what was happening in Europe very closely. Falconi was winning! Then we heard that Falconi was going to come out of seclusion and give a press conference live to the whole world. Victory was ours! The Revolution was victorious! Falconi was going to dictate terms! The world was at Falconi's feet! We knew, we just knew in our bones that we had won. I SMSed a few colleagues and friends and invited them to come over, watch the press conference on television, and celebrate. We had bottles of champagne ready." Pringsheim paused, and studied his hands, "It's pathetic when I think about it now.

"We sat there, with champagne glasses in our hands singing anarchist songs, songs of the Revolution. When Falconi appeared on the screen, we stood up and toasted him, 'To Professor Falconi, the leader of the Revolution!' Then without warning, in front of the entire world, he announced that he was calling a halt to the violence, and that people should go out into the streets and tear down the barricades. And that speech! We felt like fools! Falconi had betrayed the Revolution! How *could* he? I was disgusted. I threw my glass across the room and it smashed to pieces. That's about how I felt too, totally smashed to pieces."

"Everyone was shocked," Bernstein said soothingly, gently touching Pringsheim's shoulder.

"I certainly was," Samantha said softly, "I couldn't believe it!"

"Falconi had Europe by the throat," Pringsheim said clenching his fists. "That he abandoned us, the Cause, his whole *raison d'être* at that moment? It was unbelievable! It was incredible! What was wrong with him?! Success was at his doorstep – and **wham**! What I would have given to be in Falconi's shoes! I would have showed them!" Pringsheim said hotly. Shoulders sagging, he shot Samantha a miserable look.

"Prings, relax. Have some more beer," urged Bernstein.

Wiping his forehead with a napkin, Pringsheim picked up the glass and took a sip.

"Go on," Bernstein said encouragingly.

"When Falconi's stooges started tearing down the pictures of Proudhon and the other anarchist leaders, I thought I'd have a heart attack. You know, I had a poster of Falconi on my wall. I ripped it down and threw it away. At that moment, I hated him."

Pringsheim looked at Samantha closely. "Then *you* asked him what caused him to change so radically. And he told you – the world – that the High Priest of the Temple of Jerusalem had called him up on the telephone and told him to stop the Revolution. Just like that! 'The High Priest showed me the error of my ways,' he said. That was the famous 'phone call that saved Europe.' Falconi was the world's leading ideologue. At the moment of victory, he threw it all away! It just didn't make sense!"

Pringsheim continued, "While I was in Europe, I heard Falconi speak many times. I thought I came to know him well. You know, I even worked under him. Falconi's dialectics, his logic is ice-cold. At least it was before he went off the deep end. Sam, when I listened to your back and forth with him in Milan, and watched the 'new' Falconi, I felt like the rug was pulled out from under me. Our hero, our mentor, Professor Antonio Falconi, had publicly embraced the High Priest of Jerusalem as his guru, his spiritual leader! When Falconi started quoting Ezekiel about getting a new heart, I thought I'd die.

"Then I don't know what came over me. I suddenly got this incredible urge to visit the *Beit Hamikdash*. I tried to fight it, but I couldn't. Nothing like that ever happened to me before. I couldn't resist it and I can't explain why it happened. I'd never

184

wanted to go near the place before. And on the Temple Mount, I ran into Bernstein." Pringsheim cleared his throat and took another sip of beer.

"But what about the Levites?" Samantha asked.

"I was coming to that."

The two journalists waited patiently for him to continue.

Pringsheim began by telling them how the Levites barred the journalists from passing through the *Soreg*. Samantha already knew all about it. Gossip travels fast in the media world. Not *one* of those blowhards had gotten through. But then she had an uncomfortable feeling that had she been there, they would not have let her in either.

Pringsheim then told them about his experience that morning when he tried to enter Temple grounds in a state of impurity. He could not grasp how the Levites knew that he attended a funeral in Paris a few weeks earlier.

Looking shamefacedly at Bernstein, Pringsheim confessed that he even thought that Bernstein had tipped them off, but then he realized that that was impossible. Still, somehow the Levites had sensed that he was ritually impure.

"Guys, I have to admit that I have no reasonable explanation of how the Levites possibly could have known. If I heard this kind of story from a third party, I would not have believed it."

Pringsheim drained his glass. Raising his voice, he continued. "But I did not hear the story from a third party and I did not merely witness it. It actually happened to me," he said with a bleak smile.

"I understand," sympathized Samantha.

Pringsheim morosely jammed his feet under his chair and absent-mindedly played with his empty glass. He radiated

185

gloom. To Bernstein and Samantha, it almost seemed like a black cloud was hovering over his head.

"Sam, I don't think you *can* understand." Pringsheim said plaintively. "I know I've been repeating myself, but I still just can't wrap my mind around what happened. Suddenly Falconi, our last hope, tells the world that he accepted the High Priest as his spiritual guide! We were stunned. It just didn't make sense," he repeated, shaking his head.

"When the Falconi fiasco ended, I poured the champagne down the sink and threw the bottles in the trash. The friends I invited to celebrate our victory slunk away like whipped dogs. I haven't seen or heard from them since." His voice was slow and tired.

He admitted that he was in absolute despair when he thought of the only possible explanation for Falconi's turn around.

Bernstein and Samantha listened quietly. Samantha noticed that Pringsheim's eyes were bloodshot. She wondered how much sleep he had gotten lately, probably not very much. His face was lined with fatigue, and he was pale.

The noise level in the café rose making conversation increasingly difficult, so the three decided to decamp to a much less frequented coffee shop on the Ben Yehudah Midrachov only a few minutes' walk away. The sky was blue and cloudless, the air soft and warm but the sun was already low on the horizon. A caressing breeze was blowing and red, white, and pink hanging geraniums swayed gently in their window boxes. In front of a bank under a tree, to the delight of a swarm of laughing children, a clown-costumed man accompanied by a long-haired accordionist with a grinning monkey on his

186

shoulder, expertly twisted colored balloons into the shapes of animals. A gaggle of giggling girls took pictures.

As they walked, Bernstein turned to his two colleagues and asked, "Did you know that Jerusalem is the center of the universe?"

Pringsheim nodded grimly. A *dos* told him that once and he laughed in his face. He wasn't laughing anymore.

Samantha gave Bernstein a puzzled look, "Really? I never heard that."

"It's true. The Zohar, one of the major texts of the Kabbalah, says that when God wanted to create the universe, He took a stone called the *Even Hashetiyah*, the Foundation Stone, and threw it into the primordial abyss. That caused the universe to come into being and start expanding. The *Even Hashetiyah* merited that name because it became the foundation upon which God fashioned the entire universe. Ever since, the *Even Hashetiyah* has been the midpoint of the universe and that's where the Holy of Holies of the Temple is located. That's why the Kabbalists say that the Temple is in the center of the physical universe. They also claim that directly above the earthly Temple is a celestial Temple, and the priests there are angels. Our Temple is where Heaven and earth meet."

Frowning, eyebrows knit, Samantha stared at Bernstein, not quite comprehending what he had said. She shook her head, but kept her thoughts to herself. Reaching the café, they climbed the stairs to the upper level. They looked around and saw they had it all to themselves.

Chapter Twenty-Five

The café's airy upper level had a dozen dark Formica covered tables. Brown rattan chairs hugged the tables, and a dark imitation-parquet floor gave the room a serious feel. Tapered lights hung over the tables and black and gold framed pictures of Jerusalem scenes decorated the walls. The three journalists sat in an alcove that afforded a partial view of the Ben Yehudah Midrachov as well as the first floor of the café below. After ordering coffee and cake from a smiling Ethiopian waitress, they paused for a moment.

Samantha slowly removed her sunglasses and looked carefully at Pringsheim. It was clear that he was quite distraught. Although his shoulders dropped, he allowed himself a weak smile. Then Samantha examined her new partner Bernstein, and reviewed in her mind his recent comments about the centrality of the Temple in the cosmos. Her lips tightened, her eyes narrowed. With all due respect, this business of the Temple being the center of the universe was sheer nonsense.

"Before we can even discuss how we are going to do our story, we have to clarify what our own attitude towards the Temple is," Samantha pontificated. "Dave, you obviously have had experiences that have made you less than objective. We have to address this issue."

Pringsheim sat quietly listening, his hand pressed over his eyes.

But Samantha's unexpectedly patronizing, even insulting tone set Bernstein off. Stung by her words, Bernstein squared his shoulders and his voice acquired a hard edge. "Okay, Sam, let's be objective here. There are three points to consider. Point one: What happened to Falconi?

"Overnight the prophet of violent world revolution with millions of fanatical followers everywhere suddenly changes from a bloodthirsty anarchist rabble-rouser into a saccharine sweet Mahatma Gandhi who quotes the prophet Ezekiel about being given 'a new heart.' And the reason he gives for his radical transformation is because he had a telephone conversation with a holy man. Does that seem believable?"

"Come on, Dave!" Samantha shot back, "You know the whole world has been asking that."

"Do you remember what he said to you when you asked Falconi if the High Priest brainwashed him?"

"Of course I do." Samantha said breathlessly, "I'll never forget it. He said, 'Young woman, you cannot brainwash me with one phone call!'"

"Now realistically speaking, can you brainwash a professor of philosophy and political theory, who has written a dozen major books and hundreds of articles, with one phone call?"

"No," Samantha answered hesitantly. Realizing that she had lost control of the conversation, she looked unsure of herself.

The waitress brought their order, and Bernstein took a sip of black coffee.

189

"What about blackmail? Do you think the High Priest has something on him? Or maybe he hypnotized Falconi over the phone?" Bernstein facetiously hypothesized.

"Of course not!" she snapped impatiently as she ran her fingers along the edge of the table, "Don't be ridiculous!"

"Then what caused the change? How did the High Priest manage to win Falconi's confidence and persuade him to change course so radically? How was he able to tell Falconi about incidents from his childhood and other things that no one else could possibly have known? How was he able to sing to Falconi a lullaby sung to him by his mother when he was a baby? And in Siculu, the Sicilian dialect, no less! How did the High Priest know that?"

"I don't know," Samantha said, shaking her head. "I just don't know."

"Sam, what was your impression of Falconi at the end of the press conference?"

"I'll tell you the truth, but don't quote me. Though I was surprised when he said that he was going to ask the High Priest to offer a sacrifice on his behalf in the Temple, I thought I was looking at a different Falconi. I saw a man at peace with himself. For a minute I envied him."

"Let's go on to point two: the smoke from the sacrificial altar. How do they get it to rise straight up to the sky without scattering, even on the stormiest of days? We're talking about a phenomenon in the open air that cannot be faked. This takes place every day in an uncontrolled environment, and every day this phenomenon is witnessed by hundreds of thousands of people. I'm told that the smoke from the gold incense altar inside the Temple building behaves pretty much in the same way. I asked my contacts at the Hebrew University's physics department about it."

"What did they say?" Samantha asked slowly, half dreading the answer.

"They all said the same thing. The phenomenon of the smoke rising column-like from the open-air sacrificial altar on a windy day cannot be simulated. There can be no question about it. It is real, but on the other hand, there are no known laws of physics that can explain it. So how do we account for it? Sam, do you have any ideas?"

"No. I don't," Samantha answered, feeling a twinge of panic. Nervously running her fingers through her hair, she shifted in her chair. Samantha was uneasy with where this conversation was heading.

"Point three: Did you know that even the heaviest rains do not extinguish the fires on the sacrificial altar? And that altar is out in the open air. Jerusalem can have some real downpours in the winter, even snow. I've been caught in them more than once. But the rains never put out the fires on the altar."

"I haven't done *that* much homework." Samantha said flatly as she absent-mindedly stirred her cappuccino. "In the time frame that I had at my disposal, I didn't have time to read up on Temple ritual." She seemed to shrink into her chair.

"Okay, so I'm telling you. Do you know that the priests set out twelve large loaves of unleavened bread on a golden table every Saturday and leave them exposed to the open air? After a full week of being exposed like that, they are still as fresh as when they came out of the oven. And they do *not* use preservatives. Did you know that in the Temple Court, sacrificial meat can be left out in the hottest sun for hours, and it never spoils? Did you know that there are no flies in the Temple Court despite all the exposed meat?"

Samantha shrugged her shoulders. "No, Dave, I didn't know any of that either."

"Sam, can you give me a logical explanation how the Levite guards are able to differentiate between those who are ritually pure and those who aren't? They didn't let Pringsheim in because he was ritually impure. Can you explain to me how the Levites knew that Pringsheim went to a funeral five weeks ago in Paris and they even knew where it was held?"

Samantha, her voice rising, shot back, "You know I can't explain any of that! Just what are you trying to say?"

"Hey, Sam!" Bernstein said raising both hands in the universal "stop" position. "Ratchet it down a notch. Relax. We're on the same team now."

Samantha's brow furrowed as she looked at Bernstein closely. She shook her head as she struggled to regain her composure. "I'm sorry Dave, I overreacted. I'm a journalist, and I need to have a handle on what I'm dealing with. This whole mumbo-jumbo of magical phenomena challenges the rationalist in me. I have to admit that it's hard for me to cope with this. And it's all so new to me. It's so... bizarre."

"I know, believe me, I know. All this takes getting used to. Okay, Sam, Let's keep going. I've mentioned at least five phenomena connected to the High Priest and the Temple that defy physical laws. There are plenty of others. Do you want to hear some of them?" Bernstein paused, "Remember, we're being objective."

Samantha put down her cappuccino.

"Dave, I hear what you're saying, but what exactly are you getting at?" she asked. Though Samantha had cooled down, there was still apprehension in her voice.

Bernstein leaned forward, clasped his hands together, and began speaking very slowly. "I don't know quite how to put this. I haven't thought this all through yet, but listen to me. Sam, I think the Temple is somehow part of this world, but at the same time *not* part of this world. Remember, the Temple is not an ordinary building. It just appeared out of nowhere; it descended from heaven just as some of the early rabbis said it would.

"And you know what?" he continued, his voice becoming more animated, "I think the Temple has its own rules. I know that this sounds like science fiction, but maybe we should picture the Temple as a portal into some kind of transcendental parallel universe of sanctity, with a self-contained separate reality co-existing with our own, but obeying its own laws. It was the Danish philosopher Søren Kierkegaard who first used the expression, 'sanctity in the midst of objective reality.' Maybe that's what the Temple really is, an island of sanctity planted in the middle of our mundane universe." Bernstein paused and took a deep breath.

Pringsheim raised his head, his thoughts spinning. *Kierkegaard? Sanctity in the midst of objective reality? Our mundane Universe? Whoohoo! Bernstein is full of surprises today! A real intellectual! A philosopher even!*

Pringsheim and Samantha put their cups down and looked at Bernstein with new respect. This was a facet of his personality that they had never seen before.

"Hear me out," Bernstein continued, "Suppose the Temple really *is* where Heaven and earth meet? Suppose there really is

193

some tangible divine manifestation there? Suppose the High Priest really *is* some kind of holy man? How else could he have influenced Falconi the way he did with one phone call? And through Falconi, the world! Unless of course you think the whole thing was one gigantic set-up. I cannot accept that. Sam, you were there. I don't think you believe it was just some elaborate hoax either. The point is that I want you to have an open mind about what I am trying to say, and take it into consideration. We *are* trying to be objective, remember?"

Leaning back in her chair and swallowing, Samantha became uncomfortable as she always did when confronted with the metaphysical. She was silent but her mind was churning.

Tired from his long narrative, Bernstein stood up and stretched. He had made his point, and wanted to leave Sam and Pringsheim to cogitate. "Okay. On that note, class is dismissed," he said with a chuckle. "What do you say? Let's meet here tomorrow morning at nine to plan our course of action."

Looking at her watch, Samantha sprang to her feet. She could not wait to get out of there. She had been sitting too long. This place seemed to be closing in on her.

"Okay, let's go," Samantha said curtly grabbing her sunglasses. She exhaled sharply; she had not wanted to sound so petulant but she knew that she had. Shaking her head, she looked at Bernstein pensively. Abashed, a faint hesitant smile appeared on her lips.

Nimrod Pringsheim did not get up. Eyes closed, head in his hands, he was thinking hard. For the first time, he felt that he glimpsed something in the distance, but was not sure exactly *what* he had seen. He thought some more. Bernstein and Samantha stood there, looking expectantly at him.

194

"Sanctity in the midst of objective reality," Pringsheim whispered, nodding his head. Suddenly the pieces fell into place.

"That's it!" he exclaimed, excitedly pounding the table.

"What's it?" Samantha asked.

"Hold it. Just give me a couple minutes."

Pringsheim rested his elbows on the table and covered his eyes.

Bernstein had solved the mystery! Kierkegaard's expression, "sanctity in the midst of objective reality" explained everything! Bernstein understood the true meaning of a concept that Kierkegaard could not have understood himself. After all, what could a guy like Kierkegaard know about the Temple? Bernstein was the dwarf sitting on the shoulders of the giant! *The Beit Hamikdash is a kind of sanctified parallel universe with a self-contained separate reality coexisting with our own, but at the same time, governed by its own laws.*

He gave a start. He was amazed how clearly he could think. Bernstein's theory was not even so far-fetched. Rubbing his chin, Pringsheim looked upward and smiled; he had a strange light in his eyes.

Let's get real! Pringsheim thought. *What do we really know about our own universe?*

Nodding his head slowly, he suddenly understood *what* he had glimpsed in the distance.

Don't astrophysicists tell us that even in our *own* universe all that we can see and measure and weigh – galaxies, nubulea, planets, people – make up only 4% of what is out there and that the other unseen, unknown

96% consists of what they call "dark matter" and "dark energy?" Yet, the dark matter of which they speak, upon which their theories depend, is so rarefied a substance that after decades of research, they have not succeeded in isolating a single particle. Despite their erudition and their labratories filled with the most refined equipment imaginable, they "know" that it exists only mathematically and because of the weird effect its gravity has on light radiating from visible stars and galaxies.

What about that mysterious force called "dark energy?" The astrophysicists tell us that since the beginning of time, dark energy has been causing our universe with its hundreds of billions of galaxies to expand at an ever increasing speed. It is this infinitely powerful repulsive force that drives the very galaxies apart from each other. But even though dark energy supposedly makes up almost three-quarters of our universe's mass energy and theoretically permeates our entire universe, no one has been able to prove its existence physically. Even so, the astrophysicists contend that dark matter and dark energy are not mere speculation; they say that mathematically their existence is certain.

And even that 4%, do we really know what it is? Now quantum physicists tell us, that despite the testimony of our senses, there is no such thing as solidity at all. These theorists say that solidity itself is an illusion because deep inside every particle of every atom is a cosmic symphony with hidden dimensions and unbelievably small vibrating filaments of energy called strings. They tell us that these vibrating strings, not solid particles, are the true building blocks of everything we see in our universe.

And nowadays, even the most prominent scientists routinely speak of hidden dimensions and multiple, even infinite, parallel universes as mere components in what they now call the multiverse. They say that parallel universes can intersect, collide, and even interact with each other. Furthermore, they tell us that each parallel universe may very well possess different attributes from our own. Might not this be true of the transcendental Temple universe as well?

All that we see is *not* all that there is. There is so much more to reality than what meets the eye. Just like the stars that are blotted out by the blazing light of the sun in the daytime, there are an infinite number of unseen worlds and invisible universes out there that we cannot perceive. The sanctified, transcendental, parallel universe of the *Beit Hamikdash* must be such a universe, and it has entered *our* world.

In the parallel universe of the *Beit Hamikdash*, smoke from the altar rises heavenwards straight as a column even on the windiest day. In the parallel universe of the *Beit Hamikdash*, even the heaviest rains do not quench the fires on the sacrificial altar. In the parallel universe of the *Beit Hamikdash*, the Levites are somehow able to sniff out those who for one reason or another are not permitted or perhaps are unworthy to enter there. The High Priest of the parallel universe of the *Beit Hamikdash* is a man of such power that a single phone call from him can change history!

"Falconi is right. Salvation *is* of the Jews," he murmured dreamily to himself. He, Nimrod Pringsheim was Jewish, no question about that. Despite his somewhat sordid past, no one could take *that* away from him. Maybe Professor Falconi and

Samantha the Cat weren't, but *he* was. He was a son of the Jewish people! Funny, he had never thought of himself in those terms before. If he was Jewish, he belonged to the *Beit Hamikdash* and the *Beit Hamikdash* belonged to him!

At that moment, he sat up straighter and made a decision. Tonight, he would arrange to stay with friends in Jerusalem and early tomorrow morning, he would register at the newly-opened Purification Center that the Levite on *Har Habayit* recommended to him. He would begin the purification process so he could visit the *Beit Hamikdash* for the first time in his life, and see what it was all about. And this time, the Levites at the gate would just wave him through like every other Jew in a state of purity.

Nimrod Pringsheim would ask the *Kohanim* to offer a *korban* for the cleansing of his soul. If an anarchist gentile like Falconi could do it, a wayward Jew like Pringsheim certainly could. After all, what did that *dos* with the black hat tell him a couple of years ago? "An Israelite, even though he has sinned, remains an Israelite." A Jew is a Jew is a Jew, no matter what.

His eyes grew suddenly misty. Pringsheim slowly put down his coffee cup and gazed up at Bernstein. "Dave, we've worked together before. I'd like to do so again. You know I've written for Prince in the past. I want to be a part of this."

Astonished at Pringsheim's unexpected words, Bernstein and Samantha gingerly sat back down. They looked at Pringsheim closely. No question about it, he looked different somehow, more at ease. He didn't look so pale anymore. And his eyes – they glowed.

"Prings let me ask you a question. And please answer honestly. Can you, with your leftist background, really write

198

objectively about the High Priest and the Temple?" Bernstein asked.

"Dave, I'll be honest with you," Pringsheim answered, looking Bernstein straight in the eye. "Before Falconi's press conference, I probably would not have been able to. You know very well that we had our own agendas, but that's over now. I've just been doing some serious thinking. At this point in time, I think I could write objectively about the *Beit Hamikdash*. You'd be doing me a real favor if you'd let me try. I'll get the background material and run down any leads. And remember, I'm a *mekomi*, a local. I have a few connections that you may not have."

"Connections in Temple circles? You?" Samantha asked incredulously.

"You'd be surprised."

Bernstein looked at Pringsheim, at Samantha, then back at Pringsheim. He thought for a moment, then another. Finally he grinned, nodding his head. "Prings, you know what they say, 'you might as well be hung for a sheep as a lamb.' You're on!"

The three journalists raised their coffee cups in a toast.

"Thanks, Dave," Pringsheim said with a new buoyancy in his voice.

Suddenly though subtly, to Nimrod Pringsheim, veteran left-wing activist, journalist, and former professor of political science, the atmosphere in the café had changed. Everything seemed to look different – the few remaining patrons on the lower level, the kitschy pictures of Jerusalem on the walls, the coffee cups on the table in front of him, even Dave Bernstein fingering his Tilly-Mesh hat, and Samantha the Cat sitting across from him holding her sunglasses. He couldn't put his finger on it. Even the light inside the café intensified somehow.

Pringsheim jerked his head back. The air had a tang that did not exist even a minute ago, and it had a new fragrance, of myrrh and of frankincense. Could it be incense wafting up from the golden altar in the *Beit Hamikdash*?

Of course! What else could it be?

He took a deep breath; he never felt more alive!

"Hey! Prings, wake up!" Bernstein said snapping his fingers. "It's time to go. We'll meet back here tomorrow morning at nine."

Pringsheim looked up. "Okay. But I'm going to sit here a little longer. And tomorrow, you guys will have to start without me but I'll get here as soon as I can. There's something I have to do tomorrow morning before I can do anything else."

Samantha and Bernstein exchanged glances but said nothing.

Leaving Pringsheim still sitting at the table, they quickly descended the stairs and exited the café. It was noticeably cooler and they greedily filled their lungs with the brisk Jerusalem night air. They had been sitting a long time.

Outside, there was a fiesta starting up.

Chapter Twenty-Six

On the corner of Luntz and Ben Yehudah streets, Bernstein and Samantha encountered a large group of street musicians with flutes, guitars, trombones, accordions, and drums. As they started to play the latest *Mikdash* hit, the musicians soon were surrounded by hundreds of people singing and dancing, an eclectic mix of local Jerusalemites and *olei regel* from all over the world. In the swirling circles were shopkeepers, street peddlers, soldiers and policemen in uniform, black-hatted yeshiva students, bedraggled backpackers, university students, camera-toting tourists, businessmen, accountants, and lawyers wearing jackets and ties who had just left their offices. Like the *anshei ma'aseh* – the men of extraordinary piety – in the days of the Second Temple, some daredevils were throwing blazing torches into the air, catching them as they came down, dancing all the while.

The enthusiasm was infectious as more people poured into the streets from all sides. Music filled the air. Customers spilled out of cafés and stores, joining the throng.

Everyone sang the Hebrew words:

> How was he glorified when the people
> Gathered around him,
> In his coming out of the House of the Veil.
> So was the visage of the priest!

> He was like a morning star
> In the midst of the cloud,
> Like a full moon on festival days.
> So was the visage of the priest!

> Like the sun shining on the
> Temple of the Most High,
> Like a rainbow giving light in clouds of glory.
> So was the visage of the priest!

With ever increasing excitement, they sang it repeatedly with no letup. Their voices reverberated up and down the *midrachov*, bouncing off the stone buildings that lined Ben Yehudah. Lifting her eyes, Samantha saw people leaning out of upper windows of the buildings lining Ben Yehudah, singing and clapping to the music.

Everyone seemed to know the song and its meaning ... except for her.

"Dave, what are they singing?"

"They're singing about the High Priest, describing how awesome he was when he came out of the Holy of Holies in the Temple."

Without realizing it, she had started tapping her feet and clapping her hands in time to the music. She could not explain it, but somehow she felt in her soul a *connection* to these people. And Samantha had never felt a connection to anybody *anywhere,* and she'd been all over the world. She suddenly had an intense longing, a yearning, to join one of the swirling circles of women, but she knew she could not. She felt that somehow the women were dancing not on the mundane Ben Yehudah Midrachov of this world, but rather in the transcendental parallel universe of the Temple world where the smoke from the altar rose straight up to Heaven even on the windiest of days.

And there, she could never set foot.

Samantha stood staring silently. Juxtaposed to her feelings of strong connection with the people dancing, she felt a profound sense of loneliness. Never had she felt so alone, so empty, so isolated. But she never could admit that to Bernstein, perhaps not even to herself.

More bands appeared, adding their deafening contribution to the festivities. The crowd now numbered in the tens of thousands and was still growing rapidly, as new groups coming from the direction of King George and Jaffa Road joined in.

Like their foremothers before them who followed Miriam the dancing prophetess at the Red Sea, thousands of white-clad young women were shaking tambourines, the symbol of faith and redemption.

How Samantha wished she had one!

Now Samantha saw standard bearers wending their way through the singing crowd holding aloft enormous colorful flags, waving in the brisk Jerusalem breeze and illuminated by spotlights. They reminded her of the spectacular multi-colored tropical birds she remembered from her treks through the jungles of Belize and the swamps of the Yucatan. Circles of singing dancers ringed each flag.

"Dave, what are those flags?" she asked.

He looked at them closely.

"Those are the flags of the twelve tribes of Israel," Bernstein answered slowly.

For some reason, that made Samantha uneasy. Standing together in front of the entrance of an elegant boutique hotel, they watched the banner of the tribe of Reuven, a red mandrake-embossed flag, pass by as the crowd cheered.

It was followed by the green flag of Shim'on picturing an image of the city of Shechem and a sword. The third flag bearer carried the tricolored white, black, and red banner of the tribe of Levi highlighting the *Choshen Mishpat*, the bejeweled gold breast plate worn by the High Priest of Israel. The fourth standard bearer carried an azure flag depicting the Lion of Judah. As the flag of Judah passed in front of them, they saw in the distance Zevulun's white banner adorned with a portrayal of a ship. Behind another wave of dancers, they saw banner men raising the sun and moon embossed black flag of Yissachar – fitting symbols for the tribe of scholars who delved into the mysteries of astronomy and pondered the enigmas of the calendar.

Clapping their hands excitedly, the vast crowd burst into song again even more enthusiastically than before. Samantha heard the rhythmic beat of thousands of tambourines over the din of the dancing throng. Bobbing their heads up and down, the musicians returned to their instruments with renewed energy.

> *Baruch haba Melech Hamashi'ach!*
> *Baruch haba Melech Hamashi'ach!*
> *Baruch haba Melech Hamashi'ach!*
> *Baruch she'hechyanu ve'kiyemanu,*
> *Ve'higianu lazman hazeh!*

Welcome, Messianic King!

204

Blessed be He who has kept us alive, sustained us, and Brought us to this season!

Ashrei ha'am shekacha lo; ashrei ha'am she'Hashem Elokav...

Happy is the people who thus fare; happy is the people Whose God is *Hashem*...

"Dave, what are they singing now?" Samantha asked loudly, trying to be heard.

Awed, Bernstein was silent.

"Dave, what *is* it?"

"It's a song welcoming the Messianic King, the Messiah, *Melech Hamashi'ach*!"

"The Messiah!" she cried, "Is he here?"

"No, not yet, but they say that he can reveal himself at any moment. Hey, Sam, quick! Look over there!" Bernstein pointed excitedly.

She was astounded to see Pringsheim among the dancers. He had joined the circle dancing around Zevulun's white banner with the ship symbol. Sweat running down his face, long hair flying, singing at the top of his lungs, he was dancing with the best of them, looking like he was in another world.

"If I hadn't seen him in that circle with my own eyes, I would not have believed it!" she screamed at Bernstein, trying to make herself heard over the music.

"Me neither!"

"It's a new Pringsheim!" Samantha yelled.

"Yes, it really *is* a new Pringsheim," Bernstein repeated slowly, with wonder in his voice.

Samantha became more uneasy. Inexplicably she cast aside her journalist's instincts and uttered words that most likely never crossed the lips of a journalist before.

"Dave, we don't belong here. Let's go!"

Bernstein did not argue.

But even as they retreated up Ben Yehudah Street in the direction of King George, Samantha kept turning around and looking back at the celebrating thousands with their colorful tribal banners.

Later on that night, intensely agitated, she castigated herself for leaving. She had seen many fiestas in her career, but nothing like this.

Such spontaneous joy! Such excitement! Such enthusiasm! Such holiness! Holiness? Did I say that? Samantha exclaimed, shocked at her own thoughts.

She tried to remember some of the melodies that she heard that night, but without success. She tossed in her bed for hours. Finally, she drifted into a fitful sleep and found herself enmeshed in a whirling kaleidoscopic montage of dancers, street musicians, and colorful banners.

The image of thousands of white-clad young women shaking tambourines filled her dreams.

Chapter Twenty-Seven

The next morning, both Samantha and Bernstein arrived at the café at the same time, and they climbed the stairs together to the upper level. The quiet room was cool, and nearly empty. Although it was still early, an air conditioner hummed softly. After ordering breakfast, they started to talk. Almost by unspoken agreement, neither of them referred to the previous night's events on Ben Yehudah.

They thought that it would be a while until Pringsheim showed up. He had to have gone to sleep very late last night, that is, if he slept at all. Samantha sipped her cappuccino and looked at Bernstein.

"Dave, tell me about yourself."

He thought for a moment. "What do you want to know?" he began. "I grew up in Great Neck, New York in what they called the 'gilded ghetto.' And it really was gilded. Of course, that was before Depression II hit. I lived on Old Mill Road, a street lined with big ivy-covered mansions and old trees. They call Old Mill Road 'Synagogue Row' because there are so many big temples there – Reform, Orthodox, and Conservative. We were Reform but we almost never went. My parents are both academics, and religion was the last thing on their minds. And they liked to travel. They were always going to conferences and presenting papers somewhere or another. They've visited Europe at least twenty times. They've been to Latin America and the Far East a dozen times. And of course, they've crisscrossed America who knows how many times."

"Real travelers! How many times have they been to Israel?"

"Sam, they've never been to Israel, not even once. I think Israel's just about the only place on earth they never visited. They've even been to Tibet twice! I guess that says something, doesn't it? Anyway, I graduated from Great Neck North High School and then went on to Columbia. After getting my B.A. in English Lit with a minor in philosophy, I attended the Columbia School of Journalism. Since then, I've been knocking around the media world, and for the last ten years I've been stationed on and off in Jerusalem, representing PrinceGlobal Media. What about you, Sam?"

"I was the typical Valley Girl from the San Fernando Valley in L.A. We lived in a *faux* Spanish *hacienda* with landscaping designed to impress. We even made *Architectural Digest* one year. My dad, he passed away three years ago, was a highly respected doctor with a very lucrative private practice. My mom had an upscale art gallery on Rodeo Drive. But that was before the economy went south. Me? I was spoiled rotten and I barely made it through that bastion of academic excellence, Birmingham High School. Everyone thought I was a bit of a ditz," she grinned.

"You went to Berkeley though, didn't you?"

"That's right. I got my master's degree in journalism in Berkeley after doing a B.A. at UCLA in sociology, where I barely squeaked through. I really applied to the Berkeley School of Journalism as a joke. When my acceptance arrived, you could have knocked me over with a feather. Everyone thought it was a mistake. No one thought I'd make it through the first year. But I surprised everyone – including myself – by sticking it out and in the end, winning all the prizes. When I graduated, young and foolish, I became a war correspondent."

"Why are you called 'the Cat'?"

"Everyone asks me that. Did you know that Samantha is the most popular name for cats in America? My professional name is Samantha the Cat because everyone says that, like a cat, I have nine lives. I was wounded twice covering jihadist wars in Afghanistan and what used to be Syria and Iraq."

"A woman journalist out there? In jihadist territory? You're insane! How did you manage? They chopped off heads!"

"They sure did! They decapitated some of my best friends. Yeah, it was wild all right! Really wild! One day I'll write a book about it. The problem is that no one will believe it!

"Anyway, when I made the cover of *Time* magazine – that was before PrinceGlobal gobbled it up – the article about me was titled *The Adventures of Samantha the Cat*. Then *USA Today* and Fox News picked it up and the name stuck. Editors and newscasters loved it. They thought it was catchy, something people would remember. So I became Samantha the Cat. Actually my family name is Saraiva but practically no one remembers that anymore.

"Dave, I even had a few close calls in the recent upheavals in Europe before Falconi pulled the plug. Anyway, I like to be where the action is. At least I did."

Bernstein shot her a look.

With perhaps a slight touch of professional envy in his voice, he said, "You still seem to be where the action is. You were in Milan exactly at the right time."

"Sheer serendipity, that's all," Samantha laughed. But then, with the suddenness of a light being switched off, her whole demeanor changed. Her smile vanished, her face became rigid, and her eyes seemed to glaze over. She became very serious and shivered. "I wasn't supposed to be in Milan at all," she said breathlessly as she nervously ran her fingers through her hair.

"What do you mean?"

"I can't explain it. I was covering the fighting in Beauvais, north of Paris. A series of strange coincidences, one after the other, brought me to Falconi's press conference in Milan. I can't even begin to tell you what happened. It was almost like something was *pushing* me there. And when I got to Proudhon Hall, for some reason, the security men didn't check my passport against their list of invitees. I just walked through the outer barricade and no one paid attention. Once inside Proudhon Hall, I was standing in line with everyone else when suddenly someone literally grabbed me and hurled me through the door! I didn't know what hit me! And the security men didn't even look up! Dave, they checked and double-checked everybody else! It was as if they didn't *see* me. It was unreal. It was as like I was somehow *destined* to be at Falconi's press conference. You know, after that I felt empowered."

She continued in a staccato voice, "Then, after Falconi's press conference, we all ran to Malpensa Airport. I felt that I *had* to get to Jerusalem. Like everybody else, I wanted to interview the man who stopped Falconi and the anarchist revolution cold with one phone call. But at Malpensa, there were no tickets available, and the place was mobbed. It was so chaotic. Security had broken down everywhere. Remember, they had just re-opened. Everybody was pushing and screaming. The people in Malpensa were worse than the anarchists. Anyway, bottom line, there was no way I could get a ticket and so I turned to go. I just wanted to get out of there."

"So how did you get here?"

"Suddenly, a man came out of the crowd and shoved an envelope into my hand! I looked inside, and there was a ticket to Israel! Dave, I don't know where that man came from, and he disappeared before I could even see his face! And when I looked at the ticket again, I was stunned to see my name printed on it. It totally freaked me out.

"The next thing I knew I was on a flight to Tel Aviv. Would you believe it? The Tel Aviv flight was one of the first to take off from Malpensa after it re-opened. Dave, Malpensa is still not functioning normally. And I just heard a report that there are still thousands of people camping out there."

Shifting nervously in her chair, she sighed and finished her cup of coffee. She was soon lost in her own world, silent and unfathomable.

A few more minutes passed, and they sat in silence. They perked up when the air conditioner made a few strange belching noises. A bored waitress wearing a dark green apron and a long black pigtail refilled Samantha's empty cup. Finally, Samantha looked up and smiled wanly, "I'm back now. Sorry."

Bernstein looked up and smiled, "I'm glad. Now I have a question for you. Don't answer if you don't want to."

"It's okay. I may not answer, but you can try."

"Sam, are you married? I heard that you were but I don't see a ring."

"Just one of those rumors I guess." She paused a moment and looked into the distance, "I never found the right man."

"And I've never found the right woman," Bernstein said shaking his head wistfully. Then, noting the look in Samantha's

211

eyes, he decided it was the better part of valor to drop the subject. They looked at each other in silence for another few moments and then both of them simultaneously burst out laughing. The tension between them vanished.

"Sam, what were your parents like?"

"Distant and cold. My mom in particular always had an aura of mystery about her and she never wanted to talk about her background. But once, by accident, I saw her birth certificate and found out that she and my grandmother were born in a little village in Portugal. I asked her about it. She just got real mad and said, 'All they want to do there is remember; all I want to do is forget. Never bring that up with me again.' And I never did.

"But even though she said how much she wanted to forget her background, she sometimes did peculiar things that I always thought somehow were connected to her upbringing in Portugal. But she never wanted to talk about them."

"Such as?"

"Well, for example, she would never let me count stars. She said that if I did, I would get warts on my fingers. She always told the housekeeper never to vacuum the house from the inside toward the front door, but always from the outside to the inside. She actually fired a housekeeper who once did it 'wrong' by accident. I couldn't believe it. When she baked bread, she used to throw some pieces of the dough back into the oven. She'd crack eggs in a glass and look for bloodspots; if she saw one, she'd throw the whole egg away.

"If we passed a church, she made me look away or cover my eyes. I once saw her lighting candles in a side room in our basement one Friday night and singing to them when she thought no one was looking. When she saw me, she went ballistic! Also, we never had pork in the house because it was 'bad for our health.' Although she never gave any reasons, my dad always backed her up."

It was as if Bernstein's question opened a floodgate. Old memories surfaced.

"It was all so secretive. At first I didn't think too much about it. I just thought it was superstitious nonsense, maybe voodoo of some sort. But by the time I got to college I realized that it had to be much deeper than that. After all, my mother is a highly educated woman. Seeing her light candles in the basement like that really threw me. But she would never discuss those things with me. I felt shut out and it made me angry. In the end I just put it out of my mind. It was easier that way. I haven't thought about those things for years. You know, I never talked to anyone about this before."

"Sam, do you recall the name of the village in Portugal?"

"Yes, I do actually. Vinhateiro. It's in the northern part of the country near the Spanish border. It means 'wine grower.'"

"Have you ever been there?"

"Well, almost. About seven, eight years ago, when I was temporarily working for a European subsidiary of CNN, there was an EU trade fair in Lisbon. A couple days before it opened, our people in Portugal were hit by the big flu pandemic which swept through Europe that year so one of us had to get over there fast and cover it. No one volunteered so the boss said we could draw straws. Unfortunately, I drew the short straw and so I had to go. Anyway, while there already, I thought maybe I'd hire a cab and visit Vinhateiro and get a feel of the place. But the morning I was supposed to go it poured, and there was a snow alert for later on. So I didn't go in the end. Things being what they are, I pretty much forget about Vinhateiro until now."

Suddenly Bernstein stared at her intensely.

"Dave, what's the matter?" she asked, in a voice more demanding than she'd intended.

"Vinhateiro, you said?"

"Yes, Vinhateiro. I can't believe you've heard of it. I haven't thought about it in years."

"I've been there."

"You have?" Samantha said incredulously. "Dave, what were *you* doing there?"

"I had an assignment. I had to write a spread about the Portuguese wine industry. Northwest Portugal produces some of the world's finest wines and they have won many gold medals at international competitions. While I was there, I drove to Vinhateiro together with a Portuguese acquaintance."

"Does anyone speak English there?"

"I think that the local Catholic priest is the only one who knows any English at all, but he was the last person we were interested in seeing."

"Dave, there must be hundreds of villages in Portugal. Why Vinhateiro? What's so special about it?" asked Samantha.

"What do you know about the Inquisition?" Bernstein asked.

"I know a little," Samantha answered. "I know that the Catholic Church instituted it in the late Middle Ages, mainly in Spain and Portugal and then later in the New World, supposedly to eliminate heresy."

"Yes," Bernstein said. "But I want to ask you to elaborate, if you don't mind, and I'll explain why in a minute. If you were to give a mini-lesson to your class of one – namely me – what would you say?"

"Well," Samantha continued, "the Inquisitors started by persecuting Jews, then Muslims, and after the Reformation, Protestants. Those found 'guilty' of heresy who would not recant were tortured and burnt alive at the stake. I read somewhere that priests and monks sometimes even blessed and sprinkled holy water on their implements of torture before using them on their victims. Nobody knows how many thousands were burnt over the centuries. I remember that the Inquisitors orchestrated the expulsion of the remaining Jews from Spain in 1492 and from Portugal in 1496 so they wouldn't be a 'bad example' to those who had been forced to 'convert' to Catholicism."

"That's right," Bernstein said. "In 1391, the Catholic Church in Spain started to persecute the Jews in earnest. Most of the Jews expelled from Spain in 1492 crossed the border to Portugal where there was still a thriving Jewish community. However, shortly thereafter, Spain compelled Portugal to expel or convert her Jews, and then later, under Spanish pressure, Portugal instituted the Inquisition. But unlike the Spanish, the Portuguese were reluctant to expel tens of thousands of industrious wealth-producing Jews, so they baptized them by force. If, after an initial short period of 'grace,' they later 'backslid' or 'Judaized' they were declared 'heretics' and were subject to the full rigors of the Inquisition. Though many Jews did manage to flee Portugal, most were trapped."

"Dave, this is a very interesting history lesson but why are you telling me all this?" Samantha asked.

"Bear with me for another couple of minutes, okay?" Bernstein responded.

"All right, go ahead."

"So they did the only thing they could do. They abandoned the big cities and fled to remote villages where they hoped that the long arm of the Inquisition would not reach them. They posed as Catholics in public, but secretly practiced Judaism as best as they could. Undetected by the Inquisition, they lived in these villages this way for hundreds of years. For this reason they are called *anousim* – 'forced ones.' These *anousim* passed on to their children as much Jewish tradition as they could and – very important – married only among themselves."

Samantha put her cup down and sat as still as a statue. Only her widening eyes showed signs of life. Suddenly something clicked in her mind. "Did any of these *anousim* live in Vinhateiro?" She asked in a low whisper.

"Yes. That's exactly where I'm going. There was a group in Vinhateiro," Bernstein said, his lips curving into a smile. "Over the centuries, the *anousim* of Vinhateiro came to believe that they were the only Jews left on Earth. Even though the Portuguese government scrapped the Inquisition in the early nineteenth century, the *anousim* of Portugal remained in hiding. They were completely isolated from the outside world until the early twentieth century. Then, they were discovered only by accident."

"How did that happen?"

"After the Catholic monarchy fell in 1910, the new Portuguese government hired a Jewish mining engineer to make a geological survey of the area. While in Vinhateiro, he inadvertently came into contact with the community of *anousim*, but it took him a long time to realize that there *was* a Jewish connection there. It took him even longer to win their confidence."

"As late as the early twentieth century, they were still living underground?" Samantha asked in surprise.

"It's unbelievable, isn't it?" Bernstein responded. "But it's true. The Inquisition was officially abolished in Portugal only in 1821. And to these extremely isolated places – and you can't imagine how isolated – news travels slowly. And local attitudes change even more slowly."

"So how did the engineer win their confidence in the end?"

"Listen to this. By the early part of the twentieth century, the *anousim* of Vinhateiro didn't even know that Hebrew is the language of prayer for Jews. In fact they never even heard of the Hebrew language. Then an old woman whom they obviously respected asked the engineer to recite a Jewish prayer in Hebrew. So he recited the first verse of the *Shema*, the most well known Jewish prayer."

"That must have done the trick," Samantha said nodding her head.

"Only in a manner of speaking. The *anousim* were not familiar with the *Shema* itself, but they *did* recognize the Hebrew name of God in the passage he quoted, and on the basis of that they accepted him as Jewish and – after much hesitation – they believed what he told them: that there were millions of Jews in the outside world who practiced their religion openly."

"So, Dave, you're telling me that this single Hebrew word – *the name of God* – which they managed to preserve through five hundred years of persecution, was the key factor in bringing them back into contact with the Jewish world?" Samantha asked in amazement.

"That's exactly what I'm telling you."

217

"Unbelievable! So did they finally make contact with the Jewish world then?"

"Not then. Because of internal Portuguese politics, it wasn't until the 1980s that they were able to make contact with the outside world."

Clasping her hands together, Samantha sat there fascinated. She sat up straighter in her chair and brushed the hair out of her eyes, "Dave, what's Vinhateiro like today?"

"It's like a picture postcard. The population is about sixteen, eighteen hundred not counting the surrounding farms. Until fifteen years ago, there were no paved roads anywhere near the place. Even today, going to Vinhateiro is like entering a lost world. Very few buildings in the town were built after the 17th century. The church dates back to the 14th century. Most of the town's original surrounding walls are still there. The citadel with its fortifications is almost intact. Even the language the locals speak is closer to medieval Portuguese than it is to the Portuguese spoken today in Lisbon, although that's starting to change."

"How do the *anousim* practice Judaism today?"

"The *anousim* of Vinhateiro now have a small synagogue, and a rabbi from Israel visits them on a fairly regular basis. Recently, some of their young people have come to Israel to study and to live. At first the Israeli rabbis didn't know how to deal with them, but, with proper documentation, the *anousim* usually had no problem establishing their Jewish identity in the rabbinical courts. After what they had been through, it was obvious that their motives for wanting to return to Judaism were legitimate. As a result, more and more of them are coming forward and publicly expressing their wish to rejoin the Jewish people. Since the restoration of the Temple, the

218

rabbinical courts no longer accept converts to Judaism, but they *do* accept *anousim*, who are not considered converts."

"Dave, how many *anousim* are there?"

"No one really knows. I can only tell you that since the restoration of the Temple, the *anousim* from around the world are returning by the hundreds of thousands. And that might be only the first wave."

"Where are they?"

"There are groups all over Portugal, Spain, Palma de Mallorca, and the Azores. They're in southern Italy and Sicily, and *anousim* make up whole villages in the interior of northern Brazil. There are communities of *anousim* throughout Mexico, Columbia, Peru, and the southwestern United States. Today, the *anousim* are rejoining the Jewish people *en masse*. It's not like it used to be. Information about Judaism is only a click away and Torquemada the Grand Inquisitor, isn't looking over your shoulder anymore."

"Incredible!" breathed Samantha, her eyes widening.

"Yes, it is incredible. Samantha, if you are who and what I think you are, you are of *anousim* descent. You know the strange things you saw your mother do? She was following *anousim* customs. I'll bet your dad was of *anousim* descent too. *Anousim* always married among themselves. And I remember seeing your surname Saraiva mentioned in histories of the *anousim*. The name stuck in my mind since I have a cousin whose name is 'Sarah Eva.' Sam, there are over 45,000 extant Inquisition files in the 'Torro de Tombo,' Portugal's national archives, mostly comprised of accusations against *anousim* for 'Judaizing.' The Inquisition could bring charges against people for doing something as trivial as cleaning one's house on Friday, wearing a clean shirt on Saturday or giving one's

219

children Old Testament names. Like the Nazis, the Holy Office of the Inquisition kept meticulous records."

Samantha stared at the man sitting across from her and slowly nodded. Staggered, she was trying to absorb all she had seen and heard since she landed in Israel. In her mind's eye, she pictured a glorious cathedral with magnificent spires soaring to the very heavens. But the dank cavernous interior was filled with thousands of "converted" Jews – her ancestors – bound with thick ropes, who, with all their hearts, felt nothing but revulsion. Lurking in the shadows and barring their path, were iron-faced men in cross-embossed armor with drawn swords in their hands, soldiers of the Inquisition.

Suddenly Samantha sat up with a start. Maybe all that was happening to her was a wake-up call from God!

She remembered the inexplicable connection she had felt to the dancers on the Ben Yehudah Midrachov. She never felt connected anywhere, and she'd been just about everywhere on the planet. After hearing Bernstein's narrative, there was no doubt in Samantha's mind that she *was* of *anousim* descent. Bernstein solved the mystery that subconsciously had troubled her all her life. Bernstein's chronicle seemed to her almost like an epiphany from God. Maybe this was the real reason she came to Jerusalem! The eerie string of "coincidences" that brought her to Milan and then to Jerusalem were not coincidences at all! Dave's narrative explained so much. Shaking her head, she wondered *why* Bernstein's explanation that her mother's strange customs had their roots in some sort of tradition had never occurred to her before. Maybe the time for her to understand this had just not come.

Eyes dampening, Samantha stared across the table at Bernstein. For the first time, she thought of herself as a link in a chain, a chain that went back over six hundred years. What six hundred years? She was a link in a chain that went back three thousand six hundred years! Like the dancers on Ben Yehudah Street, like Dave Bernstein, like Nimrod Pringsheim, she was Jewish!

Samantha closed her eyes. *My God, what is it about Judaism that inspires such passionate loyalty?*

She owed it to her tenacious *anousim* ancestors and to herself to find out.

A tear rolled down her cheek. Instantly she wiped it away, hoping that Bernstein had not noticed. She looked across the table. Dave was such a sweet man. He was studying the kitschy pictures of Jerusalem on the walls; there was one of a stone windmill he could not take his eyes off of.

"Dave," Samantha asked, trying to keep her voice level, "Why were you so surprised when I mentioned Vinhateiro?"

"Because of the Vinhateiro archives. I'll tell you about them. A couple of years ago, it came to light that somewhere in the cellars of Vinhateiro, there are achieves containing genealogical tables and family trees of *anousim* going back to 1391, the year of the first nationwide pogrom in Spain. In 1492, when the Jews were expelled from Spain, the archives were smuggled into Portugal on the backs of donkeys through hidden mountain passes."

"In what language is all this recorded?"

"They're written in Spanish, Portuguese, and Latin. They're in enormous vellum bound volumes which are kept in an underground vault. The very earliest entries are in Hebrew. Because of the danger involved in recording these histories, perhaps a half a dozen people in every generation even knew about them, probably fewer. Your family may very well be

221

listed in one of those books. If you know the original Portuguese names of your grandparents and a few relevant dates, you may very well find your family history recorded there."

"Dave, do you really think so?" Samantha asked, trying to keep the excitement out of her voice.

"I think it's a real possibility. Those archives go back over six hundred years but the *anousim* of Vinhateiro never let outsiders see them. I only found about them by accident. I don't know who arranged it, but they recently allowed the Temple genealogy department to digitally scan them. If you should ever decide to try to trace your family history, let me know. Maybe I can help."

"Thank you for sharing this with me. Dave, this is a real revelation. It explains so much. I'm really overwhelmed." She paused for a minute. "Honestly, I don't know how to handle all of this."

Before she could say anything else, they heard a familiar voice.

"Sorry I'm so late. It took longer than I thought." It was Pringsheim, breathing heavily. "I wanted you guys to be the first to know. I just registered at a Temple Purification Center!"

He looked exhausted but radiant.

Then he showed Bernstein and Samantha an English edition of the *Mikdash Purification Manual for Olei Regel*. They opened the first page and began to read the introduction.

A few minutes passed and Pringsheim looked at his watch. He stood up, "Okay, I'm outta here! I want to see a Temple official I know. I think he'll be in his office now. I'll call you when I can."

Chapter Twenty-Eight

In spite of the High Priest's ban on contact with the media, worldwide interest in him and the Temple continued to mount.

The *Kohen Gadol*'s edict forbidding *Mikdash* personnel from having any contact with the media was adhered to without exception. Frustrated, journalists were reduced to scouring the *Mikdash* websites, listening to Mikdash Broadcasts to glean any information they could, and interviewing each other. Dave Bernstein, Samantha the Cat, and Nimrod Pringsheim, despite their growing expertise, were no exception.

Bernstein and Samantha sat comparing notes in the deserted upper level of the café on Ben Yehudah. The waitress had just removed the remnants of their breakfast and returned with a black coffee for Bernstein, a cappuccino for Samantha.

"Sam, can you believe it?" Bernstein blurted out, "This must be the first time in history that something like this is happening. The Temple is the source of earth-shattering news, and they've managed to totally bypass the media – except for their own – and they're getting away with it! With all the news

223

coming out about the High Priest, he hasn't given even one interview. And there hasn't been one with anyone else from the Temple either. Anyone else in the High Priest's position would be holding televised press conferences around the clock. You know, I think that the High Priest knows exactly what he's doing. He must be doing this media blackout as part of a larger strategy. He's not simply ignoring us. He's playing us like a violin, building up the tension."

Samantha did not like what Bernstein was saying, not at all. But she sensed that it was true. To show such contempt for the media – it was infuriating, and insulting. "Dave, I think I have to agree with you," she said, her head nodding slightly.

Bernstein's phone rang.

"Bernstein! Prince here!"

"Yes sir." Dave whispered to Samantha, "Here goes!"

"Good morning," came the voice over the telephone, "I hope you're having a good day."

Bernstein was shocked. In all the years that he had worked for PrinceGlobal Media, his boss had *never* spoken to him like *that.*

"Yes, I am, sir. Thank you," Bernstein replied hesitantly, not sure how to react.

"Good, I'm glad to hear it," Prince said in an uncharacteristically gentle voice. "Were you able to interview anyone at all? I hear the Temple media blackout is total."

"I'm sorry to say that the media blackout really is total. When the High Priest says no contact with the media, then there is no contact with the media. And there are no leaks from lower staff members either."

"No, there wouldn't be. You know, since Falconi's press conference, everyone wants to know about the High Priest, the

224

Temple, and what it really is. And the Temple officials are making absolutely no play to the media. None. I've never seen anything like it."

"I haven't either, sir."

"Did you hear that Falconi is coming to Jerusalem? He wants to meet the High Priest and talk to him in person."

"I heard he's coming, but I don't have details."

"Well, he is. And he's bringing a whole planeload of people with him. It should be in another three weeks or so."

"A planeload? Wow. Do you know who is he bringing?" Bernstein touched the speaker icon on his smartphone so Samantha could hear. He'd turn the speaker off when he took a turn talking.

"Who specifically, I don't know, but I understand there will be professors, writers, columnists, and government officials – real opinion molders. Anyone who's anyone in Europe is literally fighting to get on that plane. There's talk of organizing a plane from New York. There are also plenty of people here who want to join him. They say that the whole intellectual climate in the world is changing. They're calling it 'the Falconi effect.'"

Eyes widening, Bernstein leaned over and whispered to Samantha. "Sam, I've never heard him so talkative and so polite. He actually sounds thoughtful. I don't know what's gotten into him."

"Mr. Prince, think of it. All these intellectuals from Europe are making a pilgrimage to Jerusalem to meet the High Priest of a Temple that they can't even enter. Imagine that! When they arrive, the Temple will get a huge amount of publicity. That will cause even more people to visit the Temple websites and listen to the Temple broadcasts over the Internet."

Then something so extraordinary happened that Bernstein wondered if he imagined it. His boss came out with an obscure quotation in Hebrew, "*Tzadikim, melachtam na'ases al yedei acheirim.*"

Bernstein gasped, "Excuse me, sir?"

"Just something that popped into my head. Tell me, Bernstein, are you working with anyone now?"

"Yes I am, sir."

"Who?"

"Nimrod Pringsheim for one."

"Pringsheim? Hmm, we've carried his stuff before. But how do you expect him to write about the Temple? He's so anti-religious. Why him?"

"He's not the same Pringsheim," Bernstein said softly. "Falconi did something to him."

"What happened?"

Bernstein looked at Samantha. "I don't know how to describe it."

"Begin at the beginning," Prince said calmly.

Disarmed by his boss's unprecedented soft tone, Bernstein described the events that led to the dramatic change in Pringsheim: the shock that Pringsheim and his friends felt when they watched Falconi's press conference; Pringsheim's impulsive visit to the Temple Mount; Bernstein meeting him there; how and why Pringsheim's attempt to enter Temple grounds had been rebuffed by the Levite guards; Bernstein's conversation with him in the café; the shock of seeing Pringsheim among the dancers on Ben Yehudah; and finally, Pringsheim's registration at a Temple Purification Center. "He's become a totally different person now," Bernstein concluded.

Surprisingly, Prince had not interrupted him even once.

226

"So Pringsheim, ideologue of the radical Israeli left, got religion too?"

"Yes, I think so. And it seems like quite a few of his lefty friends are following his example."

"So, the Falconi effect strikes again!" Prince paused for a moment. "Is he there? Can I speak to him?"

"No. He *was* here but he's gone now. He's trying to arrange a meeting with a Temple official he knows. I hope something comes of it, but to tell you the truth, I doubt it."

"Very well. Are you working with anyone else?"

Bernstein hesitated. *Here goes*, he thought. "Samantha the Cat."

"Samantha the Cat?"

"Yes, sir."

"She wouldn't happen to be there with you now, would she?"

"Yes, sir. She is."

"Can you put her on, please?"

Bernstein turned to her and whispered: "Sam, he wants to talk to you. Now behave! This is my boss!"

"Bernstein, I always behave," Samantha said tartly, rolling her eyes heavenward.

"Mr. Prince, hello there!" she said brightly. "It's been a while!"

"Sam, it's good talking to you again after all these years. You did good in Milan, and I'm not surprised. You always were the best."

"Why, thank you very much, Mr. Prince," her eyebrows rising in surprise. "Coming from you, that's a real compliment." Putting her hand over the speaker, she whispered to Bernstein, "Dave, what's going on here? Please, thank you, compliments, and that v-e-l-v-e-t-y voice! This is the first time I ever heard him talking like a human being. Next thing you know he's going to start apologizing!"

Bernstein whispered back, "No way. He's never apologized to anybody for anything in his life and believe me, he has plenty to apologize for."

Prince cleared his throat, "Sam, you remember that spat we had in London a few years ago? It was as much my fault as yours, probably more mine. I want to apologize and wipe the slate clean. I'd like to make amends."

"Mr. Prince, I'm overwhelmed. I don't know what to say."

"Say that you'll accept my apology and let bygones be bygones."

"Of course I accept your apology. My behavior wasn't exactly exemplary either, so I hope you will forgive me too. But as far as I'm concerned, the whole thing is over and done with. So where do we go from here?" she asked, feeling a new sense of lightness.

"For now, you'll stay in Israel and work closely with Bernstein and Pringsheim," Prince responded. "We'll make the necessary arrangements. Sam, can you put me on speaker please?"

"Sure," Sam responded, as she touched the microphone icon on Bernstein's phone.

Prince continued, "Now I want both of you to pay close attention. We'll try to arrange it so we – that is, you – interview Falconi and his people when they arrive. We'll pull every string we can. Sam, he'll remember you from Milan. You will interview Falconi and Bernstein will interview the other VIPs. We've also found out that Russo, Falconi's right-hand man, spoke to the Temple administrator Chanina Abulafia several

228

times the night they got the flax fiber out of Milan. Pringsheim will deal as best as he can with the Temple authorities. Pringsheim is not exactly an unknown to them. If his recent turnabout is as sincere as Bernstein seems to think, they'll know about it. They may take that into consideration. Besides, dealing with the new Pringsheim may tickle their fancy."

"How will they know that Pringsheim is for real?" Samantha asked.

"Believe me, if his turn-about is real, they'll know," Prince answered. "I don't know how, but they'll know. And, Sam, when this mega-story is finished – the Temple, the High Priest, Falconi, all these people coming from Europe – we'll see how we can work together in the future on a more permanent basis."

"Thank you very much, Mr. Prince. I'll look forward to that."

"So do I. And again, I'm sorry I gave you a hard time."

"Hey! We wiped the slate clean, remember?"

"Yes, we did. We'll be in touch. And Samantha, thank you, and thank you Bernstein."

Prince hung up.

The two journalists stared at each other.

"Sam," Bernstein said, finally breaking the silence, "we'll talk later about what got into Prince. Right now I'd like to think through the Falconi thing." Samantha nodded. "Falconi's plane will be a chartered flight. It will most likely be landing in Mikdash Field."

"Mikdash Field? That's the restricted Temple area at the Atarot International Airport north of Jerusalem, isn't it?"

"That's right. Mikdash Field is administered directly by the Temple and the Levites handle security. We won't be able to

229

get anywhere near the place without their clearance. You know Sam, the whole time I've been based in Jerusalem, I've never seen the inside of the place even once."

"Dave, do you really think that Pringsheim can convince the Temple authorities to let us into Mikdash Field and interview these people?"

"Of course he can't. It can only be Prince dealing directly with the High Priest, if he could possibly get through to him. The High Priest sets Temple policy, not Abulafia, not Meir Hakohen. We have to call Prince back and find out exactly *how* he expects us to get clearance."

"Dave, before you say anything else, I have to know something. Prince said something that surprised you. I think it was Hebrew. What was it?"

"It *was* Hebrew; *'Tzadikim, melachtam na'ases al yedei acheirim,'* which means, 'The work of the righteous is done by others.' I'd love to know where he got that from."

"What was he trying to say?"

"I think he meant that despite the Temple's policy of total non-cooperation with the general media, they're getting all the publicity they want anyway. Everybody, everywhere, is quoting from their websites, their Internet learning programs, and listening to their broadcasts. Even without the general media, their message is getting out."

"I have to ask you. Dave, what do you think happened to Prince? 'Please,' 'thank you,' no interruptions, apologies? He's kind. He's considerate. He's going out of his way to personally try to set us up with all sorts of mega-interviews, he quotes in Hebrew... what's going on?"

"I don't know, Sam, but something else struck me. Do you remember when I finished telling him about the big change

230

that's come over Pringsheim? What was his reaction? 'So Pringsheim got religion too?' 'Too,' he said. Then he mentioned 'the Falconi effect.' Whatever the Falconi effect is, I think he's been hit with it a little himself."

"Prince?"

"So it seems. Hey, I have an idea. You remember Peter Bernard?"

"Prince's assistant?" Samantha asked.

"That's the one. I think I'll call him and ask him what's going on with Prince. He'll know."

"But will he tell you?"

"I think so. We've known each other for years."

Chapter Twenty-Nine

Later that evening Bernstein finally got through to Peter Bernard.

"Bernard, Dave Bernstein from Jerusalem here."

"Good you called. As a matter of fact, I was going to call you."

"What's happening?"

"Plenty! What do you want to know in particular?"

"About Falconi's visit, for starters."

"I don't have details yet, but there are serious negotiations going on. I can't tell you what's going on yet, but I can tell you that you'll be involved. You'll probably know soon. Just be available."

"Shall do. You know, you sound different. What's up?"

"Bernstein," Bernard responded in a booming, confident voice, "things around here *are* different. You wouldn't believe it. There's been a revolution around here. For some reason or another, the boss has suddenly become a human being. It's just unbelievable. It's a pleasure to work here now. Everything is 'please' and 'thank you' and Prince doesn't scream anymore, he talks. And when you talk, he lets you finish. And he really listens to what you have to say. Even that filthy cigar is gone.

It's amazing! And get this: there's a rabbi coming to his office every day for an hour. And when the rabbi's there, Prince doesn't take calls, and no one can see him, not even me."

"A rabbi? I didn't know Prince was Jewish."

"Nobody knew."

"I'm shocked."

"We all were. But you know what they say, 'life is full of surprises.'"

"It sure is. But let's get back to the Falconi thing. Prince said that Falconi is bringing a planeload of VIPs to Jerusalem to meet the High Priest in three weeks or so. He's trying to arrange an interview for us when they land."

"That is if the High Priest will let you do it, but I wouldn't count on it. You know as well as I do that we haven't gotten to first base with him. That's what the boss has been working on for the last few days, with no success. By the way, you said 'we.' Who else are you working with on this?"

"Samantha the Cat for one."

"You're working with Samantha? Are you crazy?"

"Bernard, relax. For your information, Samantha and Prince just had a very friendly chat, and in fact, he told her that when this Falconi business is over, he wants her to work with us on a permanent basis. I'm surprised he didn't tell you. Probably he just didn't get around to it. He even apologized for some tiff they had in London a few years ago."

"The boss apologized? To Samantha? Good Lord. Now I've heard everything. Forgive me if I faint. Wow. Bernstein, do you have any idea what happened in London?"

"Not really. I understood that they had some sort of squabble that bruised his ego."

"His ego wasn't the only thing that suffered. They met at some ultra-high profile black-tie bash. All of London society was there – cabinet ministers, members of parliament, judges, business leaders, EU officials, ambassadors, bankers, and the top media people. The Prime Minister was there. Even the royal family made an appearance. I don't know what led up to it, but the boss and Samantha got into a fight. He called her a name and she threw a glass of red wine right in his face! You should have seen him! Red wine dripping all over! In front of everybody! He was fit to be tied. It almost started a riot."

"Sam threw wine in George Prince's face?" he asked incredulously, staring at Samantha.

"She sure did. We twisted plenty of arms and paid off plenty of people so it wouldn't make the news or go viral on YouTube or Facebook. And believe me, it cost a fortune. The boss was apoplectic. A man in his position can't be made to look ridiculous.

"Bernstein, sorry I have to go, but I'll get back to you when I have any more news. Just remember, be ready to move fast when we call you."

Peter Bernard hung up.

Bernstein looked at Samantha. "Did you really throw a glass of wine in George Prince's face?" he asked, his eyebrows raised. She nodded, a sheepish grin on her face. Bernstein shook his head. "And Prince apologized to you?"

Samantha nodded again, "You heard, just now."

An astonished Bernstein fell back into his chair and started coughing.

Regaining his composure, Bernstein sat up. "Sam, let me ask you a question. Do you really blame the High Priest for not wanting to have anything to do with us?"

"What do you mean?"

"Let's face the facts. We're tainted. They're pure. Of course they don't want anything to do with us. No matter what we say, or how we say it, nobody believes what they see, read, and hear in the media. No major news outlets, cable, print or online, are credible to them, including, and maybe especially, PrinceGlobal Media."

"Aren't you being a bit harsh on all of us?" Samantha asked slowly, a slight note of rebuke in her voice.

"You think so? I'd like you to hear me out, since I've been thinking about this for a long time – how the free media is perceived by people as the bastion of a democratic society, and how we're so pompous about this role we ostensibly play. You know as well as I do that we journalists have failed in our calling, to serve the public with commitment to the values they cherish, like truth and honesty for starters.

"When I was an undergrad, and later in journalism school, they used to constantly lecture us about the importance of racial, ethnic, and gender diversity. Every group had to be 'fairly represented.' But, insidiously, in a hundred ways, they molded us to *think* in the same way. Our teachers were openly contemptuous of anyone who thought differently than they did. Their proclaimed love of diversity didn't extend to people with different values. And veracity and accuracy weren't par-ticularly important to them either even though they shouted from the rooftops how they were oh-so-dedicated to those so called hallmarks of our trade.

"And you know what? Because journalists are cranked out of the j-school system cookie cutter-like, people in every news-room in the Western world think alike. They're all in lockstep, from the editors on down. And anyone who doesn't toe the line doesn't get very far. You get yourself blackballed and no one in the media will come near you. You become a pariah. You learn that independent thinking is dangerous. It could ruin your career. You know Sam, it took me *years* to understand this. I lived in such a bubble. I thought it was all normal. I laugh when I think of it now, but at the time I thought we were all such flaming non-conformists."

"I know what you mean. Berkeley was also a haven for conforming non-conformists. I think my journalism school experience was a little different than yours, but go ahead."

Bernstein shook his head. "Sam, I'm not proud of the role that I played since I came here. Instead of doing serious research and reporting the truth, it was much easier to hang around the American Union Hotel during the day with the guys and go bar hopping at night. Did you know that at the American Union Hotel we used to fabricate anti-Israel atrocity stories and fake pictures? Our commentaries were deliberately misleading. We slanted headlines, everything. And for reasons of their own, more Israelis than you can imagine played along with us."

"Aren't you exaggerating, Dave?" Samantha asked, "Just a bit?"

"No, I'm not. Most people are convinced that journalists are politically biased, cynical, and corrupt. People believe that journalists want to be players, to *influence* events instead of reporting them honestly and fairly.

"I'll go even further. Most people think we are professional liars and manipulators. They despise us and, God help me, Sam, they're right to despise us," he said in a somber tone.

"I know," Samantha sighed.

"But listen, Sam, it paid. I know correspondents who get monthly 'expense accounts' from different NGOs, think tanks, and even governments. If they say the right things, they can go on the lecture circuit and collect six-figure fees per for spitting out what their paymasters want them to say. And don't forget the fancy vacation conferences in exotic locations held in the most luxurious five-star hotels. They're such hypocrites. They cry out how 'offended' they are and act all insulted if anyone dares to suggest that they're on the take."

Samantha gave a sad Mona Lisa smile. "I also know plenty of people like that," she said. "At least I can say that I'm not on anyone's payroll in that sense."

"Self-righteous to the core, they – no! – WE were no better than propagandists for the likes of Pringsheim. We publicized his drivel all over the world, knowing full well that most, if not all of it, was not true. I know that Pringsheim and most of his friends have changed now, but that doesn't undo all the damage they did over the years, with our help, our enthusiastic help. Sam, you know as well as I do, we fell all over ourselves in our eagerness to help them. It was so much easier and lucrative that way." Bernstein lowered his head and examined his folded hands.

"Sam, this morning I looked in the mirror and I was ashamed at what I saw. For the first time I understood the High Priest's thinking. If he or any of his people gave us interviews or cooperated with us in any way, the whole concept of the 'Beit Hamikdash,' the 'Holy Temple,' would be defiled somehow."

"Dave," Samantha said softly, "it seems that Prince was not the only one at PrinceGlobal hit by the Falconi effect."

237

"I admit it. Watching Falconi's press conference affected me far more than I realized at the time. But it started before that. The reappearance of the Temple really got me thinking. Not long afterwards, I moved out of the American Union Hotel. I couldn't stand it anymore. Sam, did you know that the laws of chemistry and physics in our universe are fine-tuned for human existence?"

"Excuse me?"

"I asked you if you knew that the laws of chemistry and physics in the universe are fine-tuned for human existence. Where there is a plan, where there is order, there is intelligence."

"Dave, you're getting philosophical on me. What are you trying to say?"

Bernstein became quiet and then, lost in thought, started humming a tune.

"Dave," Samantha observed with a smile, "your mind is in overdrive. Do you want to share?"

Chapter Thirty

Bernstein lifted his cup of coffee to his lips, but put it down without drinking.

"Well, I said that the universe is fine-tuned for human existence. It's not just random evolution of particles and forces at play."

"I've heard that, but you don't think this fine-tuning could be the result of natural development that turned out this way, but could have just as likely turned out some other way?" Samantha asked.

"No, Sam, I do not. Did you know that there are about twenty major factors – and there could be more - that govern our universe? They call them universal fundamental physical constants, and if any *one* of them was changed, ever so slightly, our universe could not exist." Samantha looked at him intently, her eyes registering real interest. "Stay with me," Bernstein continued, leaning forward, "If any of these factors were even slightly different, our universe would not be able to sustain the planets, stars, and galaxies, or any life as we know it. In fact, this 'fine-tuning' is so striking, and the 'coincidences' are so numerous, that many scientists have come to accept something called the 'anthropic principle.'"

"The anthropic principle? I never heard of it. What is it?"

"The proponents of the anthropic principle contend that the universe was brought into existence for the sole purpose of generating properties that make inevitable the emergence of intelligent life.

"Many scientists are embarrassed by this idea, but plenty of others are beginning to understand and even admit the existence of a great Cosmic Designer, a Master Intelligence. This Master Intelligence intentionally fine-tuned the physical laws in the universe to accommodate conscious life – us – even though we live on a small planet that revolves around a not very remarkable sun, located in an obscure corner of a very average galaxy."

Samantha flashed Bernstein a quizzical look, "What does all that mean?"

"I'll give you a couple of examples," Bernstein responded. "Take the force of gravity. In addition to keeping us from floating around and making it so that something we drop falls down, it's this force of gravity which governs the relationship between planets, stars, and galaxies. If the force of gravity was even slightly stronger or weaker, our universe could not exist. Same is true for the strong nuclear force that keeps the protons in the nucleus of atoms from blowing apart, or the electromagnetic force that binds atoms into molecules. If either of these were any stronger or weaker, again, our universe could not exist." Samantha nodded, but still had a quizzical look in her eyes.

"Here's another one. If our solar system was just a little bit closer to the center of our galaxy, we would be overwhelmed by the huge amounts of radiation given off by the tens of billions of stars that are concentrated there. The earth's magnetic field couldn't protect us from all that radiation, the way it protects us from our own sun's solar wind. If we were a little farther from the center of our galaxy, scientists tell us that the rocky planet we call home could not have formed at all."

"I see what you mean," Samantha nodded.

Bernstein continued, "You just have to marvel at the fine tuning of our exact position in the cosmos. The Earth revolves around the Sun in a very narrow range they call 'the Goldilocks zone.' It's like the baby bear's porridge in the story. Our Earth is not too hot and it's not too cold; it's just right. Our Earth has the exact conditions we need for life to develop."

"When you really think about it, there *do* seem to be too many 'coincidences' in our universe for it to be all chance," Samantha interjected.

"Sam, when the mathematical laws of probability are applied to biology, the odds against the incredibly organized complexity of Earth's plants, animals, and human beings evolving through blind chance – 'natural selection' – are so overwhelming that, for all practical purposes, the theory of evolution the way it is presented to us is mathematically impossible. It's like saying you threw millions of words into a drum, gave it a good spin, and out came an encyclopedia. The way that the theory of evolution is presented to us is logically impossible. This fact is a hard pill for many people to swallow – it flies in the face of their naturalist world view – but nevertheless, it's true."

"But Dave, evolution and natural development are totally accepted in the scientific community. You can't deny that," Samantha pointed out.

"I don't deny it. But you know what? Even the greatest biologist's judgment can sometimes be swayed by his personal biases. Not all scientists are as objective and rational as they pretend to be. One of the world's most famous evolutionary biologists wrote, 'Darwin made it possible to be an intellectually fulfilled atheist.' Can a man, even a scientist, who thinks this way, be really objective in interpreting his findings?"

Samantha thought for a moment. "No, I imagine he couldn't be," she answered.

Bernstein felt himself on a roll, and Samantha's expression seemed to show understanding and even agreement. "Last thing before I wrap up my mini-lecture here. Can you really believe that the human brain – conscious, thinking, flexible, theorizing, penetrating, inscrutable, subtle, and profound – maybe the most complex organism in the universe – came into being because of sheer dumb luck? No Sam, despite what ideologues with their own agendas may tell you, there is a plan here, and where there is a plan, there is a planner. Where there is a design, there is a designer, and where there is a painting, there is a painter."

"Dave, I see what you mean. What you are basically telling me is William Paley's old teleological argument proving the existence of God is true. If I remember correctly, Paley claimed that the existence of a watch implied a conscious watchmaker who crafted it."

Bernstein smiled, "Sam, you got it. In a nutshell, I'd say; 'There is no artist like our God.'"

"Is that from the Bible?"

"No, actually it's from the Talmud."

"There is no artist like our God,'" Samantha repeated slowly with a broad smile. "I like that. In fact, I like that very much."

"You know what Sam? I have a theory about that."

"About God being an artist?"

"Yes, about God being an artist. In my mind, I picture the great Artist – infinite and unknowable – 'sitting' as it were in splendid isolation but unbelievably effervescent with pulsing creative energy and power. Eons and eons passed and then one 'day,' BANG – consciously, purposefully, passionately, and according to a preconceived master plan and vision, the great Artist, by His word, unleashed unimaginably powerful forces that cumulated in the creation of our universe – and what may be beyond – with its untold galaxies, nebulae, stars, planets and all the spectacular wonders contained there. Still more astonishing if that were possible, everything throughout the universe was fine-tuned to the exact relative proportion necessary for the development of intelligent life. One of the greatest theoretical physicists of our day wrote that 'if the rate of expansion one second after the Big Bang had been smaller by even one part in a hundred thousand million, the universe would have re-collapsed before it ever reached its present size.' Talk about design! Sam, dare I say it? The great Artist – with a capital 'A' – excited and illuminated by the thrill of creation, 'couldn't help Himself!' He 'had' to do it!"

"I never heard that."

"It's not likely you would have. I told you, it's just my theory and after all I'm only a journalist working for PrinceGlobal, not a professional theologian. Anyway, where were we? I was saying that where there is a design, there is a designer, and where there is a painting, there is a painter. Where there is a building, there is an architect. When I consider our incredible universe and everything in it, I can only repeat the words of the Psalmist, 'How manifold are Thy works O Lord, in wisdom Thou have made them all.' And I came to

243

believe – and I still believe – that the act of creation was an act of Divine love so stupendous that the human mind cannot begin to fathom it and that this Divine love continues to permeate the universe. And with that idea in mind, I began to ask myself another question. What gives with the appearance of the Temple from out of the blue? It's as if – boom! Suddenly, it intrudes into our universe after all these years, and I have to ask myself why? What role does this Temple play in my life, and in everyone else's?"

Samantha studied Bernstein's serious yet animated face with intense concentration, "And what conclusion did you come to?"

"When I finally realized that I couldn't find an answer that was philosophically satisfying, I started studying the original Jewish sources. I wanted to understand what the Temple was, and what it represented. I took a few courses. I studied with rabbis. I went to public lectures about Judaism. I even started keeping kosher. I began my own spiritual journey which I'm still in the middle of. I wanted to understand what the universe was and where and how I and the Temple fit in. I wanted to understand the *why* of it all. Science says nothing about that." Bernstein realized that he had gone out on a limb sharing all this with Samantha. But it felt good. He broke into a wide smile and laughed gaily. "You know what, Sam? I don't usually talk about these things."

Samantha hesitated. "I'm not surprised," she said. "You're not going to win friends this way in certain circles."

"I don't care about my 'journalist friends' anymore. Like Pringsheim, I've moved on. Sam, if the High Priest will let me interview Falconi's people, I will do my best to get their message across as honestly and fairly as humanly possible.

244

Sam, I want my integrity back. I want to look in the mirror and be proud of what I see."

The faint music of the street musicians wafted up to them.

"Sam, I want to be worthy of entering the parallel universe of the Temple world," Bernstein said softly.

Samantha was quiet. She was twirling her spoon around the sides of her cup of cappuccino, and unconsciously tapped her toes to the music outside.

"So do I," she finally whispered.

Bernstein was humming along with the music; Samantha was silent, deep in thought.

Finally she put her cup down.

"Dave, I think you're right. What can I say? I keep thinking about the exchange I had with Falconi in Milan. How horribly arrogant I was! There I was, live, in front of hundreds of millions of people all over the world, baiting an older man, a genius – he probably has an IQ higher than the both of us put together – and ridiculing him because I didn't like his answer to my questions. Had he said that he was tearing up Europe because he's following in the time-honored anarchist tradition of violence and killing, I wouldn't have batted an eye. But let him say that he is calling for an end to bloodshed, and that people should work together in unity, trust and good will, and that he was influenced to change course by a holy man, a man of God, immediately I accuse him of being 'brainwashed.' I'm not proud of that exchange. I'll tell you the truth. Though it's made me a media superstar, I cringe every time I see a replay."

Samantha paused for a few moments and looked directly into Bernstein's eyes.

"And if I ever get the chance to meet Falconi again, I will apologize and ask his forgiveness. You know Dave, I have problems looking in the mirror myself."

Bernstein smiled. "Sam, we've done it! We've both come clean. There's an old Jewish expression that goes something like this: 'The seal of the Holy One Blessed be He is truth.' Sam, now that we've come clean, I think we're ready to do the Temple's work."

"That is, if they'll let us."

Suddenly, though subtly, the atmosphere in the cafe changed. Everything looked a little different; the patrons on the lower level; the kitschy pictures of Jerusalem vistas on the beige walls; Dave Bernstein, Tilly-Mesh hat perched on his head at a rakish angle; and Samantha the Cat slowly sipping her cappuccino. And the light inside the café! It was more intense, more luminous somehow. It was uncanny. The music wafting up from the street was intoxicating. The air had a tang that it did not have before. And there was a new fragrance in the upper level of the café, of myrrh and of frankincense.

Bernstein and Samantha both took a deep breath and looked into each other's eyes.

They never felt more alive!

Chapter Thirty-One

Holed up his office, George Prince felt frustrated and confused. This Falconi thing had really gotten to him. For the first time in his life, he wanted to do the right thing. For once, he wanted to be on the side of the angels, but he was being blocked.

It was late at night. Everyone, including Peter Bernard, had gone home. Prince rarely went home these days; he had no reason to. He frequently slept in his executive living room, off the side of his office. His magnificent penthouse apartment was empty except for the antique furniture and paintings that he had lost interest in. He had not visited his estate in Cannes in years.

Sitting at his desk with the panorama of the lit-up New York skyline at his feet, he let his mind run free. In the last twenty years, no one dared not answer his phone calls, not kings, not presidents, not the CEO's of the largest banks in the world. Even when he called their private numbers in the middle of the night, as he sometimes did to amuse himself, they hung on his every word. From those calls arose the legend that George Prince never slept. He was Big George, THE BOSS, and he was used to people fawning all over him. But his cousin Chaim didn't fawn all over him. He stood before him as an equal.

Chaim played by his own rules.

The High Priest in Jerusalem played by his own rules.

Prince had spent hours on the phone. When he finally got through to *Segan* Abulafia's office, they put him on hold. When he reached Meir Hakohen's office, they did the same. As far as Abulafia and Hakohen were concerned, he – Big George Prince, the great Media Mogul – simply did not exist. Usually it was enough for Peter Bernard to call and say the magic words, "George Prince is on the line," and no matter what they were doing, the biggest, most important people on the planet snapped to attention.

Falconi's lieutenant Eliodoro Russo finally did get back to him. Yes, Falconi's plane would be landing at Mikdash Field. No, he did not have the exact date yet. While Professor Falconi was gratified that such an important man such as George Prince thought that he was worthy of his attention, even so, unfortunately he could grant no interviews to the media without the express approval of the High Priest of the Temple of *Gerusalemme*.

Eliodoro Russo's evasive answer to Prince's personal request stunned him. No one *ever* refused a personal request of George Prince.

He had to do something.

Prince knew that a man in his position could very helpful to the Temple and to Falconi as well. The High Priest surely must know that. He *had* to know that he was trying to reach

248

him. The High Priest certainly must know that he – George Prince – wanted to put his entire media empire at the Temple's disposal. PrinceGlobal Media and Mikdash Broadcasts working together would be an unbeatable combination. Why were they stonewalling him like this? Maybe he should ask the priests in the Temple to offer up another *korban* on his behalf.

He had spoken to the rabbi who was now coming to his office every day about the whole concept of *korbanot*, sacrifices. The rabbi told him that sacrifices in the Temple, as important as they were, were not ends in themselves, but only a *means* to an end. But what exactly *was* that end? The rabbi said that *korbanot* served as a vehicle to become closer to God. He explained that the very word *korban* comes from the Hebrew root meaning "close." Snapping his fingers, Prince thought wistfully for a moment about his cousin Chaim's Shabbos table and sighed. He wished *he* could feel as close to God as Chaim did. But let's get real. Would God *have* him back after all those years of willful estrangement? What he needed was a straight communication from God Himself telling him what to do. He'd listen – if only he could figure out how to make it happen!

Sitting there in the dim light gazing at the Tanach the rabbi had left him, he remembered what his father used to do when he needed guidance. He would open a Tanach, choose a verse at random, and see how it applied to his situation. Prince decided he would do the same thing. He would follow in his father's footsteps. Maybe God would speak to him in that way too.

Prince put on the *kippa* the rabbi had given him and reached for the Tanach. Then he closed his eyes, opened the book at random, and pointed to a place on the page. Opening his eyes, he looked: First Samuel 15, verse 22. He began to read aloud.

> Hath the Lord as great delight in
> Burnt offerings and sacrifices,
> As in the harkening to the voice of the Lord?
> Behold, to obey is better than sacrifice,
> And to harken, than the fat of rams.
> For rebellion is as the sin of witchcraft,
> And stubbornness is as idolatry and *teraphim*.
> Because thou hath rejected the word of the Lord,
> He hath also rejected thee from being king...

Prince felt profoundly moved in a way that he had never been in his life. In fact, he felt as if someone just punched him in the stomach. The verse was so apropos, he couldn't believe it. It just *had* to be a message from God. Covering his eyes, he put the Tanach down and began to think feverishly. Maybe by refusing to deal with him, the High Priest was telling him that God was rejecting him from being "king." Maybe by refusing to deal with him, the High Priest was telling him that God could not be bought off by a sacrifice in the Temple – especially if it had not been offered with a contrite heart. He thought for a few minutes and came to a decision.

Tomorrow, when the rabbi came to his office, he would ask him what the message meant and what he should do about it. While he was at it, he would ask him to bring mezuzot for his office doors.

On second thought, why wait? He would call the rabbi first thing in the morning and ask him to bring the mezuzot when he came that afternoon. He would recite the *berachot* himself when they put them up. He could still read from the siddur, well, sort of. He smiled. That would set tongues wagging. In fact, many things he was going to do from now on would set tongues wagging. He laughed: the Falconi effect strikes again!

A verse from *Pirkei Avot* came to mind: "Rav Yehudah ben Tema said, 'Be bold as a leopard, light as an eagle, swift as a deer and strong as a lion to do the will of your Father in Heaven.'"

"That's the new me!" he chuckled.

Shaking his head, he said out loud, "Falconi did more than he knew."

Meanwhile he would call Eliodoro Russo back. Maybe Prince could sponsor Falconi's project anonymously. There were many groups of academics and writers all over the world who wanted to join Falconi in Jerusalem. Falconi's plane was going to be the first of many. Prince had plenty of contacts, and money was no object. If God felt that PrinceGlobal Media was not worthy of spreading the High Priest's message directly, maybe he could help out by aiding Falconi in other ways.

Dave Bernstein, Samantha the Cat, and Nimrod Pringsheim would have to wait for their instructions just a little longer.

Suddenly, though subtly, the atmosphere in the office changed. Prince looked out the window and saw the familiar spires and bright lights of Manhattan. They looked different somehow, although he couldn't say exactly why. Even the fat pigeons flapping their wings on the other side of the glass looked different. They didn't look like they were laughing at him anymore. He jerked his head backwards. Suddenly he remembered things from his youth, things that he had completely forgotten. He couldn't believe it. The Torah that he had learned in his youth was coming back!

The air had a tang that didn't exist even a minute ago. And did he smell something like the fragrance of incense from the golden altar of the *Beis Hamikdosh* in the air, myrrh and frankincense? And the light in his office – it was more luminous somehow. It was strange. It was uncanny. It was wonderful!

He never felt more alive!

He took a deep breath, smiled, and let his mind run free.

Sitting there behind his desk, he recalled a lecture given by a visiting *Rosh Yeshiva* one snowy December morning a year or so after his Bar Mitzvah. He remembered that only the senior students of the yeshiva had been invited to attend, and he was very proud to have been included. The *shi'ur* was held in a small crowded *beis midrash* on the second floor and everyone sat behind book-laden white Formica tables.

The subject of the lecture was the Biblical Chanoch – Enoch the son of Jared – who lived before the Flood. The *Rosh Yeshiva* explained that the Kabbalists taught that Chanoch had been a shoemaker, but a very special kind of shoemaker. As he worked, he pondered on how the ten *sefirot* – the ten manifestations of Divine light and energy that emanate from the *Ein Sof* – the Infinite One – interact and harmonize. By the immense power and sublime purity of his concentration, he was able to – at least temporarily – renew the previously shattered unity between the upper and lower worlds. And with each incision into the leather he made with his stitching awl, he bowed his head and said with a whole heart and perfect faith, "Blessed be the name of His glorious kingdom forever and ever."

Beaming, Prince pictured a bearded Chanoch wearing a work-stained smock hunched over an ancient wooden workbench in a shadowy room with his tools scattered in front of him. A lingering aroma of freshly mixed glue filled the air. As

252

he meditated, he sewed strips of leather together making sandals and somehow linking the upper and lower worlds.

Prince looked around his office. He thought for a moment and nodded his head.

Suddenly, clapping his hands together with considerable force, he cried out, "That's exactly what *I'm* going to do!"

I will link the upper and lower worlds together!

Buzzzzzzzzzz.

His reverie ended.

It was his ultra-private phone. George Prince had a private phone and an *ultra-private* phone. Only four people in the world had that number: his assistant Peter Bernard, his chief financial officer, and two lawyers. And all four of them had strict orders never to use it unless there was a real palpable emergency. But somehow he didn't believe that his nocturnal caller was one of the favored four. The infernal buzzing did not stop and seemed to be getting louder. Who could it be? He'd better answer it.

"Prince here."

An unfamiliar but regal voice replied, "*Shalom aleichem*, Reb Griesha Shmu'el!"

Prince took a deep breath, "Who is this? And how did you get this number?"

"Reb Griesha, I think you know the answers to both of your questions. You said that you envied Professor Falconi because I called him and not you."

Prince shuddered.

His thoughts were a jumble. Who could possibly be calling so late asking for Reb Griesha Shmu'el on this number? And who could have known what went through his mind since

Falconi's interview in Milan? It could only be...dear God. Could it really be?

"*Aleichem shalom*," Prince stammered, "Is this Rabbi Eliyahu Kagan, the High Priest?"

"Yes it is, Reb Griesha," he answered, with a smile in his voice. "You have come a long way. Your three correspondents in Jerusalem have come a long way. The time has come. There is much we have to talk about."

Like a little child, George – Griesha - Prince started to stammer, and his eyes dampened but he quickly pulled himself together. Now was *not* the time to be flustered. A term from a mishnah in the tractate *Yoma* he had once learned as a child sprung to mind.

"*Ishi Kohen Gadol*, my lord High Priest, I'm at your service. How may I serve you?"

An hour later, the High Priest finished talking. Reb Griesha slowly put down the phone. His head was spinning. And he had the distinct impression that what he had heard wasn't even the half of it.

Yes, Bernstein, Samantha and Pringsheim would be meeting Falconi's plane when it arrived and would interview the passengers. But that was small potatoes compared to what the High Priest wanted from him.

Thoroughly exhausted but ecstatic, Prince finally knew exactly what he had to do. A long-forgotten verse from the Book of Esther came to mind. For the first time he felt that he understood it. It was Mordecai's stern rebuke to Queen Esther: "Who knowest whether thou hast not come to the royal estate for such a time as this..."

He had not thought about these words since his youth, but now it all made sense. He finally understood *why* he had

254

become the Media Mogul, and *why* a penniless sixteen-year-old runaway had been so spectacularly successful at everything he did. For the first time he realized that a path had been opened before him from the very beginning. All this time, he had thought that his success was due to his own brilliance! What a fool he had been! He had been totally clueless!

He sat up straighter in his chair, raised his right hand, and made a vow.

Like Queen Esther of old, he would not let his people down.

Like Queen Esther of old, he would set wheels in motion.

After his long self-imposed exile from *Am Yisrael*, he would do a 180 degree turn-about, and instead of rejecting his people, he would actively participate in the work of redemption.

The image of the *Beit Hamikdash* and the *Kohen Gadol* filled his thoughts. Prince closed his eyes. He pictured his father robed in white gently putting his hands on his head and blessing him.

Energized, Prince swiveled in his chair and gazed at the wall behind his desk. He saw three seventeenth-century French paintings that he once picked up at an auction at Sotheby's years before. They had cost the earth. He would take them down and replace them with a big picture of the *Beis Hamikdosh* just like the one his cousin Chaim had. He'd call Chaim the first thing in the morning and ask him where he could get one.

And when it was morning in Jerusalem, he would call Bernstein and give him his instructions. He would also ask him to find him the name of a reputable real estate agent there. He would sell off the estate in Cannes and buy a house in Jerusalem. He would also look for a building or a substantial suite of offices suitable for PrinceGlobal Media's new world headquarters. Peter Bernard could run the New York office.

It was time to get his priorities straight. Chaim was right; *Eretz Yisrael* **was** calling her children home.

In a couple of hours, he would tell Peter Bernard to organize an emergency meeting of his top people. In light of what the High Priest told him, he knew that he had to present his initial proposals to the *Beit Hamikdash* as quickly as possible. In the future, his *Mikdash* contact man would be Meir Hakohen. Bernstein's contact man would be Elimelech Eizenman, the *Mikdash's* media advisor. Prince's chief financial officer would be in touch with Avi Katz, his *Mikdash* counterpart.

The *Beit Hamikdash*! How he savored the sound of those words. *Beit Hamikdash* sounded so much more *Jewish* than the generic word "Temple." He had seen temples in India. Mormons have temples. But there was only *one Beit Hamikdash*, the center of the universe, the place where Heaven and earth meet. He would make the use of the term "*Beit Hamikdash*" mandatory in all internal communications for the project the *Kohen Gadol* had tasked him to undertake. The High Priest would be referred to by his rightful title: *Kohen Gadol*. True, his subordinates didn't know Hebrew, but never mind. Let them break their teeth!

Radiantly happy, Prince pulled his keyboard over, adjusted his kippa, and started to work. It was going to be a long night.

Then Prince noticed that it was getting light outside and he paused for a moment. He looked at his watch and smiled. Reaching for his tallit and tefillin, he got up. He heard that there was a *minyan* three times a day in the office building across the street. The morning *minyan* met very early. He would join it and say Kaddish for his father. As he strode briskly towards the door carrying his tallit and tefillin, he glanced out the window. The two fat pigeons perched on the window looked at him intently. They looked like they were smiling. He saluted them on his way out.

They flapped their wings in acknowledgement.

Chapter Thirty-Two

A few hours later in Jerusalem, while he was attempting to initiate conversation with some Levites but not getting anywhere, Bernstein's phone buzzed. Excusing himself and walking well out of earshot, he took the call.

"Bernstein, Bernard here."

At the sound of Bernard's distinctive tone, Bernstein's ears perked up. A lot was at stake here.

"What's up?"

"Plenty! Listen closely. The High Priest called the boss last night and he's given the word."

"Whoa!" Bernstein interrupted. "The High Priest really called Prince? That's, that's, I don't even know what to say. It's unbelievable!"

"Well, you'd better believe it, Bernstein. Hold on to your Tilly-Mesh hat. They made up that you, Samantha, and Pringsheim will be interviewing Falconi and the other VIPs after they land in Jerusalem. Reporters from other networks will be there, but you three will do the major interviews. Someone from the High Priest's office named Elimelech Eizenman will be contacting you. He's the Director of the Temple Division of Public Affairs."

"Wow! I'm still holding on to my hat. But it's hard because my head's getting so big. We're really doing the interviews? That's phenomenal."

"Yes it is, but that's not the only reason I'm calling you. There's more, much more. The High Priest wants to reserve a two-and-a-half hour block of time on all – and I do mean all – our networks next year on October 10th in the evening, from 8:00 to 10:30 pm, Jerusalem time. He wants the whole world to watch something that will be broadcast live from Jerusalem. If we have contracts with anyone else for that time-slot, we'll have to cancel them. We either buy them out or compensate them somehow. You can imagine what kind of legal hassle that's going to be, not to mention the cost."

Bernstein whistled.

"And get this. Before the target date, we will be working in conjunction with Mikdash Broadcasts to orchestrate a publicity campaign on the Temple's behalf, the likes of which the world has never seen. The boss gave the High Priest a *carte blanche*. He agreed to every one of his conditions. I don't even know what they are. But anyway, I have an assignment for you. See if you can find out what's so important about that particular date and time. The High Priest basically said that it was still premature to say, but he did say that he would tell us when the time was right. And the boss didn't press him on it."

"Next year? October 10th, 8:00 to 10:30 pm? Offhand, I can't think why that specific time would be important."

"Well, you're the one in Jerusalem. Find out and get back to me ASAP."

"I'll do my best. But wait a minute, I have a question."

"What?"

"What are Falconi and his people going to do here once we finish interviewing them?"

"They'll be attending seminars at the new Convention Center next to the Temple Mount for a few days. Eizenman will probably tell you about it. They may want you to cover it and possibly broadcast from there as well. If they offer you the chance, grab it."

As soon as Bernard hung up, Bernstein SMSed Samantha and Pringsheim: "Big news! Can't talk about it over the phone. Meet me at 3:00 at the café." Two minutes later, Samantha texted back, "Can't wait! See you there!" Pringsheim texted back that because of prior commitments, he would be unable to make it. "But I want to know what's happening so keep me in the loop!" he concluded.

When Bernstein arrived at the cafe, he found Samantha already sitting at their usual table sipping cappuccino. Quickly joining her, he called over the waitress, and ordered black coffee.

"Dave, what's doing?"

"Sam, we're on! We're interviewing Falconi and the major VIPs. There will be representatives from other networks there but we're doing the important interviews."

Without thinking, Samantha hurriedly put down her cup, made her hands into fists and raised them high in the air, and banged them on the table with gusto. "Yeeeeeeeees!!" she cried with a shout. Then out of the corner of her eye she noticed an older couple two tables down glaring at her disapprovingly. Turning to them, she inclined her head, flashed an embarrassed smile, and shrugged her shoulders ingratiatingly. Mollified, they nodded back.

Returning her attention to Bernstein, Samantha said in a much lower voice, "That's terrific!"

"There's more," Bernstein said smiling. And in a low voice, he told Samantha all about Bernard's call.

Samantha was flabbergasted. "Worldwide coverage? Two-and-a-half hours? We're talking about multi-multi-million-dollar contracts! Man! I can't even begin to imagine what's involved here. What do you think is so special about October 10th?"

"I don't know. Bernard thought I might. He wants us to find out. Maybe we should check out the Jewish calendar and see if that gives us any clues."

"Okay."

Bernstein opened up his laptop but his train of thought was interrupted by the buzz of his cell. It was George Prince.

"Good afternoon, Bernstein. I hope you're doing well."

"Thank you, sir. I hope you're doing well too. Do you have more news for us?" Bernstein put Prince on speaker so Samantha could hear.

"Not really, I just wanted to add to what Bernard told you about covering the Falconi visit. Remember: you have to treat these *Mikdash* people with kid gloves. Don't get flippant with them for any reason. Same with Falconi and his people. If they tell you something is off limits, then it's off limits. Don't argue. Don't try to circumvent them. The *Mikdash* plays by its own rules and we have to play by them as well."

"Mr. Prince, have no fear. You can depend on us."

"Good. And Bernstein, one more thing, I want you to get me the contact info for some commercial and residential real estate companies in Jerusalem."

"No problem. I'll get right on it."

261

"Thank you! Have a good day." There was a click on the other side.

"Dave, did you notice?" Samantha pointed out. "Not a word about October 10th."

"How could I not notice?"

Bernstein went back to his computer to research the importance of October 10th.

"And did you notice?" she added, "He used the word *'Mikdash'* and not 'Temple.' Why do you think he wanted the name of a real estate agent?"

"Sam, isn't it obvious? He either wants to buy an apartment in Jerusalem or substantially upgrade our presence here. Maybe both!"

"Looks like he really *has* changed."

Bernstein went back to his laptop and started following links. Finally, he found one that led to *Shemitah*, the Sabbatical Year. He continued his research.

"Sam, look here," he said, pointing to a calendar on his screen. "Next year, the festival of Sukkot begins on the evening of the ninth of October."

Samantha's brows furrowed slightly. "But the circle is around the tenth."

"Right," Bernstein answered. "According to Jewish law, the 'day' begins at sundown, which in our case would be the evening of the ninth, and it ends the following night. Like Shabbat – you know how the busses and trains stop running Friday afternoon before sunset? That's because Shabbat, like all days in the Jewish calendar, starts when the sun sets. In the creation story in the Bible, it's written, 'It was evening, and it was morning – the first day.' That's where we get this idea of each day starting in the evening."

262

Samantha nodded.

"So if Sukkot starts on the ninth in the evening, then the day of October 10th is the first day of Sukkot. Then the evening of the 10th marks the beginning of the intermediate days of Sukkot, immediately following the Sabbatical year," Samantha nodded again. "I think we're getting warm."

Bernstein returned to his laptop and found a website describing "Hakhel." He began to read: "Hakhel (Hebrew) ('assemble') refers to the Biblically-mandated practice of assembling all Jewish men, women and children to hear the reading of the Torah by the King of Israel once every seven years. This ceremony took place at the site of the Temple of Jerusalem during Sukkot in the year following a *Shemitah* year. According to the Mishna, the mitzvah of *Hakhel* was performed throughout the years of the Second Temple era and, by inference, during the First Temple era as well. It was discontinued after the destruction of the Temple and the eviction of the Jewish people from their land."

"Here's the Biblical reference. It's in Deuteronomy 31. 'And Moses commanded them, saying: At the end of seven years, at the time of the sabbatical year, during the Sukkot festival when all Israel comes to appear before the Lord your God in the place that He shall choose, you shall read this Torah before all Israel, in their hearing. Assemble (*Hakhel*) the people, the men, the women, the small children, and your stranger who is within your gates, in order that they will hear and they will learn, and they shall fear the Lord your God, and observe to do all the words of this Torah. ... '"

Samantha looked up. "So this *Hakhel* thing is an event the Jews did during the time of the First and Second Temples. So it seems to me that now that the Temple is back, maybe they

263

would want to bring back *Hakhel* too. They've brought back so many other things."

"Makes sense, Sam. Let's keep looking. I think we're on the right track."

A website called "Maimonides/Sukkot" filled the screen. Bernstein looked further and found "Maimonides/Laws of *Hakhel, Hilchot Chagigah*, third chapter."

"Look at this!" Bernstein said, pointing to the screen. "*Hakhel* was held on the evening of the first of the intermediate days of Sukkot. I quote Maimonides. 'When do they read? At the end of the first day of Sukkot which is the beginning of the intermediate days of the holiday...'"

"So next year, the end of that first day, will be the evening of October 10th."

"Bingo! Sam, I think this is it. Next year, on the night of October 10th, the Temple is going to broadcast the *Hakhel* ceremony all over the world. And Mikdash Broadcasts and PrinceGlobal Media will carry it!"

"Dave, I think you're really on to something," Samantha said.

Bernstein continued to search, and found another text from the Mishna:

> What was the procedure in connection with the portion read by the king? At the conclusion of the first day of the Festival [of Sukkot] in the eighth year – after the end of the seventh year [the *Shemitah* year] – they used to prepare for him in the Temple court a wooden platform on which he sat, for it is written, "At the end of every seven years in the set time...(Deut. 31:10). The minister of the synagogue used to take a scroll of the Law and give it to the chief of the synagogue, and the chief of the

264

synagogue gave it to the *Segan*, and the *Segan* gave it to
the High Priest, and the High Priest gave it to the king,
and the king received it standing and read it sitting.
King Agrippa received it standing and read it standing
and for this, the Sages praised him...

"Sam, did you know that they have a synagogue in the
Temple in the Chamber of Hewn Stone? That's where the
Sanhedrin meets. The priests assemble for morning prayers
there. Do you know who's in charge of that? I guess you could
call him the chief of the synagogue."

"How would I know? Who is it?"

"Meir Hakohen. Prings ran a background check on him,
remember?"

"Good enough. Now we know the procedure," said
Samantha.

Bernstein found more information. He read from the
screen, "'The Mishna notes that the king read the prescribed
portions of the Torah in the *Azarah*, the inner Temple Court.
Already the commentaries postulate that the king read in the
Ezrat Nashim, the Court of the Women, the larger outer
courtyard of the Temple Compound.' However in the *Tosefta*, a
kind of expanded Mishna, Rabbi Eliezer ben Ya'akov is quoted
as saying that the ceremony of *Hakhel* took place on the much
larger Temple Mount outside of the Temple complex.

"So now we know *where* the ceremony will be," Bernstein
concluded.

"Dave, about that first quotation you read before. It said
that in the First and Second Temples, the King of Israel read
from the Torah on *Hakhel*. Doesn't the Mishna say the same
thing?"

"It does. So does Maimonides, Sam." Bernstein pointed to the screen, "It is the king who reads..."

"Wait, Dave. There is no King of Israel today. So who do you think will read?"

Bernstein sighed. He had been waiting for that. "Good question. Until now, I think we've been on solid ground. Now I'm going out on a limb. So hang on! Make sure your tray table is in an upright position. This is going to be a bumpy ride!"

Chapter Thirty-Three

Okay, I'm strapped in and my tray table is in an upright position. Go ahead," Samantha said.

"Ideally, the King of Israel reads. However," he scrolled down and read from the screen, "The *Tif'eret Yisrael*, a commentator on the Mishna, points out that the Torah does not specifically say that the *king* has to do it. Therefore, even when there was no king, as long as the Temple stood, they did not stop observing *Hakhel*."

"So let's go back to my original question. When there wasn't a king, who read?" Samantha asked.

"When there wasn't a king, the one who read was the most prominent person in the Jewish community, like the High Priest or the head of the Sanhedrin." Bernstein clicked a few times and read, "The *Tif'eret Yisrael* postulates that having the king read at all is a rabbinical decree designed to give honor to the Torah. It was meant to show that even the king was subject to the Law. The historian Josephus – he was an eyewitness by the way – wrote that in Second Temple times when there was no king, and that was most of the time, the High Priest read."

"So if that's the case, the High Priest can read now as well."

"Yes, he could. But you know Sam, somehow I can't see the Temple being restored after all this time and the commandment of *Hakhel* being observed for the first time in two thousand years just to have the High Priest do it. They would want to do it with a real king, the way it's really supposed to be."

"What do you mean?"

Bernstein took a breath. "Sam, listen carefully to what I am going to tell you, because what I'm going to say is going to require a quantum leap." Bernstein paused for a moment. "I think that the Anointed Messianic King of Israel, *Melech Hamashi'ach*, will read at the *Hakhel* ceremony."

Flabbergasted, Samantha paled. "The Messiah? The actual real Messiah?" she stammered.

Bernstein nodded. "Yes, the real Messiah, or in Hebrew, *Mashi'ach Tzedkeinu*, our Righteous Redeemer. The Jewish people have waited for thousands years for this. I think we're going to see the Messianic King with our own eyes. My bet is that during the ceremony of *Hakhel*, the High Priest will introduce the Messiah to the world."

"Are you serious?!"

"Yes. In the beginning of the *Hakhel* ceremony, the official in charge of conducting the morning prayers - I don't know who that will be - will give the Torah scroll to Meir Hakohen who will give it to *Segan* Chanina Abulafia. He'll give it to Eliyahu Kagan, the High Priest. Next, the High Priest will give the Torah to the King of Israel, the Messianic King."

Samantha looked puzzled. "I don't understand. Why can't the official who leads the morning prayers just give it to the king himself?"

268

"I don't know, but they say that this passing around of the Torah scroll gives more honor to the king."

"But Dave, we haven't heard anything from the Temple about any king."

"You're right. But as I understand it, many of the Jewish sages believed that the Messiah would appear when the Temple was restored. In fact, it was Maimonides, the greatest authority of them all, who contended that the Messianic King would actually rebuild the Temple."

"Excuse me for asking, but who is Maimonides?"

"Maimonides, better known as the Rambam, was a Jewish thinker who lived about nine hundred years ago. He was one of the 'greats' of Jewish history. But his real claim to fame was his codification of Jewish law, the Mishna Torah. It was a titanic achievement, and the first time it had ever been done in such a thorough manner. Maimonides has been a major influence in the development of Jewish law ever since."

"Okay, sorry to interrupt."

"No problem." Bernstein's eyes lit up. "Therefore, if Maimonides is correct, since the Temple is here, then by rights, the Messianic King should also be here. True, he hasn't given any interviews to the media, but I think he's already here working behind the scenes. There's so much going on here that we don't know. And I've come to the conclusion that he's the one pulling the strings, not the High Priest at all. I'm convinced that we're going to hear from him very soon. I'm sure of it."

"You really think so?"

"Yes I do. Samantha, mark my words, on the evening of October 10th we are going to see the Messianic King that we have been waiting for two thousand years."

Samantha was quiet. The Messiah? After all this time? But actually it *did* make sense. After all, the *Temple* was here already. And wasn't the reconstructed Temple the sure sign of the Messianic Age? This was huge. Her head was spinning. Wow! Maybe it was time for her to dismiss some of her reporter's skepticism, and allow herself to consider something that she couldn't actually see, weigh, or measure. Maybe it was time to lighten up a bit.

"Dave, is the Messiah going to ride into Jerusalem on a donkey like people say?" Samantha asked with an impish grin.

"A lot of people seem to think so Sam, but I think they're mistaken. That idea comes from a passage in the Book of Zechariah. It wasn't meant to be taken literally, I think, and that's what's led to its being misunderstood."

"I never heard of Zechariah. What does he say?"

"He was one of the later prophets. I can't download the quote right now, but the passage goes something like this, 'Rejoice greatly, O daughter of Zion, shout O daughter of Jerusalem! Behold thy king cometh unto thee, vindicated and victorious, poor and lowly, and riding on a donkey, even upon a colt, the foal of an ass.'"

"So, they're right then! According to the prophet Zechariah, the Messiah will come in riding on a donkey!"

"Not necessarily, Sam. Some of the greatest rabbinic authorities believe that the donkey motif used by Zechariah is an analogy, a metaphor, more than anything else, and that there is a much deeper meaning here than meets the eye."

"The Messiah riding a donkey is a metaphor? I never heard that."

"It's true. First of all, Maimonides doesn't even mention a donkey at all and he was the only early rabbinic authority who

270

discussed the messianic process in detail. Since he didn't mention a donkey at all, according to him, the Messiah does not *need* a physical donkey to ride on."

"So if the Messiah's donkey is only a metaphor, what *does* it represent?"

"Bear with me, Sam. We're going to get philosophical for a change, mystical anyway."

"I'm listening," Samantha said scrutinizing him closely.

"Here goes. The Gnostics and other religious groups that took their cue from them saw the physical world as inherently evil. Judaism, on the other hand, teaches that mankind's – and especially the Jew's – role on earth is not to reject the physical world but rather to sanctify it. It's written in the Midrash Tanchuma, which is an early rabbinic collection of homilies on the Torah, 'When the Holy One, Blessed be He, created the universe, He desired to have a dwelling in the lower worlds – that is the physical universe – the same way that He has a dwelling in the upper worlds.' In fact, there are authorities who posit that God's preferred 'dwelling place' is not in Heaven at all, but rather here in the 'lower worlds.' But to actualize this 'project,' so to speak, human beings must play an active role.

"In short, according to these sages, the role of humanity on earth is to prepare the 'lower world', the material world, to be a place worthy of being a dwelling place for the Shechinah, the Divine Presence. Our job is to seek holiness within the mundane, to find God within what we call the natural, and the spiritual within the physical. At the same time we must remember that God, the Transcendent, is *not* a part of His universe, but rather is *external* to it. Nevertheless, with every mitzvah that a Jew performs, with every good deed that a non-Jew does, the 'lower worlds' become that much holier and that much more suitable to be the principal 'habitat' of the Shechinah. Sam, are you with me? Do you follow me so far?"

Samantha thought for a moment. "Yes, I do. This is fascinating. I've never heard any of this before. It's beautiful. But Dave, you haven't said where the donkey fits in."

"Patience, I was just coming to that. In the Hebrew language, the words *chamor*, donkey, and *chomer*, materiality, as opposed to spirituality, are etymologically related."

"Okay," Samantha said slowly nodding her head.

"According to these sages, the Messiah's donkey, *chamor*, represents the material world, *chomer*, harnessed to accomplish spiritual purposes. Zechariah's metaphor describing the Messiah riding the *chamor* – the donkey – symbolizes that the *chomer* of the physical world can be purified, and is potentially capable of being as much as a powerful force for good – and even holiness – in the universe as the most spiritual creation. In the Messianic Age, the materiality of the physical world will be sublimated to effectuate its full potential to serve as an equal partner to the spiritual. In the Messianic Age, the dichotomy between the spiritual and the material will cease to exist."

Samantha listened and smiled. A quotation from Keats, a favorite poet from her college days, popped into her head.

> Then felt I like some watcher of the skies
> When a new planet swims into his ken…

Her eyes turned distant.

What an image Keats conjured up in those two lines! That's exactly how she felt now! In a few sentences, Dave explained so much, a whole philosophy of life! It was like discovering a new planet!

"Thank you Dave for sharing that with me," Samantha said softly.

"Sam," Bernstein said slowly, "the Messianic Age will be a whole different world. In our present state, we can't even begin to imagine what that means."

"Dave, where did you learn all this?" Samantha asked, cocking her head.

"Like I told you, when the Temple suddenly reappeared on the Temple Mount, it got me thinking. I started to go to lectures about Judaism as often as I could. And the one I heard on this subject had a tremendous impact on me."

"I can see why," Samantha said, with an intensity that surprised her.

Samantha leaned forward, put her elbows on the table and placed her chin on her laced fingers. Closing her eyes, she lapsed into thought. This was going to take some time to internalize. So much had happened to her since she'd arrived in Israel. One thing for sure, she was not the same Samantha she was when she got off the plane. She took a deep breath and reviewed Bernstein's narrative in her mind. If Bernstein was right, the Messiah, the harbinger of the new world that people prayed for and anticipated for thousands of years, was about to reveal himself. This would be the culmination of history. And God willing, she would be privileged to be part of that new world. She took another deep breath. Maybe for her sanity's sake, she should change the subject. This was heavy stuff.

Fortunately, Bernstein did it for her.

"Sam, I just thought of something else. According to tradition, the *Mashi'ach* will be preceded by Elijah the Prophet, Eliyahu Hanavi. You remember the name of the High Priest?"

"Eliyahu – Elijah – Kagan." Samantha sat up straight and grabbed the table with her hands. "Now wait a minute!" she said shaking her head, "Are you really suggesting that the High Priest is Elijah the prophet?!"

"I'm not suggesting anything. I'm just thinking out loud. Did you know that Elijah the Prophet is seen as some sort of reincarnation of Pinchas the priest? Now if he was a reincarnation of Pinchas, he would also have to be a priest. In fact, there is a reference in the Talmud that says Elijah *was* a priest."

"Who was Pinchas?"

"Pinchas was known as a real zealot. He was the grandson of Aaron, the brother of Moses. Aaron was the first High Priest. Now if Elijah the Prophet, Eliyahu Hanavi, was a priest because he was a reincarnation of Pinchas the priest, then why shouldn't his modern reincarnation, Eliyahu Kagan, be the High Priest?"

"Do you really think so?"

"It would link a few of the dots. Let's assume that it's true that Elijah must come before the *Mashi'ach*. Maybe Elijah is already here in the person of Elijah Kagan, the High Priest."

Samantha made a face. "Do you truly believe that?" Samantha asked with wonder in her voice.

"Elijah the Prophet was expected 'to bring peace and adjust all differences.' He was supposed to settle all controversies and legal disputes in Jewish law which had accumulated over the last couple of thousand years. Part of his job would be to resolve difficult ritual questions, and to reconcile passages of Scripture which at first glance seem to contradict each other.

"Eliyahu Kagan, the High Priest, has done just that. Elijah was supposed to persuade the Jews to repent. There is no question that Rav Eliyahu Kagan has done that more than anyone else in history. He's set up hundreds of yeshivot here in Israel and around the world. He's sent thousands of rabbis and teachers to Jewish communities in almost every country in the world, some communities so small they barely appear on the map. He's organized lectures and seminars on Jewish topics everywhere. He's written dozens of books covering every branch of Jewish learning. And because of his activities and writings, huge numbers of Jews have become religiously observant. Ask Prings, he'll tell you."

"I don't have to ask him," Samantha smiled, "He already told me."

"I'm not surprised," Bernstein chuckled. "The prophet Malachi speaks of Elijah's role in the Final Redemption. Listen to what he said, 'And he, Elijah, shall turn the heart of the fathers to the children and the heart of the children to their fathers.' I don't know of anyone this passage could apply to more than the High Priest. And you have to admit that he was the one who brought peace to the world, by influencing Falconi and so many other leaders."

Samantha opened her mouth to answer, but at that moment, the street musicians in the *Midrachov* started to sing loudly to the accompaniment of blaring trumpets. The music filled the café. People smiled and sat up straighter. Some started to sing along; everyone in the café seemed to know the words that the street musicians were singing. A group of young people on the lower floor of the café quickly paid their bill and ran out to join them. Samantha looked up with a gleam in her eye. With great difficulty, she restrained *herself* from running out there with them! However, sitting there and tapping her foot to the tune, she felt that her heart beat in time to the music. For the moment, that would have to suffice. Watching her, Bernstein smiled.

A new song spiraled up from the *Midrachov.*

Baruch haba Melech Hamashi'ach!
Baruch haba Melech Hamashi'ach! ...

"Dave, Isn't that the song welcoming the Messianic King?"

"Yes it is. You see? It's in the air," as he picked up his long neglected cup and sipped his coffee.

"Okay, Sam, let's backtrack for a minute. I should have mentioned this before. We were discussing *Hakhel.* Now this is very important. Do you remember the Biblical verse I read you before, the source for *Hakhel*? Here's what it says, '... Assemble (*Hakhel*) the people ... and your stranger who is within your gates - in order that they will hear and they will learn ....' Ibn Ezra, one of the classic mediaeval commentaries, contends that 'strangers' actually means non-Jews. 'Strangers' couldn't mean converts to Judaism because converts are reckoned as Jews, so they wouldn't need to be mentioned separately. Maybe that's why the High Priest wants to broadcast *Hakhel* all over the world to reach non-Jews too."

"Dave, you *do* realize that at this point, this is all conjecture. You have absolutely *no* proof," Samantha pointed out.

"I know, but you have to admit that it all hangs together."

"Well, yes, I guess it does," Samantha said slowly.

"I'm calling Bernard to tell him what we've come up with."

"Do you think he knows what *Hakhel* is?"

"Of course he doesn't. But let's be honest. We weren't exactly experts either until a few minutes ago. When I talk to him, I'll explain everything."

After he hung up, Dave Bernstein turned to Samantha, "Do you know what Bernard's exact words were? He said, and I quote, 'Good work, Bernstein. It all hangs together. I'll tell the boss.'"

Chapter Thirty-Four

Two days later, Eizenman contacted Dave Bernstein.

"Is this *Adon* David Bernstein?"

"Yes, it is. Who's calling, please?"

"This is Elimelech Eizenman, media advisor to *Segan* Abulafia. I understand you and your colleagues *Geveret* Samantha and *Adon* Pringsheim will be covering Professor Falconi's landing and the conference afterwards."

"Yes, we will be."

"May I suggest that you broadcast a brief introduction to the upcoming conference from our Communication Center this evening? We informed *Adon* Prince about the possibility of such a broadcast and he was quite enthusiastic. I understand that this is very last minute, but I think it will be quite beneficial. If the three of you will come as soon as possible to the Mikdash Communication Center – it's located in one of the side wings of our Conference Center – one of my staff will give you a tour and then afterwards we can discuss the coming conference at length. I might advise you to come as quickly as you can though; there is quite a bit of background material you should go over first. I will email you a list of the conference participants momentarily."

"Thank you. That would be excellent." Never putting stock in unsubstantiated rumors, Bernstein asked, "Excuse me, do you have adequate broadcasting facilities there?"

Bernstein thought he heard stifled laughter on the other side of the line but he wasn't certain.

"I think so. I'm quite sure that our equipment will be adequate for your needs. I don't anticipate any difficulties. Nevertheless, Levite technicians will be on hand to be of service if there are any unforeseen problems," Eizenman replied. "If you need anything or have any questions, I'll be at my office at the Mikdash Communication Center."

"I do have one question, actually. Would it be possible for us to interview you about the conference for the broadcast?"

"Of course, and at the same time, may I suggest that *Adon* Pringsheim interview Meir Hakohen, the assistant to the *Segan*, on our series *Mah Chadash Be'Mikdash?* as a guest interviewer for our Hebrew-speaking audience?"

After concluding his conversation with Eizenman, Bernstein sent three urgent SMS's. The first was to touch base with Bernard, who immediately texted back agreeing to arrange for a live broadcast from the Mikdash Conference Center that evening, and for PrinceGlobal Media to carry it worldwide. "Just let me know as soon as you have an exact time."

Bernstein's second SMS was to Samantha.

"Meet me outside the main entrance of the Mikdash Conference Center on the Temple Mount as soon as you can. We're interviewing Eizenman on Mikdash Broadcasts and PrinceGlobal Media tonight about the upcoming conference. Pringsheim will interview Meir Hakohen on Mikdash Broadcasts in Hebrew as a guest interviewer."

Bernstein then SMSed Pringsheim to tell him about the evening's broadcast. Five minutes later, Pringsheim texted back that he was on his way.

Bernstein quickly gathered what he needed, checked in the mirror to make sure he was extra presentable, and called a cab. Parking anywhere near the Temple Mount was tricky, and he didn't want to waste any time. Traffic was surprisingly light, and he arrived in record time. A couple of Levites idling in front of the Conference Center gazed at him quizzically as he hopped out of the cab.

While waiting for Samantha and Pringsheim in front of the Conference Center, Bernstein took out his smartphone and looked over the list of Falconi's VIPs and their bios which had just arrived. Falconi's list was a cross-section of the intellectual, religious, and political elite of Europe. On the list were dozens of cabinet ministers, party leaders, university presidents, and scores of prominent professors. Bernstein's jaw dropped as he continued to peruse the list, which also included internationally known philosophers, theologians, scientists, and historians. At the end of the list were the editors of major newspapers, writers, and columnists. There were even a number of well known European Islamic scholars and remorseful anarchist revolutionaries on the list.

"Unbelievable!" he said out loud.

"What's unbelievable, Dave?" said a voice.

"Hey Sam, take a look at the names on this list."

"Are these the names of Falconi's people?"

"Yes, I just got it from Eizenman. Take a look," Bernstein said as he handed his smartphone to Samantha.

"I can't believe this list!" Samantha blurted out. "I've interviewed quite a few of these people over the years. Talk about the Falconi effect!"

Then Pringsheim arrived.

Bernstein said, "We should go in already, but Prings, take a look at this first," he said, handing over his phone. "We just got Falconi's list."

Pringsheim examined the list, his eyes widening. He knew at least half of them personally through long years of political activity. All these people were coming to Jerusalem to participate in a conference on morality organized by the *Beit Hamikdash*! Shaking his head, Pringsheim laughed as he recalled the chorus of a well-known song from the 60's of the previous century: "The times, they are a-changing..."

While the three journalists were studying Eizenman's list, the doors of the Conference Center silently slid open and a Levite called out, "*Rabbotai*, excuse me. Are you *Adon* Bernstein, *Geveret* Samantha, and *Adon* Pringsheim?"

"Yes, we are."

"We've been expecting you. Please come in."

Bernstein was no longer surprised when Pringsheim touched the mezuzah on the door post and then kissed his fingertips on the way in.

"First I will take you to the Communications Center," said the Levite.

A few minutes later, they reached a pair of large, smooth bronze doors. With a serious expression on his face, the Levite slipped his right hand inside a recessed cipher box and punched in his five digit personal identification number. Within seconds, the doors of the Communication Center silently slid open. The three journalists, keenly aware that no

281

outsiders had ever been admitted before, entered the Communications Center and looked around wonderingly.

A Levite technician who was sitting at his computer terminal inside Node 3, a spacious private soundproof chamber reserved for Levites engaged in special projects, got up and greeted them warmly. After a brief introduction, he gave them an extended tour of the facility. For the amazed journalists, it was like entering a time warp into the future. The persistent rumors about "Mikbro" were true! Bernstein could not restrain himself. "Sam, look at this equipment! It must be decades ahead of anything that we use." Then laughing at himself, he said, "And I asked Eizenman if he had adequate broadcasting facilities here."

"I've never seen anything like it," Samantha agreed.

Pringsheim was speechless.

The technician smiled and explained to the three journalists that there would be simultaneous translations in seventy languages.

Bernstein and Samantha then sat down in a simply furnished side room, and discussed their upcoming interview with Eizenman.

When Meir Hakohen saw Pringsheim walk in, he did a double take. *Pringsheim of all people!* The rumors of his turnaround were true. Like so many others, he'd come a long way.

Two hours later, a green light flashed. Bernstein and Samantha's interview with Eizenman began.

Bernstein: Ladies and gentlemen, today we are broadcasting from the Temple Mount in the City of Jerusalem. This is a media first, a joint effort of *Shidurei*

Hamikdash – Mikdash Broadcasts and PrinceGlobal Media. I am your host, Dave Bernstein.

Samantha: And I am your hostess Samantha the Cat. Our subject tonight is the upcoming international conference on morality to be held here on the Temple Mount in less than three weeks. Today we are honored to be interviewing Rabbi Elimelech Eizenman, Director of the Beit Hamikdash Public Affairs Division, who will tell us about this unusual conference. Rabbi Eizenman, why has this conference captured the interest of the entire world?

Rabbi Eizenman: Thank you, Dave, and thank you, Samantha. The theme of the conference is not just morality. It is Morality for Non-Jews in the Messianic Age; the Inner Meaning of the Seven Noahide Laws and their Application Today. That covers a lot of ground. I think that quite a bit of interest has been generated because of Professor Falconi's dynamic involvement.

Samantha: Rabbi Eizenman, could you please tell us what these Seven Noahide Laws are? We've heard so much about them lately.

Rabbi Eizenman: Certainly. The name Noahide comes from Noah, as in Noah and the Flood. His descendents, who are non-Jews, are called on to abide by seven laws, which God commanded over four thousand years ago.

The first Noahide Law is a prohibition against idolatry, that is to say the deification or worship of any object, creature, human being, or power other than the one God. The second Noahide law is a blanket prohibition against blasphemy or cursing God. The third law prohibits murder. We are commanded to respect the sanctity of human life. The fourth law safeguards the integrity of marriage. The fifth law prohibits theft of any kind. We are commanded to respect the rights and property of others. The sixth law prohibits eating a limb or any meat taken from a live animal. Simply put, this law bans cruelty to animals. And finally the descendents of Noah – non-Jews – are required to create a judicial system to enforce the other six laws and any other laws that that they feel will help establish a just and healthy society. The purpose of this conference is to gain a thorough understanding of these laws and how best to implement them.

Samantha: So actually these seven laws are a distillation of the ethical values and principles upon which our civilization rests, yes?

Rabbi Eizenman: Indeed they are.

Bernstein: Rabbi Eizenman, could you tell us something about the conference itself?

Rabbi Eizenman: The original idea to have a conference of this nature actually was not even ours. It was Professor Falconi's. After consulting with some of his colleagues, he approached the High Priest, Harav Kagan. His title in Hebrew is "*Kohen Gadol*," meaning "High Priest" and "Harav" is a respectful way of saying "Rabbi." When the word got out about the conference, many European intellectuals, government leaders, writers, and religious leaders expressed interest in participating. Soon, we started getting inquiring emails by the scores. People kept signing up! We finally drew the line at five hundred and eighty two.

Bernstein: I understand that Professor Falconi and many other participants will be arriving in less than three weeks on a direct flight from Milan. What's on the schedule for them?

Rabbi Eizenman: After a brief press conference at the Mikdash airport and checking in at their lodgings, our honored guests will be welcomed at the Mikdash Conference Center by *Segan* Abulafia, his assistant Meir Hakohen, Harav Menachem, the Chief Sage and the other members of the Sanhedrin.

Samantha: Rabbi Eizenman, What about the High Priest, Harav Kagan? Won't he be on hand to welcome the participants?

Rabbi Eizenman: Because the High Priest never leaves Jerusalem, he will not meet the plane in person when it arrives. However, he looks forward to the pleasure of greeting his honored guests in Jerusalem and will of course play an active role in the conference.

Bernstein: Can you tell us something about the conference program?

Rabbi Eizenman: The conference is scheduled to last four days. The theme of the conference as I mentioned before is Morality for Non-Jews in the Messianic Age; the Inner Meaning of the Seven Noahide Laws and their Application Today. After a few welcoming speeches, there will be three keynote addresses: the first will be given by the High Priest Harav Eliyahu Kagan; the second by Harav Menachem, Chief Sage of the Sanhedrin; and the third will be given by Professor Falconi.

285

Bernstein: When will the actual sessions begin?

Rabbi Eizenman: They will begin in the afternoon, after the keynote addresses. The attendees will divide up into workshops of twenty or thirty participants. The sessions will be led by *Kohen Gadol* Harav Kagan, Harav Menachem, and various members of the Sanhedrin. There will be concurrent sessions in different rooms, with lecturers giving half-hour presentations followed by questions and open discussion.

Samantha: Rabbi Eizenman, what will be broadcast?

Rabbi Eizenman: Only the keynote addresses, the greetings, and the concluding summaries by some of the participants will be carried live by Mikdash Broadcasts as well as PrinceGlobal Media. All of the sessions, including panel discussions, roundtables, workshops and tutorials, will be closed to the press and the public. We have found that cameras and recording equipment can have a chilling effect. But there will be ample opportunity to interview the participants during the breaks.

Bernstein: Will synopses of the sessions be available during the conference?

Rabbi Eizenman: Absolutely. Synopses of all sessions will be posted daily on the *Mikdash* website, and people can read and download them at their leisure. In addition, at the end of the conference, the presentations will also be transcribed and published in hardcopy.

The interview continued for another ten minutes. At the end, Eizenman noted that the *Kohen Gadol*, Harav Eliyahu Kagan, was elated that world interest in the coming conference was so great, even though there had been comparatively little publicity about it.

After the interview, Eizenman summoned them to his ultra-orderly spanking white office. "Let me show you something."

He flicked a switch and a screen lit up. "Take a look. This is the number of people who are currently visiting our websites. Look at the dramatic increase since your broadcast started. The numbers speak for themselves," Eizenman said with a grin.

However, before they could say anything, there was a knock on the door and Pringsheim walked in. He had just concluded his interview with Meir Hakohen on *Mah Chadash Be'Mikdash?*

"I'm glad you're finished, *Adon* Pringsheim. You need to hear this too. We have to discuss what the three of you will be doing when Professor Falconi's plane arrives and as well as the procedures you will follow during the conference.

"As you know, Falconi's plane will be arriving at Mikdash Field. About two hours before his scheduled arrival, you, together with three *Mikdash* officials, will board a *Mikdash* helicopter at the helipad located behind this building. I'll show it to you on the way out. The helicopter will take you to Mikdash Field in the early afternoon. I will meet you there. To facilitate your preparations for the interviews, Levite technicians will be available if you need them. *Geveret* Samantha will interview Professor Falconi and you will interview some of our other guests. You and *Geveret* Samantha will be broadcasting in English on Mikdash Broadcasts and

PrinceGlobal Media. *Adon* Pringsheim will broadcast in Hebrew on *Shidurei Hamikdash*. I will be in touch with you the day before to finalize everything."

During the next few days, the Internet, YouTubes, radio, television, and newspapers throughout the world carried Bernstein's and Samantha's interview with Eizenman, as well as stories about the upcoming conference in Jerusalem. The number of visits to the *Mikdash* websites continued to soar. "Falconi's Temple Conference on Morality" continued to be the major topic for columnists, talk shows, bloggers and chat rooms everywhere.

Chapter Thirty-Five

Upon landing at Mikdash Field, Professor Falconi and his entourage swiftly exited the aircraft, and entered a large reception room. Thunderous applause greeted them. As they took their places at the dais, the *Chacham Muflag* raised his hand for silence, then he and the members of the Sanhedrin recited the *berachah* that the halachah ordains upon seeing a great non-Jewish scholar, first in Hebrew and then in English.

> Blessed art Thou, O Lord, our God, King of the universe, who has imparted of His wisdom to flesh and blood.

The sound of hundreds of people simultaneously answering "Amen" pierced the air.

Acknowledging the applause and the blessing, Falconi stepped to the podium and stood silently. Shafts of fading sunlight shone through clerestory windows set high in the terminal walls.

In a melodious voice, the former anarchist leader began to speak. "*Signore e signori*, ladies and gentlemen, many people have asked why we have come to Jerusalem. It is simple. We have come to witness with our eyes, we have come to fulfill something very important, and most crucially, we have come to learn.

"The prophet Isaiah said: 'And it shall come to pass in the end of days that the mountain of the House of the Lord shall be established as the chief of the mountains. And it shall be exalted above the hills; and all nations shall flow unto it. And many peoples shall go and say: Come ye and let us go up to the mountain of God, to the house of the God of Jacob,'" Falconi looked up. "This house, my friends, is the Temple of Jerusalem. I continue with Isaiah's words, 'and He will teach us of His ways and we will walk in His paths. For out of Zion shall go forth the law and the word of the Lord from Jerusalem.'

"We are here to fulfill that prophecy.

"Our teachers will be High Priest Rabbi Eliyahu Kagan of the Temple of Jerusalem, Chief Sage Rabbi Menachem, and the distinguished sages of Israel. We are honored that we have this privilege. Many thanks to Rabbi Eliyahu Kagan, Rabbi Chanina Abulafia, and Rabbi Meir Hakohen and everyone else who has helped us so much and organized this conference that we are about to attend. We know that it will be the first of many. *Dio vi benedica!* God bless you all."

When Professor Falconi finished speaking, he began to clap. Within seconds, everyone in the hall joined in. When the applause started to wind down, Eizenman nodded to Samantha. She approached Falconi, microphone in hand. She knew that the eyes of the world were upon her. A smile of recognition played on Professor Falconi's face.

Modestly, almost bobbing a curtsey, her eyes bright and her face flushed with exhilaration, Samantha said softly, "Professor Falconi, before I begin, I want to apologize for treating you with such disrespect during your press conference in Milan. I know now that your words then were only the beginning of something much greater, something I could not and would not understand at the time. But I *am* beginning to understand it now. I want to tell you that every time I see a replay of our exchange in Milan, I feel ashamed."

Dave Bernstein was amazed. What a woman! Sam said she was going to apologize to Falconi, and by Heaven, she did – in front of the entire world.

In his New York office, newly graced by an enormous framed picture of the *Beit Hamikdash,* George Prince took a deep breath and sat there open-mouthed.

Nodding his head, Falconi looked at Samantha and smiled.

"*Signorina,* young woman, it is nothing! We have *all* come a long way in the last few months. *Signorina,* today, I am fulfilling my destiny. Now, it is your turn. You must begin to fulfill your own destiny!"

And at that moment, under Falconi's gaze, Samantha made a decision: after the conference, she would fly back to Los Angeles and confront her mother about her family's past. She would solve the mystery of Vinhateiro and find out who and what she really was. But in her heart, she already knew.

"I will, Professor Falconi, I promise."

"I know you will. And *Signorina,* don't be a stranger!"

With an enigmatic smile on his face, for the second time, Eizenman signaled to Samantha to begin the interview. After Samantha finished interviewing Professor Falconi, Dave Bernstein and Nimrod Pringsheim stepped forward and interviewed select people previously chosen from Falconi's entourage. Finally, the journalists representing the other networks were permitted to ask questions.

Finally Eizenman called a halt to the questioning and made a few concluding remarks. Professor Falconi and his colleagues boarded the gold and white streamlined light-rail that would take them directly to the Chomot Yerushalayim Hotel where they would be staying during the conference. The three representatives of PrinceGlobal Media hopped aboard. Within seconds, the doors of the train whooshed shut. The train started moving, slowly at first, then gathered speed. The train swayed softly as it raced towards Jerusalem. Bernstein, Samantha, and Pringsheim found themselves a table with four empty seats near one of the entrances of the car. Bernstein's phone started buzzing.

It was George Prince.

"You did a good job, Bernstein."

"Thank you, sir. The Temple authorities could not have been more cooperative."

"I'm glad to hear it. Where are you now?"

"The ceremonies at Mikdash Field are over and we're on the light-rail to Jerusalem. The conference officially starts tomorrow early afternoon, though there will be a welcoming banquet tonight. Eizenman said that aside from the closed sessions, we'll have free run of the place. He's really been very accommodating. We are scheduled to interview *Segan* Abulafia and Meir Hakohen again during the next few days."

"Great! Is Samantha there?"

"Yes."

"Would you put her on, please?"

"My pleasure," he said, as he passed the smartphone to Samantha.

Samantha put her cold drink down on the table. From the other side of the car, they heard an outburst of happy laughter.

292

"Yes, Mr. Prince."

"Sam, you did an amazing thing there with Falconi, in front of the entire world. We were all moved."

"Thank you, sir."

"You know, Samantha, I've underestimated you in the past. I won't do that again."

"Thank you again sir, but I can barely hear you. I'm going to have to get off. We'll call you back as soon as we can."

"Okay, we'll talk later."

Falconi shared a table with the *Segan*, the Prime Minister of Italy, and the Irish deputy prime minister. Meir Hakohen shared a table with the Spanish Minister of Culture, the rector of the Universidad Carlos III de Madrid, and the vice-president of the Russian Federation.

Three French writers who knew Pringsheim from his days in Paris recognized him despite his new beard and *kippa*. They invited him to join them at their table. They wanted to hear the story of how he had changed from an anti-religious leftist ideologue to a veritable *protégé* of the High Priest. Pringsheim was more than happy to oblige. In fact, Pringsheim soon became the center of attention of many Francophones during the reception.

The Irish Deputy Prime Minister faced the *Segan*. He was deeply troubled that the flax fiber the *Mikdash* had ordered from a firm in his country had ended up in Canada instead of Jerusalem.

In a lilting though subdued Irish brogue, he said, "Your Eminence Abulafia, I'm so glad that I have this opportunity to speak to you before the conference begins. In the name of our government, I'd like to apologize for the terrible mishap about the flax fiber. It should never have happened and, indeed, we were all mortified."

"Do not trouble yourself unduly, Your Excellency. It all worked out for the best."

"Nevertheless, it should not have happened. We will gladly pay any indemnity, compensation, or damages that you feel just."

"That won't be necessary," the *Segan* assured him.

"Thank you, Your Eminence. But there is also another reason I wanted to speak to you. I am authorized to make a proposal to the Temple of Jerusalem in the name of the government of the Irish Republic and the Irish people. You know that flax is the very fabric of Ireland. The combination of fine raw materials, skilled weavers, advanced loom technology, and careful finishing has brought Irish linen a reputation as being the finest in the world. We are very proud of this reputation. Our home grown flax is truly the best in the world, and for this reason we feel that it is only appropriate that the priests of the Temple of the Lord be clothed in linen vestments woven from the very best Irish flax. For this reason, we request the honor of supplying all the Temple's flax needs in the future, *gratis*, in perpetuity. And of course we will strictly follow every specification you may have."

"Sir, you are very gracious."

"Not nearly as gracious as you will be if you grant our request, Your Eminence."

"Very well. As *Segan*, and as deputy to the High Priest, in the name of the Temple of Jerusalem, we accept the very generous offer of the people of Ireland with great appreciation. May they be blessed from Heaven."

The Irishman's eyes lit up with joy. "Thank you, Your Eminence."

Falconi, the don from Oxford University, the Irish deputy prime minister, and the *Segan* smiled and the four shook hands. As Falconi shook hands with the Irish Deputy Prime Minister, the *Segan* thought again of how the flax stuck in Milan had been miraculously released and sent to the *Mikdash*. Smiling, the *Segan* remembered the prescient words of the *Kohen Gadol* and the commentary of Rav David Altschuler, the Metzudat David: "The House of My Glory, this is the *Beit Hamikdash,* which will be glorified by the gifts the nations joyfully will bring to it."

Slowing down as it approached the northern Jerusalem suburbs, the high-speed train pulled into the domed Har Habayit station. As he was getting off the train, Pringsheim thought he heard someone calling his name. He turned around. It was Falconi, addressing him in French, with a gentle smile.

"*Monsieur* Pringsheim, I thought it was you. But with your altered appearance, and your *kippa*, I wasn't sure."

"Yes, it's me." Pringsheim replied somewhat abashed, "I'm surprised you remember me."

"*Monsieur*, don't be so modest. Of course I remember you. You are not so easily forgotten. We *did* work together in Paris for many years. We also had some long and very stimulating conversations. Now it seems we meet again, but under somewhat different circumstances," Falconi smiled, his eyes sparkling.

"So it seems."

"*Monsieur*, I used to read your articles with great interest."

"I appreciate your kind words, Professor Falconi. As you know, I always considered you my mentor," Pringsheim said.

"Thank you," Falconi said softly.

Pringsheim nodded his head.

"*Monsieur*," Falconi continued, "As we both travel on the parallel paths that have been providentially opened before us, you as an observant Jew and I as a *Ben Noach*, a righteous gentile who observes the Seven Noahide Laws, I hope you still can consider me a mentor."

"Yes, of course, Professor Falconi. I want to tell you that I owe you more than I can say," Pringsheim replied with feeling.

"You are gracious, *Monsieur*. And I must tell you that I owe the High Priest Harav Kagan more than *I* can say. But consider *Monsieur*: the prophet Isaiah has already described seekers such as us:

> The people that walked in darkness
> Have seen a great light.
> They that dwelt in the land of the shadow of death,
> Upon them hath the light shined.

"*Monsieur*, we've both come a long way, but remember, our parallel journeys have not ended; they have only begun," and with a wave, Falconi vanished into the crowd.

Pringsheim smiled broadly as he watched the professor leave.

It was the unanimous verdict of all who attended the conference that it was an unqualified success. Everyone commented on the high intellectual level of the sessions, the seriousness of purpose of the participants, and their intense involvement. Everyone noted the unusual rapport between the sages of Israel and their European guests. It was clear that this was no ordinary academic gathering, and that the seminars merely whetted the appetite of the participants for future conferences. Towards the end of the conference, the *Segan* announced that *Shidurei Hamikdash,* Mikdash Broadcasts, the Mikdash websites, and the Mikdash Committee for Universal Education would be considerably expanded.

Bernstein, Samantha and Pringsheim were kept busy dashing around the Convention Center interviewing part-icipants, getting their reactions, and broadcasting. Mikdash Broadcasts and PrinceGlobal Media carried the proceedings live.

The final speeches of the conference were over.

Elimelech Eizenman had just finished making a few concluding remarks, the representatives of the media were turning off their recording equipment and putting their cameras away when unexpectedly Professor Falconi returned to the podium and raised his hand for silence. Instantly, the hall was quiet. All the digital recording equipment and cameras were flipped back on. Samantha, Bernstein and Pringsheim inched forward.

Chapter Thirty-Six

Falconi began, *"Signore e signori,* ladies and gentlemen, please bear with me for a few moments," He opened an English Bible, turned to his European colleagues, and slowly began to read from the Book of Zechariah.

"'And it shall come to pass, that everyone that is left of all the nations that came against Jerusalem shall go up from year to year to worship the King, the Lord of Hosts, and to keep the Feast of Sukkot.'" Falconi looked up from his Bible to make eye contact with his listeners. "If this is so," Falconi continued, "then we must *all* come to Jerusalem next year to observe the Feast of Sukkot, the Feast of Tabernacles. I myself plan to come. Let all those who hear my voice, both here in this room and everywhere around the world, join me in Jerusalem, the City of Truth, and celebrate the Feast of Sukkot as the prophet has said!"

The *Segan,* Meir Hakohen, and Elimelech Eizenman stared at each other. *That* was not on the program!

In a secluded room on the Temple Mount, Harav Eliyahu Kagan and the King of Israel, *Melech Hamashi'ach,* were watching Falconi's speech on a large wall screen.

"*Hod Malchutechah*, Your Majesty, he has invited the entire world to Jerusalem!"

"And so he should, *ishi Kohen Gadol*. Professor Falconi has been chosen to do just that. He is helping to fulfill the prophecies of our *nevi'im*. He is causing the nations to flow to Jerusalem! Yermiyahu said, 'At that time, they shall call Jerusalem *kisei Hashem*, the throne of the Lord; and all the nations shall be gathered to it...'"

Smiling, Harav Eliyahu Kagan, the *Kohen Gadol*, nodded his head in assent.

After the conference, Falconi and his colleagues returned to Europe.

A week later, the *Segan*, Meir Hakohen, Eizenman, Bernstein, Samantha, and Pringsheim met in the *Segan*'s office to discuss ideas for future conferences.

Looking at the three journalists, Eizenman commented, "Hundreds of millions of people all over the world listened to your broadcasts from the Mikdash Conference Center. We are gratified that our message is getting out."

The *Mikdash* public relations chief paused for a moment, his eyes twinkling.

"Incidentally, I called your boss in New York and told him that you did a superb job and that we were pleased with your work." The three journalists glowed with pride. Accolades of this sort are rare in the media world.

The *Segan* commented that the conference spurred some of the attendees to suggest topics for future consideration. Glancing at his notes he reported, "During the conference, the Governor of the Bank of England asked me if we could organize a conference devoted to banking law. I told him that we would consider it very seriously. The halachah has a great deal to say

299

about finances. It's a very important subject. Some of the top bankers in America, Asia, and Europe have already expressed interest."

Meir Hakohen read an email from the rector of the Faculty de Medicine de l'Université Paris-Sud, "My colleagues and I wondered if it would be possible to have a conference in Jerusalem devoted to bioethics. Since we do a great deal of medical research, we would be interested to know what the sages of Israel have to say about the ethical and moral implications of the new biological discoveries and biomedical advances."

"Can you do it?" Samantha asked.

"I think we can," answered the *Segan*. "Many members of the Sanhedrin and our other top scholars have extensive medical backgrounds."

"It would be a wonderful idea," Samantha said enthusiastically.

"For a number of years, Harav Menachem, the *Chacham Muflag* of the Sanhedrin, has conducted seminars for Israeli physicians and medical students on the Torah's view on bioethics. Students and doctors from some of the top medical schools and hospitals in America have participated."

"I attended some of Harav Menachem's seminars last year," Meir Hakohen interjected, "I remember one in particular. He discussed the halachic ramifications that can arise when serious complications or adverse effects stem from incorrect medical treatment or advice."

"You mean iatrogenesis?" Samantha asked.

"Uh ... yes. How did you know that?" Meir Hakohen asked incredulously.

"Aside from his private practice, my father also led seminars in bioethics at Berkeley."

"I see," Meir said.

The *Segan* cleared his throat to get the meeting back on track.

"Some of my old friends wanted to know about halachah and political theory," said Pringsheim.

The *Segan* nodded. "*Adon* Pringsheim, not surprisingly, that's precisely the field that interests Professor Falconi. We've already decided that halachah and political theory will be the theme of the next conference."

The *Segan* confirmed that similar conferences were planned for groups from the United States, Russia, Canada, Turkey, India, China, the Asian rim, and Latin America. Americans from academia, the arts, government officials and religious leaders were already registering for the forthcoming *Mikdash* conference. While the conference which had just concluded had been run in a more or less *ad hoc* manner, in the future a new office directly responsible to Meir Hakohen would coordinate these events.

"Apparently when the attendees returned home, they gave good reports to their colleagues," the *Segan* chuckled. "It will be necessary to enlarge the Conference Center considerably. I suspect that within two or three years, we'll be running three or four such conferences for world leaders simultaneously. We will have to significantly expand our facilities and augment our roster of lecturers."

"From what I saw of this conference and the reactions of the participants, I'm not surprised in the least," Samantha said.

"You might be interested to know that PrinceGlobal Media will be sponsoring the next conference."

The three journalists stared at each other in disbelief. Despite their boss's recent changes, they still found this hard to believe.

The *Segan* adjourned the meeting.

As everyone got up, Bernstein leaned over to the *Segan* and asked in a low voice. "Is it possible for Samantha and me to have a word with you please?"

The *Segan* nodded his assent. Samantha looked puzzled.

The door closed. Only the *Segan*, Bernstein, and Samantha remained in the office.

"What can I do for you?" the *Segan* opened, as they resumed their seats. Altogether pleased with the way the meeting went, he had a benevolent look in his eyes.

"Your Eminence, you know my work takes me all over the world," Bernstein began.

"I'm sure it does. Not like a harried Temple official!" the *Segan* laughed.

Bernstein continued. "One of the places I've visited in my travels is a village in northern Portugal called Vinhateiro."

Looking up, Samantha sat straighter in her chair. The *Segan*'s face suddenly became serious, and his demeanor became distant and formal.

"Vinhateiro? Why are you telling me this?" asked the *Segan* curtly.

"I know the history of the *anousim* there," Bernstein said.

The *Segan* sat impassively behind his desk with a stern look on his face, waiting for Bernstein to continue.

"Your Eminence, today the history of the *anousim* of Vinhateiro is public knowledge, and as you know, there is even a synagogue there. Only after my visit did I find out about the Vinhateiro archives. I know that the archives are kept in

302

vellum-bound volumes in an underground vault. I also know that while the originals are still in Vinhateiro, there are digital copies of them in the Temple archives."

Samantha was taken aback, even angry. Bernstein had not told her he planned to do this. But then she remembered what she had promised herself when Falconi challenged her to pursue her destiny. She would fly back to Los Angeles and confront her mother about her past, and once and for all solve the mystery of Vinhateiro. She would find out who and what she really was.

Her eyes were on the *Segan,* her mind in turmoil.

"Who told you about the Vinhateiro archives?" the *Segan* asked slowly.

"I found out purely by accident. But I assure you that no matter what your answer might be to our request, the knowledge of their very existence will go no further. We have not told a soul about them, nor will we, unless you authorize us to do so. We understand their great importance and the need for discretion."

The *Segan* relaxed and sighed with relief. "I'm very glad to hear that. As we speak, there are some very delicate negotiations going on. We want to bring them here where they belong. They have fulfilled their purpose in Vinhateiro. Now they must become part of the history of not only the *anousim* but of all *Am Yisrael.* They can only do that if they are here in Jerusalem."

"Understood!"

"Good. I have no doubt that at a later date, we will ask you to write about them, but not yet. Now, *Adon* Bernstein and *Geveret* Samantha, what exactly is your interest in the Vinhateiro archives?" the *Segan* asked.

Bernstein's eyes focused on Samantha, "We have reason to believe that Samantha is descended from the *anousim* of Vinhateiro. Though her mother has refused to discuss her background with her, Samantha has seen documents that verify that both her mother and her maternal grandmother were born in Vinhateiro."

"*Geveret* Samantha," the *Segan* said slowly, "you are rather quiet. *Adon* Bernstein has been doing all the talking. Are these documents in your possession?"

"Not right now but I can get them, Your Eminence."

"Where are they?"

"My mother has them."

"And where does your mother live?"

"In Los Angeles."

"*Geveret* Samantha, most of the people who live in Vinhateiro are ordinary Portuguese Catholics, not *anousim*. What makes you think that you are of the *anousim*? Were there any unusual and perhaps inexplicable customs observed in your mother's house?"

"Well ..." Samantha began hesitantly.

"Go on, Samantha," Bernstein said, "tell *Segan* Abulafia what you told me."

She began by telling the *Segan* that no matter how much her mother said that she wanted to forget her background, she had performed strange rituals that Samantha had always thought were somehow connected to her upbringing in Portugal. She gave examples.

"At home, the housekeeper was never permitted to vacuum the house from the inside toward the front door. She always had to go from the outside to the inside. I was never allowed to look at churches. While baking my mother would

304

throw some pieces of dough back into the oven, and she'd crack eggs into a glass and hold the glass up to the light to look for blood spots. If she found any, she would discard the egg."

Bernstein said, "Your Eminence, Samantha's surname is Saraiva."

The *Segan* thought for a moment. "It's true; Saraiva *is* a very old and honorable name among the *anousim*."

"Yes, *Adon* Bernstein told me that," said Samantha.

"Please continue, *Geveret* Saraiva" the *Segan* said in a gentle voice.

"One Friday night, I found my mother in the basement, lighting candles and singing over them. Also we never had pork in the house because it wasn't 'healthy.'"

And this was a woman who said that she wanted to forget about Vinhateiro!

The *Segan* nodded his head. "*Geveret* Saraiva, if all this is true, you may indeed be of the *anousim*. The next time you visit your mother, please make copies of any relevant documents and get them notarized by the local Rabbinical Court, the local *Beit Din*. I will give you the name of a rabbi to contact in Los Angeles. Get any other information that you think relevant, and be as accurate and detailed as possible. Finally, and this is very important, write an exact account of all the customs you witnessed in your mother's house, and anything else your mother can tell you."

"I hope to fly to California within the next few days."

"*Geveret* Saraiva, it *is* possible that your mother's family is indeed recorded in the archives. If you find out her original Portuguese name and that of your grandparents and great-grandparents, plus a few relevant dates, we can do a search.

305

The information should not be hard to find. The archives are now digitized and easy to access."

Getting up, the *Segan* said, "When you return to Israel with the necessary information, please call my office and we'll see what we can do for you."

Samantha was shaking with excitement.

"Your Eminence, I want to be part of the Jewish people. I mean *really* part of the Jewish people, and I want to do it right." Her voice was dulcet, her cheeks were flushed, and her eyes twinkled as she smiled.

Bernstein looked at her again. This was a new Samantha!

The *Segan* smiled. "I'm not surprised. Many *anousim* are rejoining *Am Yisrael* today. But nevertheless, you – as all *anousim* must – will have to appear before the *Beit Din* and convince them of the authenticity of your documentation."

"Even if our names are recorded in the Vinhateiro archives?"

"Even then. But if they are recorded in the archives, it will make things much easier. Since the restoration of the Temple, we no longer accept converts, but *anousim* are not considered converts."

"But Your Eminence, if my mother's family is recorded in the archives, I wouldn't have had to convert anyway. I would be Jewish, wouldn't I?"

"*Geveret* Saraiva, it's not quite so simple. What we call 'personal status' is under the jurisdiction of the *Batei Din*, the Rabbinical Courts. But if the history of your mother's family is recorded in the Vinhateiro archives, the judges will take that into consideration. However, the final authority in these matters rests with the *Batei Din*, not with me."

"I understand, Your Eminence."

"However," the *Segan* added, "if you are found to be of the *anousim*, a lifetime of obligation and responsibility lies before you. Being part of *Am Yisrael* is far more than just having your family's history recorded in ancient archives, as important as that might be. *Am Yisrael* is a living people and it lives only by virtue of our connection to the Torah. You are going to have to do some serious thinking about your own future. The prophet Amos tells us; 'You – *Am Yisrael* – only have I known of all the families of the earth. Therefore I will visit upon you all your iniquities.' That's what the *Beit Din* is going to tell you, that you will be responsible for any transgressions of Jewish law. This is no small thing. Have you thought about it – and all the implications of formally rejoining the Jewish people?"

Have I thought about it? All the years of my life, maybe even from before I was born, this has been part of me; for six hundred years, I have been waiting only for this, to close the circle and rejoin my people and re-connect with my God.

She recalled the soul connection she felt to the dancers on Ben Yehudah. With a shiver, she remembered that she never felt a connection to anybody *anywhere*.

Even before Dave told me who and what I was, in my heart I already knew.

As Samantha began to speak, Bernstein's attention riveted on her. Sam was usually so detached; but she was not detached now. She was radiant.

Chapter Thirty-Seven

She began, "Your Eminence, I've thought of almost nothing else since *Adon* Bernstein first told me about the *anousim* of Vinhateiro and their history. I just *know* we're listed in those archives! I've done quite a bit of reading and I *do* feel that I am connected to the Jewish people. I realize that I have a long path ahead of me. But I am committed to taking that path. And I realize that there's a package deal in joining the Jewish people. I will have responsibilities as well as privileges. However, I am willing to be held accountable for my actions. I've already started learning Hebrew. And a rabbi I spoke with promised to give me an additional reading list, but I do have some questions," Samantha said anxiously. "May I take a few more minutes of your time please?"

"Of course. If I can help you, I'll be happy to do so."

Samantha's shoulders relaxed a bit. She took a breath. "I am beginning to see God's direction in my own life but I really don't know who or what He is. Where are such things explained?"

"Though some of our sages have written about this, unlike many other religions, we typically do not dwell on 'analyzing the nature of God.' That is a subject well beyond our comprehension. Our primary concern is what He – as our King – expects from us. Our focus is to lovingly observe His c ommandments, and live a good and righteous life, as He wants us to live. In doing so we are able to become ever closer to Him."

"Then how do I know what good and evil are?"

"The definition of good and evil is defined in our Torah, both oral and written. The Torah is all-inclusive and contains the answers to our philosophical, religious and ideological questions. But, it takes far more than a lifetime to learn it, it is so deep. Nevertheless, that does not excuse us from trying as best as we can to study the Torah on our own level. The great sage Hillel said, 'It is not upon you to finish the work, but neither are you free to desist from it.' We connect to God by enveloping ourselves with His wisdom."

"So what is different now that the Temple has been rebuilt?"

"Our Prophets told us that society would come to a particular point when it would enter a new phase of development and awareness. In fact, now that the Third Temple is standing and the *avodah* is being performed, the focus of humanity *already* is changing. Mikdash Broadcasts together with PrinceGlobal Media and other companies are spreading our message to every part of the world. Every day many hundreds of millions of people tune in everywhere. And most important, they are listening to what we say and are beginning to take it to heart."

"That's for sure!" Bernstein interjected.

"Our constantly expanding websites can barely handle the torrent of visitors. There already has been a radical, fundamental – I would say even metaphysical – transformation of all human activity and inter-relationships. People are striving to lead moral and meaningful lives in a way they never did before. The anarchist revolution – as violent and yes, as bloody as it was – was the last necessary catharsis to bring that about. It was necessary to clear the air, and it was a learning experience for the entire world. People saw what it was like for society to totter at the edge of the abyss. Having seen that, people are more willing to work together. The spirit of increasing universal cooperation on every level is becoming more evident every day."

"Why is that?"

"Because the tension between people primarily derived from struggles for power and material things. But, now that the Temple – and this is critical, not the physical building and not even the *avodah*, but what they *stand* for – is becoming the world's focus."

"What about the Messiah? We think he's already here though he has not revealed himself publicly. What is his role in all this?" Samantha queried.

"A great deal. But first I must emphasize that the Messiah – *Mashi'ach* – is a human being, not a divine or semi-divine figure. He is appointed and anointed by God to be the King of Israel and the entire world. He will unite the peoples of the world under God's rule."

"So, the Messiah is basically God's man on the job? I mean, he is God's agent, no? What is so special about this man?" Samantha gave a small smile, "Or might the Messiah be a woman?"

"*Mashi'ach* is a man; don't get confused," the *Segan* answered with a chuckle. "God has assigned different roles for men and for women. Our *mekorot* speak of 'ben David,' the son of David not 'bat David,' the daughter of David. *Mashi'ach* will be the facilitator of God's ultimate plan for human society. He is a great Torah scholar, and will teach, lead, and rule. He will be the charismatic human King of Israel and teacher of all mankind. But do not picture him as simply some sort of dictator shoving morality down our throats. On the contrary, the nations of the world will willingly accept his authority. An incorruptible judge, he will be recognized by the nations of the world as the leader of humanity by his sheer moral power."

Samantha leaned forward in her chair.

"In the messianic era there will be world peace. There will be an end to civil unrest, crime, substance abuse, disease, and famine. Most important, the hearts of men and women everywhere will change. In fact, as you see, it is already happening. The coming of *Mashi'ach* will substantially advance God's purpose in creation: for humankind to make an abode for Him in the lower worlds. He will reveal the inherent spirituality in our material universe."

Samantha looked deep in thought, as she considered the *Segan's* words. The wheels in Bernstein's head were turning as well, and he asked a question that had coalesced in his mind during the *Segan's* explanation of the Messiah's role, "Your Eminence, will we go back to absolute monarchies?"

"Will there be no more democracy?" Samantha asked.

"You are both investigative journalists with worldwide reputations. You are not naïve. You, more than most of the so called experts, understand how modern societies function, especially modern political societies. You are able to peer beneath the surface and see what's lurking below. Can you really say that there is democracy in our world today? Are there not powerful, absolutist trends in government structures

311

in *all* the so called democratic countries that strive toward uniformity and ultimate absolute control of the lives of the average citizen? Is not the real power in so called democratic countries embodied in complex, computerized, faceless, ideologically-driven, byzantine self-serving bureaucracies where no one takes responsibility, and the average man or woman is less than dust?"

"It's true," Samantha sighed.

"*Geveret* Saraiva, people everywhere seek justice; all they receive is the right to vote for corrupt politicians every few years. It is not the same thing. And realizing the futility of it all, fewer and fewer people bother. There is a great dichotomy between the shining image of what we call 'democracy' and its realistic practicality in the real world in which we live. Everything Professor Falconi said was true. He just went about it in the wrong way. Revolutions inevitably create more problems than they solve."

"But at least in the democratic system, the average citizen, man or woman, can aspire to political office and try to affect change," Samantha countered.

"*Geveret* Saraiva, are you sure of that? With the rarest of exceptions, candidates for high political office everywhere are multi-millionaires or are totally beholden to the special interests who own them. Totally enamored by the trappings of wealth, these people are hardly average. For the most part they emerge from a paper-thin, self-selected, worldwide ruling class and they have their own agendas. Despite what they may say, they have absolutely no interest in the welfare of the common people or in improving their lot in any way. It rarely makes the slightest difference to the struggling average man or woman which party or which politician hold the reins of power.

312

Internationally well connected, they have a mutually beneficial relationship with the leading lights of academia, trendy intellectuals, bogus religious leaders, oligarchs, the top bankers, so called labor leaders, high profile entertainers, and the media elite. Despite appearances to the contrary, they all run interference for each other. Genuine dissident is easily identified and neutralized."

"Do you really think they are all part of a worldwide ruling class?"

"Yes, I do. For the most part these people come from the same background. They graduate from the same kind of universities, and increasingly even marry among themselves. This emerging elite in all its manifestations has succeeded in becoming a true hereditary ruling class in the feudal sense of the word. In this new international aristocracy – and make no mistake, that is exactly what it became – national origins and even race play little part. Nor do morality or ethics for that matter. The occasional bright young man or woman with a lower class background worthy of notice is easily co-opted into the ruling class and rapidly forgets his or her origins."

"What about Professor Falconi? Where did he fit in?"

"Professor Falconi was one of the very rare exceptions. He had a vision. Fired by a molten passion, he could not be bought nor could he be co-opted. His heart remained pure. Despite his violent rhetoric, he radiated integrity and compassion. People everywhere instinctively understood this and were drawn to him. For this reason he was chosen to play such a pivotal role."

Samantha asked quietly, "But how will the Messiah establish his kingdom on earth? Will he use force?"

"*Geveret* Saraiva, he will not have to. Very few people are content with the present 'democratic' political system. Though most people were lulled to sleep by the all-pervasive totalitarian ideologically-driven mass media - drugged if you will - they instinctively understood that the hypocritical power-hungry politicians who presume to represent them, and the venal police and egotistical judges who ostensibly protect them from injustice, have nothing but contempt for them. There was a universal feeling of frustration, hopelessness, and anger. Why do you think Falconi was so successful?"

"He succeeded because his message resonated in the hearts of men and women all over the world," Samantha whispered.

"Exactly right. People want truth. They yearn for it. But they couldn't find it. Their leaders, aside from a very few honorable exceptions, were simply master manipulators. Protected by the media, they specialized in deception and falsehood. A self-perpetuating elite, unlike ordinary citizens, they were invariably shielded from the consequences of failure. Men and women everywhere finally came to understand that and were tired of being constantly lied to. They felt that they had no recourse."

"I saw that."

"Compare this with what our prophets tell us about *Mashi'ach*, a leader of spiritual stature that the world has never seen." The *Segan* laughed, "When he reveals himself, the world will be literally engulfed by a spiritual tsunami! People will instinctively turn to *Mashi'ach* and hear his voice. His unique personality, wisdom, and charismatic leadership – with God's help – will be so great that mankind will be inspired to change direction. And no one will have to force them; they will do it on their own volition. Look around you," the *Segan* smiled, "the process has already started!"

314

"But what will be the role of the Jewish people in all this?"

"The Jewish people will continue fulfilling the task that we have been given since the days of Abraham, to be the teachers and guides of humanity."

Samantha noticed that *Segan* surreptitiously glanced at his watch and she shot Bernstein a glance. Bernstein nodded, and with broad smiles on their faces, they got up.

"Thank you so much, Your Eminence, for answering our questions and spending so much time with us."

"It has been my pleasure. *Geveret* Saraiva," the *Segan* said with a slight nod. "When you return from California, please call my office and make an appointment to see me. There are some people I'd like you to meet. They will examine the documents you bring back and they will do a search of our copy of the Vinhateiro archives. They will also help you organize things in your own mind and answer any questions you may have before you appear before the rabbis of the *Beit Din*. But remember, their decision is final."

He walked towards his office door, and held it open.

"Thank you again, Your Eminence. I look forward to meeting them when I return," Samantha smiled as she glided euphorically out the door. Bernstein followed her, shaking his head in wonder. He had been doing some serious thinking himself, but he had no idea that Samantha had been thinking so much too, and was so strongly affected.

This was definitely a new Samantha. He looked at her again; his face lit up.

Chapter Thirty-Eight

Now that the Falconi conference was over, Meir Hakohen hoped to catch up on his routine day-to-day work. He had spent so much time preparing the *Mikdash* for the *chagim* and organizing the Falconi conference that he had fallen far behind. Today he wanted to review requests submitted by various *Mikdash* committees and officials for his approval, and pass his recommendations on to the *Segan*. Meir turned on his computer and clicked his way to the folder labeled "Requests."

One committee recommended the building of three new *mikva'ot* for the *Kohanim* who served in the *Mikdash*. There were a number of *mikva'ot* located beneath the *Beit Hamokeid*, the large domed building north of the *Azarah* which lodged the *Kohanim* on duty. The *Kohanim* who served on the early shift in the *Mikdash* slept in the *Beit Hamokeid* the night before. In the morning they immersed in these *mikva'ot* before donning their priestly garments. Meir noted that the request for the additional *mikva'ot* was certainly reasonable; there had been crowding recently as the number of *Kohanim* serving in the *Mikdash* increased. This was a cut-and-dried case: approved!

Next Meir reviewed a request from Harav Naphtali for a new oven to bake the *lechem ha'panim*. The *lechem ha'panim* were the twelve loaves of unleavened bread baked weekly by the *Kohanim* of Beit Garmu, and then carefully arranged on an especially dedicated golden table in the *Heichal*. Harav Naphtali, the sometimes cantankerous patriarch and Master Baker of Beit Garmu, submitted the request over a month ago and was getting impatient. He adamantly insisted that they needed a new oven, although he couldn't say exactly why. Shaking his head, Meir searched for "Beit Garmu" in his computer and found what he was looking for. Only three months before, Yannai, the *Mikdash* Chief Engineer had inspected Beit Garmu's oven at their request, and given it a perfect bill of health. However, as Meir well knew, the oven used by Rav Naphtali and his bakers for the *lechem ha'panim* was not an ordinary oven, just as the *lechem ha'panim* they baked was not just ordinary bread. Carefully prepared according to ancient specifications handed down in their family for countless generations, the *lechem ha'panim*, which never grew stale even after being exposed to the open air in the *Heichal* for a week, was one of the permanent miracles that took place in the *Mikdash*.

Meir thought for a minute. This could be delicate. Shaking his head, Meir added Harav Naphtali's request to the list of things he would have to go over later in greater detail. First he would review the Chief Engineer's evaluation of the oven.

Meir's train of thought was broken by a knock on the door.

"Come in."

It was the *Segan.*

Meir invited him to sit down and said, "Reb Chanina, I wanted to show you this." The *Segan* removed a box filled with old computer printouts from the chair nearest Meir's work table and made himself comfortable. Meir turned his computer screen toward him, and pointed to the request next to the cursor. "The conductor of the Levitical choir, Rav Reuven ben Tzvi, wants to order forty-two new musical instruments immediately. He insists that he can't manage without them."

"Forty-two instruments at one time?" The *Segan* took a deep breath and coughed. "That's a lot even for him. May I see the list, please?" Moving his chair a little closer, he began to read the tender submitted by *HaGitit of B'nei Braq: Purveyors of Fine Musical Instruments to the Beit Hamikdash*. Included in the list were various types of flutes, harps, lyres, cymbals, and trumpets. As he reviewed the list, the *Segan* chuckled.

"Meir, have you ever visited *HaGitit*'s workshop in B'nei Braq?"

"No, I haven't. Who has time?"

"Well, you should make time. It's a fabulous place. And it's a pleasure to watch them work. They are real perfectionists. Every day, we hear the results."

The quality of *HaGitit*'s work was not the problem. Meir knew that every instrument that they supplied to the *Mikdash* was handmade by the finest craftsmen in the world. Shifting in his chair and tapping his foot, he went over the list again.

The first problem was that Meir had a soft spot for the Levitical choir since the first time he heard them. He just couldn't be objective when it came to that choir; he was so entranced by their music. He looked at the order again, topped by *HaGitit*'s elegant logo, and let his mind run free: *The shirah – the music and song – of the Levites is as important as the service of the Kohanim. The Holy Zohar asks: "Why were the Levites selected to sing in the Beit Hamikdash? They were chosen because the name Levi means 'cleaving.' The soul of him who heard their singing at once cleaved to God."*

318

The Levites sang with such feeling, and played their musical instruments so beautifully, that they reminded Meir of the angelic choir in Heaven. He literally trembled when he heard the Levites sing. They were that good! Meir knew that the *Segan* felt the same way. How could he not?

The second problem was that Choirmaster Reuven ben Tzvi was well on his way to exceeding his budget again.

Sighing, Meir shook his head slowly. Avi Katz, the Chief Financial Officer, was not going to like this.

Giving the *Segan* an appraising look, Meir asked in a sweet voice, "Reb Chanina, do you remember the Gemara in *Tamid*, 'There is no poverty in the place of wealth?' Couldn't that apply in this particular case?"

The *Segan* mulled over Meir's words for a moment and nodded his head. "Reb Meir, it's entirely possible. You know, sometimes genius simply must be coddled."

"Approved," the two conspirators smiled at each other. Grinning, the *Segan* stood up. "Could you come over to my office, Meir?" the *Segan* asked.

The two *Kohanim* strolled down the hall.

Once in the *Segan*'s office, the two *Kohanim* began to review some of the enormous logistical problems that the *Mikdash* would face in another nine months when the Sabbatical Year would draw to a close. They discussed *Hakhel*, when the Messiah, the anointed King of Israel, would read from the Torah to *Am Yisrael* and to the entire world.

When Mikdash Broadcasts and PrinceGlobal Media jointly announced that the Messiah himself would preside over the upcoming *Hakhel* ceremony on the Temple Mount, there was indescribable excitement everywhere. Even though the restoration of the *Beit Hamikdash* pointed to this upcoming

319

reality, people were still in shock. Finally! The Messiah! Just the word alone was enough to send chills up the spines of hundreds of millions of people. Millions of people from all over the world had already declared their intention to come to Jerusalem to witness the event with their own eyes. And *Hakhel* was still nine months away!

Jerusalem was going to be the epicenter of a veritable migration of nations!

Humanly speaking, it would not only be a logistical nightmare, but a sheer impossibility. There was no natural way that Jerusalem could hold so many people. But the *Kohen Gadol* had ordered that no restrictions whatsoever were to be placed on the number of people coming to Jerusalem.

"Let them come!" he said.

And though the *Segan* and Meir Hakohen had absolute faith in the *Kohen Gadol* and kept quoting to each other the *pasuk*, "No man said to his fellow, 'The place is insufficient for me to stay overnight in Jerusalem,'" their stomachs did somersaults every time they thought of it.

Meir, who had had his hands full, preparing the *Mikdash* for Yom Kippur and Sukkot, not to mention Falconi's conference, had not given *Hakhel* much thought.

"Well, Meir, maybe you *should* start thinking about *Hakhel* because you are going to be chairman of the Hakhel Committee," the *Segan* said. "This is the first time that *Am Yisrael* will be fulfilling the mitzvah of *Hakhel* in two thousand years, and masses of people want to be here to take part. And thanks to Professor Falconi and his colleagues, not only *Am Yisrael* is interested. The *Segan*'s voice grew tremendous with enthusiasm as he leaned back in his chair.

320

"We've already been approached by representatives of scores of foreign countries inquiring about their heads of state visiting Jerusalem during Sukkot. We're talking about kings, presidents and prime ministers! All of them will be coming with large entourages. Just the Emperor of Japan wants to bring ten planeloads of VIPs. Meir, that's only the tip of the iceberg. Tens of thousands of ordinary Japanese citizens have already visited our website and registered. And that's only the beginning!"

Meir beat a meditative soft tattoo on the edge of the table as he sat there trying to take all of this in.

"Meir, I think we're going to see the fulfillment of a number of very extraordinary prophecies. Take a look at some of these emails."

The *Segan* turned his monitor towards Meir, and he began to read an email from Aliza from Denver. "...our entire (Jewish) community is scheduled to make aliyah in two years and, *im yirtzeh Hashem*, we will be moving into our new homes in Ramot Gil'ad. But what I really wanted to write you about is *Hakhel*. We thought that the idea of participating in the first *Hakhel* in 2000 years, and joining with *Am Yisrael* in watching *Melech Hamashi'ach* fulfill this wonderful mitzvah, was so exciting that my husband and I ran to our respective bosses and asked them for three weeks leave during the *chagim* – the time frame that will include Yom Kippur, Sukkot and, of course, *Hakhel*.

"My boss (not Jewish) asked me why I was asking for time off so far in advance. I told him that we wanted to go up to Jerusalem for Sukkot and sacrifice in the Temple. I also told him about *Hakhel* and what seeing the Messianic King meant to us. He looked at me closely said, 'I would very much like to join

321

you if I may and I'll bet there would be quite a few here in the office who would want to come as well.' He was right! Quite a few of my co-workers, and they're not even Jewish, *did* want to come with us! Who would have believed it? It seems like going up to Jerusalem is the only topic of conversation in our office these days. I couldn't help but think of Zechariah 8:23, 'In those days it shall come to pass, that ten men shall take hold of the skirt of him that is a Jew, saying; 'We will go with you for we have heard that God is with you.' Zechariah's prophecy is really happening!"

The *Segan* broke in, "Meir, airline reservations are already almost impossible to come by. We have to inform the airlines that they will have to arrange many more flights. And you know what? We're going to have to expand the capacity of the Timna/Eilat Airport radically."

Meir nodded.

"We're going have to explore the possibility of laying down temporary runways. I suspect that in the end we're going to have to divert quite a few flights there. We can't put this off. Our existing airports are simply incapable of handling such a massive influx of people."

"I agree," Meir said, as he jotted down a few notes.

"We're also going to have to radically increase the number of trains on the Eilat/Jerusalem line to transport the *olei regel* deplaning at Timna to Jerusalem. In fact, we may have to consider laying down new tracks altogether. The infrastructure in the south is simply not adequate. And we're going to need more rolling stock! Before we go any further on this subject, let's schedule a meeting with Chief Engineer Yannai, and get his input before we contact the Minister of Transport. After all, Yannai and his staff will have to do the preliminary research and write up the proposals. And it will have to be done double time. Meir, this will have to be a national priority. We don't have a day to lose!"

After a quick exchange of emails it was decided that the meeting would take place later that afternoon.

That done, Meir pulled up another email, from Susan of Englewood, New Jersey. "I wanted to share with you an incident that happened to me yesterday. I work out at a gym near me and one of the regulars, not Jewish, came over to me and said, 'It must be a wonderful thing to belong to God's people.'

"Before I could even answer, she asked me if we had gone on pilgrimage to Jerusalem this year for the Feast of Tabernacles. I told her that unfortunately we were unable to go this year, but we've already signed up for next year. 'So you'll be there for *Hakhel*,' she said. I was surprised (though I shouldn't have been), that she knew exactly what *Hakhel* was! Like many of her friends, every day she downloads lectures on ethics, morality, and the Seven Noahide Laws from the Mikdash Committee for Universal Education program. Then she told me that her family, her two brothers, and their families were all moved by the spirit. Like Professor Falconi, they want to fulfill the words of Zechariah, the prophet who called on all the peoples of the world to worship God in Jerusalem during the Feast of Tabernacles.

"P.S. I wanted to add that all our children are married and live in Israel. God willing, we will be joining them in a year and a half. We count the days!"

"Meir, we are getting thousands of emails like this from all over the world, not to mention all the comments in Facebook," said the *Segan*. "And because of the increasing publicity, we are getting thousands more every day. In fact, we're bringing in

323

dozens of additional Levites to help cope with the flood of emails. *Hakhel* will be the greatest media event in history. George Prince of PrinceGlobal Media - he calls himself Griesha Shmu'el Pressman now - is making sure of that."

"Griesha Shmu'el Pressman?"

"That's right. George Prince changed his name back to Griesha Shmu'el Pressman, his given name."

"When did this happen?"

"Right before the *chagim*. Meir, I can't believe that you didn't see the publicity. It was everywhere! That, and the new policies of PrinceGlobal Media have sparked a revolution in the media world. Even the Internet and the social networks have undergone a profound change for the better."

"I was so busy preparing the *Mikdash* for the *chagim*. And then there was the Falconi conference. And aside from being interviewed by Pringsheim on *Shidurei Hamikdash*, I wasn't involved with the media at all. Besides, who had time to keep up with the news?"

"Meir," the *Segan* sighed, "I know you're devoted to the *Mikdash*, but sometimes you have to come up for air. There were interviews all over the place and tremendous publicity. I can't imagine how even *you* missed it. It was a great *kiddush Hashem*, a sanctification of the name of God. Do you know who Griesha Pressman's father was?"

"How would I know?"

"George Prince, or rather Griesha Pressman's, father was Harav Yehudah Pressman, *alav ha'shalom*."

"George Prince's father was Rav Pressman? *Ha'avodah*! He wrote amazing *sefarim*. I've seen them in the *Mikdash* library and on our websites. I can't believe it!"

"Hard to believe, but true nevertheless. Griesha Pressman is now a *chozer be'teshuvah* in the fullest sense of the word. He has become a major supporter of the *Mikdash* and Torah institutions everywhere. He's helping to sponsor the international conferences that we'll be holding. And he supports countless charities in virtually every country on earth. You know Meir, he was quite an *ilui* before he went off the rails.

"Anyway, all PrinceGlobal Media affiliates will be carrying *Hakhel*. But that's not all. By the time Pressman is through, media outlets everywhere will be carrying *Hakhel*, including the European, Russian, Chinese, Indian and even the African networks. Nine months to prepare for such a big project is not a lot of time. But Meir, rest assured that all of our resources will be at your disposal, and we will be hiring more staff so that you can delegate more of the work."

Meir took a deep breath.

Chapter Thirty-Nine

Nine months had passed since that meeting.

It was the day before Yom Kippur. The Sabbatical Year was drawing to a close and all the technical preparations for *Hakhel* were complete. Even the components of the large wooden platforms required for the ceremony were ready and waiting in a storeroom adjacent to *Har Habayit*. Yehoshua, the *av bayit*, noted with satisfaction that it took his Levites forty-three minutes to transport and assemble all the components.

During the early afternoon, two young *Kohanim* climbed an enormously tall specially constructed ladder and hung a large red strip of wool over the entrance to the *Bayit*.

Night had come, and the normally bustling city of Jerusalem was eerily quiet; it was *erev* Yom Kippur, the eve of the holiest day of the year.

The *Beit Hamikdash*, glowing gold and white under the silver moon, was deserted except for *Kohanim* standing guard and Levites on their nightly rounds. But high above the *Sha'ar Hamayim*, the Water Gate in the southern wall of the *Azarah*, two sages sat with their heads together. In the illuminated studio-workshop of the master spice apothecaries of Beit Avtinas, Harav Eliyahu Kagan reviewed the technicalities of the incense offering with his old *chavruta* and friend, Harav Azariah, the Master Perfumer. Finishing their consultations, they descended to the *Lishkat Hagazit* where the *Kohen Gadol*

326

lectured through the night on various aspects of the *avodah* of Yom Kippur to a select group of *Kohanim* and scholars. Tomorrow, Harav Eliyahu Kagan, the High Priest of Israel, would enter the *Kodesh Hakodashim* to offer incense before *Hakadosh Baruch Hu.*

By 4:00 a.m. Yom Kippur morning, the *Azarah* was packed. Dave Bernstein, Nimrod Pringsheim and Griesha Pressman stood excitedly in the crowd. It was their first Yom Kippur in the *Beit Hamikdash.*

By 4:30, Rav Kagan already immersed for the first time in the *mikvah*, arrayed himself in the eight golden high priestly garments, and slaughtered the *Tamid shel Boker,* the obligatory morning sacrifice. The *Segan,* Meir Hakohen, and Chief *Shochet* Binyamin did not leave his side. When the *Kohen Gadol* began slaughtering the lamb, Binyamin effortlessly grasped the knife in the middle and finished the cut. The *Kohen Gadol* caught the lamb's blood in a gold round-bottomed *Mikdash* vessel. He approached the altar, and splashed blood on the northeast and southwest corners. He entered the Sanctuary and offered the daily offered incense expiation and cleaned and re-lit the lamps of the Menorah. Exiting the *Bayit*, he completed the *Tamid shel Boker* sacrifice together with its accompanying meal offerings and wine libation. Then he offered the additional sacrifices, one bullock and seven lambs.

When the *Kohen Gadol* sacrificed the *Mussafin*, the additional holiday offerings, Rav Reuven ben Tzvi and his Levites outdid themselves with the magnificence of their *shirah.*

By 8:40, the *Kohen Gadol* immersed a second time, changed into white garments, and confessed his sins and those of his wife over a bullock that he himself had purchased. As he placed his hands on its head, he said:

> O God, forgive the iniquities, transgressions, and sins which I have committed and transgressed and sinned before Thee, I and my house, as it is written in the law of Thy servant Moses, "For on this day shall atonement be made for you to purify you: from all your sins shall ye be clean before the Lord."

When the *Kohanim* and the people heard the *Shem Hameforash*, the Ineffable Four-Lettered Name of God, from the lips of the *Kohen Gadol*, the myriads standing in the *Azarah* knelt, and falling on their faces they cried out, "Blessed be the name of the glory of His kingdom forever and ever."

The *Kohen Gadol* raised his hands in blessing and answered, "May you be purified!"

He walked quickly to the eastern gate of the *Azarah* where identical he-goats were positioned near a small table upon which a gold urn containing two gold lots had been placed. One lot was inscribed "*Lashem*," to God, and the other was written "*La'azazel*," to *Azazel*. The goat chosen by lot for God would be sacrificed on the altar. The he-goat chosen for *Azazel* – the *sa'ir hamishtalei'ach*, known as the "scapegoat" – would be led to the wilderness and hurled over a cliff, effecting atonement for the sins of the Jewish people. Contemplating the massive gold facade of the *Bayit* for a moment, he stood behind the goats. Every eye in the *Azarah* focused on him.

The *Kohen Gadol* slipped his hands into the urn and drew out the two golden lots simultaneously. As he felt them in his hands, he recalled the Gemara, "Throughout the forty years that Shim'on HaTzadik ministered [as *Kohen Gadol*], the lot

Lashem always came up in the right hand." He offered a silent prayer and took a deep breath. Slowly, he opened his hands and looked down. The lot *Lashem* was in his right hand! A true sign of Divine grace! Grasping the *Lashem* lot tightly, he handed it to Meir HaKohen who raised it for all to see. A spirit of rejoicing and exaltation swept through the vast crowd.

Energized, he joyously approached the two goats and bound one ribbon of crimson wool on the goat that was to be sent to *Azazel,* and another around the neck of the goat dedicated to *Hashem.* He then turned to his bullock, which he would offer as a sacrifice for himself, his family, and all *Kohanim.* He placed his hands on its head, and pressed down.

> O God, forgive the iniquities, transgressions and sins which I have committed and transgressed and sinned before Thee... as it is written in the law of Thy servant Moses, "For on this day shall atonement be made for you to purify you: from all your sins shall ye be clean before the Lord."

And as before, when the people heard the *Kohen Gadol* utter the *Shem Hameforash*, they fell down on their faces, prostrated themselves, and cried out, "Blessed be the name of the glory of His kingdom forever and ever." The *Kohen Gadol* raised his hands in benediction and answered, "May you be purified!"

With the assistance of Binyamin the Master *Shochet*, the *Kohen Gadol* slaughtered his bullock. As Binyamin finished the cut, the *Kohen Gadol* received the blood in the Temple vessel and handed it to Meir Hakohen. Meir stirred the blood so it would not coagulate and become unfit.

Rav Kagan ascended the ramp of the sacrificial altar and filled a long-handled gold fire pan with glowing coals. Descending the ramp and laying down the fire pan, he cupped both of his hands together, filled them with *ketoret*, and poured the contents into a large gold incense ladle. He then took the fire pan in one hand, and the incense ladle in the other.

It was with great trepidation that the *Kohen Gadol* entered the *Bayit* and then disappeared behind the curtain that divided the *Heichal* from that sacred chamber, from which even the angels are barred, the *Kodesh Hakodashim*. [In the days of the Second Temple, two curtains separated the *Heichal* from the *Kodesh Hakodashim* because there was a question whether the space in between the curtains was part of the *Heichal* or the *Kodesh Hakodashim*. In the Third Temple, such uncertainties will be clarified and therefore, there will be no need for two curtains.]

The *Kohen Gadol* placed the fire pan before the *aron habrit* and poured the incense in the ladle on to the glowing coals causing redolent columns of billowing smoke to rise from the sizzling coals. As he perceived the awesome holiness of *Hakadosh Baruch Hu*, he saw the exalted letters of the *Shem Hameforash* wafting upwards in the midst of a great light to Heaven. There they succeeded in binding the upper and lower worlds together in a perfect unity.

Arrayed in pure white, the *Kohen Gadol* bowed his head before the *aron habrit*, the Ark of the Covenant, and worshipped.

Exiting the *Bayit*, he left the smoking fire pan in the *Kodesh Hakodashim*, and retrieving the vessel containing the blood of his bullock from Meir Hakohen, he returned to the *Kodesh Hakodashim*.

Standing in front of the *aron habrit*, he sprinkled the blood of his bullock once upward and seven times downward. When he finished, he left the *Kodesh Hakodashim* and placed the vessel with the remaining blood on a stand before the curtain. Then he slaughtered the goat dedicated to *Hashem*. Reentering the *Kodesh Hakodashim* for the third time, he sprinkled the goat's blood, one time upward and seven times downward in front of the *aron habrit* and then placed the vessel with the remaining blood on a second stand before the curtain. Once again he sprinkled the bullock's blood once upward and seven times downward before.

The *Kohen Gadol* spilled the blood of the bullock into the vessel containing the blood of the he-goat and then poured the contents of the full vessel into the empty one, thereby mixing the blood of the two sacrificial animals.

He walked to the golden incense altar, and gently placed drops of the mixed blood on the horns of the altar. He cleared away the ashes from the top of the golden incense altar, exposing the gold surface and sprinkled seven drops of blood on the clean surface.

There was a spirit of anticipation in the air when the *Kohen Gadol* exited the *Bayit* and stood before the *sa'ir hamishtalei'ach*. Harav Kagan trembled when he placed his hands on the animal's head and confessed the sins of *Am Yisrael*.

> O God, forgive I pray, the iniquities, and transgressions and sins which Thy people, the House of Israel, have committed, transgressed, and sinned before Thee; as it is written in the law of Thy servant Moses, "For on this day shall atonement be made for you to cleanse you: from all your sins shall you be purified before the Lord."

331

When the people heard the *Shem Hameforash* pronounced by the *Kohen Gadol*, they fell on their faces, and cried out, "Blessed be the name of the glory of His kingdom forever and ever."

The *ish iti*, the "designated man" and his entourage, led the *sa'ir hamishtalei'ach*, the bearer of Israel's sins, out of the *Azarah*, out of Jerusalem, in the direction of the wilderness.

The *Kohen Gadol* swiftly began removing the *emurim*, the sacrificial portions of the bullock and the goat previously slaughtered, to burn them on the altar. He dismembered the carcasses and twisted their limbs around carrying-poles; they would later be carried outside of Jerusalem and burned.

Time passed. There was an air of tension in the *Azarah*. Everyone was waiting for word that the *ish iti* reached the wilderness.

The *ish iti* and his escort led the goat ever deeper into the wilderness. Finally, they reached their destination, a wild isolated ravine to the east of Jerusalem. Pausing, the *ish iti* removed the red strip of wool from between the horns of the goat and divided it in half. He fastened one piece to a nearby rock and the other he re-tied to the goat's horns. With a silent prayer, the *ish iti* pitched the goat over the jagged cliff.

Many centuries before, the great sage Rav Yishma'el taught that if *Am Yisrael*'s sins were forgiven, the moment the *ish iti* pushed the *sa'ir hamishtalei'ach* over the cliff, the red strip of wool that the *Kohanim* hung above the entrance of the *Bayit* would turn white.

And so it happened!

Suddenly, the *Azarah* fell silent. Then there was a shout, then an earth-shaking roar. Gasping with emotion, the hundreds of thousands of people in the *Azarah* excitedly pointed at the piece of wool hanging at the entrance of the *Bayit.*

The red ribbon had turned white! The sins of Am Yisrael had been forgiven!

Supremely exalted at this open miracle, the people in the *Azarah* started singing over and over, "Though your sins be as scarlet, they shall be as white as snow." They formed long lines and started to dance around the *Azarah* as they sang.

In a secluded niche overlooking the *Azarah, Melech Mashi'ach,* the anointed King of Israel, sat and watched approvingly. It happened! *Am Yisrael* connected to their Father in Heaven! The sins of *Am Yisrael* are forgiven! In only a few more days, he, *Melech Hamashi'ach,* would reveal himself to the world. His heart beat faster just thinking about it. He recalled the words of the prophets:

> In that day I will restore David's fallen tent, I will repair its broken places, repair its ruins, and build it as it used to be …. The days are coming, declares *Hashem,* when the reaper will be overtaken by the plowman, and the planter by the one treading grapes. New wine will drip from the mountains and flow from the hills. I will bring back my exiled people Israel; they will rebuild the ruined cities and live in them. They will plant vineyards and drink their wine; they will make gardens and eat their fruit. I will plant Israel in their own land, never again to be uprooted from the land I have given them, says *Hashem* your God.
>
> Sing and rejoice, O daughter of Zion; for, lo, I come, and will dwell in the midst of thee, saith *Hashem.* And many nations shall join themselves to *Hashem* on that day, and

shall be My people, and I will dwell in the midst of thee; and you shall know that the Lord of Hosts has sent me unto thee...

I shall ascend to the highest point of the *Beit Hamikdash* and I shall cry out to *Am Yisrael* with a loud voice that will be heard from one end of the earth to the other: *Anavim, anavim, higi'a zeman ge'ulatchem!*

Humble ones; the time for your Redemption has come!

And it shall come to pass that, of which was said unto them, "You are not My people, it shall be said to them, 'You are the children of the Living God.'"

It has been so long.

Melech Hamashi'ach put his hands over his eyes and bowed his head in the direction of the *Kodesh Hakodashim* praying that he would be worthy.

The *Azarah* was quiet again. It took a long time for the *Kohanim* to persuade the excited crowds to end the exuberant singing and dancing so that the *Avodah* could continue.

The rest of Yom Kippur passed like a dream.

After *Ne'ila*, the concluding service, the *Kohen Gadol*, the *Segan,* and Meir Hakohen broke their fast in a side room. The *Kohen Gadol* was exhausted. Slipping a pillow under his head, they let him rest for an hour. Finally, the *Segan* nudged him, "*Ishi Kohen Gadol*, you must get up now. *Am Yisrael* wants to see their *Kohen Gadol!* You cannot disappoint them."

An hour later, surrounded by an accompanying honor guard of young *Kohanim*, the *Kohen Gadol*, the *Segan*, Meir Hakohen, Reb Azariah of Beit Avtinas, Harav Naphtali of Beit Garmu, and Meshullam Hamalbish exited the *Mikdash* and stepped into the brisk night air. Once outside, they were joined by the members of the Sanhedrin, and Reuven ben Tzvi and his Levites.

To the ecstatic cheers of the multitudes, the entourage slowly passed through the Eastern Gate of the *Mikdash* compound. Everyone who had been in the *Mikdash* courtyard had gone home, broken their fast, rested a few minutes and returned. Even people who had not spent Yom Kippur in the *Mikdash* were there; men, women and children. Filling the vast *Har Habayit* plaza and all the adjoining streets, the white-clad throng was rapidly growing. Everyone wanted to celebrate the man who had come forth safely from the *Kodesh Hakodashim* and obtained forgiveness of the sins of *Am Yisrael*.

As the priestly entourage slowly inched forward through the adoring crowd, the masses of doting people started jumping up and down with excitement. With a spirit of exaltation, they spontaneously burst into enthusiastic song.

> How was he glorified when the people
> Gathered around him,
> In his coming out of the House of the Veil.
> So was the visage of the priest!
>
> He was like a morning star
> In the midst of the cloud,
> Like a full moon on festival days.
> So was the visage of the priest!
>
> Like the sun shining on the
> Temple of the Most High,
> Like a rainbow giving light in clouds of glory.
> So was the visage of the priest!

Like a flower of roses on new-moon days,
So was the visage of the priest!
Like a lily by springs of water.
Like a shoot of Lebanon on summer days.
So was the visage of the priest

Like fire and incense upon the censor.....

Then suddenly the heavens lit up; gold, silver, pink, blue, purple, every color of the rainbow. The sky filled with sparkling celestial wheels, palm trees, waterfalls; there was a barrage of globes, shooting stars, and chrysanthemums.

"In the old days, *Am Yisrael* used to greet their *Kohen Gadol* after Yom Kippur carrying torches," smiled Harav Eliyahu. "Today, they greet him with fireworks and a laser show!"

Chapter Forty

Two days after Yom Kippur, in the early afternoon...

"The voice of mirth and the voice of gladness; the voice of the bridegroom and the voice of the bride ..."

Several hundred people – all in a state of ritual purity – filled a magnificent spacious veranda overlooking *Har Habayit*. It was part of an apartment complex purchased by Griesha Pressman in Yerushalayim Bein Hachomot several months before. The admiring guests, milling around the veranda nibbling refreshments, came to celebrate the wedding of Dave Bernstein and Samantha–Shulamit Saraiva. The ceremony had not yet begun, and the guests were enjoying the lavish reception buffet. The massive gold and white structure of the *Beit Hamikdash* dominated the horizon.

That morning Bernstein, accompanied by Pringsheim, brought an *olah* to the Temple. Facing the *Bayit*, he placed both hands on the lamb's head and pressed down as the halachah ordains. As he recited words of praise he grinned, *"Lately I've had a lot to be thankful for!"* He also brought two calves to offer as *shelamim*. After burning the sacrificial portions of the *shelamim* on the altar, the *Kohanim* removed what was due to them, and gave the remaining meat to Bernstein to be taken to Griesha Pressman's home to be roasted. As Bernstein and Pringsheim left the *Azarah*, they walked backwards, as is the custom, so not to turn their backs on the *Bayit*.

Samantha's mother, Dave's parents, Griesha's mother Menucha, and his cousin Chaim and his family were there. The *Segan*, Meir Hakohen, Meshullam Hamalbish, Elimelech Eizenman, the Mikdash Chief Financial Officer Avi Katz, and many other prominent *Mikdash* personalities were among the invitees. Griesha Pressman flew Samantha's extended family from Vinhateiro in for the wedding and for the first time, the new bride met her *anousim* relatives. They bore ancient surnames such as Costa, Da Silva, Saraiva and Teixeira. And like Samantha, all of them – newly restored to *Am Yisrael* – were able to trace their unblemished Jewish lineage back to the terrible days of 1391, 1492, and 1496.

Everyone was elated to hear that the *Kohen Gadol* himself would honor them by performing the marriage ceremony. But it was understood that he could not stay more than a short time due to the extreme sanctity of his office.

As the guests continued to arrive, Menucha noticed a dignified woman sitting alone at a side table. Menucha knew about Samantha's family background, and realized that the woman at the table must be Samantha's mother. She was dressed as was fitting for a mother of the bride, in a deep garnet brocade gown. Menucha decided to approach her.

"I am Menucha Pressman. Are you Mrs. Saraiva, Samantha's mother?"

"Yes I am. I am Fortuna Gracia Saraiva," she said, smiling, "Are you Griesha Pressman's mother?"

Mrs. Saraiva had heard from her daughter all about the cast of characters connected to the wedding, and she realized that the older woman in the dark tailored suit who had approached her must be Griesha's mother.

338

"Yes, I am," Menucha said. "Mrs. Saraiva, I wish you mazal tov. It's a wonderful thing to marry off a child."

"Thank you so much. As you can imagine, I have been looking forward to this day for a long time. But I'll tell you the truth, it's not exactly what I had expected." She motioned to the chair next to her, "Please sit down."

"Thank you."

"Please call me Fortuna," she said smiling.

"And you can call me Menucha."

"It was very generous of your son to offer us his beautiful home for my daughter's wedding. And you know he flew all our relatives in from Vinhateiro, and put them up in hotels so they could participate in the wedding."

Menucha glowed.

"Mrs. Pressman, I read how Griesha left the Jewish community and built up PrinceGlobal Media. The article mentioned that since your son returned to Judaism, he has become a major philanthropist. Did you know that last month he gave five million dollars to a children's hospital in Los Angeles? The only reason I know that is because I am the chair of the hospital's fundraising committee."

"No, I did not know. The new Griesha is modest, and doesn't tell his mother all the details of his *tzedakah* work. And I do wish you'd call me Menucha. Griesha gave up the day-to-day administration of PrinceGlobal Media for the most part, but he still sets policy. Nowadays, he spends most of his time studying Torah and on charitable endeavors."

"I heard the interview he gave when he announced that he was changing his name from George Prince back to Griesha Shmu'el Pressman. I found it very inspiring."

"Thank you. I was very proud of him."

"It must have been very hard when Griesha ran away like that when he was so young."

"Yes. It was devastating. My late husband always believed that he would come back one day, and *baruch Hashem*, he has. Unfortunately, my husband didn't live to see it."

"I know that that must have been terribly hard for you, Menucha. But look what Griesha has done in just the last year. The news media worldwide is far cleaner and more truthful. Even the social media has improved. You know that's all Griesha's doing! Look what he's doing to publicize the Temple's message to the world, and the *Hakhel* ceremony as well. He could not have done any of that if he wasn't in the position that he built up for himself at PrinceGlobal. If he had become one of the greatest Talmudic scholars of the generation, as I'm sure you and your husband hoped he would, he could not have accomplished any of that. Menucha, don't you see? As painful as it was for you and your husband, he had to run away to grow into the man he eventually became."

Menucha had a faraway look in her eyes and then she began to smile. "You know, I never thought of it that way, Fortuna."

"Menucha, my late husband used to say that when children reach a certain stage of development in their lives, and you don't always know when that is, you can't steer them anymore. You shouldn't even try. My husband was not a religious man but he used to say, 'Children, like birds, must learn how to fly. And when they do, all you can do is to love them, trust them, be there for them if they ask for your help, pray for them, and leave the rest to God.'"

"Your husband was a wise man."

"You must excuse a mother getting sentimental at her only daughter's wedding, and saying things that perhaps she shouldn't say. I left Vinhateiro when I was nineteen and built a new life for myself in America. Though I married a man of *anousim* descent, we kept our distance from the *anousim* organizations. Even though we followed many *anousim* customs, we made no effort to pass them on and we never spoke to Samantha about her – our – background. Looking back now, I see we made a serious mistake. We deprived her of her heritage, and that was wrong." Fortuna paused, deep in thought.

"Please continue," Menucha said softly.

"Do you remember Professor Falconi's press conference in Milan, when he announced that he was calling a halt to the anarchist revolution?"

"Of course! Who could forget it?"

"After Professor Falconi told Samantha at the press conference that he was stopping the revolution at the behest of the High Priest, she came to Israel. She couldn't understand how a High Priest of a Temple in Jerusalem could have such influence over Falconi."

Menucha nodded her head vigorously in agreement, "At the time nobody understood it."

"She wanted to interview the High Priest and find out why. She wasn't able to interview him of course, but once in Israel, she met up with Dave Bernstein, an old acquaintance. Somehow, he showed her that she might be of *anousim* descent. I can't imagine how the subject even came up. But that conversation lit a spark. It got her thinking. Samantha, you should know, is a woman of deep thoughts. She was always that way, even when she was an unsettled adolescent. In the

341

end, she decided to investigate her background and uncover her roots. I suppose it's not surprising for an investigative reporter to want to investigate her own family background. In any event, one thing led to another, and she ended up appearing before the rabbinical court and officially rejoining the Jewish people. Menucha, she's asked me to do that too."

Menucha nodded. "How do you feel about it?"

Fortuna sighed. "To tell you the truth, I'm ambivalent about the whole thing. We really haven't been part of the Jewish community for over five hundred years. I can understand why Samantha and hundreds of thousands of other people of *anousim* descent are changing their lives so radically, but I don't know if I'm ready to take such a drastic step. But I look at Samantha. She has an inner peace she never had before. I see it in her eyes, and it's beautiful to see. Samantha says that if I don't return to the Jewish people now that I have the opportunity to do so, what I am saying by my actions, or inaction really, is that the struggles of our *anousim* ancestors to preserve what Judaism they could throughout the centuries were in vain. It would mean that as I far as I'm concerned, the Inquisition won. And you know what? She's right. But for me personally to take on the obligations of Jewish observance... I don't know if I can."

"Fortuna, I can understand your ambivalence."

"You can?"

"Of course I can," Menucha said. "It's no small thing to change your life around." Then Menucha pointed to a strange phenomenon in the distance. "Look at the smoke from the sacrificial altar rising straight up to the heavens. The smoke does not allow the wind to deter it from its chosen path. Like Samantha, like the smoke rising from the altar, you have to

342

embark on your own spiritual journey. But in the end, your journey will be a straight path which is clear and makes sense for you. This journey is something only you can do, and only when you're ready. Fortuna, you can't know what the future holds. Samantha followed her own path and now you must follow yours."

"Yes, I know. And I would never interfere with the path that Samantha has chosen. I just don't want her to throw away everything she's worked for all these years. I don't feel she should just abandon her career."

"I don't think anyone is asking her to abandon her career, Fortuna. Maybe once she's married, and God willing, has other responsibilities, she won't be able to travel all over the world at the drop of a hat, but she certainly can continue to work as a journalist. She has more opportunities here than you may think."

"Do you really think so?"

"Yes I do. Since Griesha moved PrinceGlobal Media's head office to Jerusalem, Israel is now the media capital of the world. Being based in Jerusalem will be a great advantage to her. And most important, Samantha will have a wonderful husband to share her life with!"

Fortuna smiled, with her lips and her eyes. "Yes, she will. Who would have thought? My Samantha! The war correspondent, a blushing bride! You've made me feel so much better, Menucha. Thank you for talking to me."

"You have it wrong. Thank *you* for talking to me, Fortuna. You've helped me see Griesha and his journey in a new light."

As the meat of the *shelamim* roasted over open grills, people took turns giving *divrei Torah,* which were simultaneously translated into Portuguese for the guests. The

Segan led off. Gazing at the *anousim* sitting before him, the *Segan* began by analyzing a passage from the prophet Amos: "For lo, I will command, and I will sift the House of Israel among all the nations, like corn is sifted in a sieve, yet not the least grain will fall upon the earth." When the translator rendered the passage into Portuguese, the eyes of the *anousim* glowed. Newly rejoined to *Am Yisrael*, they understood the prophet's message perfectly: they had *lived* it.

Abruptly the sound of wedding music filled the air. From the veranda the guests saw an approaching procession; it was Samantha and her attendants. As brides in ancient Israel were escorted to their weddings in the days before the destruction of the Second Temple, Samantha - now Shulamit - was being carried to her wedding in an *aperion*, a gorgeous roofed litter with a covered and curtained couch designed to carry a passenger of special importance. The canopied litter had a cedar framework with long extended poles for the bearers to grasp. Braid embellished golden curtains flowed from the canopy and rich purple velvet lined the litter's interior. Led by a harpist in royal purple, the litter was borne by four broad shouldered men wearing dark blue and gold robes.

Behind the pulled back curtains, the guests could see a gold-embroidered throne upon which Shulamit sat. On either side of the bearers, marching musicians clad in light blue robes played wind instruments and beat drums. Dozens of singing and clapping young women and girls trailed behind them shaking tambourines as they danced. Shulamit was arrayed in elaborate white tulle, and wore a striking *Yerushalayim shel Zahav* – Jerusalem of Gold – tiara. Many guests smiled; they recalled that in the days of the Second Temple and even some time after its destruction, it was customary for bridegrooms to

344

give their brides a coronet, a small crown, called a "Jerusalem of Gold" on their wedding day. A representation of the city of Jerusalem was embossed on the coronet. The tradition had been renewed since the restoration of the Temple.

Her tiara glistening in the sun, Shulamit excitedly leaned forward when the bearers stopped at a short distance from the wedding canopy and carefully lowered the four supports of the litter to the ground. There her *chatan* Dave Bernstein stood waiting for her, robed in a white *kittel* and wearing the *ateret chatanim*, the once more traditional wreath worn by bridegrooms. With a broad grin, he opened the latticed door of the litter and watched Shulamit gracefully descend. He approached her and gently covered her face with her veil. Bending over, he whispered something in her ear which made her quiver with delight. Then, escorted by his parents, he resolutely walked to the canopy of bridegrooms, a dome-shaped crimson silk and gold structure supported by four slender cedar pillars. Shulamit was escorted to the canopy by her mother and dozens of singing young women shaking tambourines.

Without warning, the music stopped, and everyone looked up; the *Kohen Gadol* and his entourage had just arrived. The few who were seated rose in their honor. The others looked in their direction, and bowed slightly.

Facing the *Kohen Gadol* arrayed in white, the couple felt pure as the driven snow. And they were: for like a king at his coronation and a sage at his ordination, the sins of a married couple are forgiven on their wedding day. With twinkling eyes, Samantha, followed by her mother and mother-in-law to be, circled her *chatan* seven times, symbolizing the six days of creation and the Sabbath, and the new world that Dave and Shulamit Bernstein were creating for themselves.

Under the canopy, the *Kohen Gadol* lifted up a glass of wine and recited the *berachah: borei pri ha'gafen*, followed by a second *berachah* that thanked *Hakadosh Baruch Hu* for giving the Jewish people the laws of holiness and purity. After Bernstein and Shulamit drank from the cup, Bernstein held up a smooth gold ring in the sight of the two witnesses, Griesha Pressman and Nimrod Pringsheim. Gazing intently at his bride, Bernstein recited the ancient formula: "Behold you are sanctified to me with this ring, according to the Law of Moses and Israel." Then he placed it on the forefinger of Samantha's right hand.

Griesha Pressman expertly read aloud the *ketubah*, the marriage contract.

Taking a second glass of wine, the *Segan* recited the first of the *Sheva Berachot*, the "seven blessings" recited for the bride and groom. Next, Meir Hakohen was given the cup and he chanted the second *berachah*. Elimelech Eizenman sang the third. Griesha's cousin Chaim chanted the fourth. Griesha Pressman proudly recited the fifth. Upon receiving the cup, Mordecai Da Silva chanted the sixth *berachah*; he was a long-lost uncle of Samantha's who had been living in Israel for many years. Nimrod Pringsheim took the cup and slowly and meticulously read aloud the last *berachah*. He was very pleased with himself, as this was the first time he had ever participated in a religious wedding.

The *Kohen Gadol* smiled. "This is the time," he said, passing his eyes over the hundreds of guests, then back at Samantha and Bernstein, "when, for almost two thousand years, Jewish bridegrooms the world over broke a glass in commemoration

346

of the destruction of the *Beit Hamikdash*. Many people had the additional custom of spreading ashes on the bridegroom's forehead. *Baruch Hashem*, we have lived to see the restoration of the *Beit Hamikdash* in all its glory. Nevertheless, though the days of mourning are behind us, we still remember and we still revere Jerusalem. David and Shulamit, please say with me the words of the psalmist, 'If I forget thee, O Jerusalem, let my right hand lose its cunning. Let my tongue cleave to the roof of my mouth if I do not remember thee; if I do not set Jerusalem above my highest joy.'"

The ceremony concluded, the musicians began to play and they escorted the young couple out with singing and dancing. Accompanied by the beat of tambourines, they entered a private room, away from the crowd. Awaiting them were plates laden with an array of delicate pastries and cold drinks set in crystal decanters. Shulamit and Dave broke their traditional wedding day fast together, as they spent a short time in precious seclusion which symbolized their new status of living together as husband and wife.

The guests found their places for the meal, and before they recited *ha'motzi* over the bread, they performed *netilat yad-ayim*, the ritual hand washing before eating bread. However, as the halachah ordains, they also immersed their hands in a *mikvah* before eating the meat of the *shelamim*. There was no difficulty there. Like so many other inhabitants of Yerushalayim Bein Hachomot, Griesha had a *mikvah* on his premises.

Griesha Pressman, his cousin Chaim, and even Nimrod Pringsheim rose and gave short *divrei Torah* during the meal. Then, having returned to the festivities from their seclusion, David and Samantha-Shulamit Bernstein added their own words of Torah. The high level of their *divrei Torah* surprised everyone except for the *Segan*. He knew better than anyone how far they had advanced on their spiritual odyssey together. The dancing was especially joyous, and both Samantha and Bernstein were lifted on to chairs and danced around in circles. It was an unusual wedding: the music was a blend of the traditional songs and the centuries-old ballads of the *anousim*. At the end of the meal, Griesha poured a cup of wine for *Birkat Hamazon*, the grace after meals. The *Segan*, as the senior *Kohen* still present, was honored with leading *Birkat Hamazon*.

> *Devai ha'seir ve'gam charon,*
> *Ve'az ileim be'shir yaron...*
>
> Remove distress, and also wrath,
> Then the dumb will burst forth in song;
> He shall lead us in straight paths,
> Accepting the blessing of the children of *Yeshurun*....

At the end of the *Sheva Berachot*, Griesha mixed the wine from the two cups, the original cup from *Birkat Hamazon* and the *Kos shel Berachah* – the cup of blessing – from the *Sheva Berachot,* and gave one to David Bernstein and the other to Shulamit.

Chapter Forty-One

Sukkot marking the end of the Sabbatical Year had arrived. Though Jerusalem had never been so crowded, somehow, miraculously, there was room for everyone. No one could explain it; Meir Hakohen, chairman of the *Hakhel* Committee certainly could not. But perhaps even more miraculously, nobody complained about their accommodations.

All Meir's preparations were finally complete. Mikdash Broadcasts and PrinceGlobal Media were on standby. After the conclusion of Yom Tov, the first day of Sukkot, the voices of Dave Bernstein, Samantha-Shulamit, and Nimrod Pringsheim would be heard around the world.

As he sat in Griesha Pressman's magnificent Sukkah overlooking *Har Habayit*, the words of a Psalm came to Pringsheim's mind.

> A song of ascents. Out of the depths have I called to Thee O Lord. My God, hearken unto my voice; let Thine ears be attentive to the voice of my supplications. If Thou Lord were to mark iniquities, O Lord, who could stand?

> That certainly describes my own life, full of iniquities. I was the classic *tinok shenishba* – a baby raised in an atmosphere hostile to Torah. And like Yerav'am ben Nevat – Jereboam the son of Nevat – who rebelled

against the House of David and spurned the *Beit Hamikdash* that King Solomon built, I not only sinned myself but caused others to sin as well. But *baruch Hashem*, the merit of the *Beit Hamikdash* brought me to the Torah way of life.

We read on Yom Kippur just a few days ago, "Though your sins be as scarlet, they shall be forgiven and be as white as snow." And because of me, *baruch Hashem*, others followed my lead. *Teshuvah* not only can bring about forgiveness but can enable the *ba'al teshuvah* to rise to great spiritual heights. "The place where penitents stand, even the completely righteous cannot stand there." In a roundabout way, it seems that a person's spiritual descent is really the preparation for an even higher ascent. May it be Your will, that all of us rise together to ever higher spiritual levels. It is the heart that has the power to cause repentance to be acceptable to God.

For on that day He shall give you atonement, to cleanse you of all your sins; you shall be purified before *Hashem*.

Unseasonably cool though sunny, a steady breeze was blowing from the west. Pringsheim watched the smoke from the sacrificial altar – unaffected by the wind – rise heavenward as straight as the trunk of a mighty date palm. He smiled; he was at peace with himself.

Night had fallen. *Yom Tov*, the first day of Sukkot, had ended. It was the eve of the second day of Sukkot; the long anticipated day of *Hakhel* had arrived.

Millions of singing, white-clad *olei regel* from *Eretz Yisrael* and from all over the world began marching down Jaffa Road and all of the other streets leading to Yerushalayim Bein Hachomot and *Har Habayit*. Young women by the hundreds of thousands were shaking tambourines as they marched. People from cities, towns, and settlements across *Eretz Yisrael* marched as organized groups carrying colorful streamers. Massive groups of students from yeshivot, seminaries, youth movements, and schools from Israel and abroad, marched together with their *rabbanim* and teachers. Hasidim marched with their *rebbei'im*; university students marched with their professors. Even a huge contingent of former radical leftists was in the crowd. They, like their mentor, Nimrod Pringsheim, had seen the error of their ways and were not ashamed to admit it.

The energy and exaltation of the marchers was incredible. Everyone knew that they were making history. This was the first *Hakhel* in two thousand years! Everyone wanted to see the face of *Melech Hamashi'ach*!

Griesha Pressman declined the *Segan's* offer to sit in the VIP grandstand overlooking *Har Habayit*. Instead he chose to join his cousin Chaim and his family – newly ensconced in the garden city of Har El – as they marched with their friends and neighbors. With one of his grandchildren perched on his shoulders squealing with delight, the usually reserved Chaim and his wife Yehudis danced their way along.

Holding torches aloft, hundreds of thousands of *olei regel* from Ir David, Kiryat Melech Rav, Klilat Yofi, and many of the newer neighborhoods, entered Yerushalayim Bein Hachomot through the enlarged Sha'ar Ha'ashpot. Tens of thousands of others – denizens of Makor Baruch, Ge'ula, Me'ah She'arim, Shmu'el Hanavi and adjacent neighborhoods – entered Yerushalayim Bein Hachomot through Sha'ar Shechem.

Hundreds of standard-bearers and their entourages hoisted colorful tribal banners aloft as they marched. The jubilant throngs stepped aside to let them pass. As they went by, the exuberant crowd roared its approval. In the distance people in the crowd noticed a banner that they never saw before.

It was the royal banner of *Melech Hamashi'ach*!

At the sight of the messianic ensign, the crowd became respectfully silent. Larger than the others, it was royal purple and white, emblazoned with a golden crown and harp, as befitting the Davidic King.

Then they broke their silence and burst into song.

Baruch Haba Melech Hamashi'ach!

The unending rivers of white-clad *olei regel* flowed through the brightly lit up stone alleyways of Yerushalayim Bein Hachomot on their way to *Har Habayit*. And, as in the days of *Bayit Sheini*, they were greeted by thousands of white-clad *Kohanim* standing on the ancient crenellated walls blowing golden trumpets.

Overhead, there were spectacular fireworks displays.

Shaking their heads, the *Segan* and Meir Hakohen looked incredulously at the masses of people. It seemed to them that the laws of physics had been rescinded.

They had.

Though it was physically impossible for so many people to occupy so little space, somehow everyone squeezed in!

Every nation in the world was represented on *Har Habayit*.

Professor Antonio Falconi was there as he had promised, flanked by his aides and virtually all those who had attended his conferences in Jerusalem. As Falconi surveyed the vast crowds on the Temple Mount, he had a vision.

The Messianic Age will be one where all nations of the earth will come together to create a better world built on trust, morality, and love. There will be a feeling of worldwide unity, even though individuals and peoples will retain their intrinsic identities and their own cultures. It will be a time when the unity of God will be seen in our world.

When King Solomon dedicated the First Temple, he said:

Concerning the stranger that is not of Thy people Israel, when he shall come out of a far country for Thy name's sake – for they shall hear of Thy great name, and of Thy mighty hand and of Thine outstretched arm – when he shall come and pray towards this house; hear Thou in Heaven Thy dwelling-place, and do according to all that the stranger calleth to Thee for; that all the peoples of the earth may know Thy name, to fear Thee, as doeth Thy people Israel ...

For out of Zion shall go forth the law and the word of the Lord from Jerusalem. And He will judge between the nations, and shall decide for many peoples; and they shall beat their swords into plowshares and their spears into pruning hooks. Nation shall not lift sword against nation. Neither shall they learn war any more. But they shall sit every man under his vine and fig tree: and none shall make them afraid....

The sages of Israel say that Adam brought his offerings to God in the place which in years to come would be the site of the Temple altar. Indeed Adam, the ancestor of all humanity, was created from the dust of the earth from the very place that eventually would bring about atonement. So too, may the merit of the Temple bring about atonement to *all* of Adam's children.

I will bring them to My holy mountain, And make them joyful in My house of prayer; Their burnt offerings and their sacrifices willingly shall I accept on My altar, For My house shall be called a house of prayer for all peoples.

Bowing his head, Falconi recalled the mysterious blind man who had blessed him so many years before, and who had had such a powerful influence on his life.

Mio padre, forgive me, I did not understand the true meaning of your words. I believed that governments were evil because they violated the principles of freedom and justice. I believed that governments were corrupt and corrupting. I preached revolution, the violent overthrow of venal societies everywhere by fire and sword, by deception, cyberwarfare, bombings and assassinations. In my arrogance I thought we could build a new world of peace and justice by purifying the old with the blood of our enemies. I was wrong. Such a world where the most bestial passions of men are released and indeed glorified could never be the basis of a just and equitable society. *Mio padre*, do you not see now that my original question to you was a valid question? When you spoke to me so long ago, I asked you what did I know of purity and rebuilding? It was a valid question, because despite my erudition and my plethora of university degrees, it turned out that I knew nothing. I only knew how to ravage and destroy. God of *Rabbino* Eliyahu Kagan, High Priest of the Temple of *Gerusalemme*, I stand before You now. Teach me how to help build *Your* new world, a world of truth, a world of purity!

354

The former anarchist leader raised his eyes heavenward and whispered words of the prophet Zechariah, "Not by might, nor by power, but by My spirit saith the Lord of Hosts."

The millions of people standing on *Har Habayit* waited in anticipation.

Thousands of years before, the prophet Jeremiah had envisioned this day:

> Unto Thee shall the nations come
> From the ends of the earth, and shall say:
> Our fathers have inherited naught but lies,
> Vanity and things wherein there is no profit.

> Shall a man make unto himself gods,
> And they are no gods?
> Therefore, behold, I will cause them to know...
> My hand and My might;

> And they shall know that My name is the Lord.

Finally, that day had come.

Chapter Forty-Two

On that day Aliza from Denver, her boss, and her co-workers fulfilled their wish; they and their families came to Jerusalem for the great *Hakhel*. Susan from Englewood, her friend from the gym, her two brothers, their families, and millions of non-Jews like them fulfilled the prophecy of Zechariah and ascended to Jerusalem.

Pilgrims from Africa, Kazakhstan, and Pakistan were there, sent by their tribes and villages to represent them. Indians from isolated tribes deep in the heart of the Amazon rain forests joined them. Sophisticates from Paris clasped hands with peons from Peru; engineers from China and the Asian rim joined hands with Cajuns from the steamy bayous of southern Louisiana; coffee growers from Brazil joined hands with watchmakers from Switzerland and factory workers from Russia; sheep herders from Australia joined hands with physicists from the Silicon Valley; nomads from the mountains of Afghanistan joined hands with fishermen who spread their nets in the Ganges River in India. There were men and women from every nation in the world in Jerusalem and they, like the *olei regel* gathered together from all over the Jewish world, stood on *Har Habayit*.

Precisely at 9:00 p.m., a grand parade of thousands of white-clad *Kohanim* exited the *Mikdash* compound through the Eastern Gate. Led by the *Segan*, Meir Hakohen, Harav Azariah and the master spice apothecaries of Beit Avtinas, Harav Naphtali and the expert bakers of Beit Garmu, Meshullam Hamalbish and his weavers walked together. A special twinkle in their eyes, Meshullam Hamalbish and his weavers proudly surveyed the white sea of *Kohanim* wearing their expertly made garments, and smiled. Chief Financial Officer Avi Katz and his accountants, Chief Engineer Yannai and his technicians followed them with Binyamin, the Chief *Shochet*, and his staff close behind. *Av bayit* Yehoshua with his artisans, stone masons, and maintenance men were next in line. Singing as they marched, choirmaster Reuven ben Tzvi and the Levitical choir, instruments in hand, were escorted by the gate keepers, the Levite security men, technicians, and drivers.

A beaming *Melech Hamashi'ach*, splendidly arrayed in royal purple and crowned with a gold diadem, and Harav Eliyahu Kagan, *Kohen Gadol*, resplendent in his eight golden high priestly garments, took their place at the head of the procession. They were met by the *Chacham Muflag* and the sages of the Sanhedrin, wearing sky-blue robes with white sashes. Together they all filed into the vastly expanded *Har Habayit* plaza.

As *Melech Hamashi'ach* came into view, the vast multitude burst into song that pierced the heavens:

> *Ashrei ha'am shekacha lo; ashrei ha'am*
> *She'Hashem Elokov....*
> *Baruch haba Melech Hamashi'ach!*
> *Shehechiyanu ve'kiyemanu ve'higiyanu la'zeman ha'zeh ...*

As *Melech Hamashi'ach*, the *Kohen Gadol*, the *Segan*, Meir Hakohen, select *Kohanim*, the *Chacham Muflag* and members of the Sanhedrin slowly ascended the stairs of the huge wooden platform, the thousands of white-clad *Kohanim* standing on the crenellated stone walls of the *Mikdash* once more sounded their golden trumpets in unison. As the venerable company took their seats, the *Kohanim* and the crowd became silent. A magnificently carved wood and gold *aron kodesh* stood in the center of the platform. The ark contained one of the original Torah scroll written by Moshe Rabbeinu himself which had miraculously reappeared the day *Am Yisrael* dedicated the new *Mikdash*.

The *chazzan* of the *beit knesset* in the Chamber of Hewn Stone slowly opened the *aron kodesh*, bowed and then took out the *Sefer Torah*. Everyone rose to their feet and, led by the Levite choir, they began to sing:

> *Vayehi binso'a ha'aron, va'yomer Moshe...*
> When the Ark would travel, Moses would say;
> Arise O Lord and let your foes be scattered,
> Let those who hate You flee from you.

> For from Zion will come forth the Torah, and the word
> Of *Hashem* from Jerusalem.
> Blessed is He who gave the Torah to His people Israel in
> His holiness....

> Blessed art Thou O Lord, our God, Who redeemed Israel.

Then led by the *Chacham Muflag*, everyone recited the *Shehechiyanu*, the blessing recited at joyous occasions. They thanked *Hakadosh Baruch Hu* for being privileged to participate in this unique mitzvah and see the face of *Melech Hamashi'ach*.

Blessed art Thou, O Lord, our God, King of the universe, who has kept us alive, sustained us, and brought us to this season!

They recited the *berachah* ordained by the Sages upon seeing a great Torah scholar.

Blessed art Thou, O Lord, our God, King of the universe, who has apportioned of His knowledge to them who fear Him.

And for the first time in thousands of years, *Am Yisrael* was able to recite the unique blessing enacted by the Sages upon seeing the King of Israel.

Blessed art Thou, O Lord, our God, King of the universe, who has imparted of His glory to them who fear Him.

They recited the mystical *berachah* said when six hundred thousand Jews gather together in one place.

Blessed art Thou, O Lord, our God, King of the universe, Knower of secrets.

Billions of people around the globe watching the ceremony in their homes, workplaces, and schools, listened reverently and bowed their heads.

Griesha Pressman, standing with the men of Har El, gave free reign to his thoughts:

Baruch Hashem, because of the merit of the *Beis Hamikdash*, I've returned to my roots. Even so, the pain that I inflicted on my parents can never be forgiven. I want to set up a worldwide charitable organization in their name. At least, as much as humanly possible, I can make up at least a little for the hurt that I caused them. Thank God, my mother had the *nachas,* the satisfaction, of seeing her son return to a life of Torah and mitzvos.

In the age of *Mashi'ach,* PrinceGlobal Media must be a force for good and purity in the world. Like the sacrifices in the *Beis Hamikdash,* PrinceGlobal Media must not be an end in itself but rather a *means* to an end, a vehicle to help transform this world of *sheker* – falsehood - into the world of *emes* – truth. May this world be worthy to be a true resting place for the Shechinah. *Baruch Hashem,* I'm in a position that I can help bring this about.

George Prince has died, unmourned, but *baruch Hashem,* Griesha Shmu'el Pressman, son of Harav Yehudah and Rabbanit Menucha Pressman, has been reborn. *Baruch Hashem!*

"But what about me, personally?" Griesha asked himself. He thought of his cousin Chaim's family, Chaim's children and grandchildren. He thought of his two wonderful protégés, Dave and Samantha-Shulamit Bernstein, who were just beginning their married lives together in Jerusalem. How he had come to love those two phenomenal people! What precious jewels! "Grant perfect joy to these loving companions, as you did your creations in the Garden of Eden," he prayed.

As he thought of his own life of solitude and loneliness, a familiar passage from the Torah came to mind, "It is not good for man to be alone."

The *chazzan* reverently gave the Torah scroll to Meir Hakohen. Meir Hakohen lifted it high in the air, so that as many people as possible standing on *Har Habayit*, and around the world, could see it.

> The first time I performed *Nisuch Hayayin*, the wine libation, in the *Beit Hamikdash* and poured wine on the altar as the *korbanot* were offered, I used wine made by my father from vines that I myself helped cultivate and prune. My father was so excited, and so was I. I love the *Beit Hamikdash* and every day I give thanks to *Hakadosh Baruch Hu* that it was returned to us in my lifetime. I pray that I may continue to have the merit of serving *Hakadosh Baruch Hu* in His *Beit Hamikdash*, the earthly resting place of the Shechinah, in purity and holiness.

> One thing have I asked from *Hashem*, that will I seek after: that I may dwell in the House of *Hashem* all the days of my life, to behold the graciousness of *Hashem* and to visit in His Temple.

Meir Hakohen then passed the Torah scroll to Chanina Abulafia, *Segan*; he in turn lifted the Torah up high in the air.

> Many years have passed since that day when my *rebbe* called me into his office and told me that I had to leave the yeshiva and learn how to administer large institutions. And what years they turned out to be! It never occurred to me that he was thinking of the *Beit Hamikdash*!

> Today, we are reaching a new stage in the history of *Am Yisrael* and the entire world. After all this time, *Mashi'ach is finally here*! Perhaps when the transitional period is completed, and *Mashi'ach's* kingdom on earth is firmly established, I can step down from being *Segan* and go back to learning Torah full time. How I yearn to return to the *beit midrash*! I have still so much to learn! I

361

am a sojourner on the earth; hide not Thy commandments from me.

The *Segan* lowered the Torah Scroll, and clung to it for a
brief moment before giving it reverently to the *Kohen Gadol*.

The *Kohen Gadol* clutched the scroll to his breast tightly for
a few moments and recalled the words of the Rambam.

> The sages and the prophets did not yearn for the
> Messianic era so that they might rule over the nations,
> nor to be exalted by the nations. They did not yearn for
> the Messianic era in order that they may eat, drink and
> be merry; but only to be free to study the Torah and its
> wisdom, without anyone to oppress and disturb them...

> In the Messianic era there will be neither famine nor
> war, neither envy nor strife, because good will emanate
> in abundance and all delightful things will be accessible
> as dust. The one preoccupation of the entire world will
> be solely to know God....

He recalled the words of the prophets.

> In those days, and at that time, will I cause the Branch of
> righteousness to grow up unto David; and he shall
> execute judgment and righteousness in the land.

> In those days shall Judah be saved, and Jerusalem shall
> dwell safely: and this is the name wherewith she shall
> be called, The Lord is our righteousness.

> The *navi* Yermiyahu prophesized: Behold the days
> come, saith the Lord, that I will make a new covenant
> with the house of Israel and the house of Judah ... and I
> will be their God, and they shall be My people, and they

shall teach no more their neighbor, and every man his brother saying: 'Know the Lord; for they shall *all* know Me from the least of them to the greatest of them, saith the Lord ...

Kein yehi Ratzon. So may it be His will.

The *Chacham Muflag* intoned, *"Ya'amod Melech Hamashi'ach ben David*! Let the Messianic King, son of David arise!"

As the *Mashi'ach* approached, the *Kohen Gadol*, trembling with emotion, handed him the *Sefer Torah.*

With the *Kohen Gadol* and the *Chacham Muflag* of the Sanhedrin on his right and the *Segan* and Meir Hakohen on his left, *Melech Hamashi'ach* walked to the white-draped *bimah* in the center of the platform. Bowing down, as the halachah mandates the King of Israel to do before reading from the Torah, *Melech Hamashi'ach* began to chant the prerequisite *berachot.*

The waiting millions of *olei regel* quietly standing on *Har Habayit* mentally prepared themselves to receive and internalize the message of *Melech Hamashi'ach.* Countless parents lifted their children up high above their heads to give them a better of view of *Melech Hamashi'ach* fulfilling the ancient and now renewed mitzvah of *Hakhel.*

From a newly constructed studio on the roof of the Mikdash Conference Center on *Har Habayit* high above the crowds, Dave and Samantha-Shulamit Bernstein, and Nimrod Pringsheim began broadcasting. Elimelech Eizenman and his expert staff provided commentary and simultaneous translations into seventy languages.

While Eizenman spoke, Dave Bernstein gazed at his *bashert* across the array of broadcast equipment that filled the studio.

I remember a quote that I heard in *shi'ur* a couple of months ago: "When a person builds a house, he makes the windows narrow on the outside and wider within. But when King Solomon built the first Holy Temple he made the windows narrow within and wide without, so that its light could radiate to the entire world." Can anyone deny that the light of the *Beit Hamikdash* circles the globe and brightens up the Jewish and non-Jewish world alike? If it did this even before *Mashi'ach* revealed himself, imagine what will happen now when *Mashi'ach* is revealed!

Bil'am, the prophet of the nations, said concerning *Mashi'ach*, "I shall see him, but not now; I shall look at him, but it is not near; a star has come out of Jacob; a scepter-bearer has risen from Israel, and he shall pierce the nobles of Moab and undermine the children of Seth. Edom shall be a conquest and Seir shall be the conquest of his enemies – Israel will attain success.

After thousands of years of waiting, that time has come.

And best of all, the merit of the *Beit Hamikdash* caused me to find my *bashert*; she whom my soul loveth!

I am my beloved's, and my beloved is mine ...
Thou art beautiful, O my love, as Tirtzah,
Comely as Jerusalem, and as awe inspiring
As an army with banners.

364

Standing next to a cluster of broadcasting equipment and holding her tambourine close to her heart, Samantha-Shulamit looked at her husband with dancing eyes and with smiling lips.

So much has happened to me over the last year. I feel like I've been in the middle of a whirlwind. And I have! I have been united with my *bashert*, he whom my soul loveth, and at the same time, *baruch Hashem*, the *anousim*, wherever they may be, are returning to our people.

Samantha raised her eyes heavenward.

May it be His will that all *Am Yisrael* be reunited to their people and to their God.

And may it be His will that just as we *anousim* are returning to *Torat Yisrael, Am Yisrael,* and *Eretz Yisrael* from *our* hidden exile, so may we - very soon - be privileged to see all our brothers and sisters of the lost tribes of Israel wherever *they* may be, return to us from *their* hidden exile, and once again, as in the days of King David, the ancestor of *Melech Hamashi'ach*, our nation will be one.

Thus saith the Lord God, 'Behold I will take the children of Israel from among the nations ... and will gather them on every side, and bring them into their own land, and one king shall be king to them all...

And it shall come to pass on that day,
That a great shofar shall be blown;
And they shall come, that were lost
In the land of Assyria,
And they that were dispersed in the land of Egypt,
And they shall worship the Lord in the holy mountain of Jerusalem.

♦

His face glowing with an unearthly splendor, *Melech Hamashi'ach* – who was just as the *Midrash* described him "greater than Abraham, higher than Moses, and loftier than the ministering angels" – finished chanting the prerequisite *berachot*. Then once again he bowed down as he began to chant the sections of the Torah traditionally recited at *Hakhel*. And yet … without electronic amplification, all the millions standing on *Har Habayit* and even Jews still residing outside of the Land of Israel – for them it was still *yom tov* and they were not permitted to use electronic devices – miraculously heard and understood every word.

> See, I have taught you decrees and ordinances as *Hashem* my God has commanded me, to do so in the midst of the Land which you come to possess it. You shall safeguard them and perform them…, for it is your wisdom and discernment in the eyes of the peoples, who shall hear all these decrees and who shall say, 'Surely a wise and discerning people is this great nation.' For which is a great nation that has a God who is close to it, as is *Hashem*, our God, whenever we call upon Him? And which is a great nation that has righteous decrees and ordinances such as this entire Torah that I place before you this day?

> Blessed art thou in the city and blessed be you in the field. Blessed shall be the fruit of your womb and the fruit of your ground. …

> Blessed shall you be when you come in and blessed shall you be when you go out. *Hashem* shall cause your

enemies who rise up against you to be struck down before you.

Hashem will confirm for Himself as a holy people, as He swore to you...Then all the peoples of the earth will see that the name of *Hashem* is proclaimed over you, and they will revere you... "

But this time *Hakadosh Baruch Hu* supplied the fireworks.

Unexpectedly, undulating ribbons of white light shimmered in the sky like glowing, dancing curtains. Spectacularly bright red, green, blue, yellow, and orange flames of incredible intensity and wondrous beauty shot through the heavens. A hush fell over *Har Habayit* as millions of men, women, and children raised their eyes and open-mouthed, gazed heavenward at the breathtaking explosion of light over their heads.

"Meir, what is *that?*" the *Segan* asked excitedly, looking at Meir, to the sky, and back.

"*Ha'avodah*! I don't know!"

"It's the aurora borealis," replied the *Kohen Gadol* with a gleam in his eye.

"The aurora borealis? But it's never seen this far south, and it never, never shines so brightly," Meir said with a puzzled expression.

"Reb Meir, you are right. It *is* never seen so far south, and it *is* never so bright, unless it is a truly extraordinary sign of Divine favor," *Melech Hamashi'ach* explained with a smile.

מי ימלל גבורות ה' ישמיע כל תהילתו.

367

Hakarat Hatov - Acknowledgements

It is impossible for me to mention everyone who helped me to research and write this book. I am deeply indebted to all of them, ranging from beloved teachers who taught me Torah and *chochmat chaim* in my younger days, to dear friends who offered constructive criticism as the book progressed, to editors who made invaluable suggestions in the final stages.

I would like to thank Harav Chaim Blumberg of Baltimore for reviewing the halachic content of the book. If any errors remain, I take full responsibility for them.

I would like to thank Yehoshua Friedman and Channa Coggan for their astute and perceptive comments, and Reuven Prager for sharing his expertise about how weddings were conducted during *Mikdash* times.

Special thanks to Daniel Gwirtzman, who constantly encouraged me as I wrote this book. Although I was tempted to shelve the entire project more than once, Daniel kept me on track with strong moral support, and would not let me desist from my task especially in the early stages.

Special thanks to Reuven Brauner, my "technical advisor," who introduced me to the bewildering world of computers and formatting. He dragged me – kicking and screaming – into the 21st century. And the importance of his unfailing help in editing important passages, as well as his insightful comments about style, cannot be overestimated.

I am indebted to Shifrah Devorah Witt who saw the manuscript in its truly raw state and did not flinch.

I want to thank Jolie Greiff for her sage editing advice, her cheerful professionalism, and for helping me to "lighten up," not to mention her unfailing droll sense of humor. She managed to get

368

inside my head, no small thing to say about an editor! It was a joy working with her. I also appreciate the meticulous efforts of Judy Shafarman who served as copyeditor, formatter, and cover designer.

I am incredibly indebted to the many thousands of people in Israel, the United States and Canada, who over the years, have attended my lectures on various *Mikdash* topics and read (and responded) to my weekly column in the OU's Torah Tidbits, *Yibaneh Hamikdash*. I owe you more than I can say.

I would like to acknowledge my debt to Mesorah Publications, (the ArtScroll Series, the Stone Chumash) and the Jewish Publication Society for permission to make use of their very beautiful translations of the Torah and the books of the Tanach. I would like to thank Dr. Robert Hayward for allowing me to quote passages from his beautiful English rendition (from the Greek) of the Wisdom of Jesus ben Sira.

Finally, I want to thank my wife Heidi who has been a constant source of strength and support over the years. *Tzofia halichot beitah!*

May *Hakadosh Baruch Hu* – *ha'notein le'ya'eif koach* – be gracious to all *Am Yisrael* in these difficult times and may we all merit seeing the restoration of the *Beit Hamikdash* speedily in our days!

Glossary

The following glossary provides a partial explanation for some of the Hebrew, Aramaic, and Yiddish terms that that appear in this book.

Abba. "Dad" or "Father"

Adon. Mister

Adoni. Sir, my lord, Excellency

Alav Hashalom. Literally, peace be upon him; equivalent to "May he rest in peace."

Aliyah. Literally, to ascend; in normal usage, a Jew who leaves the Diaspora and settles in the Land of Israel "makes aliyah."

Am Ha'aretz. Ignoramus

Am Hashem. Literally, the People of God; the Jewish people

Am Yisrael. The people of Israel, the Jewish people

Anousim. Literally, the "forced ones." Also called Crypto-Jews or *Marranos*, Jews of Spain, Portugal and their colonial possessions who were forced to convert to Catholicism during the Inquisition in the Middle Ages. They continued to observe Jewish customs in secret to the best of their ability.

Anshei Ma'aseh. Men of extraordinary piety

Anshei Chen. Adepts of the Hidden Wisdom, the **Kabbalah**

Aron Habrit. The Ark of the Covenant. Ex. 19:20; 24:18

370

Aron Kodesh. *pl.* **Aronot Kodesh** Holy Ark in which the Torah scrolls are kept in the synagogue

Av. A month in the Jewish calendar, roughly equivalent to August

Av Bayit. Chief custodian

Avodah. The Temple service

Azarah. The inner Temple Court accessible only to **Kohanim,** priests

Ba'al Teshuvah. *pl.* **Ba'alei Teshuvah.** Non-observant Jew who has returned to full observance of the Jewish religion

Bar Mitzvah. When Jewish boys reach the age of 13 and are responsible for observing the precepts of Judaism

Baruch Attah. "Blessed art Thou...;" first words of a blessing

Baruch Hashem. Literally; Bless God, colloquial for "thank God"

Bashert. The divinely destined marriage partner (Yiddish)

Batei Knesset. Synagogues (Singular: **Beit Knesset**)

Bayit. Literally, the house; the main Temple building

Bayit Rishon. The First Temple, built by King Solomon 957 BCE and destroyed by the Babylonians in 587 BCE.

Bayit Sheini. The Second Temple, built after the Babylonian Exile, 530 BCE, and destroyed by the Romans, 70 CE.

Bayit Shelishi. The Third Temple

Be'ezrat Hashem. With God's help

Beis Hamikdosh. The Holy Temple of Jerusalem (Ashkenazic pronunciation)

Beis Din Shel Ma'alah. The Heavenly Tribunal (Ashkenazic pronunciation)

Beit Avtinas. The priestly family that prepared the Temple incense

Beit Garmu. The priestly family that prepared the showbread

Beit Hamikdash. The Holy Temple of Jerusalem

Beit Hamokeid. The Chamber of the Hearth, a hospice for priests located on the north side of the Temple court

Ben Noach. Literally, a son (or descendent) of Noah, a non-Jew who is obligated to observe the Seven Noahide Laws, the basis of all morality.

Bigdei Kehunah. The priestly garments

Bigdei Lavan. The white garments worn by the High Priest during the Yom Kippur service when he entered the Holy of Holies.

Bigdei Zahav. The "golden garments" worn by the High Priest during the Yom Kippur service as well as when he officiated in the Temple the rest of the year.

Birkat Hamazon. Grace after meals

Borei Pri Ha'gaffen. Blessing made over wine

Berachah. *pl.* **Berachot.** Blessing

Chagim. Holidays

Chacham Muflag. The chief sage and chairman of the **Sanhedrin**

372

Challot. Twisted loaves of bread eaten on the Sabbath and holidays

Chamor. Donkey

Chas Veshalom. God forbid!

Chatan. Bridegroom

Chavitim. Wafers or a sort of cake offered in the Temple

Chavruta. Study partner (Aramaic)

Chaza"l. Acronym for the Sages of blessed memory

Chatat. A sin offering

Chazzan. The leader in communal prayer in the synagogue

Chesed. Loving kindness, benevolence

Cheder. School for young boys

Chol Hamo'ed. The intermediate days of the Passover and Sukkot festivals

Chomer. Materiality

Chozer Be'teshuvah. A formerly non-observant Jew who has returned to full observance of the Jewish religion

Chupah. Wedding canopy

Daven. Pray (Yiddish)

Dinei Tum'ah Ve'tahorah. The laws of impurity and purity

Divrei Chullin. Secular matters

Divrei Torah. Lectures based on Torah

Dos. *pl.* **Dosim.** A contemptuous term for a religious person

Eichah. The Biblical Book of Lamentations, chanted in the synagogue on **Tisha B'av**

Eineklech. Grandchildren (Yiddish)

Eishet Chayil. "Woman of Valor," hymn sung by Jewish men to their wives on Sabbath Eve. (Prov. 31:10-31)

Elul. A month in the Hebrew calendar, roughly equivalent to September

Emurim. The parts of sacrificial animals burnt on the altar

Ezrat Nashim. Literally, the Court of the Women, the outer Temple court where women as well as men were permitted to enter.

Ezrat Yisrael. The Temple court where ordinary Israelite men (as opposed to priests) were permitted to enter

Eretz Benyamin. The Land of [the Biblical tribe] Benjamin, that area of the Shomron immediately north of Jerusalem

Eretz Yisrael. The Land of Israel

Erev. The eve of ...

Etrog. *pl.* **Etrogim.** Citron; one of the "four kinds" upon which a special blessing is made on the *Sukkot* holiday. The fruit of the "beautiful tree" (Leviticus 23:40) is traditionally believed to be the **Etrog,**

Gan Eden. The Garden of Eden, paradise

Gemara. The *Gemara* is an extensive commentary on the **Mishna;** together they make up the Talmud or a book of the Talmud

Gerusalemme. Jerusalem (Italian)

Geveret. Madam

Golus. Exile (Ashkenazic pronunciation)

Goyim. Non-Jews

Goyishe. Non-Jewish (Yiddish)

Ha'avodah! By the Divine Service!

Haga'on. Literally, "The genius," an honorific title for a very eminent and learned rabbi

Hakadosh Baruch Hu. The Holy One, Blessed be He, God

Hakhel. Biblically ordained custom based on the mandated practice in the Torah of assembling all Jewish men, women and children to hear the reading of sections of the Torah by the King of Israel once every seven years. (Deut. 31)

Haktarat Ketoret. The act of offering incense in the Temple

Halachah. *pl:* **Halachot.** Torah Law

Hamotzi. The blessing recited before eating bread

Hanavi. The prophet

Harav. The Rabbi, an honorific term

Har Habayit. The Temple Mount

375

Hashem. Literally, "the Name," God

Hashkafah. Spiritual outlook, perspective

Hassidim. Modern Hasidim are Orthodox Jews that believe in a more mystical interpretation of the fundamentals of Judaism than do non-Hasidic Jews. The various Hasidic groups usually follow a *Rebbe*, a charismatic religious leader.

Hatov Ve'hameitiv. Literally, "He (God) who is good and does well," a prayer recited upon hearing good news

Havdalah. Ceremony performed at the conclusion of the Sabbath separating it from the six days of the week, recited over a glass of wine, a braided candle, and spices.

Heichal. The Temple sanctuary, a large area within the **Bayit** containing the incense altar, the Menorah, and the table for the Showbread.

Ilui. A young genius, a child prodigy

Im Yirtzeh Hashem. God willing

Ishi Kohen Gadol. My lord, High Priest

Kabbalah. The Jewish mystical tradition

Kablan. Israeli building contractor

Kehunah. The priesthood

Kaddish. The "Mourners' Kaddish," an Aramaic prayer said as part of the mourning ritual in Judaism in all prayer services as well as at funerals and memorials.

Kaddish De'rabbanan. Special **Kaddish** said by mourners after learning Torah

Kavod Harav. "Your Excellency," an honorific term used to address an eminent rabbi

Kavod Hakohen. "Your Excellency," an honorific term used to address an eminent priest

Ketoret. Incense offered in the Temple

Kiddush. Prayer recited over wine on Sabbath and holidays

Kiddush Hashem. Sanctification of God's name

Kinderlach. Children (Yiddish)

Kippa. Skullcap

Klezmer Music. A genre of joyous Jewish music that developed in Eastern Europe

Kodashim. Sacrificial meat, also that order of the **Mishna** which discusses the Temple service

Kodesh Hakodashim. Holy of Holies, the most sacred area of the Temple. No one could enter the Holy of Holies except for the High Priest during the Yom Kippur service.

Kohen. *pl.* **Kohanim.** Priest

Kohen Gadol. High Priest

Korban. *pl.* **Korbanot.** Sacrifice offered in the Temple

Kos Shel Berachah. Literally, the "Cup of Benediction," cup of wine drunk on festive occasions

Kriyah. The cutting or tearing of a garment as a sign of mourning

Kriyat Shema. The recitation of the **Shema** prayer

Lechem Hapanim. Showbread, literally, "Bread of the Presence," the twelve loaves of unleavened bread which were always present on a specially dedicated golden table in the **Heichal** in the Temple (Lev. 24: 5 - 6). One of the miracles of the Temple was that even though the **Lechem Hapanim** was exposed to the open air for an entire week before being replaced by new loaves, they remained as fresh as the moment the loaves were removed from the oven.

Levy. Levite

Lishkat Hagazit. Chamber of Hewn Stone, seat of the **Sanhedrin**

Lishkat Hashemanim. Chamber in southwest corner of the **Ezrat Nashim** used for storing of olive oil and wine used in the Temple service

Lulavim. Ripe green closed fronds of the date palm tree, one of the "four kinds" upon which a special blessing is made on the **Sukkot** holiday (Lev. 23:40)

Ma'ariv. The evening service

Masechet. Mishnaic or Talmudic Tractate

Mashi'ach. Literally, the "Anointed One," the Messiah

Matan Torah. The giving of the Torah

Mehudar Etrogim. **Etrogim** (citrons) of an exceptionally high quality

Mei Niddah. "Water of impurity" is spring water mixed with the ashes of the Red Heifer used in purification rites in the Temple. In

Num. 19, the Torah describes the ritual of the Red Heifer: the ritual slaughter of a blemish-free red heifer and its burning together with cedar wood, hyssop, and red thread. The ashes of this heifer are mixed with spring water and are used as part of a seven-day ritual to purify Israelites who have come in contact with death and thereby acquired the severe form of impurity **Tum'at Meit**. Those upon whom this "water of impurity" (**Mei Niddah**) are sprinkled become ritually pure.

Meitim. Dead people

Mekubalim. Kabbalists, adepts of the Kabbalah, the mystical tradition in Judaism

Melech Hamashi'ach. The Messianic King, the Messiah

Menachot. Meal offerings in the Temple usually consisting of fine wheat flour mixed with olive oil with a touch of frankincense (Lev. 2)

Mentch. A highly ethical, kind, gracious person (Yiddish)

Menorah. Seven branched golden candelabra in the Temple lit daily by the **Kohanim** in the Temple

Metzudat David. The pen name of the classical Biblical commentator R. David Altschul

Mezuzah. *pl.* **Mezuzot.** A piece of parchment hand written by a scribe, usually contained in a protective case, inscribed with two portions of the Torah (*Shema* Deut. 4-9 and *Vehaya* Deut. 11:13-21) affixed to the doorposts of Jewish homes.

Middot. The tractate of the **Mishna** that deals with the measurements of the buildings, courtyards and the sacrificial altar Temple

Midrachov. Pedestrian mall

Midrash Rabbah. Collection of rabbinical homiletical commentaries on the books of the Bible

Midrash Tanchuma. An early homiletic commentary on the Torah attributed to Rabbi Tanchuma bar Abba (circa 370 CE)

Mikdash. The Holy Temple of Jerusalem

Mikdash Me'at. A miniature sanctuary

Mikvah. *pl.* **Mikva'ot.** "Purity pool," constructed according to complex specifications as defined in Jewish law; a facility built for the purpose of ritual purification in Judaism. *Mikvah* waters are commonly chest high and kept at a comfortable temperature.

Mincha. The afternoon service

Minyan. Quorum of ten adult males needed for public prayer

Mishna. The first authorized written compilation of the Jewish Oral Law; also paragraph in the Mishna.

Mitzvah. *pl.* **Mitzvot.** (**Mitzvos:** Ashkenazic pronunciation) commandments, good deeds

Mizbei'ach. Altar

Motzei Shabbos. Saturday night, the conclusion of the Sabbath; Ashkenazic pronunciation

Nachas. Pleasure, gratification; Ashkenazic pronunciation

Navi. *pl.* **Nevi'im.** Prophet

Ne'ila. Literally, "Locking," The concluding prayers of the *Yom Kippur* service

Neshamah. Soul

Netilat Yadayim. Ritual washing of hands before eating bread

Nevu'ah. Prophecy

Nigun. *pl.* **Nigunim.** Melodies

Nisuch Hayayin. Wine libation. Most sacrifices brought in the Temple were accompanied by pouring a prescribed measure of undiluted wine on the altar.

Olam Haba. The world to come

Oleh Regel. *pl.* **Olei Regel.** A pilgrim who ascends to Jerusalem

Parah Adumah. The Red Heifer, ashes of which are used in Temple purification rites (Num. 19)

Parochet. The one curtain that separate the Sanctuary and the Holy of Holies in the Third Temple.

Parshan. Biblical or Talmudic commentator

Parshat Hashavu'a. The weekly portion of the Torah read in the synagogue on the Sabbath

Pasuk. Biblical verse

Perek. Literally, chapter. Also shortened form for **Pirkei Avot**, Ethics of the Fathers, a Mishnaic tractate

Pesach. Passover

Peyos. Side locks (Ashkenazic pronunciation) worn by some men and boys in the Orthodox community based on an interpretation of the Biblical injunction against shaving the "corners" of one's beard.

Pirkei Avot. Mishnaic tractate Ethics of the Fathers is a compilation of the ethical teachings and maxims of the authorities quoted in the Mishna.

Rabbanim. Rabbis

Rabbanit. Wife of rabbi, an honorific term

Rav. Rabbi

Rebbe. Affectionate term for teacher, also the charismatic leader of a Hasidic group

Rebono Shel Olom. Literally, Master of the Universe, God

Rosh Chodesh. The new month

Rosh Yeshiva. The dean of a yeshiva, a Talmudical academy

Ruach Hakodesh. The Holy Spirit

Sabbatical Year. The seventh year of the seven year agricultural cycle ordained by the Torah. During the Sabbatical year (*Shemitah*), the land is left to lie fallow and all agricultural activity, including plowing, planting, pruning and harvesting, is forbidden by Jewish law. Other cultivation techniques (such as watering, fertilizing, weeding, spraying, trimming and mowing) may be performed as a preventative measure only, not to improve the growth of trees or other plants.

Salvezza. Salvation (Italian)

Sanhedrin. The supreme Torah tribunal and legislative body. It meets in the Temple chamber, the **Lishkat Hagazit**, the Chamber of Hewn Stone.

S'chach. Palm leaves or other greens used to roof a **Sukkah**

Sefer. *pl.* **Sefarim.** A holy book

Sefer Torah. A hand written Torah scroll on parchment containing the Five Books of Moses

Segan. Administrative assistant to the **Kohen Gadol**, the High Priest

Se'udah. A festive meal

Sha'ar Hamayim. The Water Gate; one of the entrances to the **Azarah,** the inner Temple Court located on the southern side of the Temple complex.

Shabbat. The Holy Sabbath (**Shabbos**, Ashkenazic pronunciation)

Shacharit. The morning service

Shalom Aleichem. Literally, "Peace unto you," a greeting; also a Sabbath eve hymn

Shas. A set of the Talmud

Shechinah. The Divine Presence

Shehechiyanu. Blessing made at a joyous occasion

Shekel. Unit of Israeli currency

Shelamim. Peace offering, a sacrifice offered in the Temple, part of which is burnt on the altar, part eaten by the priests, and part eaten by the person who brought the offering, his family and friends.

Shema. The central prayer of Judaism affirming God's absolute unity (*Shema* Deut. 4-9 and *Vehaya* Deut. 11:3-21)

Shemen Hamishchah. The holy anointing oil prepared by Moses, (Lev. 8)

Sheva Berachot. The Seven Blessings recited during the marriage service and during the grace after meals after the ceremony (**Sheva Berochos,** Ashkenazic pronunciation)

Sheva Mitzvot B'nei Noach. The seven ethical commandments ordained by God to be followed by all humanity

Shidurei Hamikdash. Temple Broadcasts

Shirah. The singing of Psalms with musical accompaniment by the Levitical choir in the Temple

Shir Hama'alot. Literally, A Song of Ascent (Psalm 126) recited or sung before **Birkat Hamazon,** grace after meals. "When the Lord brought back that those that returned to Zion, we were like unto those that dream. Then was our mouth filled with laughter, and our tongue with singing ..."

Shi'ur. A class or lesson on a Jewish religious topic

Shiva. The week long period of intense mourning after the death of close relatives: father, mother, son, daughter, brother, sister, or spouse. All normal activity is interrupted.

Shloshim. The first 30 days of mourning following the funeral (The **Shloshim** includes the **Shiva** period)

Shemitah. The **Sabbatical Year**

Shochet. Ritual slaughterer

Shofar. Ram's horn

Shuk. Market

Shomron. Samaria

Shtibel. *pl.* **Shtebelach.** Small one room synagogue (Yiddish)

Shul. Synagogue (Yiddish)

Siddur. *pl.* **Siddurim.** Prayer book

Solet. Fine wheat flour required for meal offerings in the Temple

Soreg. The low wall surrounding the Temple compound

Sukkah. *pl.* **Sukkot.** Booth built for the Feast of Tabernacles, Lev. 23:42 et seq, A Sukkah may be any size, so long as it is large enough to fulfill the commandment of "dwelling" in it. The roof of the **Sukkah** must be made of material referred to as **S'chach** (literally, covering) and must be something that grew from the ground and was cut off, such as tree branches, bamboo reeds, sticks, or two-by-fours. In Israel palm branches are usually used.

Sukkot. The Feast of Tabernacles; usually falls in October. The word "Sukkot" means "booths," and refers to the temporary dwellings that Jews are commanded to live in during this holiday in memory of the period of wandering in the wilderness after the Exodus from Egypt. (Lev. 23:33 et seq.) No work is permitted on the first day of the holiday (in Israel). Work is permitted on the remaining days. These intermediate days on which work is permitted are referred to as **Chol Hamo'ed**, as are the intermediate days of Passover.

Tallit. Fringed prayer shawl worn by Jewish men during morning services. (**Tallis**, Ashkenazic pronunciation)

Talmid. *pl.* **Talmidim.** Student

Talmid Chacham. Literally; "student of the wise," a Torah scholar

Tamid Shel Boker. The obligatory early morning burnt offering sacrificed in the Temple

Tanach. Jewish Bible

Tammuz. A month in the Hebrew calendar; roughly equivalent to July

Tanna. Authority quoted in the Mishna

Tanta. Aunt (Yiddish)

Tashmishei Kedusha. Judaica, ritual objects used in the Jewish Religion

Tati. "Daddy" (Yiddish)

Tefillah. Literally, prayer, the *Shemoneh Esrei*, the "Eighteen benedictions" prayer

Tefillin. A set of two cubic black leather boxes containing hand written parchment scrolls inscribed with Biblical verses with leather straps and worn by Jewish men during weekday morning prayers. (Deut.6:8)

Tehillim. Psalms

Temei'im. People who are ritually impure

Tikkun. Spiritual rectification

Tikkun Chatzot. Service of lamentation recited at midnight in commemoration of the destruction of the First and Second Temples and the exile of the **Shechinah.**

Tirzah. A city in ancient Israel renowned for its beauty

Tisha B'av. The 9th day of the Jewish month of *Av*, the anniversary of the destruction of the First and Second Temples, the expulsion of the

Jews from Spain in 1492, the uprooting of Gush Katif, and many other tragic events in Jewish history.

Torat Yisrael. The Torah of Israel

Tosefta. A collection of Tannaitic traditions that goes into greater detail than does the **Mishna.**

Tum'at Meit. Corpse impurity, the most severe form of ritual impurity. The seven day rite of purification included contact with **Mei Niddah**

Tzadik. A righteous man

Tzefat. Safed, a city in the upper Galilee

Ulam. Entrance hall to the **Bayit,** the main Temple building

Urim Ve'tumin. The Temple oracle worn by the High Priest

Yahadut. Judaism

Yechezkel. The prophet Ezekiel

Yiddishkeit. Judaism (Yiddish)

Yehudah. Judea

Yemei Hamashi'ach. The Messianic Age

Yerushalmi. *pl.* **Yerushalmim.** Jerusalemite, Jerusalem Talmud

Yerushalyim. Jerusalem

Yerushalyim Bein Hachomot. Literally "Jerusalem within the walls," the Old City of Jerusalem

Yeshiva. *pl.* **Yeshivot.** Talmudic college

Yeshiva Bochur. Yeshiva student (Yiddish)

Yeshiyahu. The prophet Isaiah

Yehoshua Bin Nun. Joshua the son of Nun, disciple of Moses, conqueror of Canaan.

Yiddishe Mispocho. A "Jewish family" (Yiddish)

Yisgadal Ve'yishkadash Shmei Rabba. "Magnified and sanctified be His great name" First line of **Kaddish** prayer. (Aramaic, Ashkenazic pronunciation)

Yisrael. An Israelite, a Jew

Yom Kippur. The Day of Atonement, the holiest day of the year

Zechuyot. Merits (Ashkenazic pronunciation: **Zechuyos**)

Zephaniah Hanavi. The prophet Zephaniah

Zeicher Le'mikdash. A pious act performed in remembrance of the Temple

Zohar. Major text of the **Kabbalah**; attributed to the **tanna** Rabbi Shimon bar Yochai

Made in the USA
San Bernardino, CA
09 July 2016